TEEN BOAT!

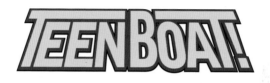

TEEN BOAT!

*The **ANGST** of being a Teen–the **THRILL** of being a Boat!*

BY **DAVE ROMAN** AND **JOHN GREEN**

Clarion Books | Houghton Mifflin Harcourt | Boston New York   2012

Lead colorist:
WES DZIOBA

Additional colors by
BRADEN D. LAMB
DOUGLAS HOLGATE
RIKKI SIMONS

Color flats by
MEGAN BRENNAN
NASEEM HRAB
GALE WILLIAMS

Letters by
JOHN GREEN

Clarion Books
215 Park Avenue South
New York, New York 10003

Text and illustrations copyright © 2012
by Dave Roman and John Green

For information about permission to reproduce selections from this book,
write to Permissions, Houghton Mifflin Harcourt Publishing Company,
215 Park Avenue South, New York, New York 10003.

Clarion Books is an imprint of Houghton Mifflin Harcourt Publishing Company.

www.hmhbooks.com
www.teenboatcomics.com

Library of Congress Cataloging-in-Publication Data is available.
LCCN 2011940658

Manufactured in China
LEO 10 9 8 7 6 5 4 3 2 1
4500338200

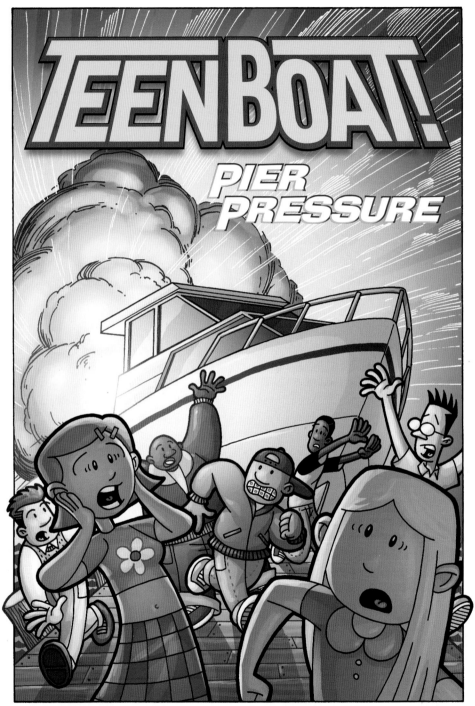

TEEN BOAT!
PIER PRESSURE

The **ANGST** of being a Teen—the **THRILL** of being a Boat!

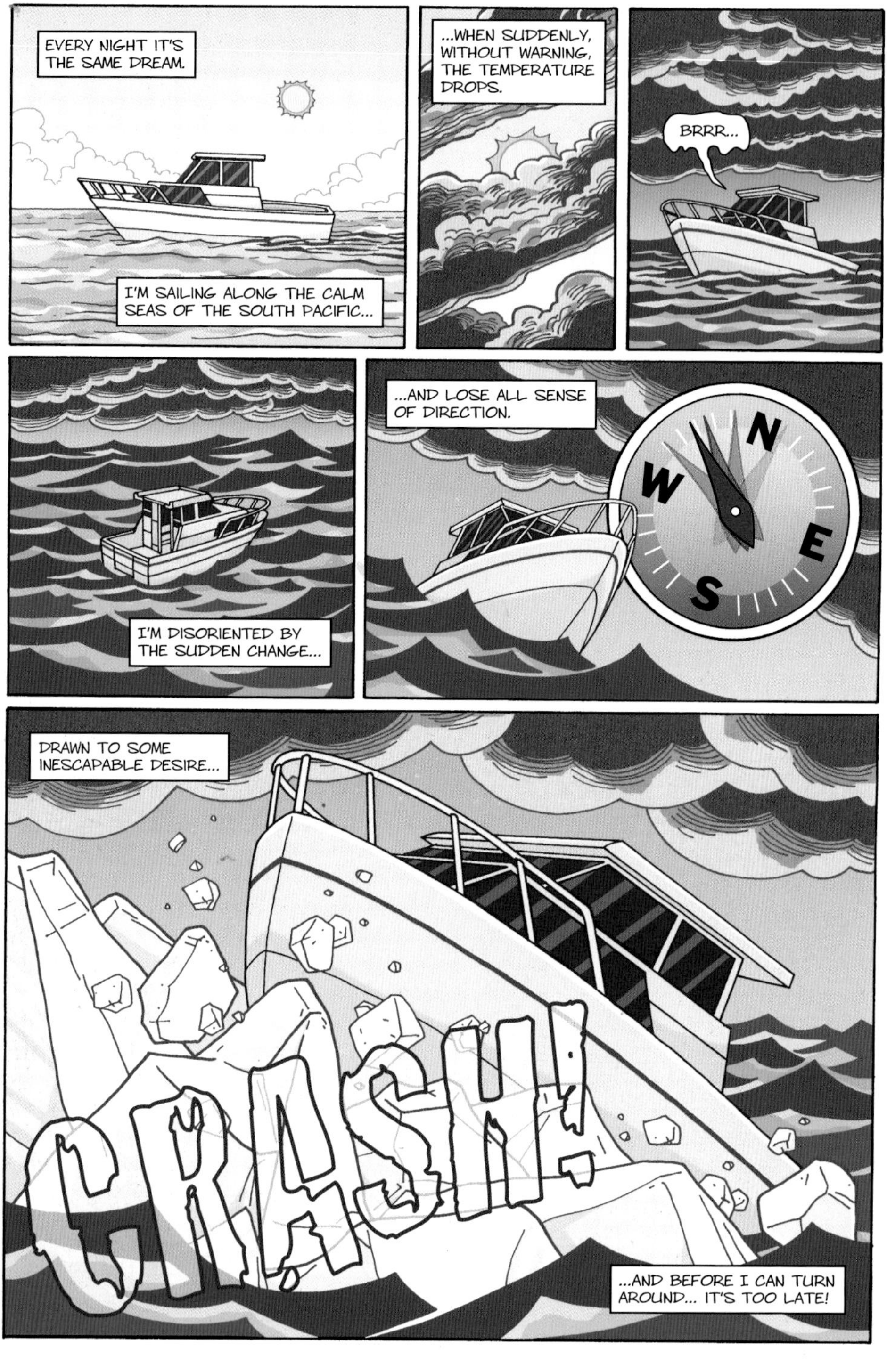
EVERY NIGHT IT'S THE SAME DREAM.
I'M SAILING ALONG THE CALM SEAS OF THE SOUTH PACIFIC...
...WHEN SUDDENLY, WITHOUT WARNING, THE TEMPERATURE DROPS.
BRRR...
I'M DISORIENTED BY THE SUDDEN CHANGE...
...AND LOSE ALL SENSE OF DIRECTION.
N
W
E
S
DRAWN TO SOME INESCAPABLE DESIRE...
CRASH!
...AND BEFORE I CAN TURN AROUND... IT'S TOO LATE!

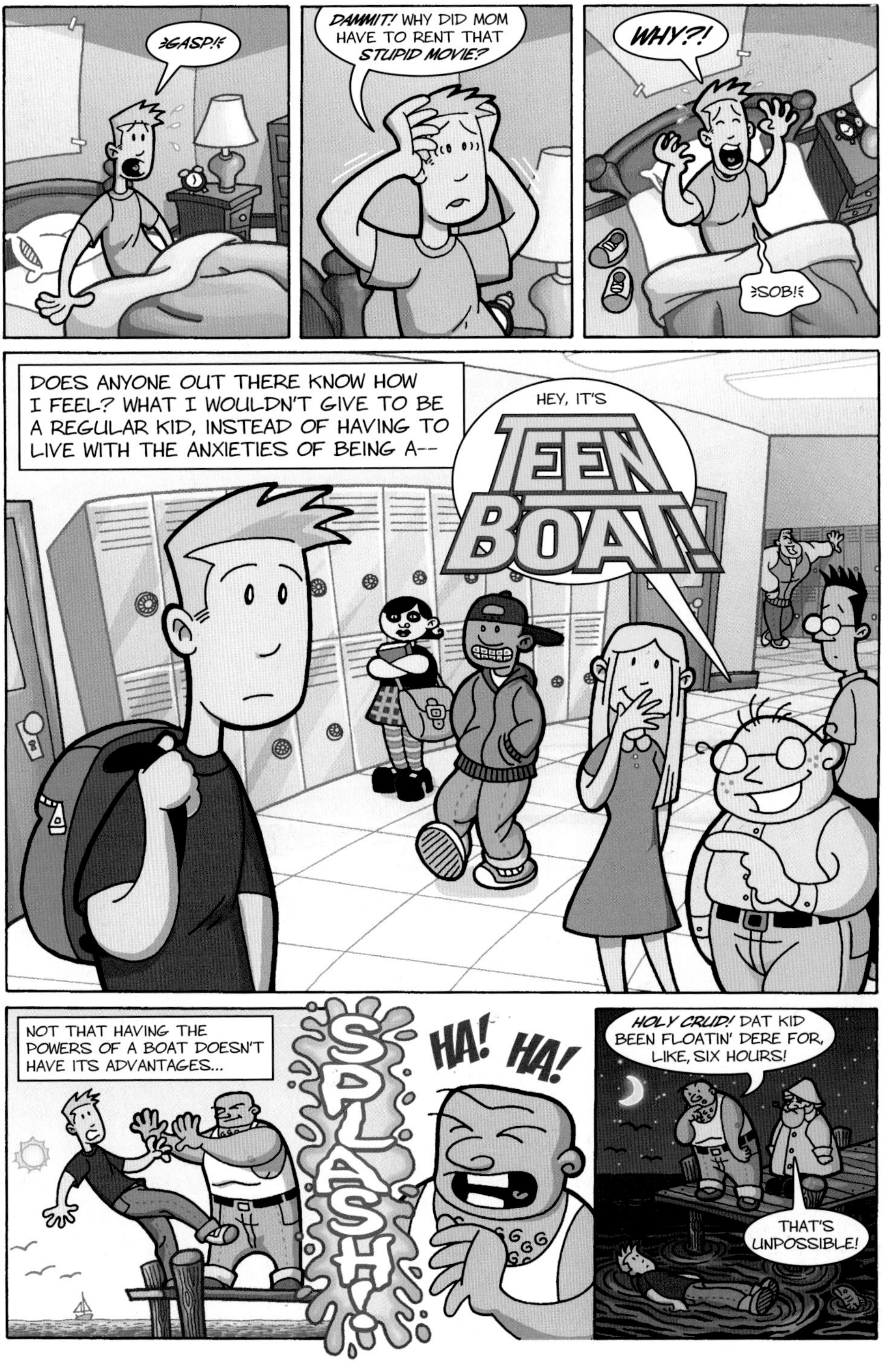

GASP!
DAMMIT! WHY DID MOM HAVE TO RENT THAT STUPID MOVIE?
WHY?!
SOB!
DOES ANYONE OUT THERE KNOW HOW I FEEL? WHAT I WOULDN'T GIVE TO BE A REGULAR KID, INSTEAD OF HAVING TO LIVE WITH THE ANXIETIES OF BEING A--
HEY, IT'S TEEN BOAT!
NOT THAT HAVING THE POWERS OF A BOAT DOESN'T HAVE ITS ADVANTAGES...
SPLASH!
HA! HA!
HOLY CRUD! DAT KID BEEN FLOATIN' DERE FOR, LIKE, SIX HOURS!
THAT'S UNPOSSIBLE!

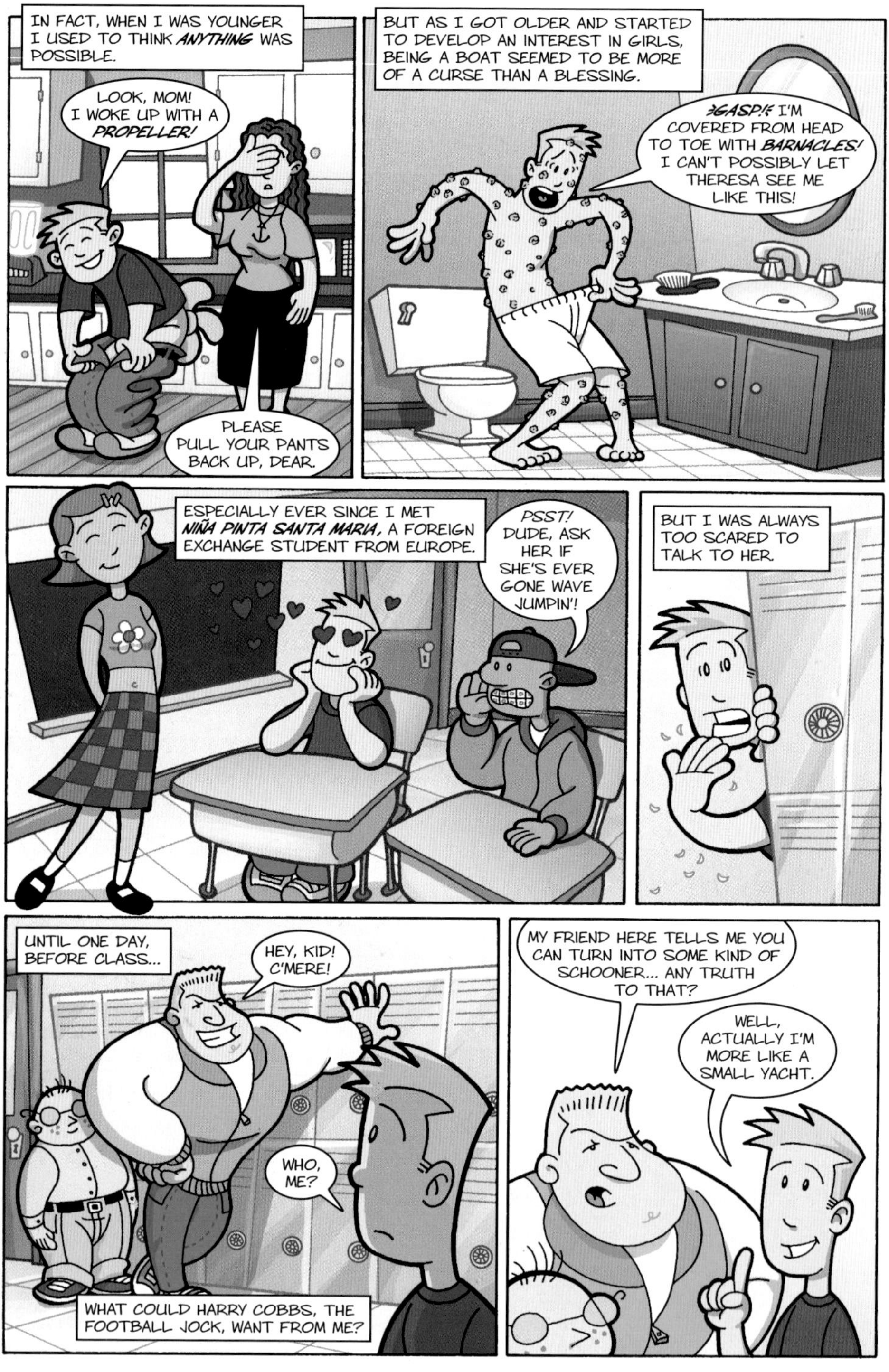
IN FACT, WHEN I WAS YOUNGER I USED TO THINK *ANYTHING* WAS POSSIBLE.
LOOK, MOM! I WOKE UP WITH A *PROPELLER!*
PLEASE PULL YOUR PANTS BACK UP, DEAR.
BUT AS I GOT OLDER AND STARTED TO DEVELOP AN INTEREST IN GIRLS, BEING A BOAT SEEMED TO BE MORE OF A CURSE THAN A BLESSING.
GASP! I'M COVERED FROM HEAD TO TOE WITH *BARNACLES!* I CAN'T POSSIBLY LET THERESA SEE ME LIKE THIS!
ESPECIALLY EVER SINCE I MET *NIÑA PINTA SANTA MARIA,* A FOREIGN EXCHANGE STUDENT FROM EUROPE.
PSST! DUDE, ASK HER IF SHE'S EVER GONE WAVE JUMPIN'!
BUT I WAS ALWAYS TOO SCARED TO TALK TO HER.
UNTIL ONE DAY, BEFORE CLASS...
HEY, KID! C'MERE!
WHO, ME?
WHAT COULD HARRY COBBS, THE FOOTBALL JOCK, WANT FROM ME?
MY FRIEND HERE TELLS ME YOU CAN TURN INTO SOME KIND OF SCHOONER... ANY TRUTH TO THAT?
WELL, ACTUALLY I'M MORE LIKE A SMALL YACHT.

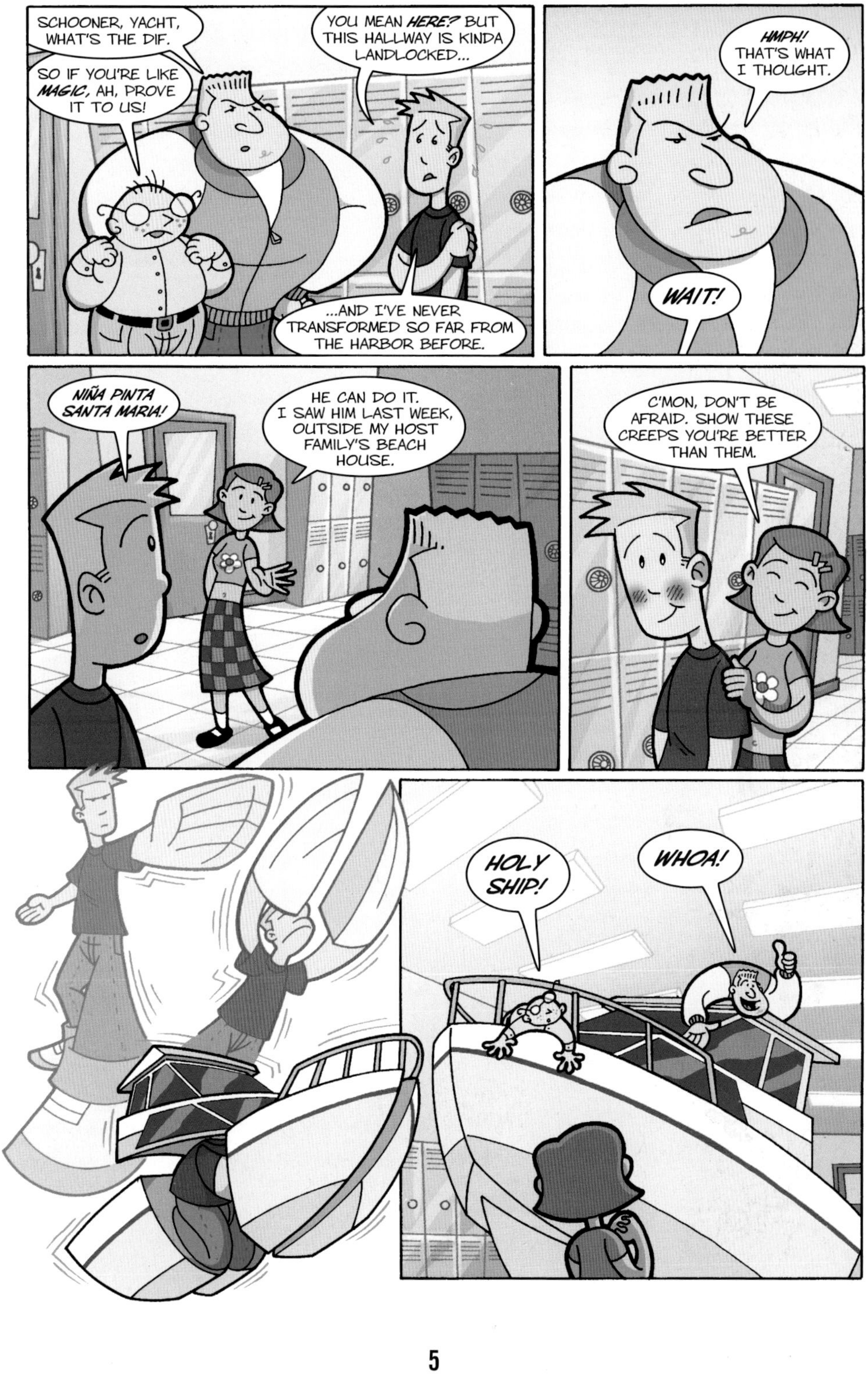
SCHOONER, YACHT, WHAT'S THE DIF.
SO IF YOU'RE LIKE *MAGIC,* AH, PROVE IT TO US!
YOU MEAN *HERE?* BUT THIS HALLWAY IS KINDA LANDLOCKED...
...AND I'VE NEVER TRANSFORMED SO FAR FROM THE HARBOR BEFORE.
HMPH! THAT'S WHAT I THOUGHT.
WAIT!
NIÑA PINTA SANTA MARIA!
HE CAN DO IT. I SAW HIM LAST WEEK, OUTSIDE MY HOST FAMILY'S BEACH HOUSE.
C'MON, DON'T BE AFRAID. SHOW THESE CREEPS YOU'RE BETTER THAN THEM.
HOLY SHIP!
WHOA!

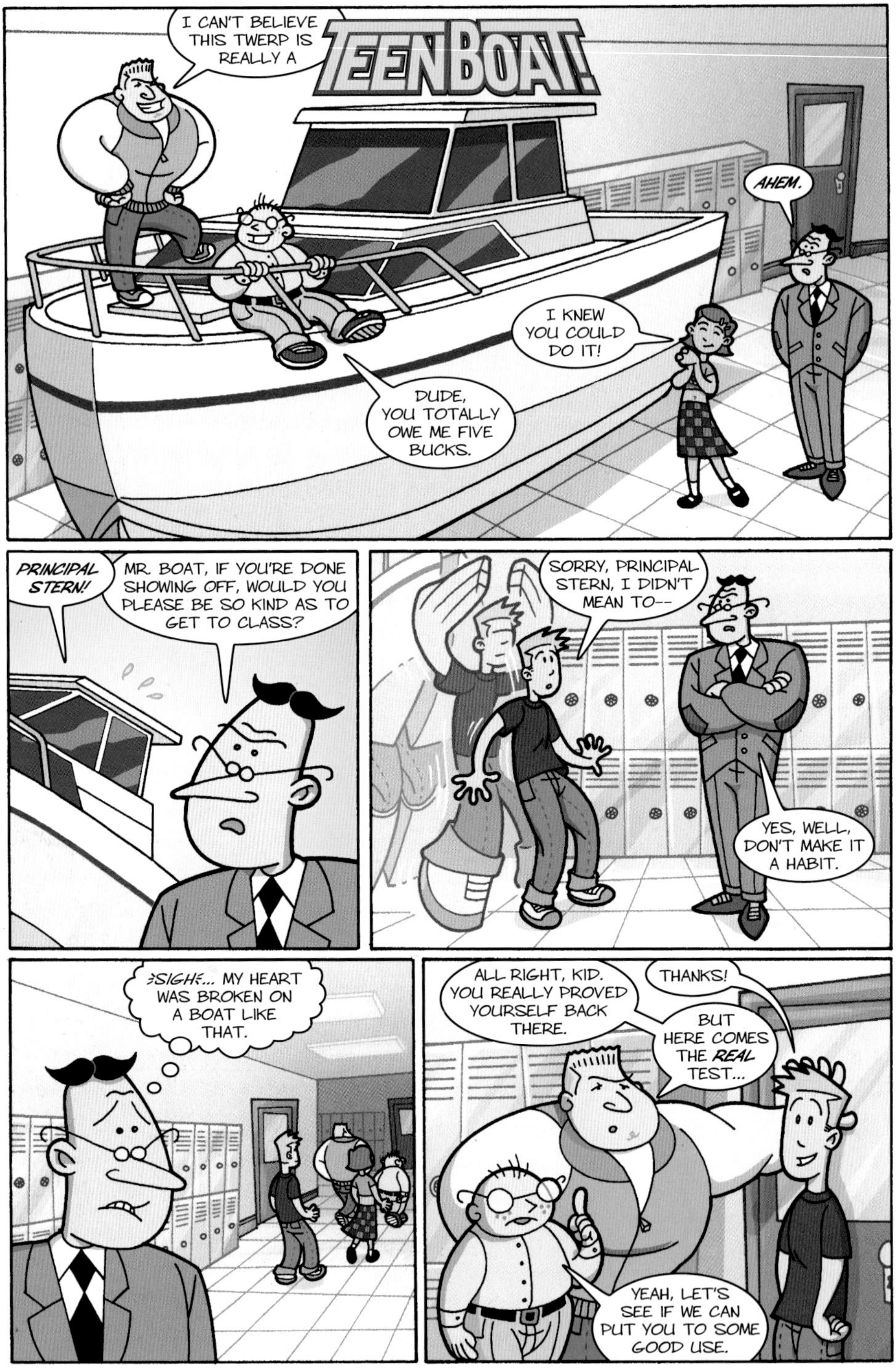
I CAN'T BELIEVE THIS TWERP IS REALLY A
TEEN BOAT!
AHEM.
I KNEW YOU COULD DO IT!
DUDE, YOU TOTALLY OWE ME FIVE BUCKS.
PRINCIPAL STERN!
MR. BOAT, IF YOU'RE DONE SHOWING OFF, WOULD YOU PLEASE BE SO KIND AS TO GET TO CLASS?
SORRY, PRINCIPAL STERN, I DIDN'T MEAN TO--
YES, WELL, DON'T MAKE IT A HABIT.
SIGH... MY HEART WAS BROKEN ON A BOAT LIKE THAT.
ALL RIGHT, KID. YOU REALLY PROVED YOURSELF BACK THERE.
THANKS!
BUT HERE COMES THE REAL TEST...
YEAH, LET'S SEE IF WE CAN PUT YOU TO SOME GOOD USE.

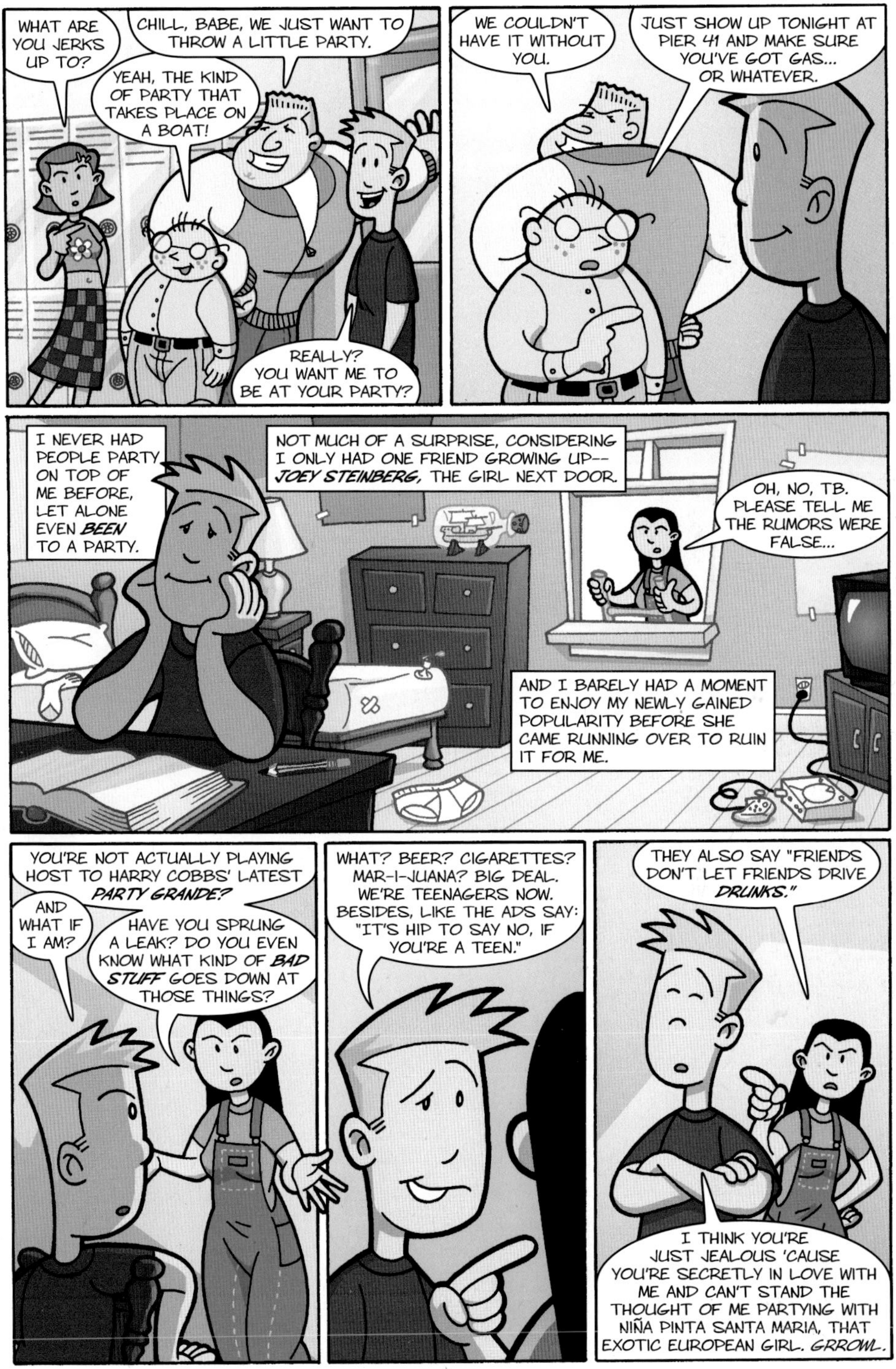
WHAT ARE YOU JERKS UP TO?
CHILL, BABE, WE JUST WANT TO THROW A LITTLE PARTY.
YEAH, THE KIND OF PARTY THAT TAKES PLACE ON A BOAT!
REALLY? YOU WANT ME TO BE AT YOUR PARTY?
WE COULDN'T HAVE IT WITHOUT YOU.
JUST SHOW UP TONIGHT AT PIER 41 AND MAKE SURE YOU'VE GOT GAS... OR WHATEVER.
I NEVER HAD PEOPLE PARTY ON TOP OF ME BEFORE, LET ALONE EVEN *BEEN* TO A PARTY.
NOT MUCH OF A SURPRISE, CONSIDERING I ONLY HAD ONE FRIEND GROWING UP-- *JOEY STEINBERG,* THE GIRL NEXT DOOR.
OH, NO, TB. PLEASE TELL ME THE RUMORS WERE FALSE...
AND I BARELY HAD A MOMENT TO ENJOY MY NEWLY GAINED POPULARITY BEFORE SHE CAME RUNNING OVER TO RUIN IT FOR ME.
YOU'RE NOT ACTUALLY PLAYING HOST TO HARRY COBBS' LATEST *PARTY GRANDE?*
AND WHAT IF I AM?
HAVE YOU SPRUNG A LEAK? DO YOU EVEN KNOW WHAT KIND OF *BAD STUFF* GOES DOWN AT THOSE THINGS?
WHAT? BEER? CIGARETTES? MAR-I-JUANA? BIG DEAL. WE'RE TEENAGERS NOW. BESIDES, LIKE THE ADS SAY: "IT'S HIP TO SAY NO, IF YOU'RE A TEEN."
THEY ALSO SAY "FRIENDS DON'T LET FRIENDS DRIVE *DRUNKS.*"
I THINK YOU'RE JUST JEALOUS 'CAUSE YOU'RE SECRETLY IN LOVE WITH ME AND CAN'T STAND THE THOUGHT OF ME PARTYING WITH NIÑA PINTA SANTA MARIA, THAT EXOTIC EUROPEAN GIRL. *GRROWL.*

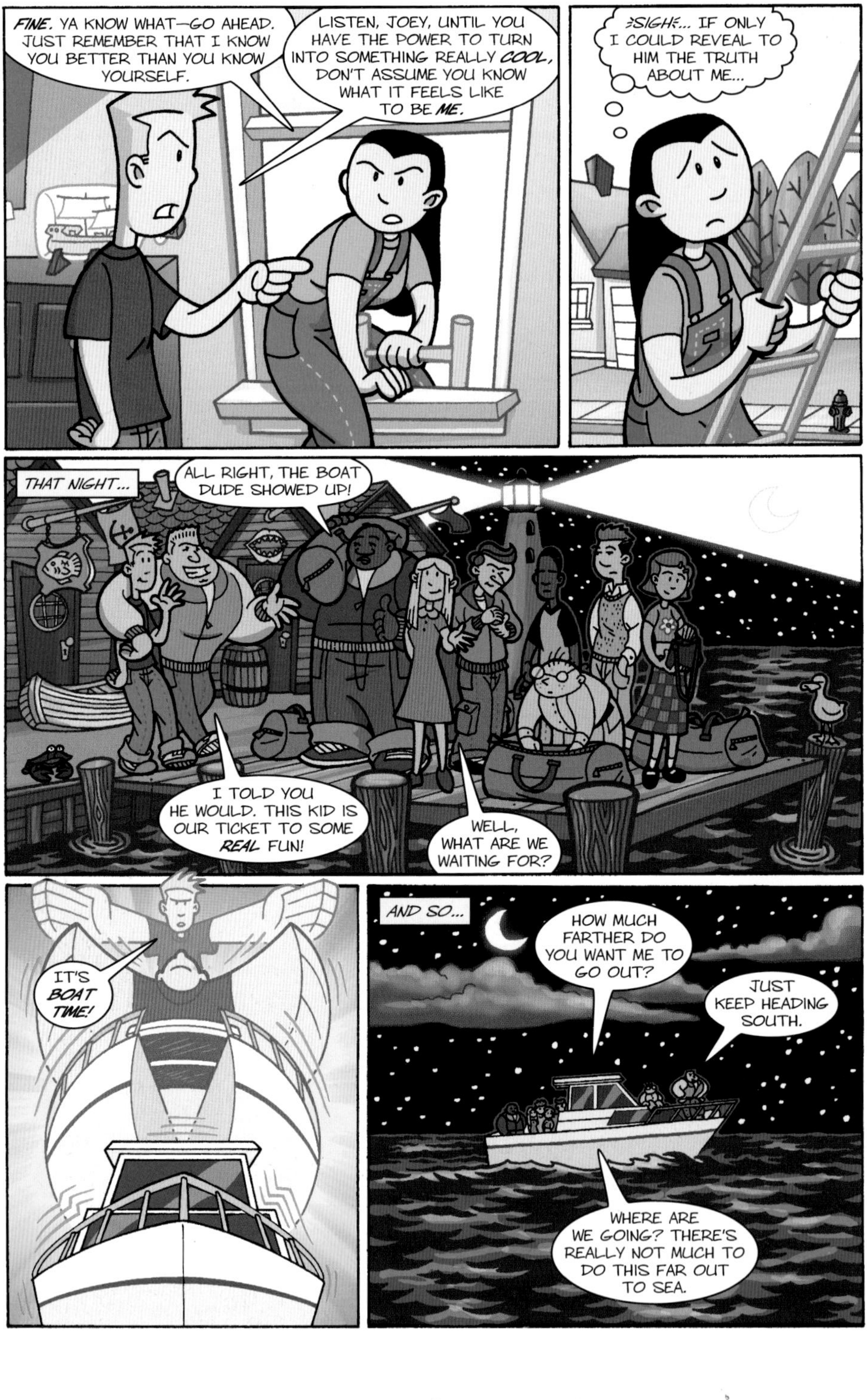
FINE. YA KNOW WHAT—GO AHEAD. JUST REMEMBER THAT I KNOW YOU BETTER THAN YOU KNOW YOURSELF.
LISTEN, JOEY, UNTIL YOU HAVE THE POWER TO TURN INTO SOMETHING REALLY COOL, DON'T ASSUME YOU KNOW WHAT IT FEELS LIKE TO BE ME.
SIGH... IF ONLY I COULD REVEAL TO HIM THE TRUTH ABOUT ME...
THAT NIGHT...
ALL RIGHT, THE BOAT DUDE SHOWED UP!
I TOLD YOU HE WOULD. THIS KID IS OUR TICKET TO SOME REAL FUN!
WELL, WHAT ARE WE WAITING FOR?
IT'S BOAT TIME!
AND SO...
HOW MUCH FARTHER DO YOU WANT ME TO GO OUT?
JUST KEEP HEADING SOUTH.
WHERE ARE WE GOING? THERE'S REALLY NOT MUCH TO DO THIS FAR OUT TO SEA.

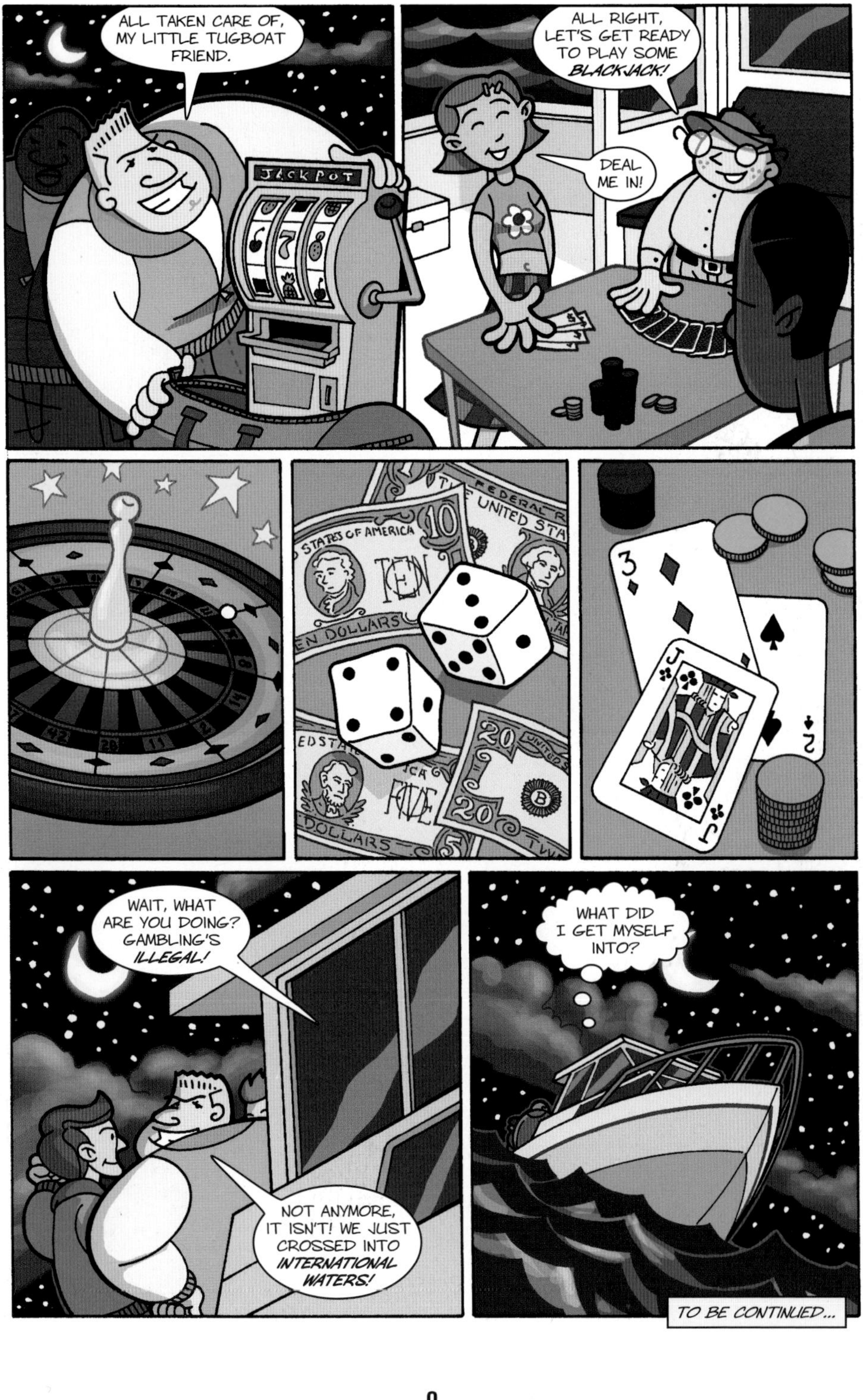
ALL TAKEN CARE OF, MY LITTLE TUGBOAT FRIEND.
JACKPOT
ALL RIGHT, LET'S GET READY TO PLAY SOME BLACKJACK!
DEAL ME IN!
WAIT, WHAT ARE YOU DOING? GAMBLING'S ILLEGAL!
NOT ANYMORE, IT ISN'T! WE JUST CROSSED INTO INTERNATIONAL WATERS!
WHAT DID I GET MYSELF INTO?
TO BE CONTINUED...

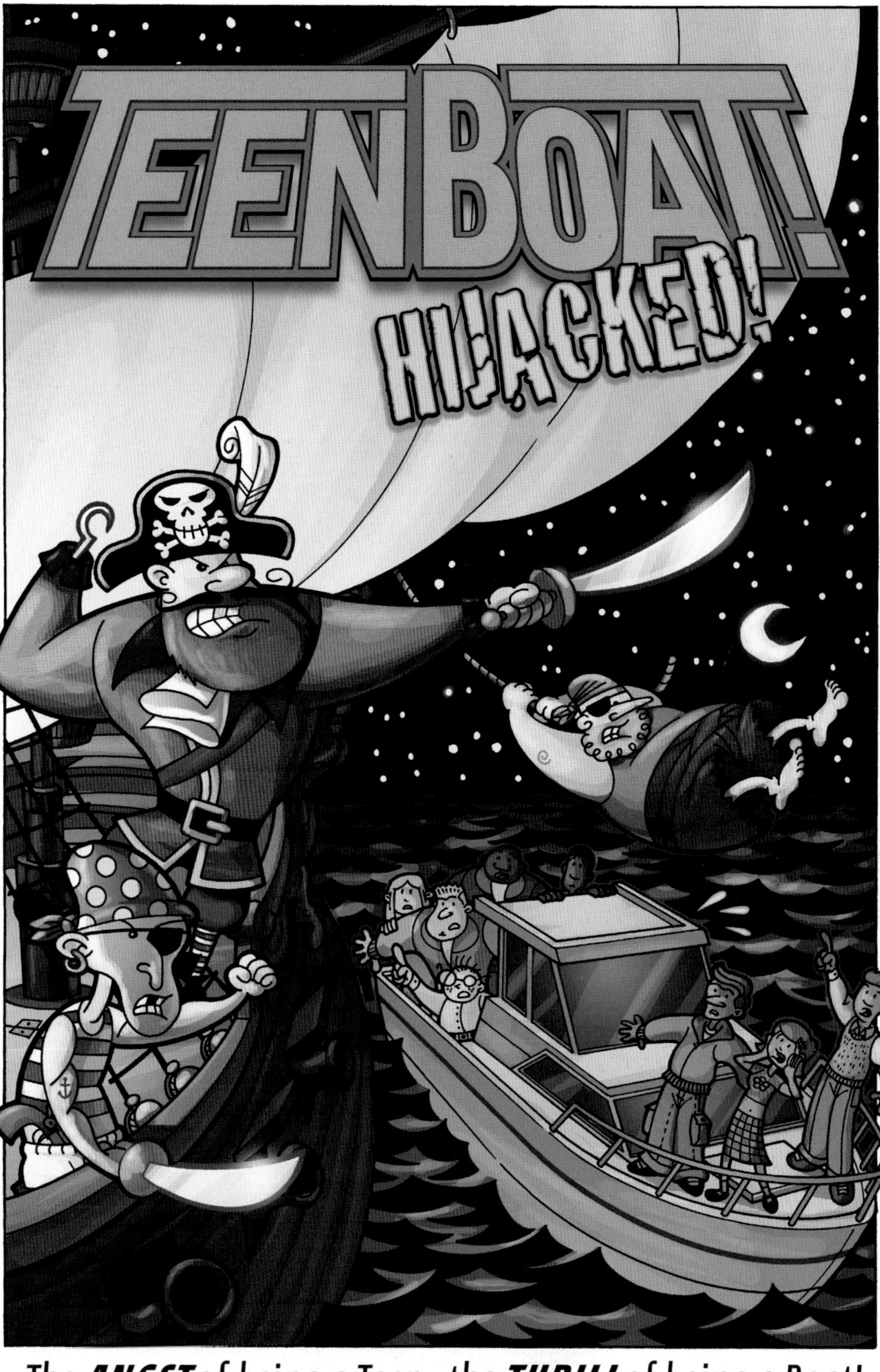
TEENBOAT!
HIJACKED!

The ***ANGST*** of being a Teen—the ***THRILL*** of being a Boat!

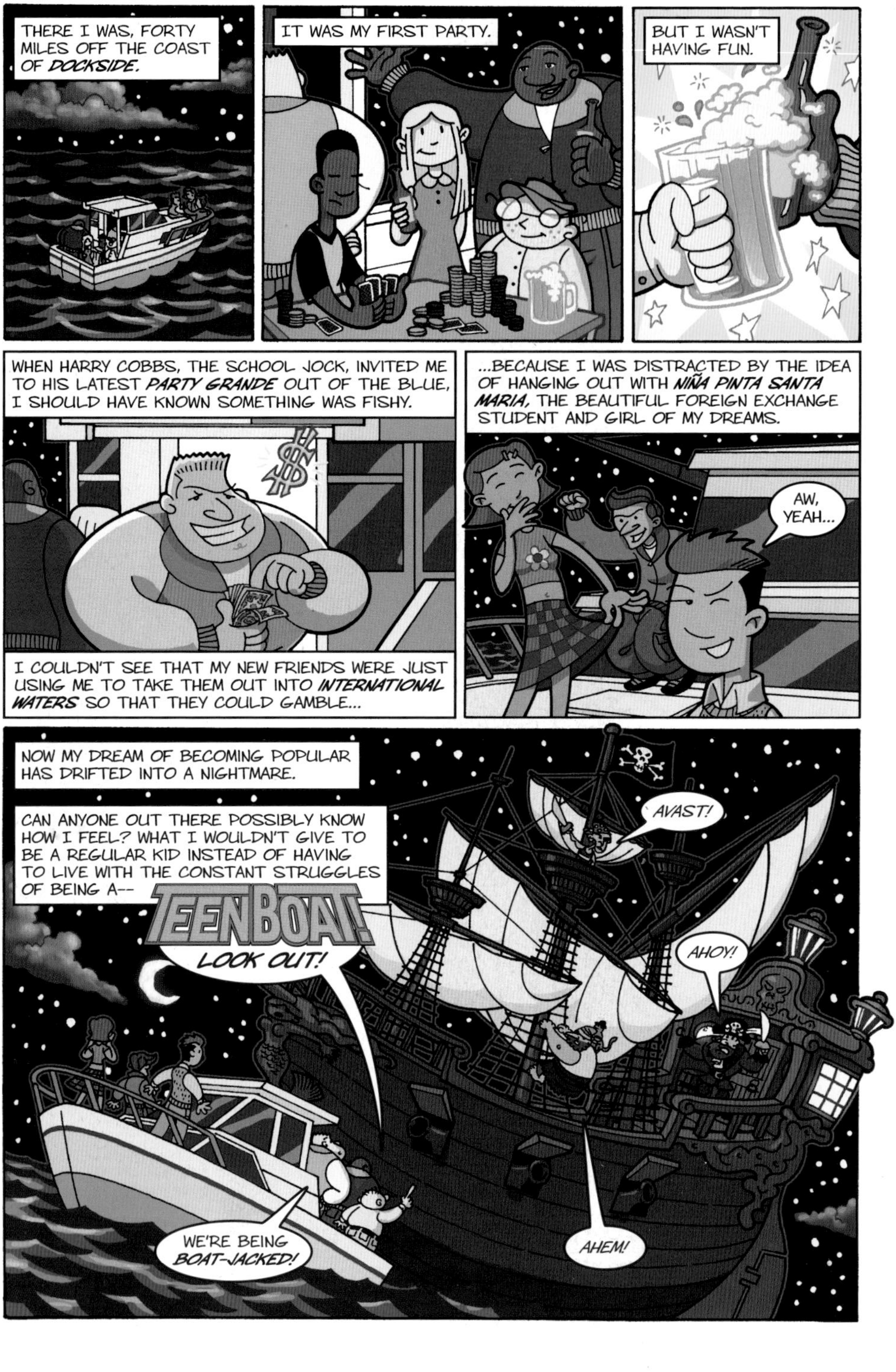
THERE I WAS, FORTY MILES OFF THE COAST OF DOCKSIDE.
IT WAS MY FIRST PARTY.
BUT I WASN'T HAVING FUN.
WHEN HARRY COBBS, THE SCHOOL JOCK, INVITED ME TO HIS LATEST PARTY GRANDE OUT OF THE BLUE, I SHOULD HAVE KNOWN SOMETHING WAS FISHY.
I COULDN'T SEE THAT MY NEW FRIENDS WERE JUST USING ME TO TAKE THEM OUT INTO INTERNATIONAL WATERS SO THAT THEY COULD GAMBLE...
...BECAUSE I WAS DISTRACTED BY THE IDEA OF HANGING OUT WITH NIÑA PINTA SANTA MARIA, THE BEAUTIFUL FOREIGN EXCHANGE STUDENT AND GIRL OF MY DREAMS.
AW, YEAH...
NOW MY DREAM OF BECOMING POPULAR HAS DRIFTED INTO A NIGHTMARE.
CAN ANYONE OUT THERE POSSIBLY KNOW HOW I FEEL? WHAT I WOULDN'T GIVE TO BE A REGULAR KID INSTEAD OF HAVING TO LIVE WITH THE CONSTANT STRUGGLES OF BEING A--
TEENBOAT!
AVAST!
LOOK OUT!
AHOY!
WE'RE BEING BOAT-JACKED!
AHEM!

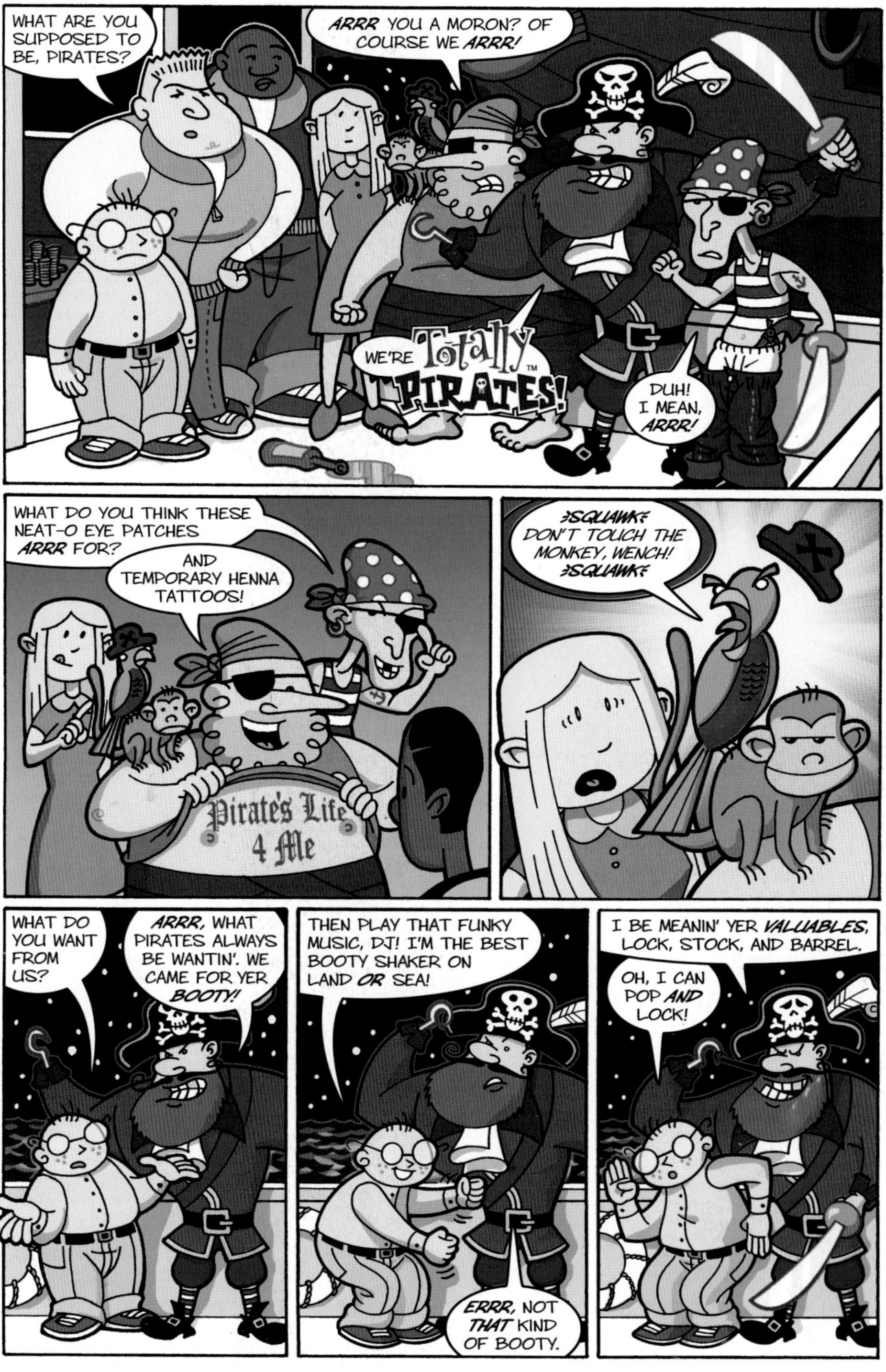
WHAT ARE YOU SUPPOSED TO BE, PIRATES?
ARRR YOU A MORON? OF COURSE WE ARRR!
WE'RE Totally PIRATES!
TM
DUH! I MEAN, ARRR!
WHAT DO YOU THINK THESE NEAT-O EYE PATCHES ARRR FOR?
AND TEMPORARY HENNA TATTOOS!
Pirate's Life 4 Me
SQUAWK DON'T TOUCH THE MONKEY, WENCH! SQUAWK
WHAT DO YOU WANT FROM US?
ARRR, WHAT PIRATES ALWAYS BE WANTIN'. WE CAME FOR YER BOOTY!
THEN PLAY THAT FUNKY MUSIC, DJ! I'M THE BEST BOOTY SHAKER ON LAND OR SEA!
ERRR, NOT THAT KIND OF BOOTY.
I BE MEANIN' YER VALUABLES, LOCK, STOCK, AND BARREL.
OH, I CAN POP AND LOCK!

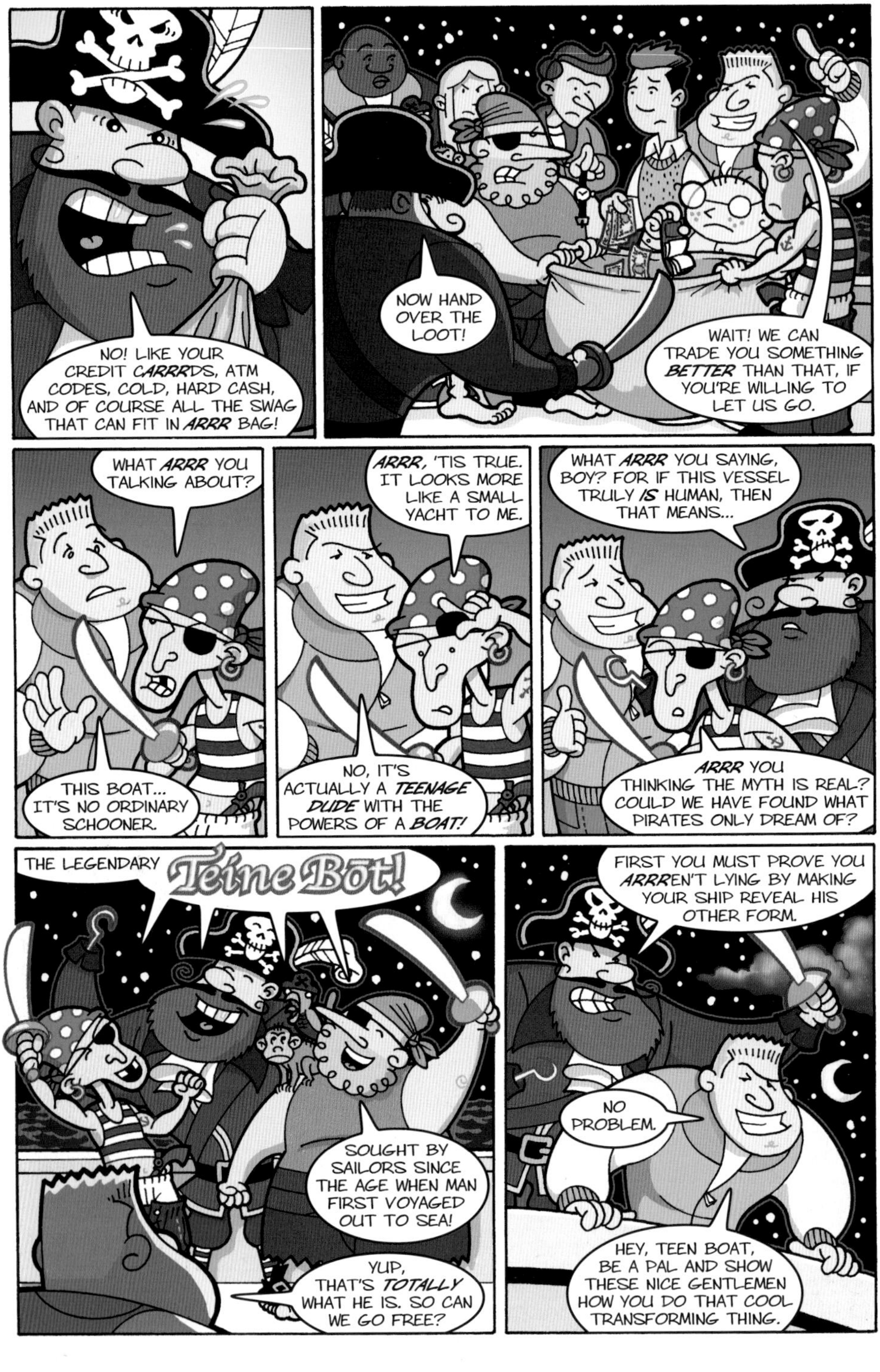
NO! LIKE YOUR CREDIT CARRRDS, ATM CODES, COLD, HARD CASH, AND OF COURSE ALL THE SWAG THAT CAN FIT IN ARRR BAG!
NOW HAND OVER THE LOOT!
WAIT! WE CAN TRADE YOU SOMETHING BETTER THAN THAT, IF YOU'RE WILLING TO LET US GO.
WHAT ARRR YOU TALKING ABOUT?
THIS BOAT... IT'S NO ORDINARY SCHOONER.
ARRR, 'TIS TRUE. IT LOOKS MORE LIKE A SMALL YACHT TO ME.
NO, IT'S ACTUALLY A TEENAGE DUDE WITH THE POWERS OF A BOAT!
WHAT ARRR YOU SAYING, BOY? FOR IF THIS VESSEL TRULY IS HUMAN, THEN THAT MEANS...
ARRR YOU THINKING THE MYTH IS REAL? COULD WE HAVE FOUND WHAT PIRATES ONLY DREAM OF?
THE LEGENDARY Teine Bot!
SOUGHT BY SAILORS SINCE THE AGE WHEN MAN FIRST VOYAGED OUT TO SEA!
YUP, THAT'S TOTALLY WHAT HE IS. SO CAN WE GO FREE?
FIRST YOU MUST PROVE YOU ARRREN'T LYING BY MAKING YOUR SHIP REVEAL HIS OTHER FORM.
NO PROBLEM.
HEY, TEEN BOAT, BE A PAL AND SHOW THESE NICE GENTLEMEN HOW YOU DO THAT COOL TRANSFORMING THING.

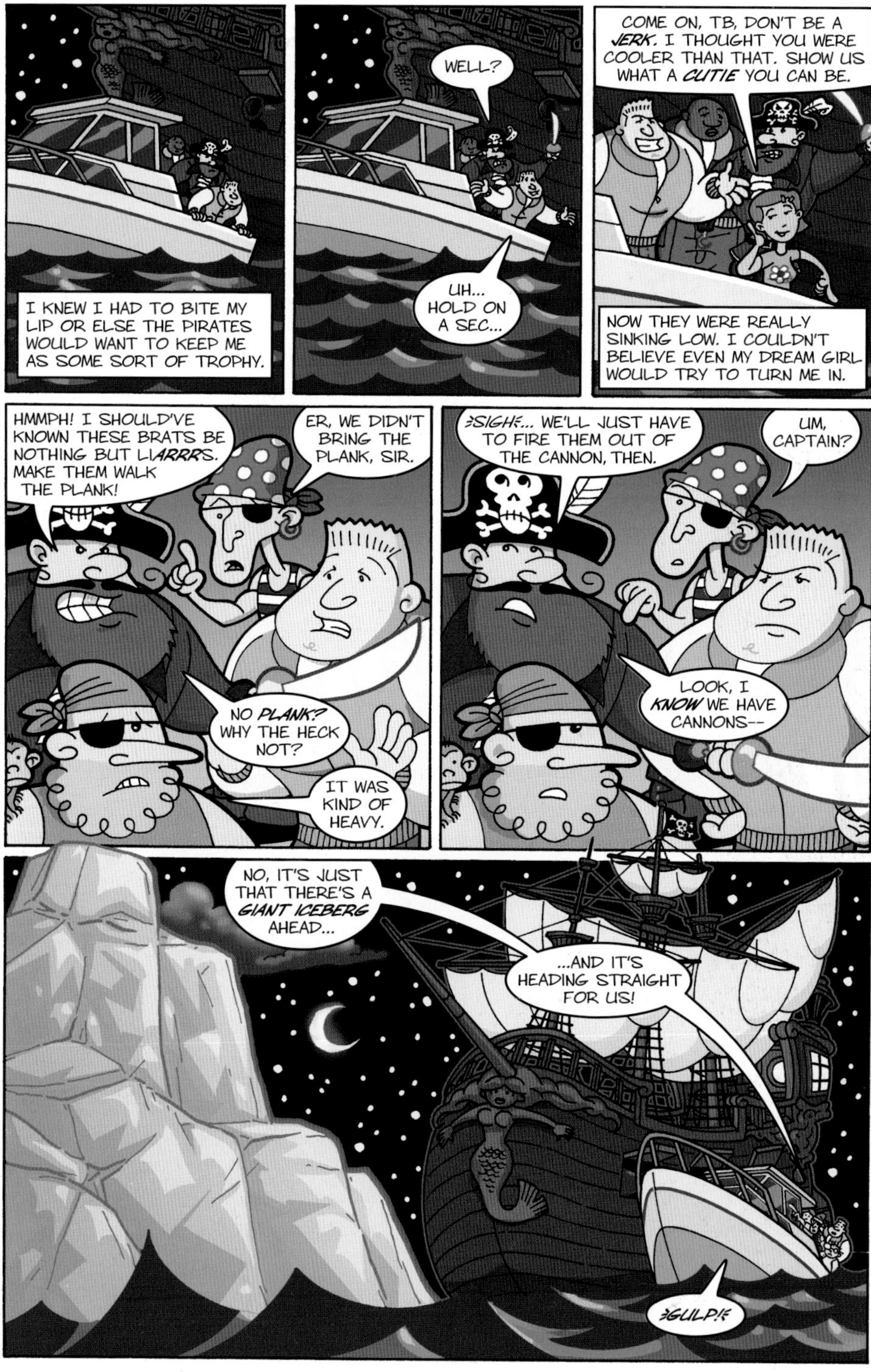
I KNEW I HAD TO BITE MY LIP OR ELSE THE PIRATES WOULD WANT TO KEEP ME AS SOME SORT OF TROPHY.
WELL?
UH... HOLD ON A SEC...
COME ON, TB, DON'T BE A JERK. I THOUGHT YOU WERE COOLER THAN THAT. SHOW US WHAT A CUTIE YOU CAN BE.
NOW THEY WERE REALLY SINKING LOW. I COULDN'T BELIEVE EVEN MY DREAM GIRL WOULD TRY TO TURN ME IN.
HMMPH! I SHOULD'VE KNOWN THESE BRATS BE NOTHING BUT LIARRRS. MAKE THEM WALK THE PLANK!
ER, WE DIDN'T BRING THE PLANK, SIR.
NO PLANK? WHY THE HECK NOT?
IT WAS KIND OF HEAVY.
SIGH... WE'LL JUST HAVE TO FIRE THEM OUT OF THE CANNON, THEN.
UM, CAPTAIN?
LOOK, I KNOW WE HAVE CANNONS--
NO, IT'S JUST THAT THERE'S A GIANT ICEBERG AHEAD...
...AND IT'S HEADING STRAIGHT FOR US!
GULP!

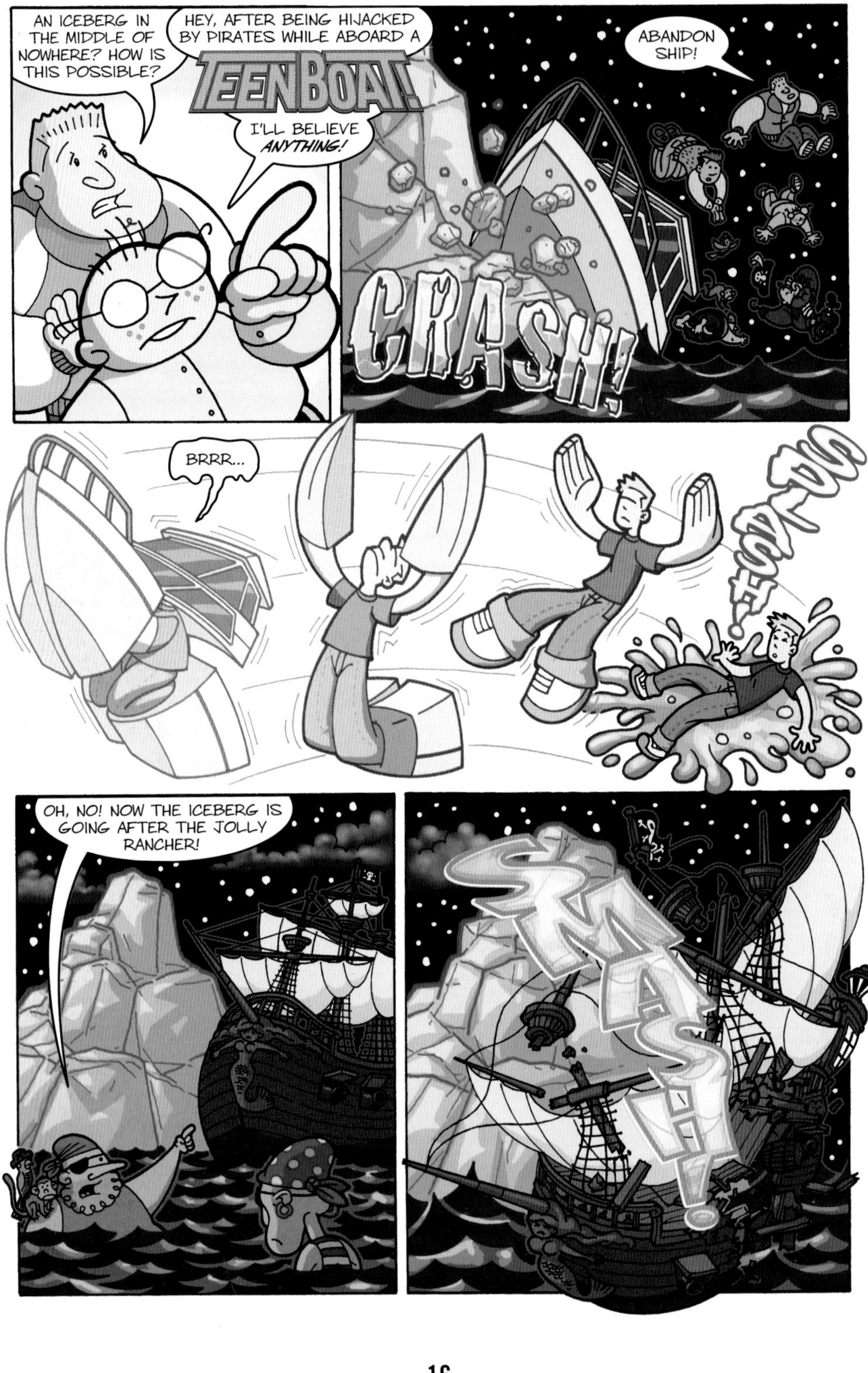
AN ICEBERG IN THE MIDDLE OF NOWHERE? HOW IS THIS POSSIBLE?
HEY, AFTER BEING HIJACKED BY PIRATES WHILE ABOARD A
TEENBOAT!
I'LL BELIEVE ANYTHING!
ABANDON SHIP!
CRASH!
BRRR...
SPLASH!
OH, NO! NOW THE ICEBERG IS GOING AFTER THE JOLLY RANCHER!
SMASH!

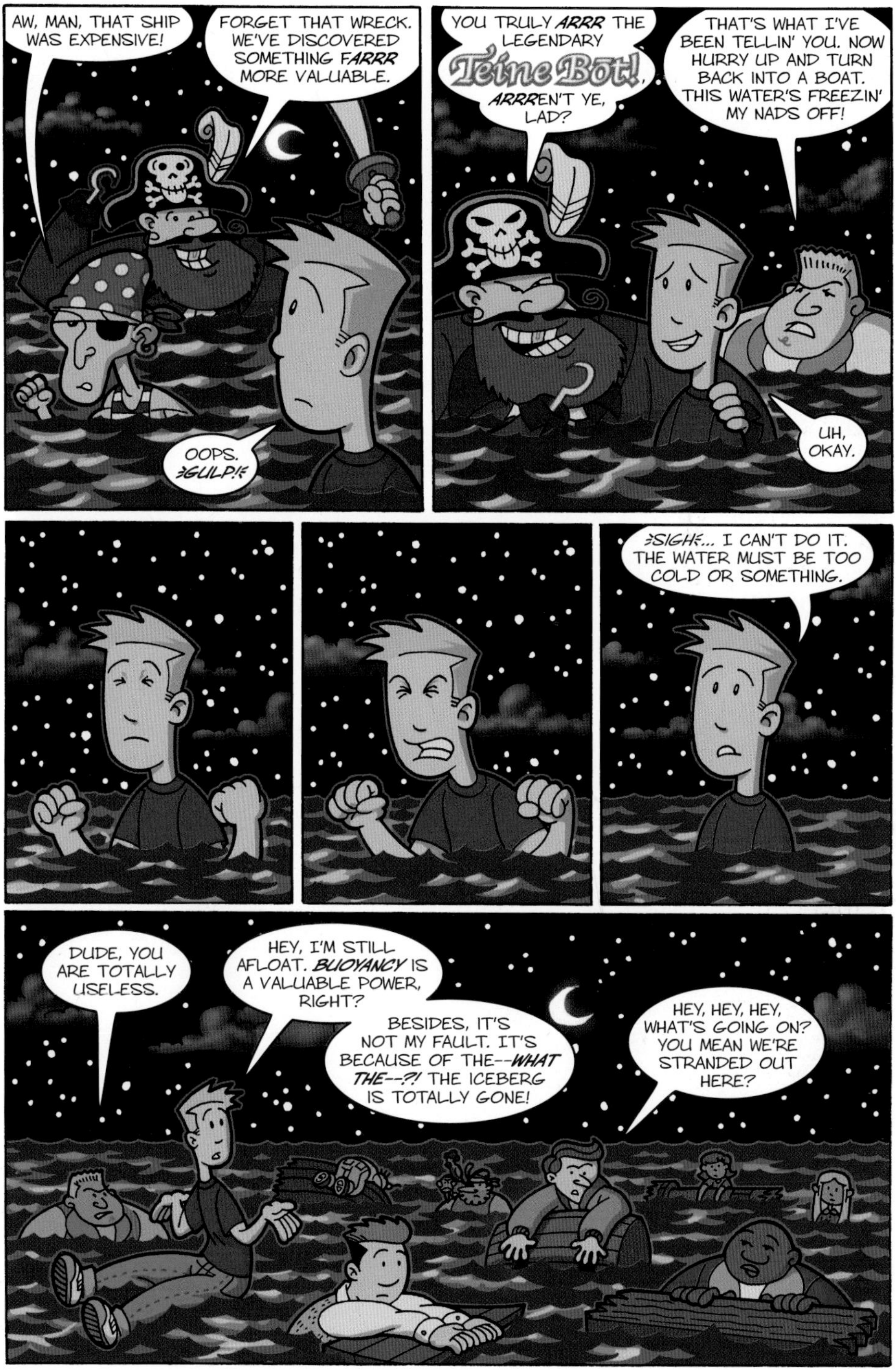
AW, MAN, THAT SHIP WAS EXPENSIVE!
FORGET THAT WRECK. WE'VE DISCOVERED SOMETHING FARRR MORE VALUABLE.
OOPS. GULP!
YOU TRULY ARRR THE LEGENDARY Teine Bot!, ARRREN'T YE, LAD?
THAT'S WHAT I'VE BEEN TELLIN' YOU. NOW HURRY UP AND TURN BACK INTO A BOAT. THIS WATER'S FREEZIN' MY NADS OFF!
UH, OKAY.
SIGH... I CAN'T DO IT. THE WATER MUST BE TOO COLD OR SOMETHING.
DUDE, YOU ARE TOTALLY USELESS.
HEY, I'M STILL AFLOAT. BUOYANCY IS A VALUABLE POWER, RIGHT?
BESIDES, IT'S NOT MY FAULT. IT'S BECAUSE OF THE--WHAT THE--?! THE ICEBERG IS TOTALLY GONE!
HEY, HEY, HEY, WHAT'S GOING ON? YOU MEAN WE'RE STRANDED OUT HERE?

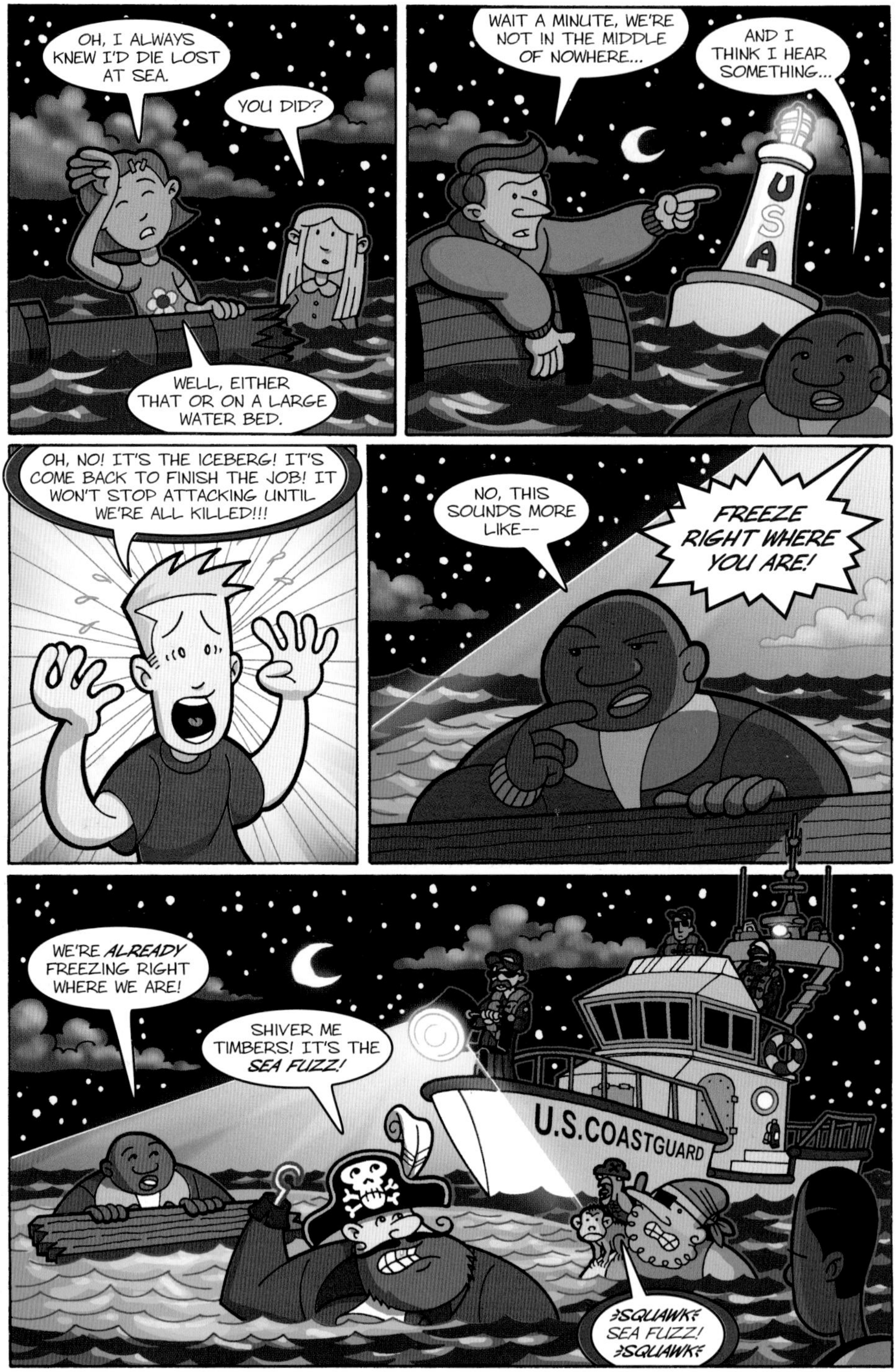
OH, I ALWAYS KNEW I'D DIE LOST AT SEA.
YOU DID?
WELL, EITHER THAT OR ON A LARGE WATER BED.
WAIT A MINUTE, WE'RE NOT IN THE MIDDLE OF NOWHERE...
AND I THINK I HEAR SOMETHING...
USA
OH, NO! IT'S THE ICEBERG! IT'S COME BACK TO FINISH THE JOB! IT WON'T STOP ATTACKING UNTIL WE'RE ALL KILLED!!!
NO, THIS SOUNDS MORE LIKE--
FREEZE RIGHT WHERE YOU ARE!
WE'RE ALREADY FREEZING RIGHT WHERE WE ARE!
SHIVER ME TIMBERS! IT'S THE SEA FUZZ!
U.S.COASTGUARD
SQUAWK SEA FUZZ! SQUAWK

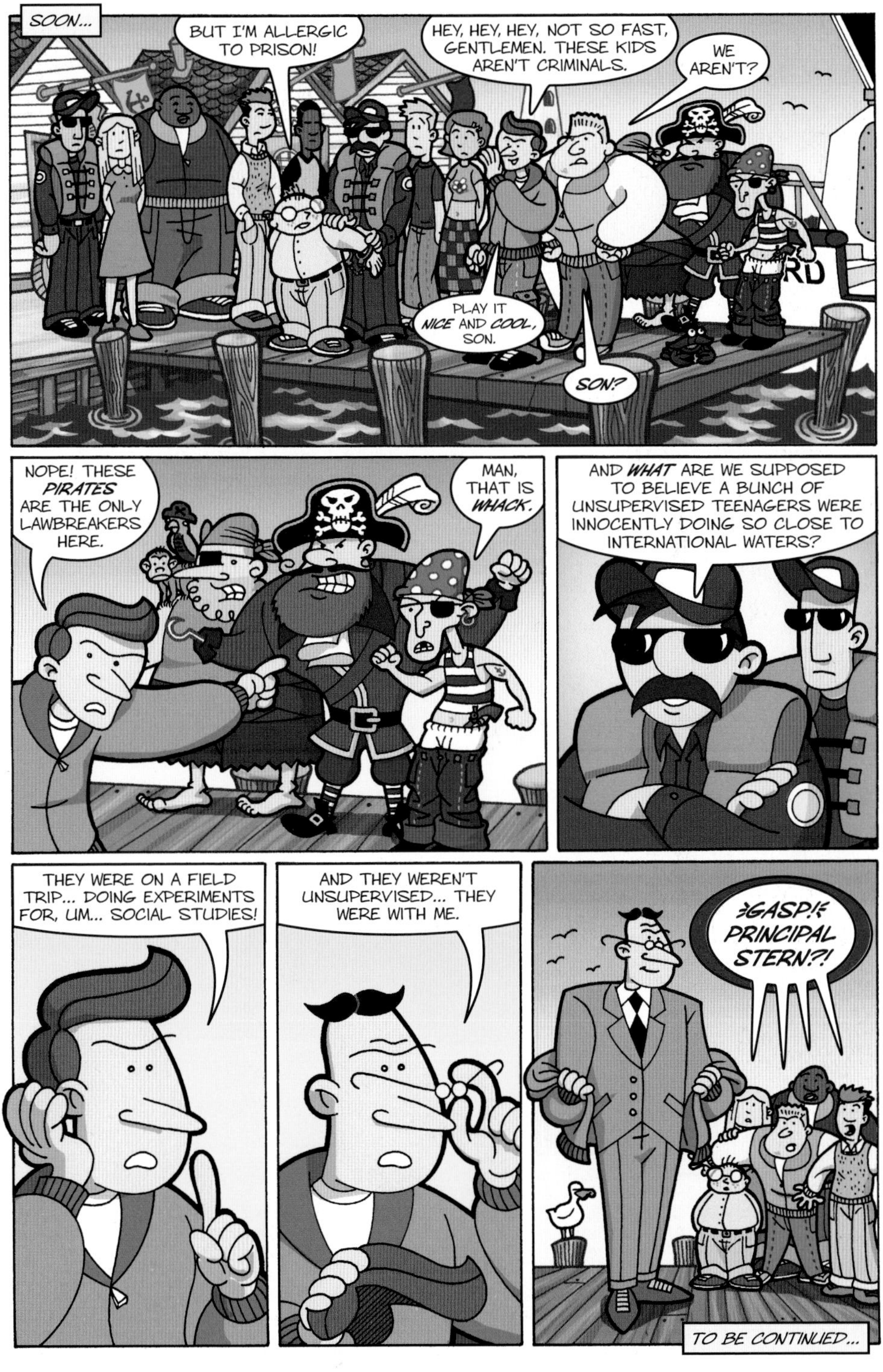
SOON...
BUT I'M ALLERGIC TO PRISON!
HEY, HEY, HEY, NOT SO FAST, GENTLEMEN. THESE KIDS AREN'T CRIMINALS.
WE AREN'T?
PLAY IT *NICE* AND *COOL*, SON.
SON?
NOPE! THESE *PIRATES* ARE THE ONLY LAWBREAKERS HERE.
MAN, THAT IS *WHACK.*
AND *WHAT* ARE WE SUPPOSED TO BELIEVE A BUNCH OF UNSUPERVISED TEENAGERS WERE INNOCENTLY DOING SO CLOSE TO INTERNATIONAL WATERS?
THEY WERE ON A FIELD TRIP... DOING EXPERIMENTS FOR, UM... SOCIAL STUDIES!
AND THEY WEREN'T UNSUPERVISED... THEY WERE WITH ME.
GASP! PRINCIPAL STERN?!
TO BE CONTINUED...

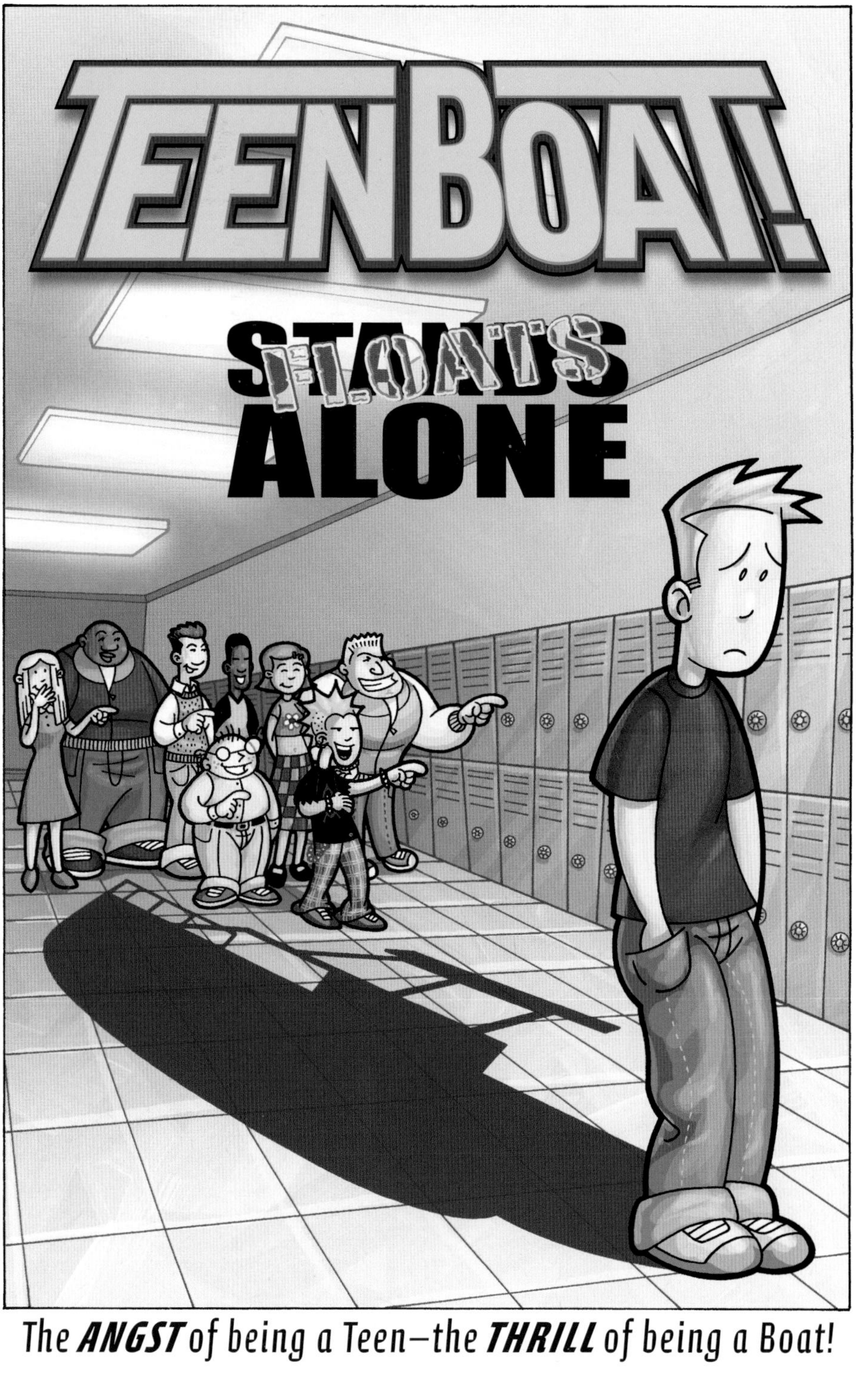

TEEN BOAT!
STANDS
FLOATS
ALONE

The ***ANGST*** of being a Teen—the ***THRILL*** of being a Boat!

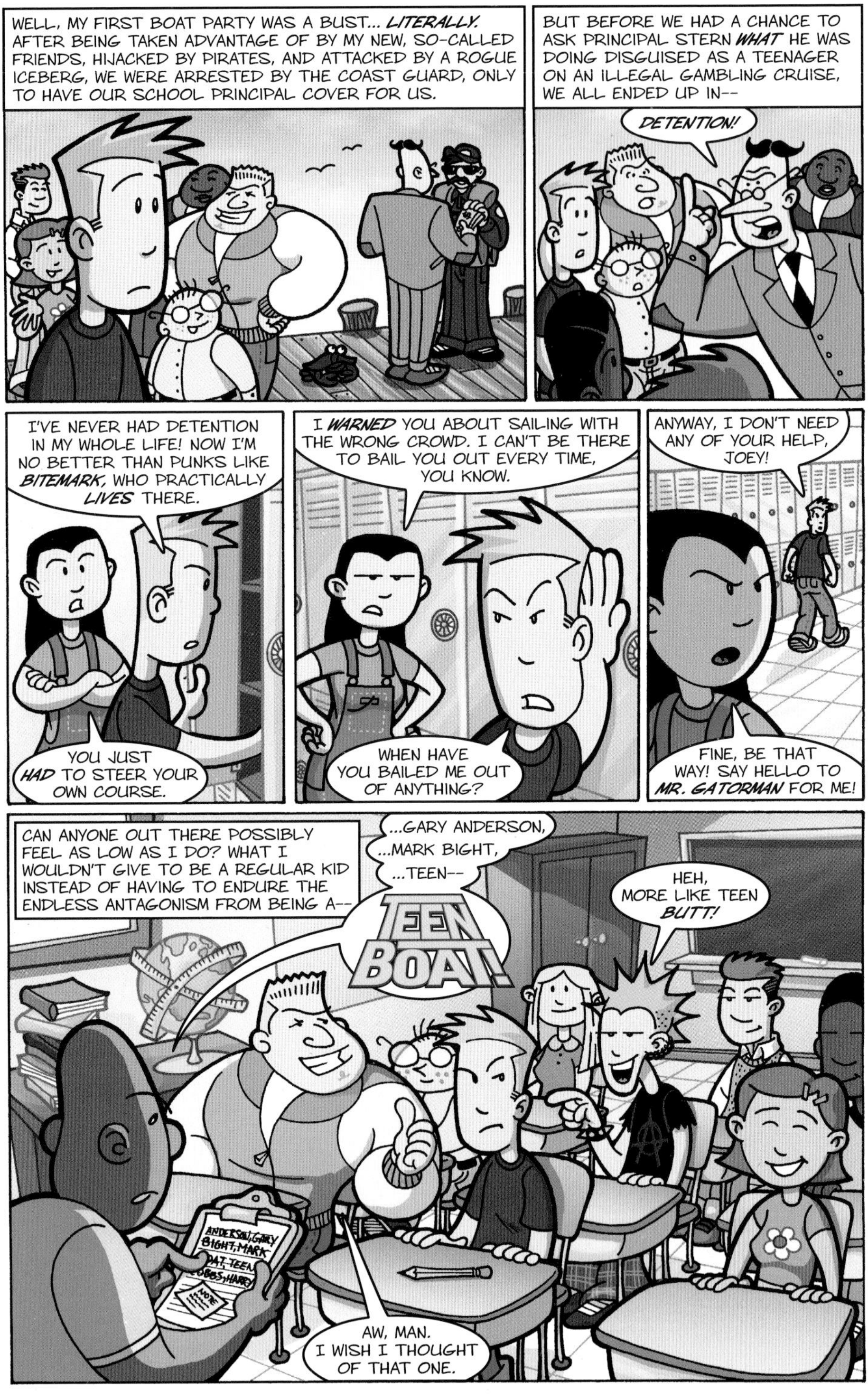
WELL, MY FIRST BOAT PARTY WAS A BUST... LITERALLY. AFTER BEING TAKEN ADVANTAGE OF BY MY NEW, SO-CALLED FRIENDS, HIJACKED BY PIRATES, AND ATTACKED BY A ROGUE ICEBERG, WE WERE ARRESTED BY THE COAST GUARD, ONLY TO HAVE OUR SCHOOL PRINCIPAL COVER FOR US.
BUT BEFORE WE HAD A CHANCE TO ASK PRINCIPAL STERN WHAT HE WAS DOING DISGUISED AS A TEENAGER ON AN ILLEGAL GAMBLING CRUISE, WE ALL ENDED UP IN--
DETENTION!
I'VE NEVER HAD DETENTION IN MY WHOLE LIFE! NOW I'M NO BETTER THAN PUNKS LIKE BITEMARK, WHO PRACTICALLY LIVES THERE.
YOU JUST HAD TO STEER YOUR OWN COURSE.
I WARNED YOU ABOUT SAILING WITH THE WRONG CROWD. I CAN'T BE THERE TO BAIL YOU OUT EVERY TIME, YOU KNOW.
WHEN HAVE YOU BAILED ME OUT OF ANYTHING?
ANYWAY, I DON'T NEED ANY OF YOUR HELP, JOEY!
FINE, BE THAT WAY! SAY HELLO TO MR. GATORMAN FOR ME!
CAN ANYONE OUT THERE POSSIBLY FEEL AS LOW AS I DO? WHAT I WOULDN'T GIVE TO BE A REGULAR KID INSTEAD OF HAVING TO ENDURE THE ENDLESS ANTAGONISM FROM BEING A--
...GARY ANDERSON,
...MARK BIGHT,
...TEEN--
TEEN BOAT!
HEH, MORE LIKE TEEN BUTT!
AW, MAN. I WISH I THOUGHT OF THAT ONE.

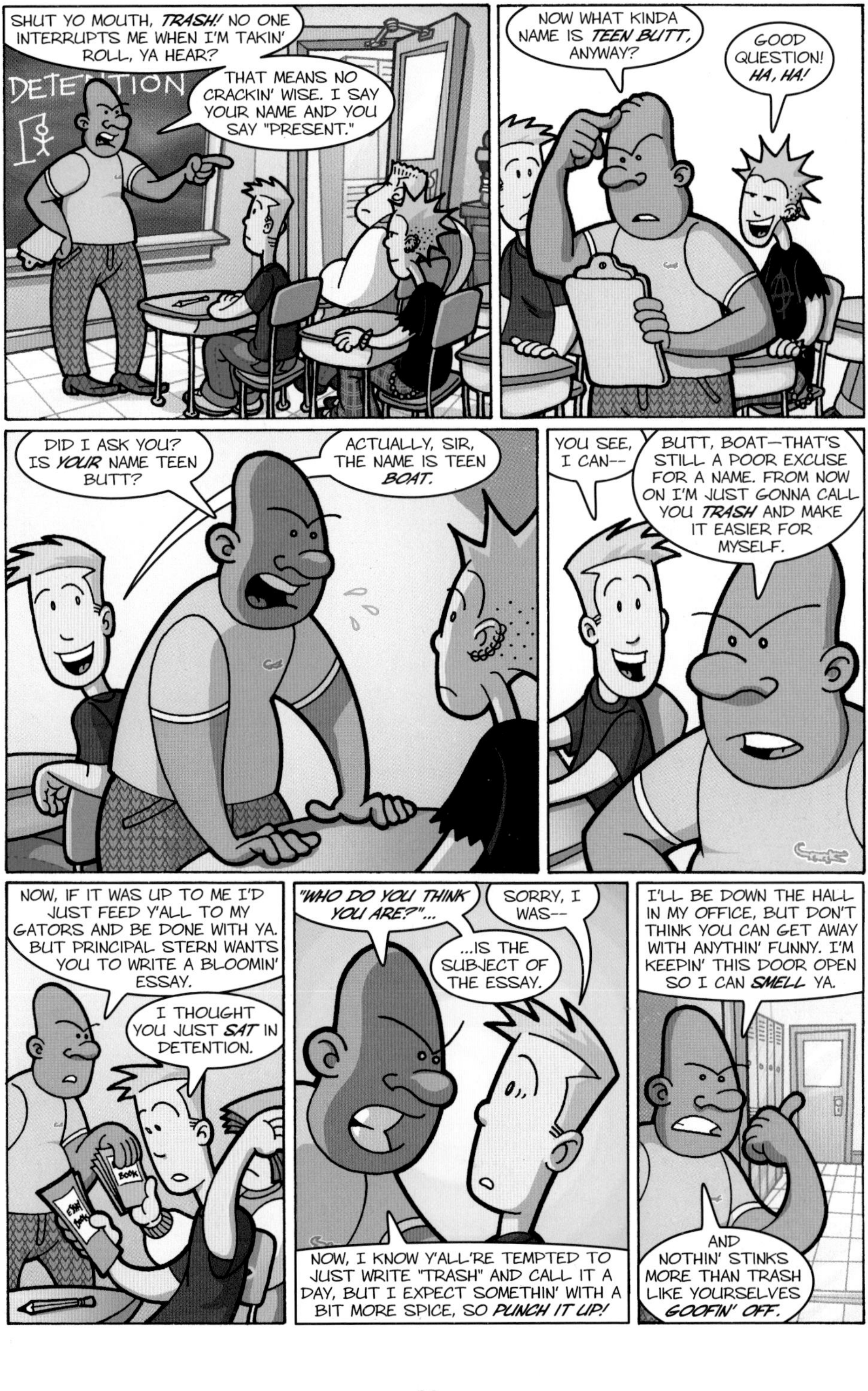
SHUT YO MOUTH, TRASH! NO ONE INTERRUPTS ME WHEN I'M TAKIN' ROLL, YA HEAR?
DETENTION
THAT MEANS NO CRACKIN' WISE. I SAY YOUR NAME AND YOU SAY "PRESENT."
NOW WHAT KINDA NAME IS TEEN BUTT, ANYWAY?
GOOD QUESTION! HA, HA!
DID I ASK YOU? IS YOUR NAME TEEN BUTT?
ACTUALLY, SIR, THE NAME IS TEEN BOAT.
YOU SEE, I CAN--
BUTT, BOAT—THAT'S STILL A POOR EXCUSE FOR A NAME. FROM NOW ON I'M JUST GONNA CALL YOU TRASH AND MAKE IT EASIER FOR MYSELF.
NOW, IF IT WAS UP TO ME I'D JUST FEED Y'ALL TO MY GATORS AND BE DONE WITH YA. BUT PRINCIPAL STERN WANTS YOU TO WRITE A BLOOMIN' ESSAY.
I THOUGHT YOU JUST SAT IN DETENTION.
BOOK
"WHO DO YOU THINK YOU ARE?"...
SORRY, I WAS--
...IS THE SUBJECT OF THE ESSAY.
NOW, I KNOW Y'ALL'RE TEMPTED TO JUST WRITE "TRASH" AND CALL IT A DAY, BUT I EXPECT SOMETHIN' WITH A BIT MORE SPICE, SO PUNCH IT UP!
I'LL BE DOWN THE HALL IN MY OFFICE, BUT DON'T THINK YOU CAN GET AWAY WITH ANYTHIN' FUNNY. I'M KEEPIN' THIS DOOR OPEN SO I CAN SMELL YA.
AND NOTHIN' STINKS MORE THAN TRASH LIKE YOURSELVES GOOFIN' OFF.

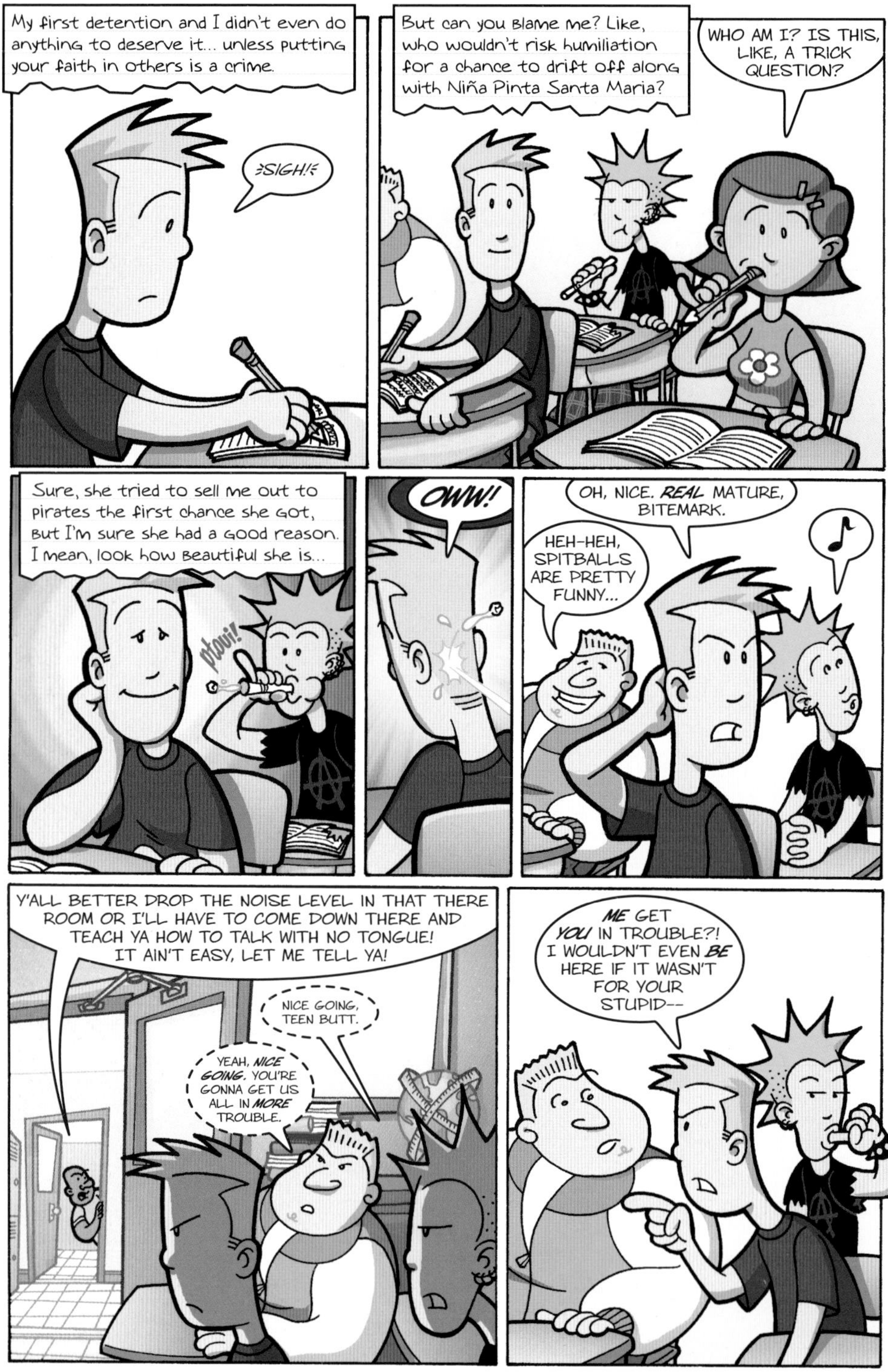
My first detention and I didn't even do anything to deserve it... unless putting your faith in others is a crime.
SIGH!
But can you blame me? Like, who wouldn't risk humiliation for a chance to drift off along with Niña Pinta Santa Maria?
WHO AM I? IS THIS, LIKE, A TRICK QUESTION?
Sure, she tried to sell me out to pirates the first chance she got, but I'm sure she had a good reason. I mean, look how beautiful she is...
ptoui!
OWW!
OH, NICE. REAL MATURE, BITEMARK.
HEH-HEH, SPITBALLS ARE PRETTY FUNNY...
Y'ALL BETTER DROP THE NOISE LEVEL IN THAT THERE ROOM OR I'LL HAVE TO COME DOWN THERE AND TEACH YA HOW TO TALK WITH NO TONGUE! IT AIN'T EASY, LET ME TELL YA!
NICE GOING, TEEN BUTT.
YEAH, NICE GOING. YOU'RE GONNA GET US ALL IN MORE TROUBLE.
ME GET YOU IN TROUBLE?! I WOULDN'T EVEN BE HERE IF IT WASN'T FOR YOUR STUPID--

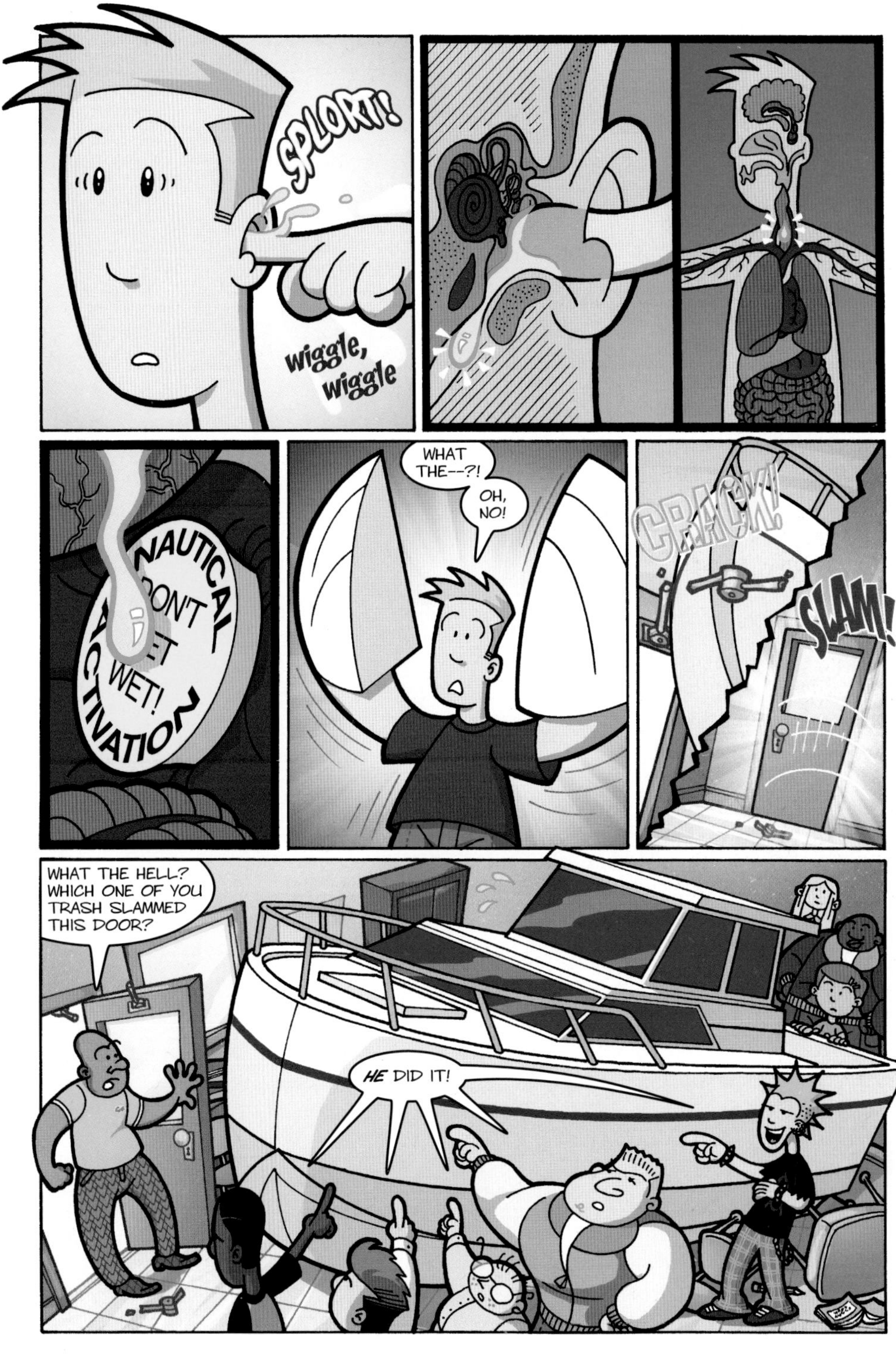
SPLORT!
wiggle, wiggle
NAUTICAL ACTIVATION
DON'T GET WET!
WHAT THE--?!
OH, NO!
CRACK!
SLAM!
WHAT THE HELL? WHICH ONE OF YOU TRASH SLAMMED THIS DOOR?
HE DID IT!

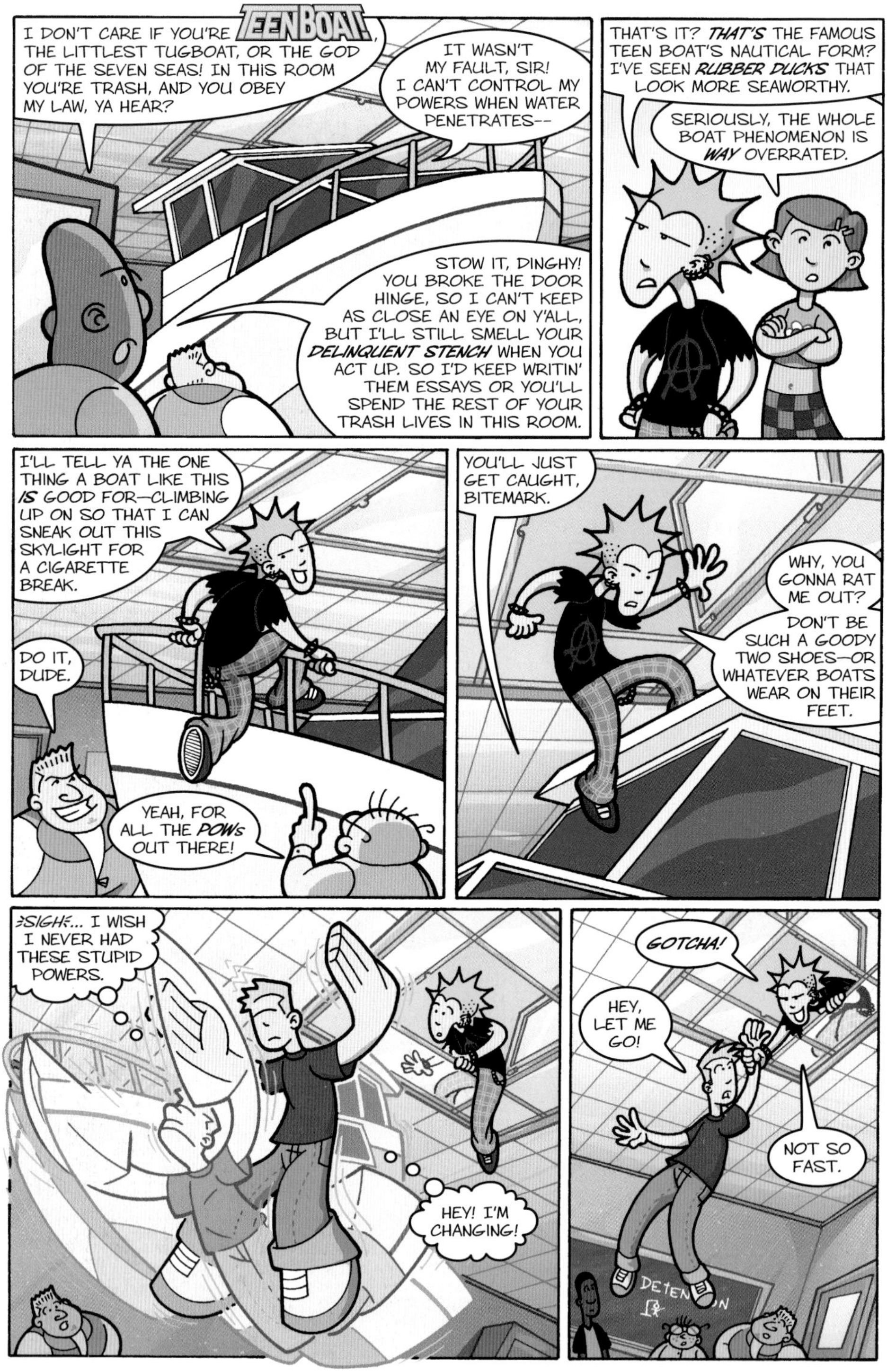
I DON'T CARE IF YOU'RE TEEN BOAT! THE LITTLEST TUGBOAT, OR THE GOD OF THE SEVEN SEAS! IN THIS ROOM YOU'RE TRASH, AND YOU OBEY MY LAW, YA HEAR?
IT WASN'T MY FAULT, SIR! I CAN'T CONTROL MY POWERS WHEN WATER PENETRATES--
STOW IT, DINGHY! YOU BROKE THE DOOR HINGE, SO I CAN'T KEEP AS CLOSE AN EYE ON Y'ALL, BUT I'LL STILL SMELL YOUR DELINQUENT STENCH WHEN YOU ACT UP. SO I'D KEEP WRITIN' THEM ESSAYS OR YOU'LL SPEND THE REST OF YOUR TRASH LIVES IN THIS ROOM.
THAT'S IT? THAT'S THE FAMOUS TEEN BOAT'S NAUTICAL FORM? I'VE SEEN RUBBER DUCKS THAT LOOK MORE SEAWORTHY.
SERIOUSLY, THE WHOLE BOAT PHENOMENON IS WAY OVERRATED.
I'LL TELL YA THE ONE THING A BOAT LIKE THIS IS GOOD FOR—CLIMBING UP ON SO THAT I CAN SNEAK OUT THIS SKYLIGHT FOR A CIGARETTE BREAK.
DO IT, DUDE.
YEAH, FOR ALL THE POWs OUT THERE!
YOU'LL JUST GET CAUGHT, BITEMARK.
WHY, YOU GONNA RAT ME OUT?
DON'T BE SUCH A GOODY TWO SHOES—OR WHATEVER BOATS WEAR ON THEIR FEET.
SIGH... I WISH I NEVER HAD THESE STUPID POWERS.
HEY! I'M CHANGING!
GOTCHA!
HEY, LET ME GO!
NOT SO FAST.
DETEN ON

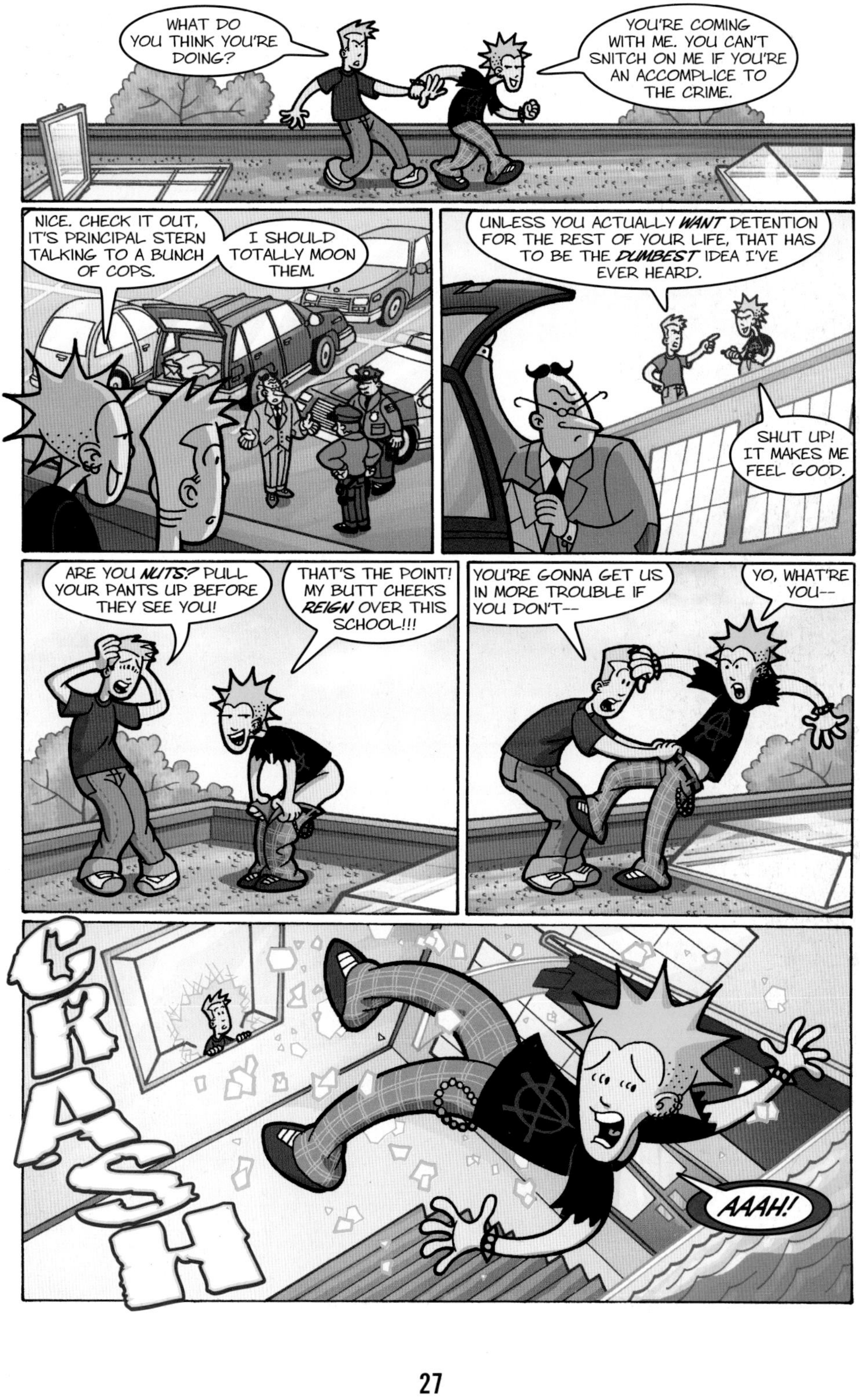
WHAT DO YOU THINK YOU'RE DOING?
YOU'RE COMING WITH ME. YOU CAN'T SNITCH ON ME IF YOU'RE AN ACCOMPLICE TO THE CRIME.
NICE. CHECK IT OUT, IT'S PRINCIPAL STERN TALKING TO A BUNCH OF COPS.
I SHOULD TOTALLY MOON THEM.
UNLESS YOU ACTUALLY WANT DETENTION FOR THE REST OF YOUR LIFE, THAT HAS TO BE THE DUMBEST IDEA I'VE EVER HEARD.
SHUT UP! IT MAKES ME FEEL GOOD.
ARE YOU NUTS? PULL YOUR PANTS UP BEFORE THEY SEE YOU!
THAT'S THE POINT! MY BUTT CHEEKS REIGN OVER THIS SCHOOL!!!
YOU'RE GONNA GET US IN MORE TROUBLE IF YOU DON'T--
YO, WHAT'RE YOU--
CRASH
AAAH!

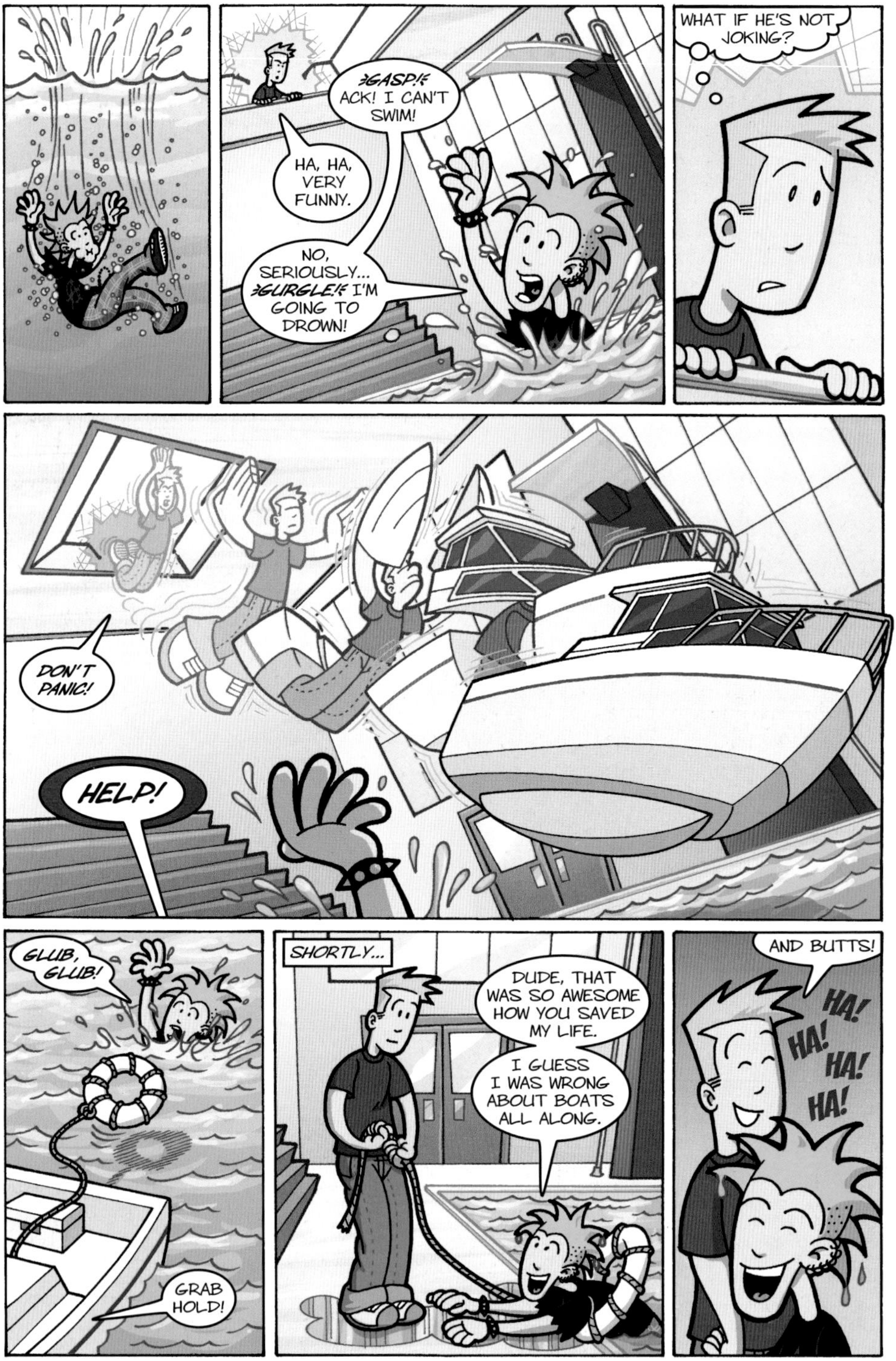

ÆGASP!Æ ACK! I CAN'T SWIM!
HA, HA, VERY FUNNY.
NO, SERIOUSLY... ÆGURGLE!Æ I'M GOING TO DROWN!
WHAT IF HE'S NOT JOKING?
DON'T PANIC!
HELP!
GLUB, GLUB!
GRAB HOLD!
SHORTLY...
DUDE, THAT WAS SO AWESOME HOW YOU SAVED MY LIFE.
I GUESS I WAS WRONG ABOUT BOATS ALL ALONG.
AND BUTTS!
HA! HA! HA! HA!

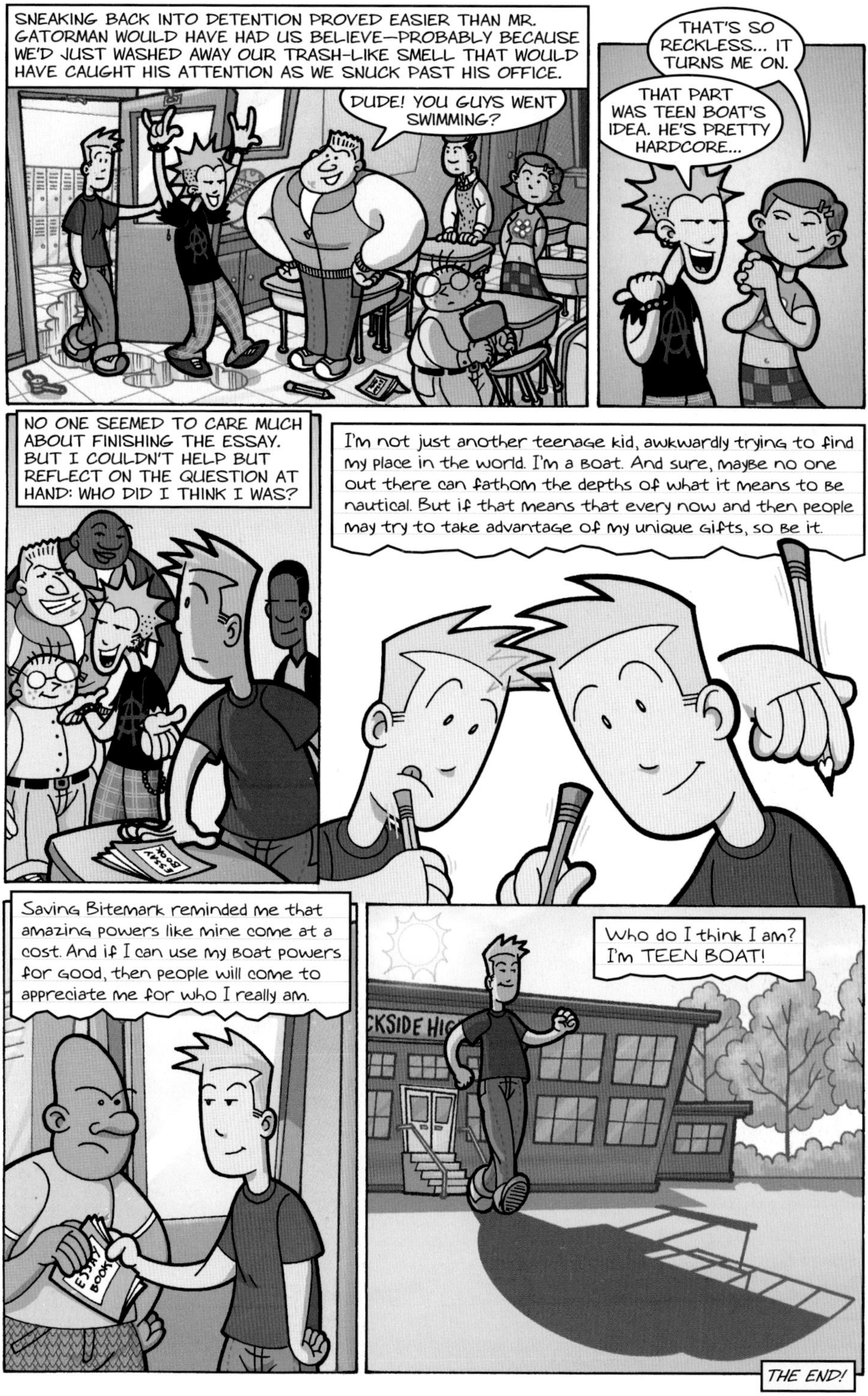
SNEAKING BACK INTO DETENTION PROVED EASIER THAN MR. GATORMAN WOULD HAVE HAD US BELIEVE—PROBABLY BECAUSE WE'D JUST WASHED AWAY OUR TRASH-LIKE SMELL THAT WOULD HAVE CAUGHT HIS ATTENTION AS WE SNUCK PAST HIS OFFICE.
DUDE! YOU GUYS WENT SWIMMING?
THAT PART WAS TEEN BOAT'S IDEA. HE'S PRETTY HARDCORE...
THAT'S SO RECKLESS... IT TURNS ME ON.
NO ONE SEEMED TO CARE MUCH ABOUT FINISHING THE ESSAY. BUT I COULDN'T HELP BUT REFLECT ON THE QUESTION AT HAND: WHO DID I THINK I WAS?
ESSAY BOOK
I'm not just another teenage kid, awkwardly trying to find my place in the world. I'm a boat. And sure, maybe no one out there can fathom the depths of what it means to be nautical. But if that means that every now and then people may try to take advantage of my unique gifts, so be it.
Saving Bitemark reminded me that amazing powers like mine come at a cost. And if I can use my boat powers for good, then people will come to appreciate me for who I really am.
ESSAY BOOK
Who do I think I am? I'm TEEN BOAT!
CKSIDE HIG
THE END!

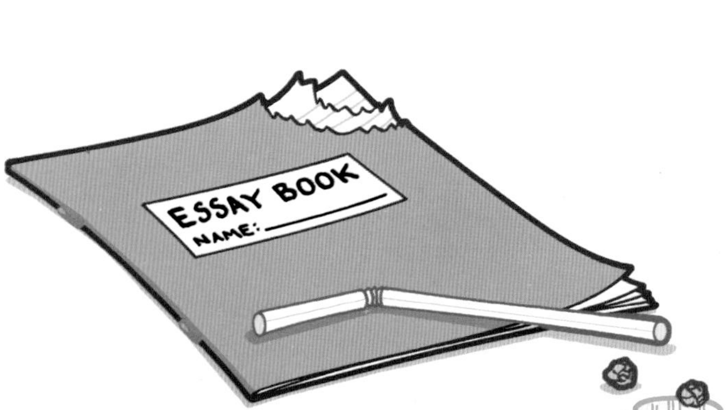
ESSAY BOOK
NAME:

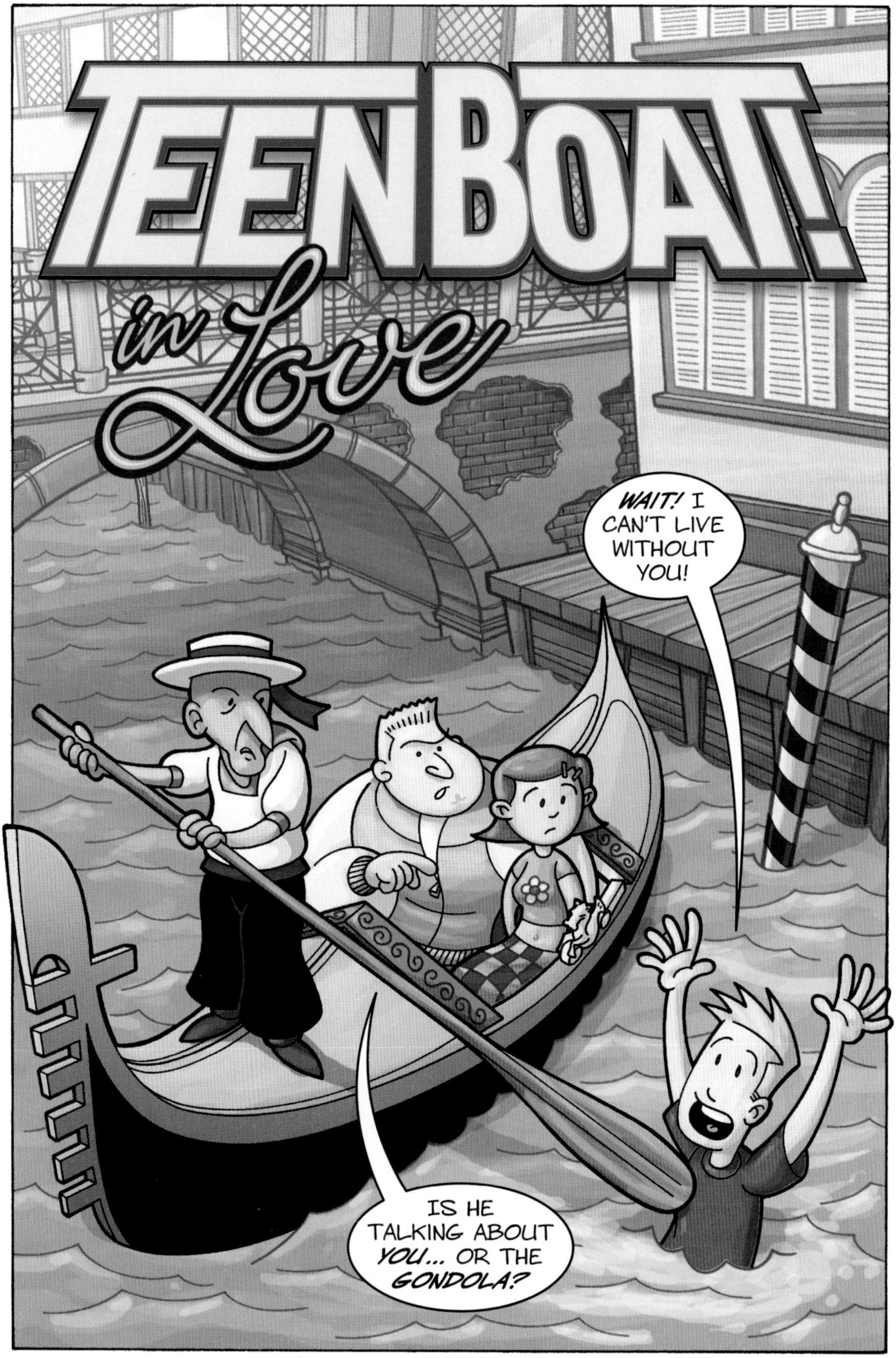
TEEN BOAT!
in Love
WAIT! I CAN'T LIVE WITHOUT YOU!
IS HE TALKING ABOUT YOU... OR THE GONDOLA?

The **ANGST** of being a Teen—the **THRILL** of being a Boat!

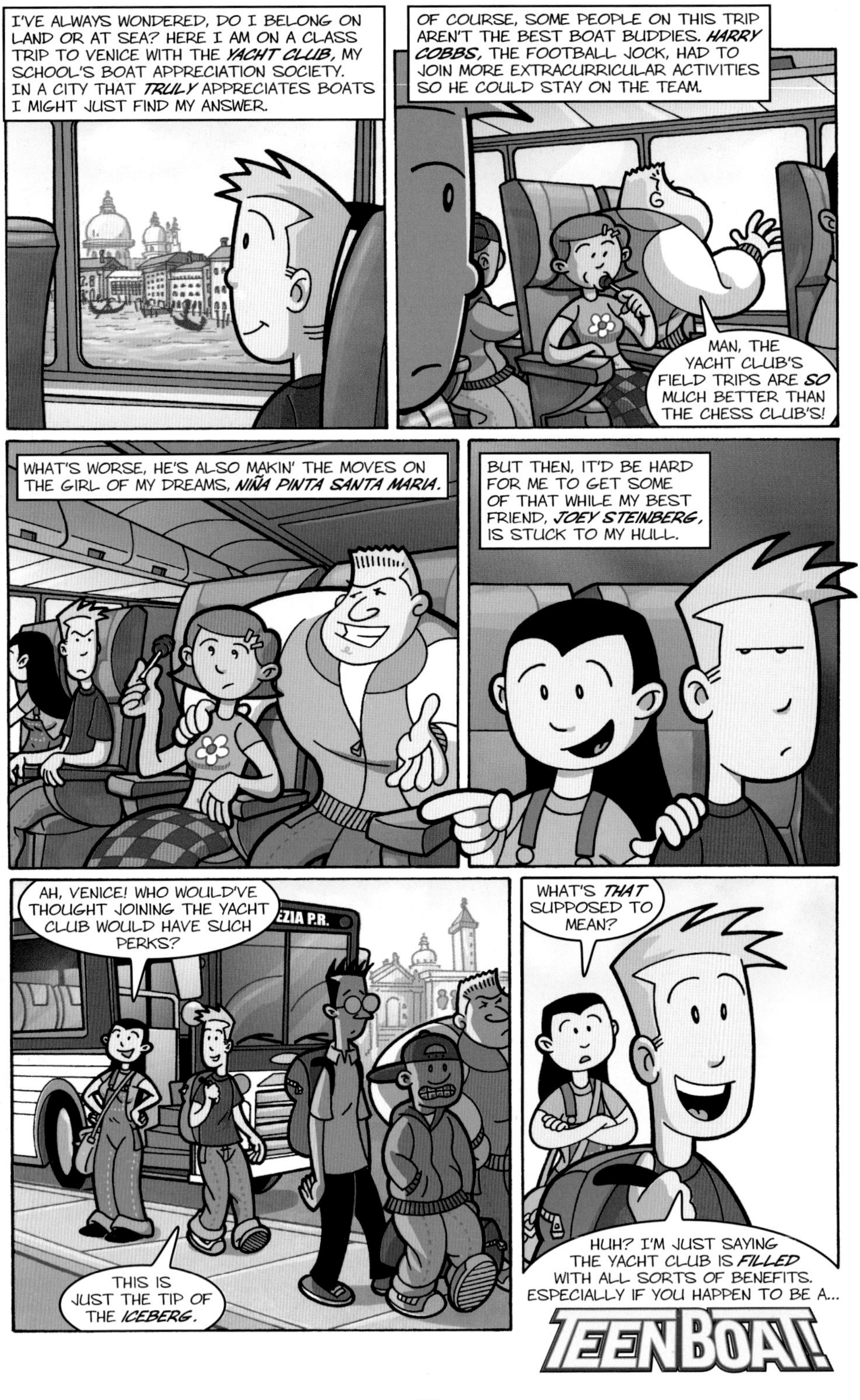

I'VE ALWAYS WONDERED, DO I BELONG ON LAND OR AT SEA? HERE I AM ON A CLASS TRIP TO VENICE WITH THE YACHT CLUB, MY SCHOOL'S BOAT APPRECIATION SOCIETY. IN A CITY THAT TRULY APPRECIATES BOATS I MIGHT JUST FIND MY ANSWER.
OF COURSE, SOME PEOPLE ON THIS TRIP AREN'T THE BEST BOAT BUDDIES. HARRY COBBS, THE FOOTBALL JOCK, HAD TO JOIN MORE EXTRACURRICULAR ACTIVITIES SO HE COULD STAY ON THE TEAM.
MAN, THE YACHT CLUB'S FIELD TRIPS ARE SO MUCH BETTER THAN THE CHESS CLUB'S!
WHAT'S WORSE, HE'S ALSO MAKIN' THE MOVES ON THE GIRL OF MY DREAMS, NIÑA PINTA SANTA MARIA.
BUT THEN, IT'D BE HARD FOR ME TO GET SOME OF THAT WHILE MY BEST FRIEND, JOEY STEINBERG, IS STUCK TO MY HULL.
AH, VENICE! WHO WOULD'VE THOUGHT JOINING THE YACHT CLUB WOULD HAVE SUCH PERKS?
EZIA P.R.
THIS IS JUST THE TIP OF THE ICEBERG.
WHAT'S THAT SUPPOSED TO MEAN?
HUH? I'M JUST SAYING THE YACHT CLUB IS FILLED WITH ALL SORTS OF BENEFITS. ESPECIALLY IF YOU HAPPEN TO BE A...
TEEN BOAT!

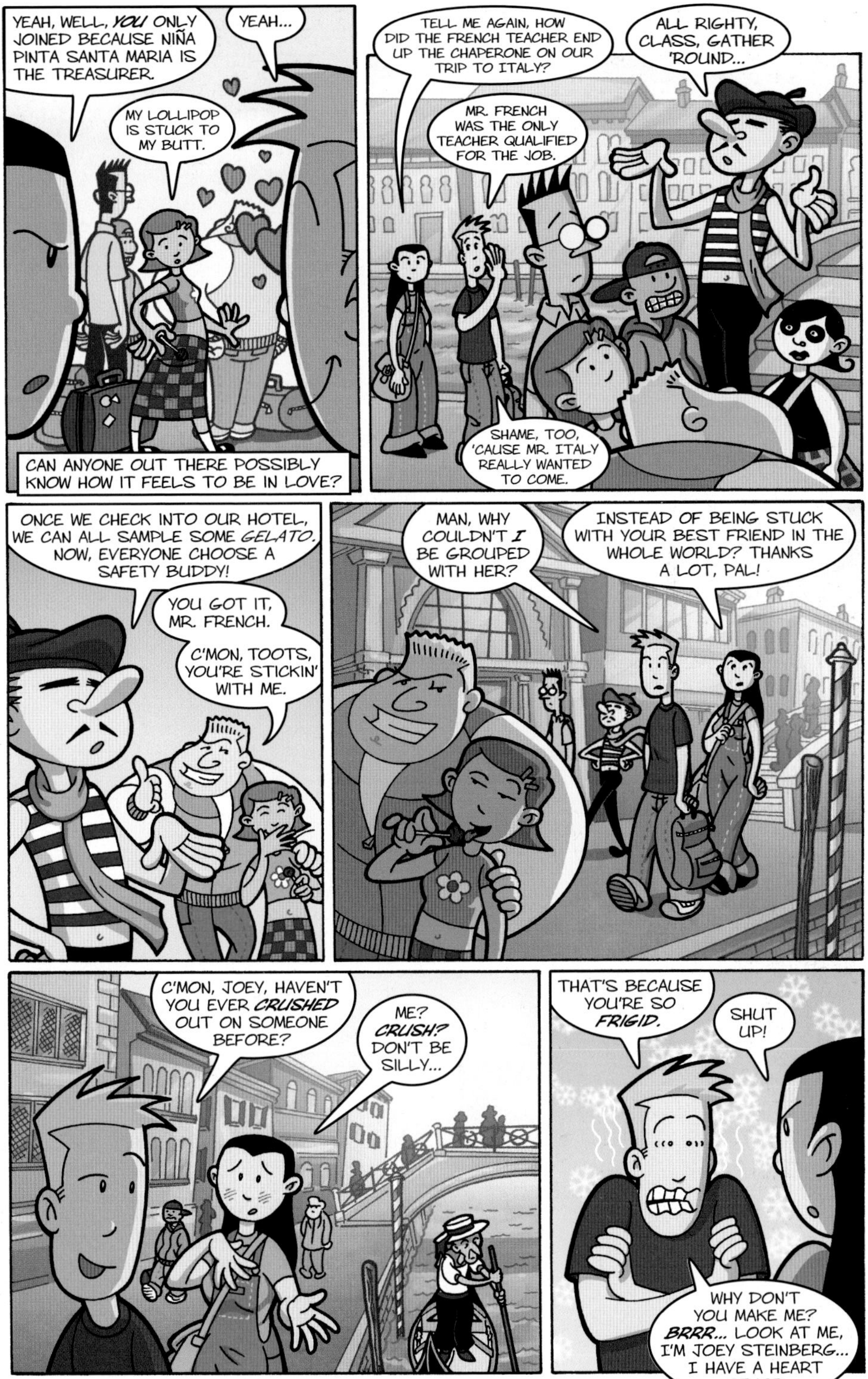
YEAH, WELL, *YOU* ONLY JOINED BECAUSE NIÑA PINTA SANTA MARIA IS THE TREASURER.
YEAH...
MY LOLLIPOP IS STUCK TO MY BUTT.
CAN ANYONE OUT THERE POSSIBLY KNOW HOW IT FEELS TO BE IN LOVE?
TELL ME AGAIN, HOW DID THE FRENCH TEACHER END UP THE CHAPERONE ON OUR TRIP TO ITALY?
ALL RIGHTY, CLASS, GATHER 'ROUND...
MR. FRENCH WAS THE ONLY TEACHER QUALIFIED FOR THE JOB.
SHAME, TOO, 'CAUSE MR. ITALY REALLY WANTED TO COME.
ONCE WE CHECK INTO OUR HOTEL, WE CAN ALL SAMPLE SOME *GELATO*. NOW, EVERYONE CHOOSE A SAFETY BUDDY!
YOU GOT IT, MR. FRENCH.
C'MON, TOOTS, YOU'RE STICKIN' WITH ME.
MAN, WHY COULDN'T *I* BE GROUPED WITH HER?
INSTEAD OF BEING STUCK WITH YOUR BEST FRIEND IN THE WHOLE WORLD? THANKS A LOT, PAL!
C'MON, JOEY, HAVEN'T YOU EVER *CRUSHED* OUT ON SOMEONE BEFORE?
ME? *CRUSH?* DON'T BE SILLY...
THAT'S BECAUSE YOU'RE SO *FRIGID*.
SHUT UP!
WHY DON'T YOU MAKE ME? *BRRR...* LOOK AT ME, I'M JOEY STEINBERG... I HAVE A HEART OF ICE.

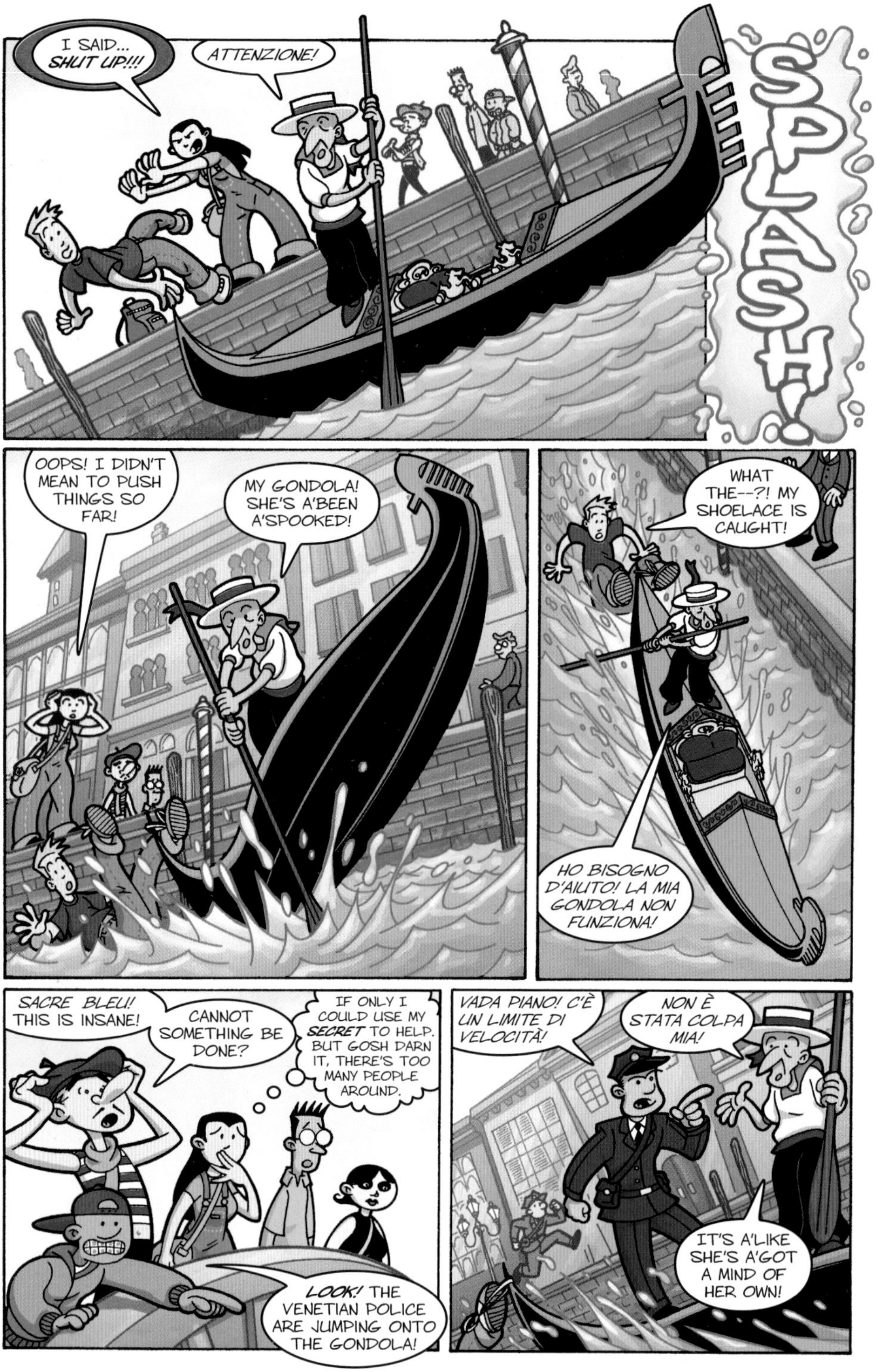
I SAID... SHUT UP!!!
ATTENZIONE!
SPLASH!
OOPS! I DIDN'T MEAN TO PUSH THINGS SO FAR!
MY GONDOLA! SHE'S A'BEEN A'SPOOKED!
WHAT THE--?! MY SHOELACE IS CAUGHT!
HO BISOGNO D'AIUTO! LA MIA GONDOLA NON FUNZIONA!
SACRE BLEU! THIS IS INSANE!
CANNOT SOMETHING BE DONE?
IF ONLY I COULD USE MY SECRET TO HELP. BUT GOSH DARN IT, THERE'S TOO MANY PEOPLE AROUND.
LOOK! THE VENETIAN POLICE ARE JUMPING ONTO THE GONDOLA!
VADA PIANO! C'È UN LIMITE DI VELOCITÀ!
NON È STATA COLPA MIA!
IT'S A'LIKE SHE'S A'GOT A MIND OF HER OWN!

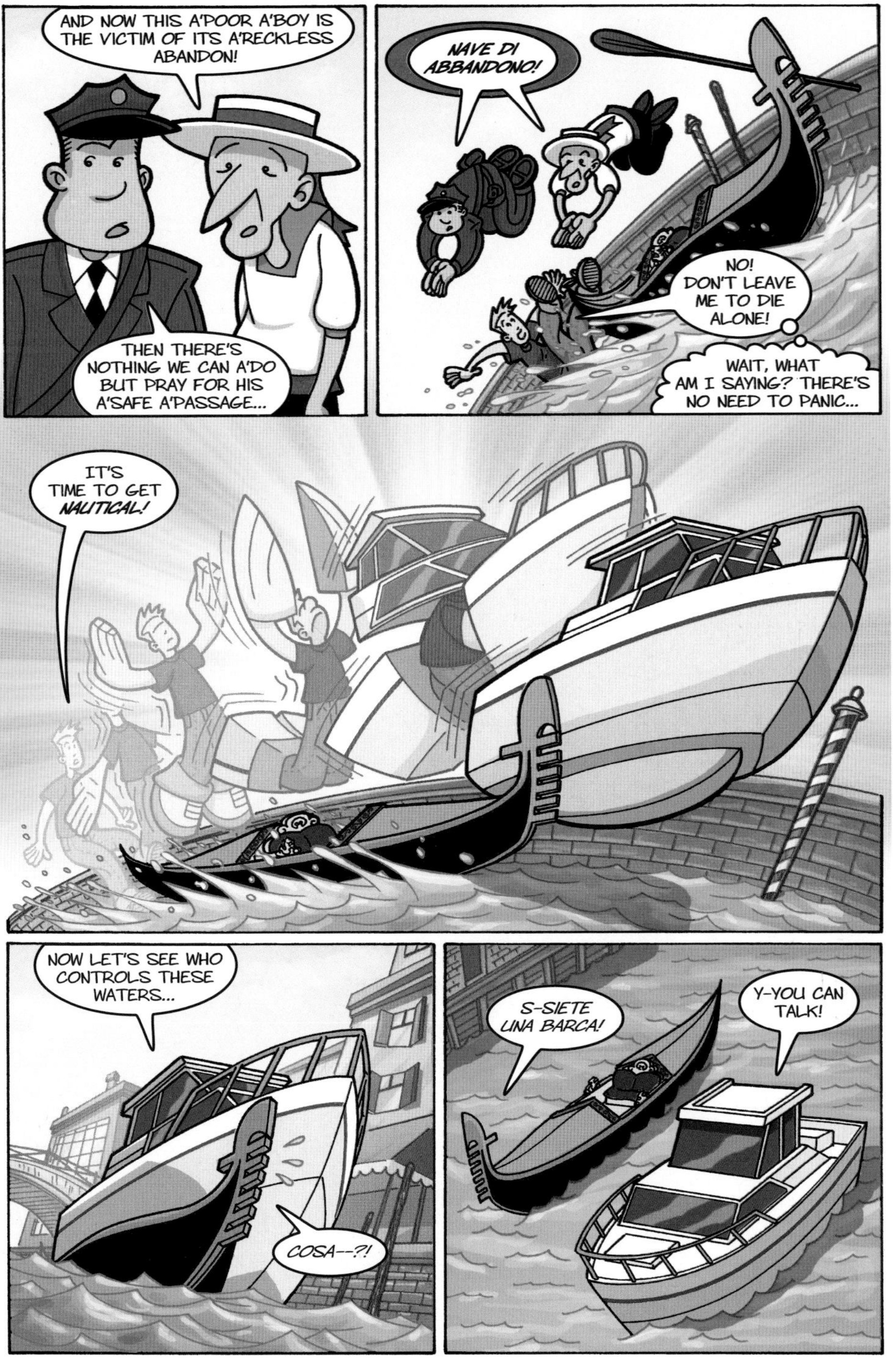
AND NOW THIS A'POOR A'BOY IS THE VICTIM OF ITS A'RECKLESS ABANDON!
THEN THERE'S NOTHING WE CAN A'DO BUT PRAY FOR HIS A'SAFE A'PASSAGE...
NAVE DI ABBANDONO!
NO! DON'T LEAVE ME TO DIE ALONE!
WAIT, WHAT AM I SAYING? THERE'S NO NEED TO PANIC...
IT'S TIME TO GET NAUTICAL!
NOW LET'S SEE WHO CONTROLS THESE WATERS...
COSA--?!
S-SIETE UNA BARCA!
Y-YOU CAN TALK!

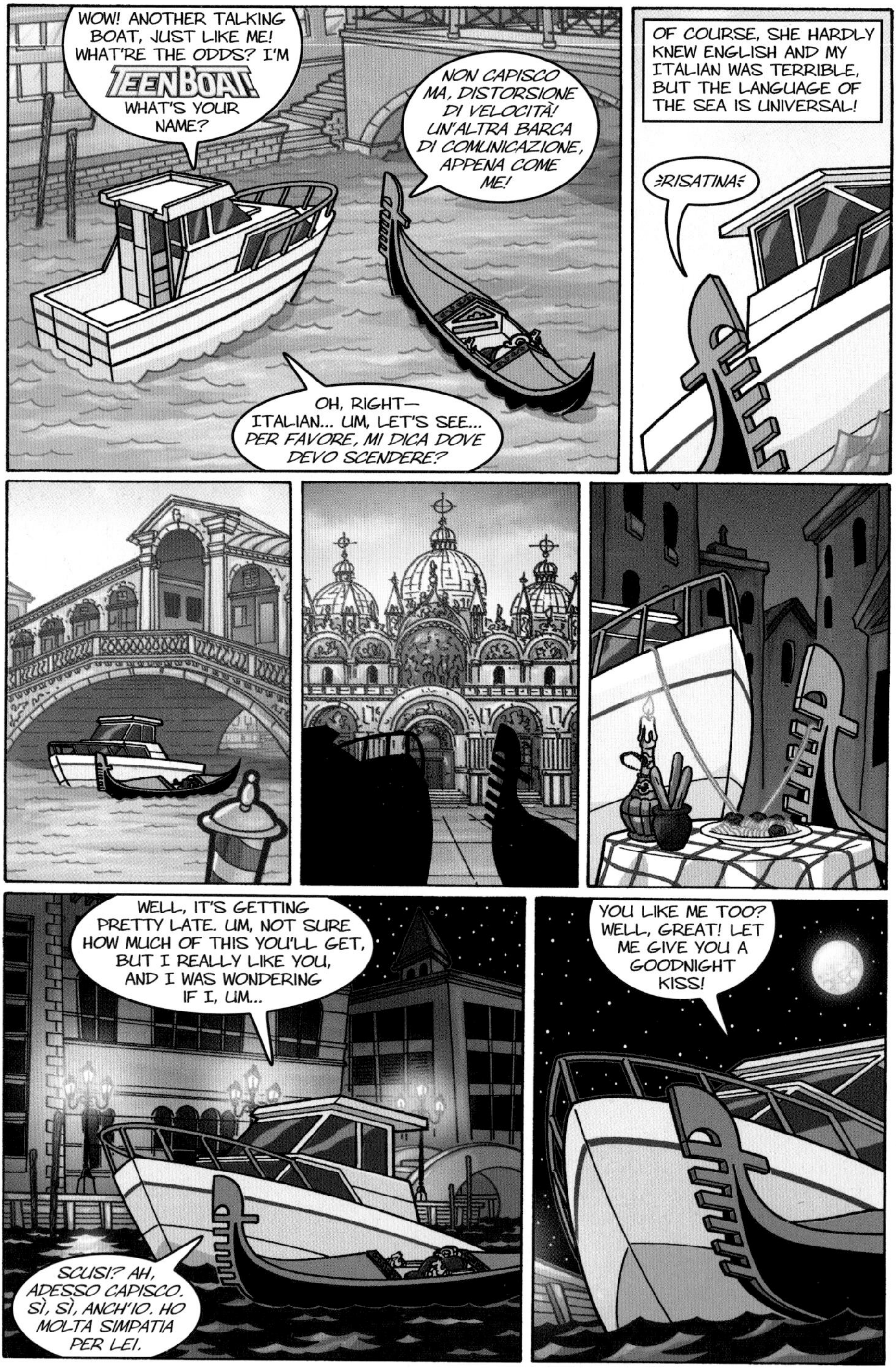
WOW! ANOTHER TALKING BOAT, JUST LIKE ME! WHAT'RE THE ODDS? I'M TEEN BOAT! WHAT'S YOUR NAME?
NON CAPISCO MA, DISTORSIONE DI VELOCITÀ! UN'ALTRA BARCA DI COMUNICAZIONE, APPENA COME ME!
OH, RIGHT— ITALIAN... UM, LET'S SEE... PER FAVORE, MI DICA DOVE DEVO SCENDERE?
OF COURSE, SHE HARDLY KNEW ENGLISH AND MY ITALIAN WAS TERRIBLE, BUT THE LANGUAGE OF THE SEA IS UNIVERSAL!
RISATINA
WELL, IT'S GETTING PRETTY LATE. UM, NOT SURE HOW MUCH OF THIS YOU'LL GET, BUT I REALLY LIKE YOU, AND I WAS WONDERING IF I, UM...
SCUSI!? AH, ADESSO CAPISCO. SÌ, SÌ, ANCH'IO. HO MOLTA SIMPATIA PER LEI.
YOU LIKE ME TOO? WELL, GREAT! LET ME GIVE YOU A GOODNIGHT KISS!

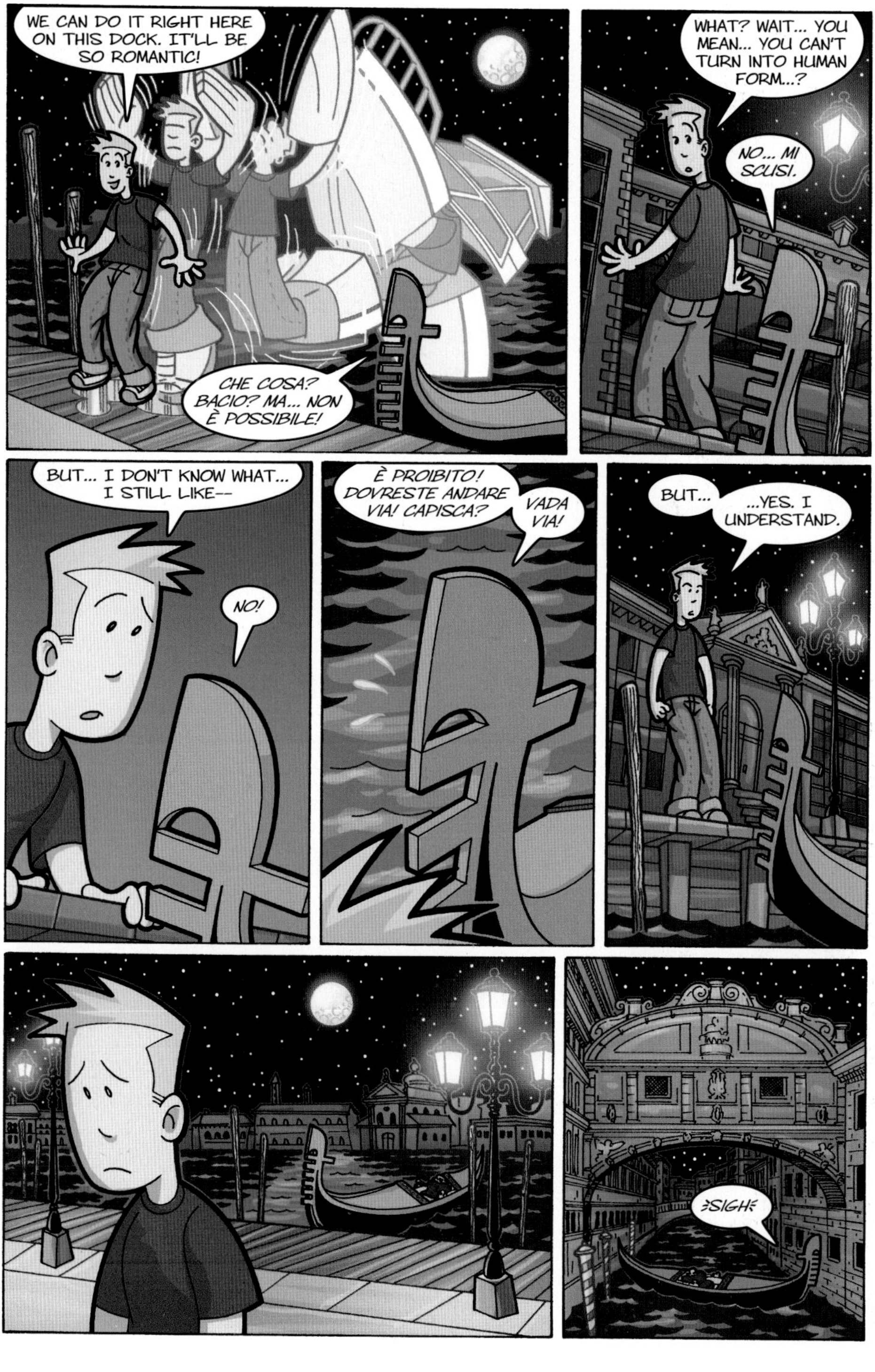

WE CAN DO IT RIGHT HERE ON THIS DOCK. IT'LL BE SO ROMANTIC!
CHE COSA? BACIO? MA... NON È POSSIBILE!
WHAT? WAIT... YOU MEAN... YOU CAN'T TURN INTO HUMAN FORM...?
NO... MI SCUSI.
BUT... I DON'T KNOW WHAT... I STILL LIKE--
NO!
È PROIBITO! DOVRESTE ANDARE VIA! CAPISCA?
VADA VIA!
BUT...
...YES. I UNDERSTAND.
SIGH

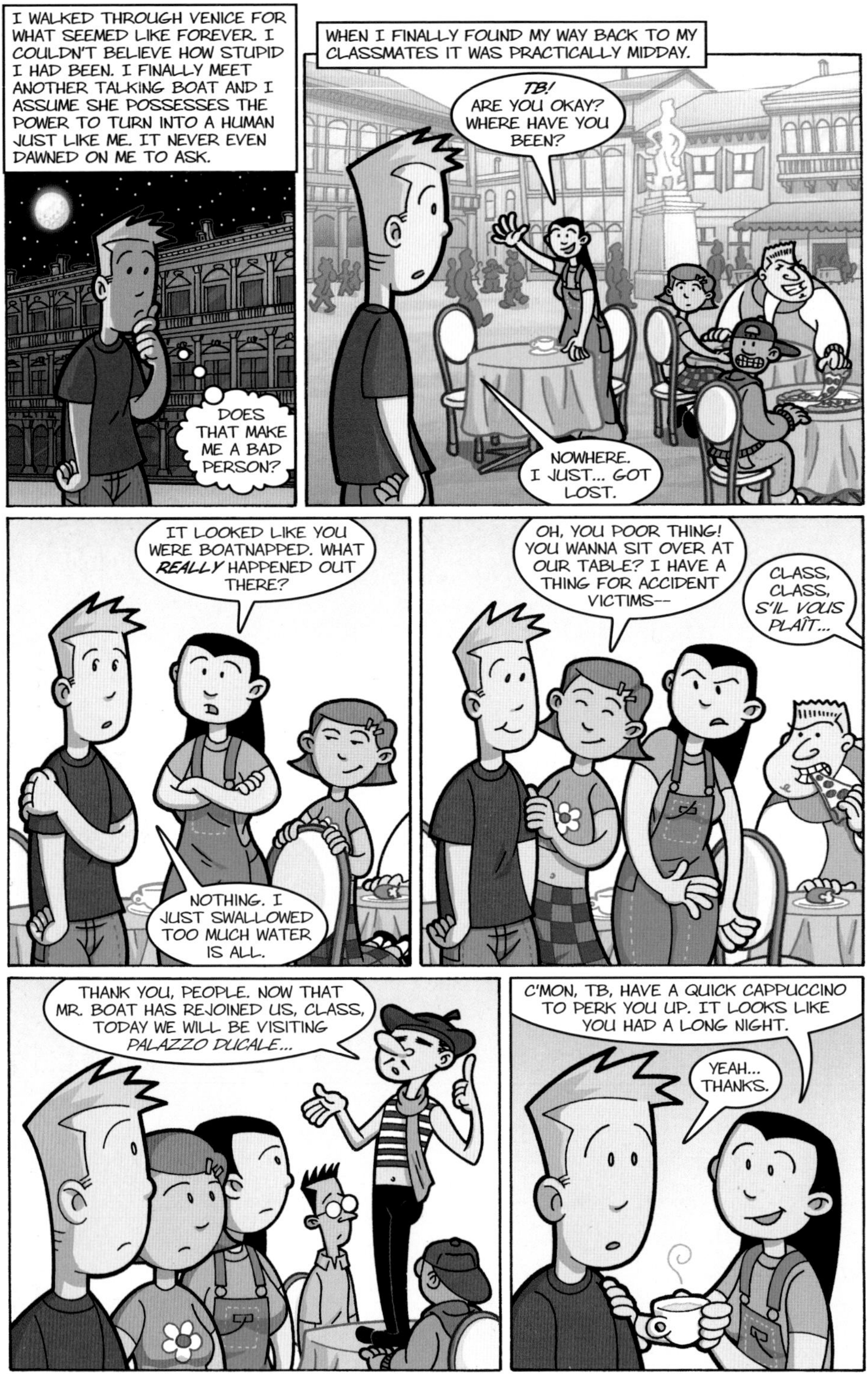
I WALKED THROUGH VENICE FOR WHAT SEEMED LIKE FOREVER. I COULDN'T BELIEVE HOW STUPID I HAD BEEN. I FINALLY MEET ANOTHER TALKING BOAT AND I ASSUME SHE POSSESSES THE POWER TO TURN INTO A HUMAN JUST LIKE ME. IT NEVER EVEN DAWNED ON ME TO ASK.
DOES THAT MAKE ME A BAD PERSON?
WHEN I FINALLY FOUND MY WAY BACK TO MY CLASSMATES IT WAS PRACTICALLY MIDDAY.
TB! ARE YOU OKAY? WHERE HAVE YOU BEEN?
NOWHERE. I JUST... GOT LOST.
IT LOOKED LIKE YOU WERE BOATNAPPED. WHAT *REALLY* HAPPENED OUT THERE?
NOTHING. I JUST SWALLOWED TOO MUCH WATER IS ALL.
OH, YOU POOR THING! YOU WANNA SIT OVER AT OUR TABLE? I HAVE A THING FOR ACCIDENT VICTIMS--
CLASS, CLASS, *S'IL VOUS PLAÎT...*
THANK YOU, PEOPLE. NOW THAT MR. BOAT HAS REJOINED US, CLASS, TODAY WE WILL BE VISITING *PALAZZO DUCALE...*
C'MON, TB, HAVE A QUICK CAPPUCCINO TO PERK YOU UP. IT LOOKS LIKE YOU HAD A LONG NIGHT.
YEAH... THANKS.

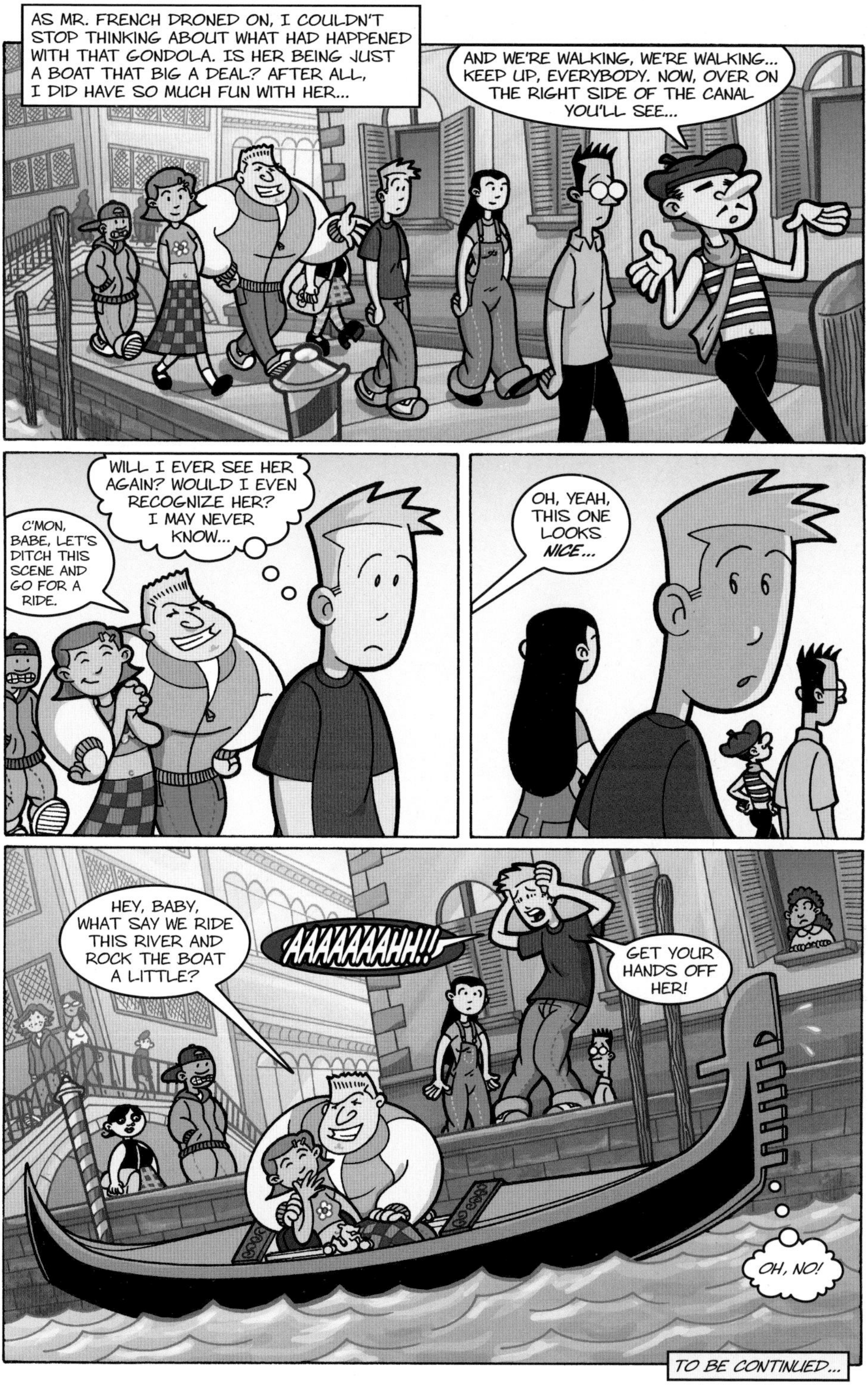
AS MR. FRENCH DRONED ON, I COULDN'T STOP THINKING ABOUT WHAT HAD HAPPENED WITH THAT GONDOLA. IS HER BEING JUST A BOAT THAT BIG A DEAL? AFTER ALL, I DID HAVE SO MUCH FUN WITH HER...
AND WE'RE WALKING, WE'RE WALKING... KEEP UP, EVERYBODY. NOW, OVER ON THE RIGHT SIDE OF THE CANAL YOU'LL SEE...
C'MON, BABE, LET'S DITCH THIS SCENE AND GO FOR A RIDE.
WILL I EVER SEE HER AGAIN? WOULD I EVEN RECOGNIZE HER? I MAY NEVER KNOW...
OH, YEAH, THIS ONE LOOKS *NICE*...
HEY, BABY, WHAT SAY WE RIDE THIS RIVER AND ROCK THE BOAT A LITTLE?
AAAAAAAHH!!
GET YOUR HANDS OFF HER!
OH, NO!
TO BE CONTINUED...

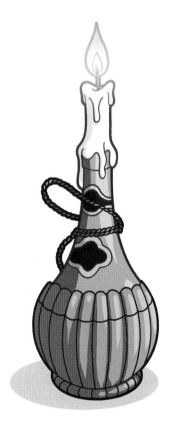

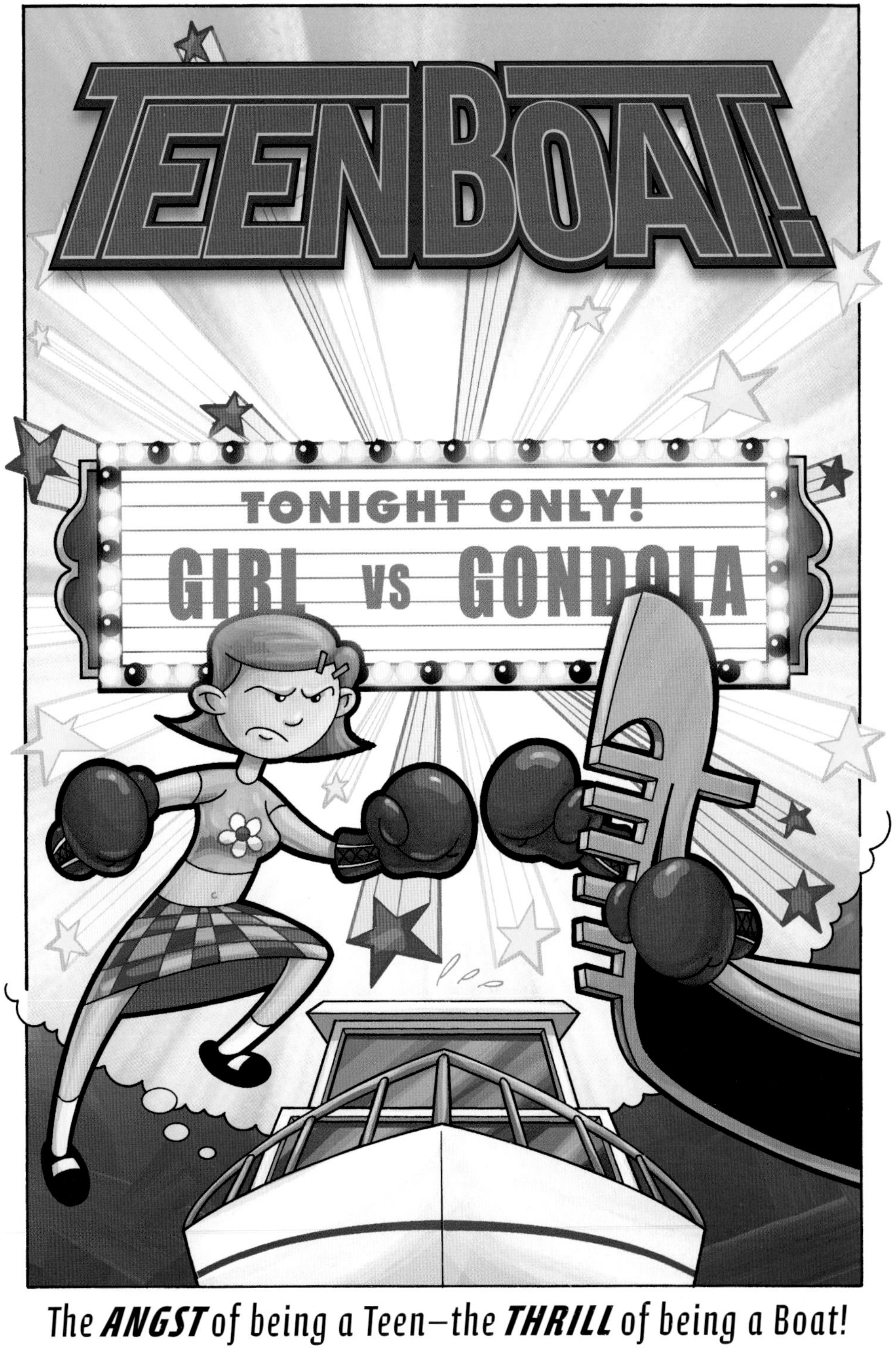
TEENBOAT!
TONIGHT ONLY!
GIRL vs GONDOLA

The ***ANGST*** of being a Teen—the ***THRILL*** of being a Boat!

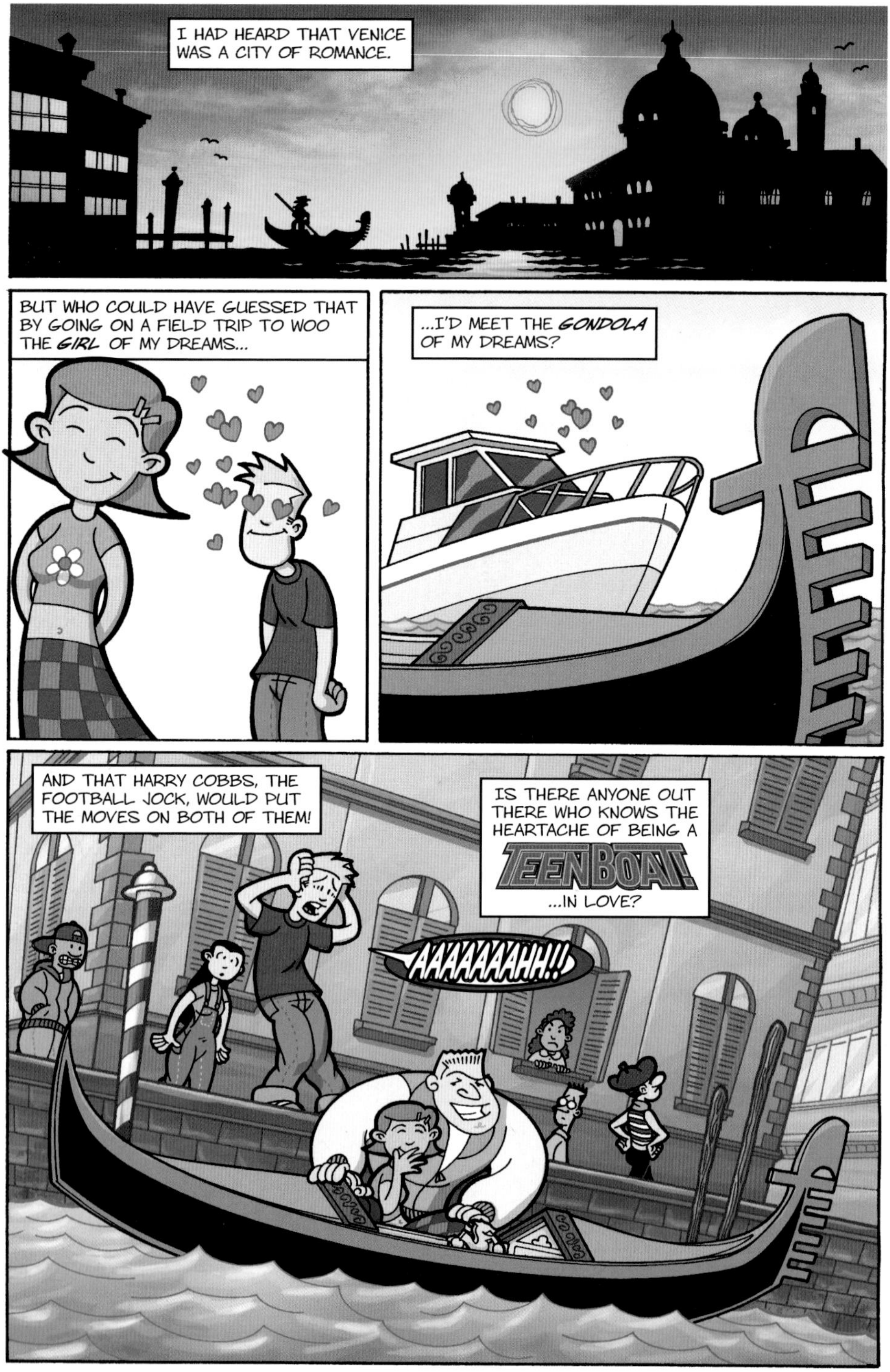
I HAD HEARD THAT VENICE WAS A CITY OF ROMANCE.
BUT WHO COULD HAVE GUESSED THAT BY GOING ON A FIELD TRIP TO WOO THE *GIRL* OF MY DREAMS...
...I'D MEET THE *GONDOLA* OF MY DREAMS?
AND THAT HARRY COBBS, THE FOOTBALL JOCK, WOULD PUT THE MOVES ON BOTH OF THEM!
IS THERE ANYONE OUT THERE WHO KNOWS THE HEARTACHE OF BEING A
TEENBOAT!
...IN LOVE?
AAAAAAAHH!!!

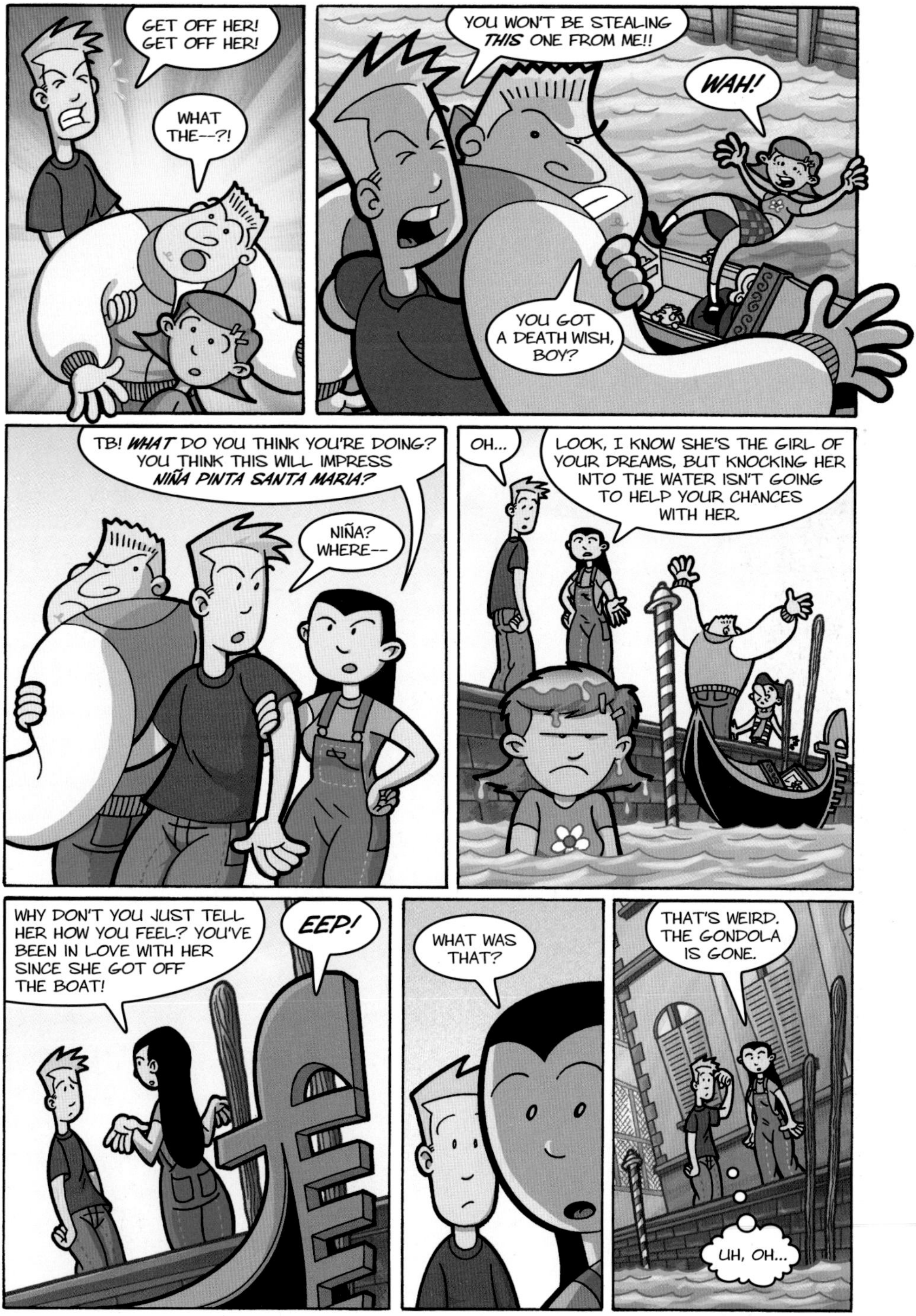
GET OFF HER! GET OFF HER!
WHAT THE--?!
YOU WON'T BE STEALING *THIS* ONE FROM ME!!
WAH!
YOU GOT A DEATH WISH, BOY?
TB! *WHAT* DO YOU THINK YOU'RE DOING? YOU THINK THIS WILL IMPRESS *NIÑA PINTA SANTA MARIA?*
NIÑA? WHERE--
OH...
LOOK, I KNOW SHE'S THE GIRL OF YOUR DREAMS, BUT KNOCKING HER INTO THE WATER ISN'T GOING TO HELP YOUR CHANCES WITH HER.
WHY DON'T YOU JUST TELL HER HOW YOU FEEL? YOU'VE BEEN IN LOVE WITH HER SINCE SHE GOT OFF THE BOAT!
EEP!
WHAT WAS THAT?
THAT'S WEIRD. THE GONDOLA IS GONE.
UH, OH...

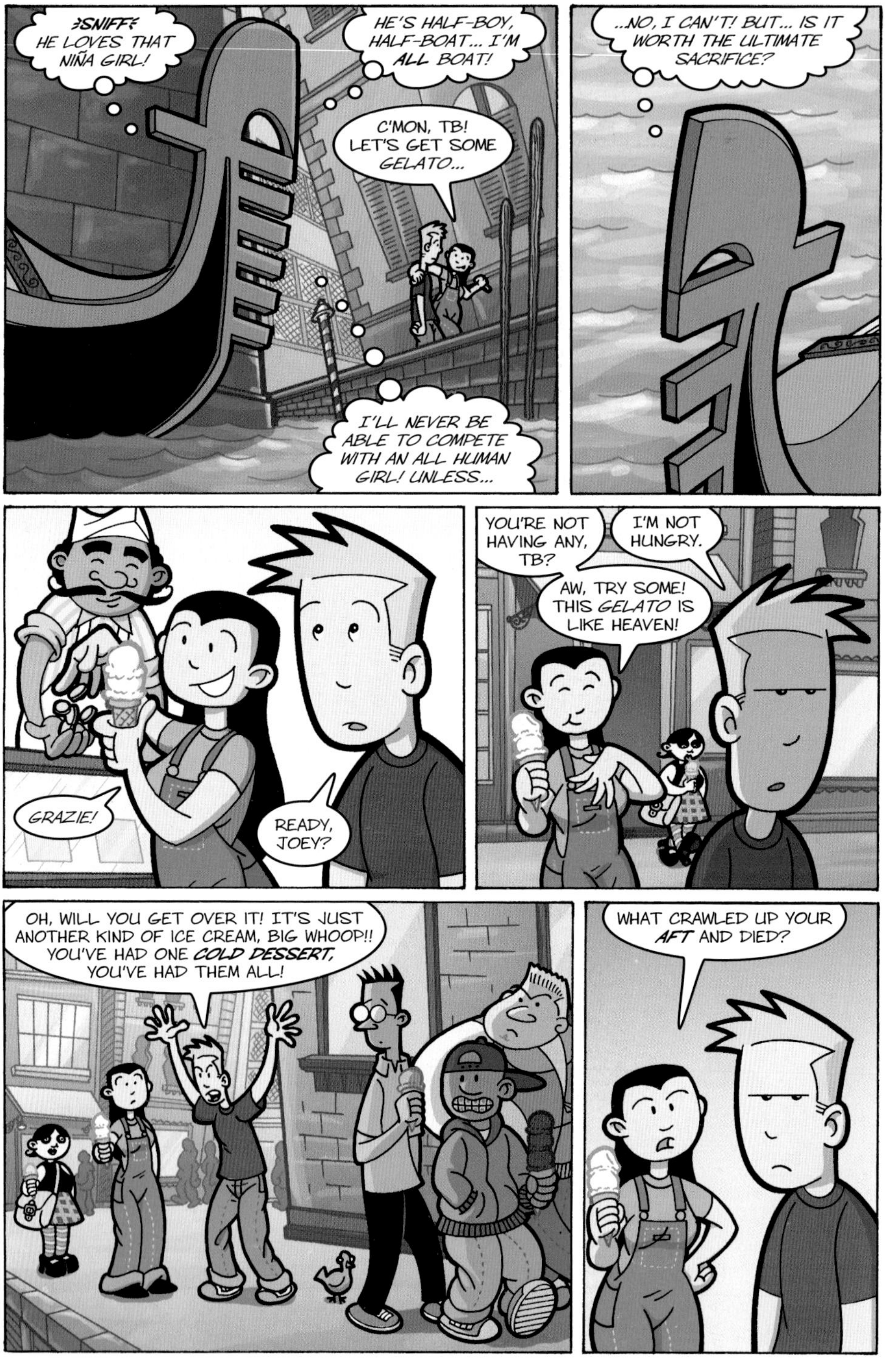

SNIFF HE LOVES THAT NIÑA GIRL!
HE'S HALF-BOY, HALF-BOAT... I'M ALL BOAT!
C'MON, TB! LET'S GET SOME GELATO...
I'LL NEVER BE ABLE TO COMPETE WITH AN ALL HUMAN GIRL! UNLESS...
...NO, I CAN'T! BUT... IS IT WORTH THE ULTIMATE SACRIFICE?
GRAZIE!
READY, JOEY?
YOU'RE NOT HAVING ANY, TB?
I'M NOT HUNGRY.
AW, TRY SOME! THIS GELATO IS LIKE HEAVEN!
OH, WILL YOU GET OVER IT! IT'S JUST ANOTHER KIND OF ICE CREAM, BIG WHOOP!! YOU'VE HAD ONE COLD DESSERT, YOU'VE HAD THEM ALL!
WHAT CRAWLED UP YOUR AFT AND DIED?

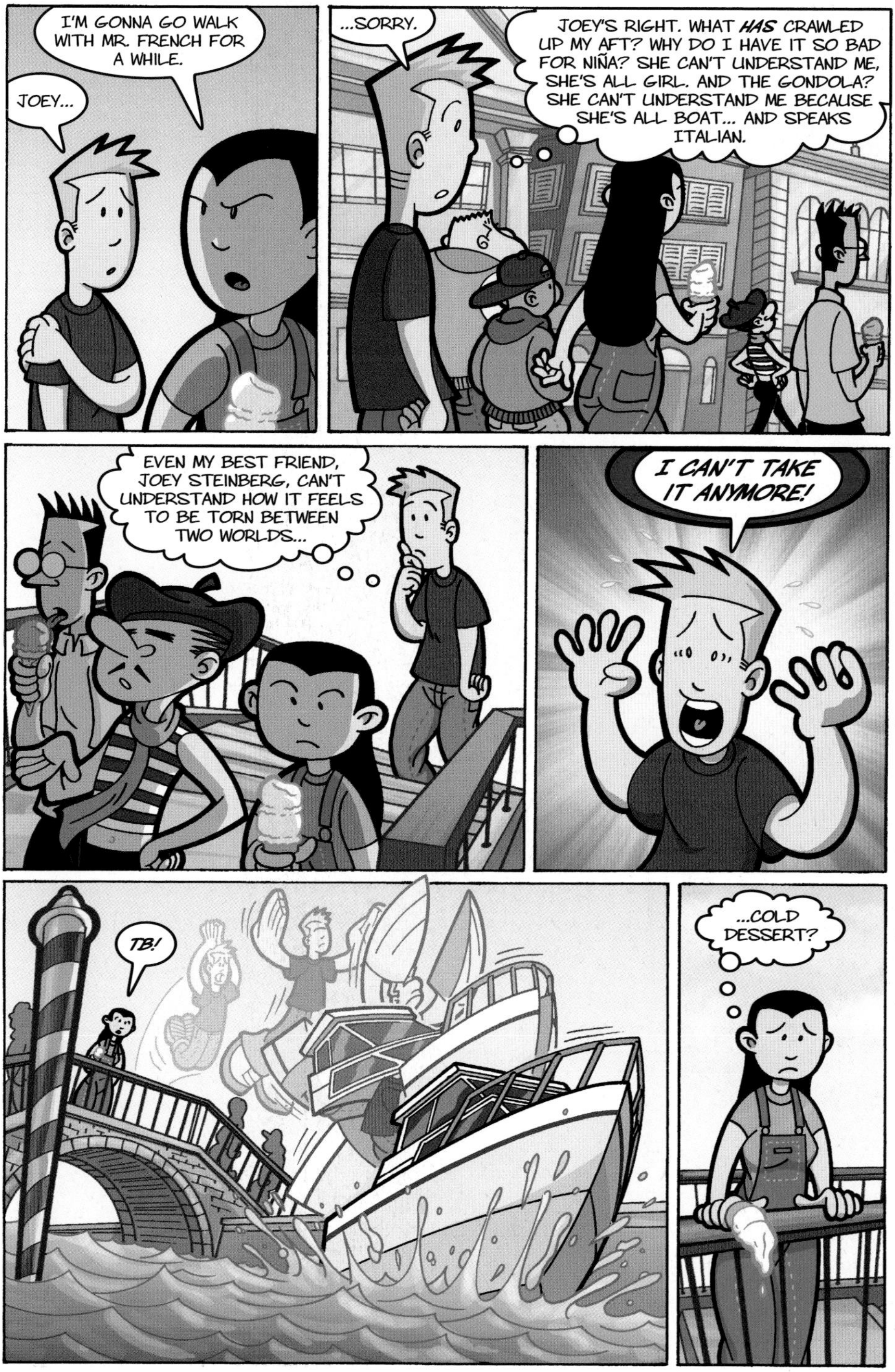
JOEY...
I'M GONNA GO WALK WITH MR. FRENCH FOR A WHILE.
...SORRY.
JOEY'S RIGHT. WHAT *HAS* CRAWLED UP MY AFT? WHY DO I HAVE IT SO BAD FOR NIÑA? SHE CAN'T UNDERSTAND ME, SHE'S ALL GIRL. AND THE GONDOLA? SHE CAN'T UNDERSTAND ME BECAUSE SHE'S ALL BOAT... AND SPEAKS ITALIAN.
EVEN MY BEST FRIEND, JOEY STEINBERG, CAN'T UNDERSTAND HOW IT FEELS TO BE TORN BETWEEN TWO WORLDS...
I CAN'T TAKE IT ANYMORE!
TB!
...COLD DESSERT?

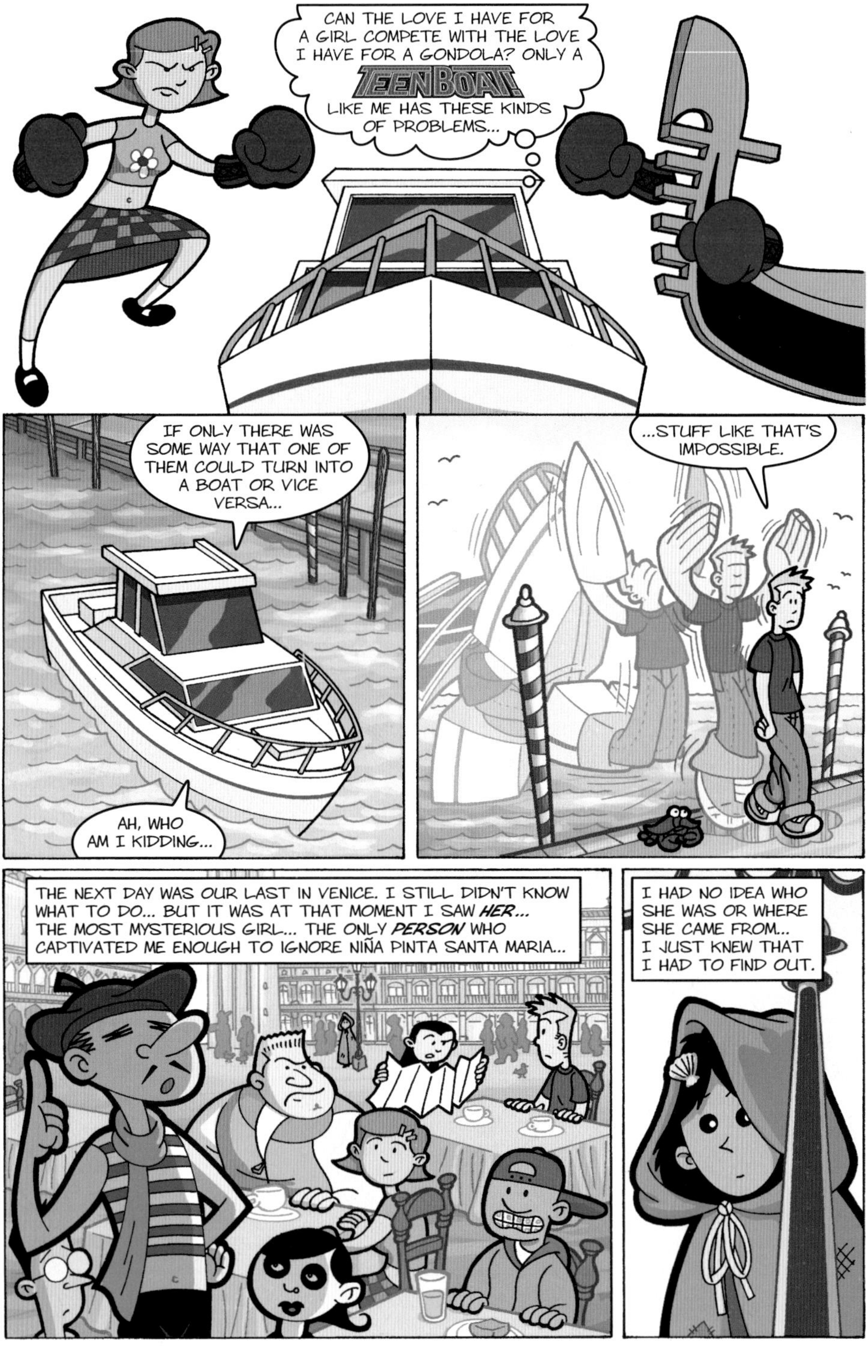

CAN THE LOVE I HAVE FOR A GIRL COMPETE WITH THE LOVE I HAVE FOR A GONDOLA? ONLY A
TEEN BOAT!
LIKE ME HAS THESE KINDS OF PROBLEMS...
IF ONLY THERE WAS SOME WAY THAT ONE OF THEM COULD TURN INTO A BOAT OR VICE VERSA...
AH, WHO AM I KIDDING...
...STUFF LIKE THAT'S IMPOSSIBLE.
THE NEXT DAY WAS OUR LAST IN VENICE. I STILL DIDN'T KNOW WHAT TO DO... BUT IT WAS AT THAT MOMENT I SAW *HER...* THE MOST MYSTERIOUS GIRL... THE ONLY *PERSON* WHO CAPTIVATED ME ENOUGH TO IGNORE NIÑA PINTA SANTA MARIA...
I HAD NO IDEA WHO SHE WAS OR WHERE SHE CAME FROM... I JUST KNEW THAT I HAD TO FIND OUT.

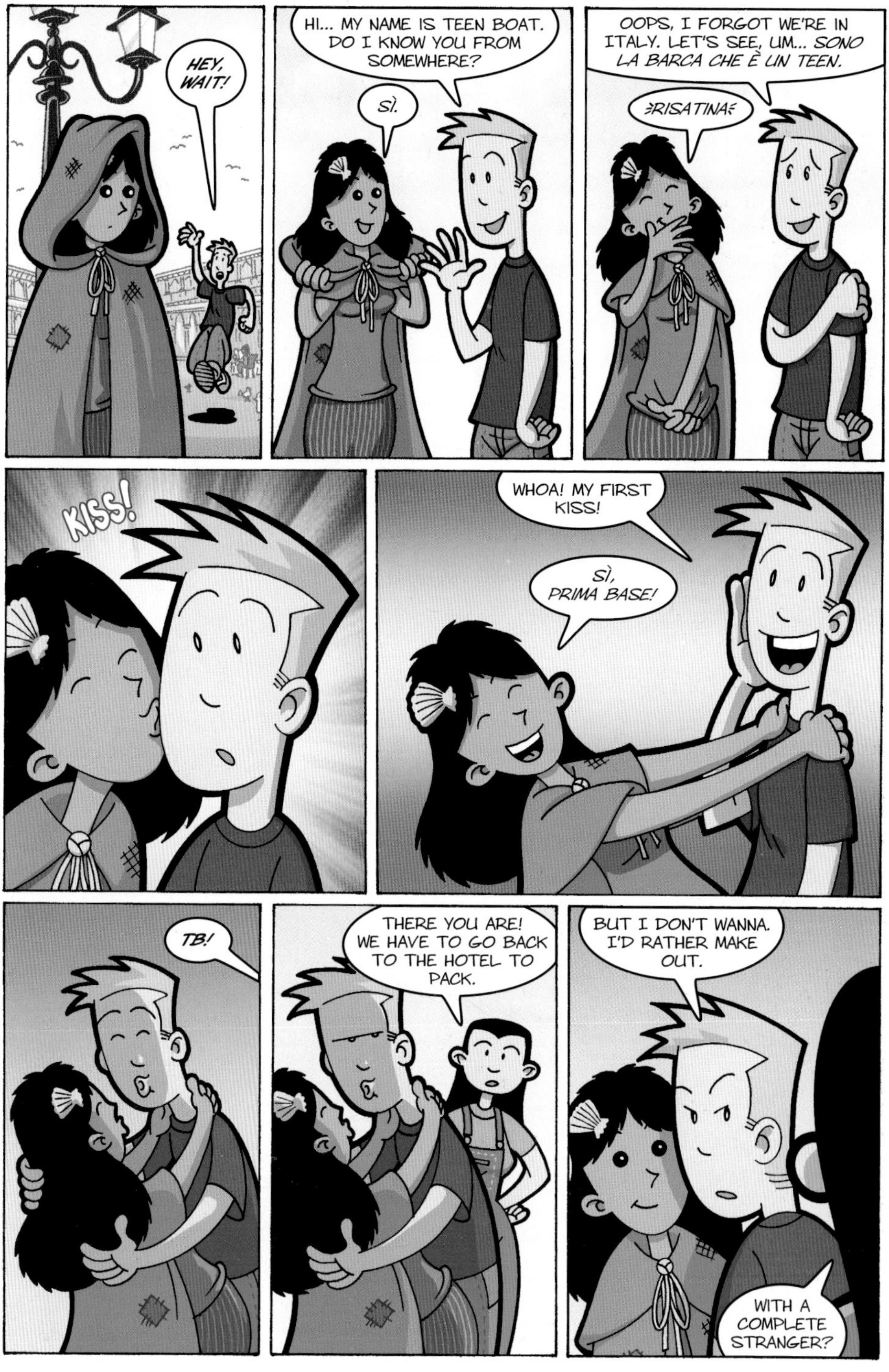
HEY, WAIT!
HI... MY NAME IS TEEN BOAT. DO I KNOW YOU FROM SOMEWHERE?
SÌ.
OOPS, I FORGOT WE'RE IN ITALY. LET'S SEE, UM... SONO LA BARCA CHE È UN TEEN.
RISATINA
KISS!
WHOA! MY FIRST KISS!
SÌ, PRIMA BASE!
TB!
THERE YOU ARE! WE HAVE TO GO BACK TO THE HOTEL TO PACK.
BUT I DON'T WANNA. I'D RATHER MAKE OUT.
WITH A COMPLETE STRANGER?

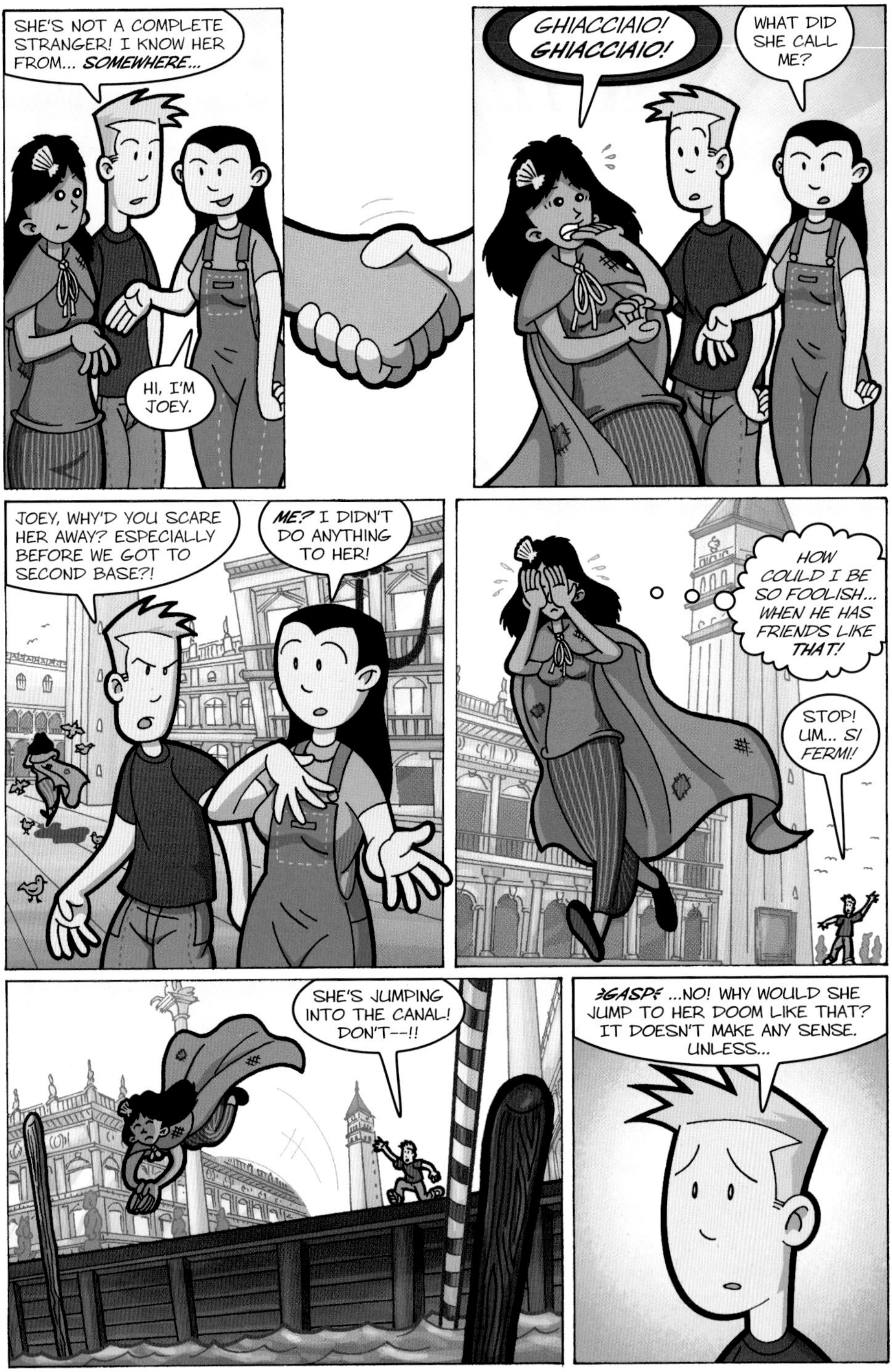
SHE'S NOT A COMPLETE STRANGER! I KNOW HER FROM... SOMEWHERE...
HI, I'M JOEY.
GHIACCIAIO! GHIACCIAIO!
WHAT DID SHE CALL ME?
JOEY, WHY'D YOU SCARE HER AWAY? ESPECIALLY BEFORE WE GOT TO SECOND BASE?!
ME? I DIDN'T DO ANYTHING TO HER!
HOW COULD I BE SO FOOLISH... WHEN HE HAS FRIENDS LIKE THAT!
STOP! UM... SI FERMI!
SHE'S JUMPING INTO THE CANAL! DON'T--!!
GASP ...NO! WHY WOULD SHE JUMP TO HER DOOM LIKE THAT? IT DOESN'T MAKE ANY SENSE. UNLESS...

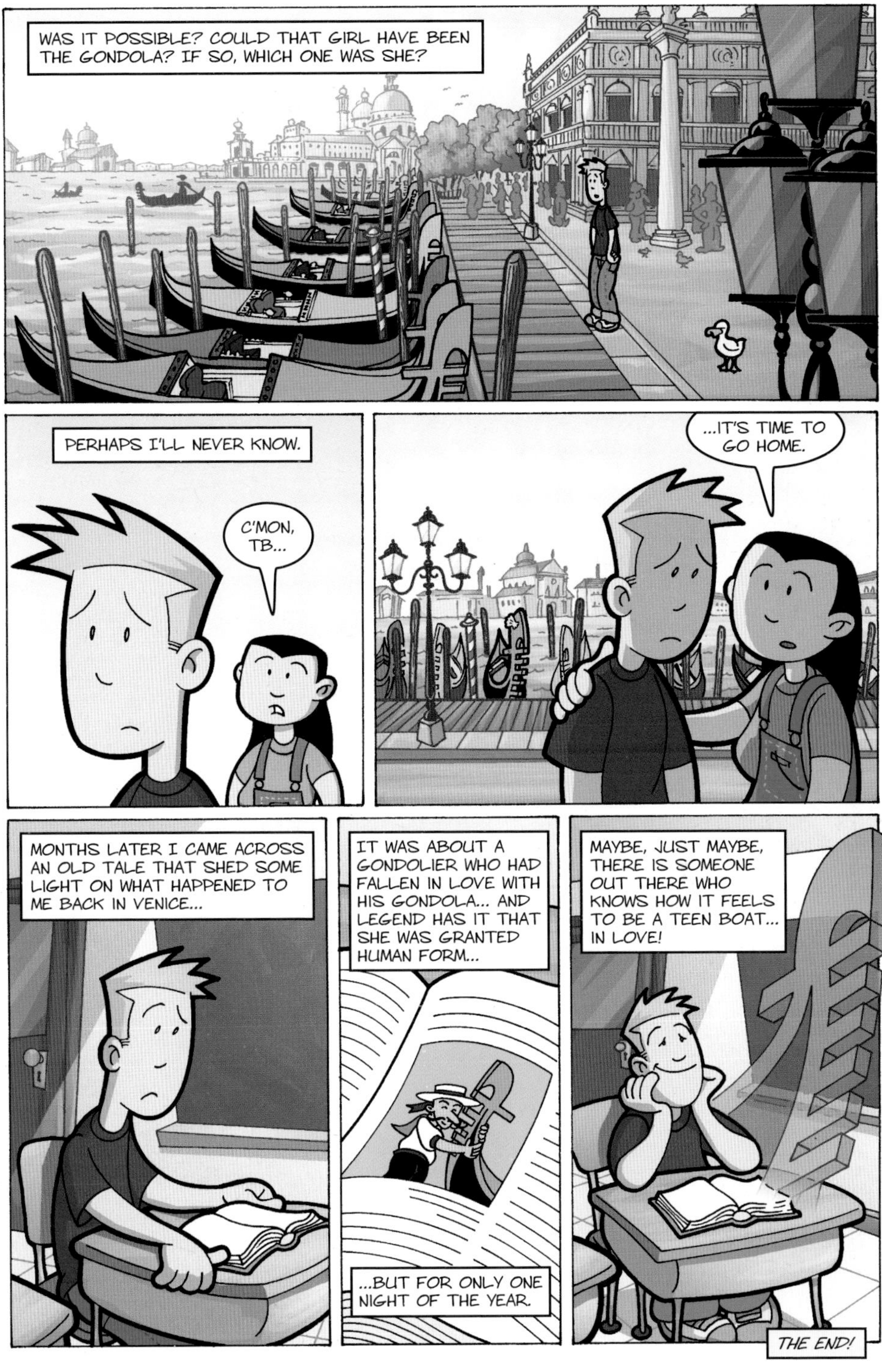
WAS IT POSSIBLE? COULD THAT GIRL HAVE BEEN THE GONDOLA? IF SO, WHICH ONE WAS SHE?
PERHAPS I'LL NEVER KNOW.
C'MON, TB...
...IT'S TIME TO GO HOME.
MONTHS LATER I CAME ACROSS AN OLD TALE THAT SHED SOME LIGHT ON WHAT HAPPENED TO ME BACK IN VENICE...
IT WAS ABOUT A GONDOLIER WHO HAD FALLEN IN LOVE WITH HIS GONDOLA... AND LEGEND HAS IT THAT SHE WAS GRANTED HUMAN FORM...
...BUT FOR ONLY ONE NIGHT OF THE YEAR.
MAYBE, JUST MAYBE, THERE IS SOMEONE OUT THERE WHO KNOWS HOW IT FEELS TO BE A TEEN BOAT... IN LOVE!
THE END!

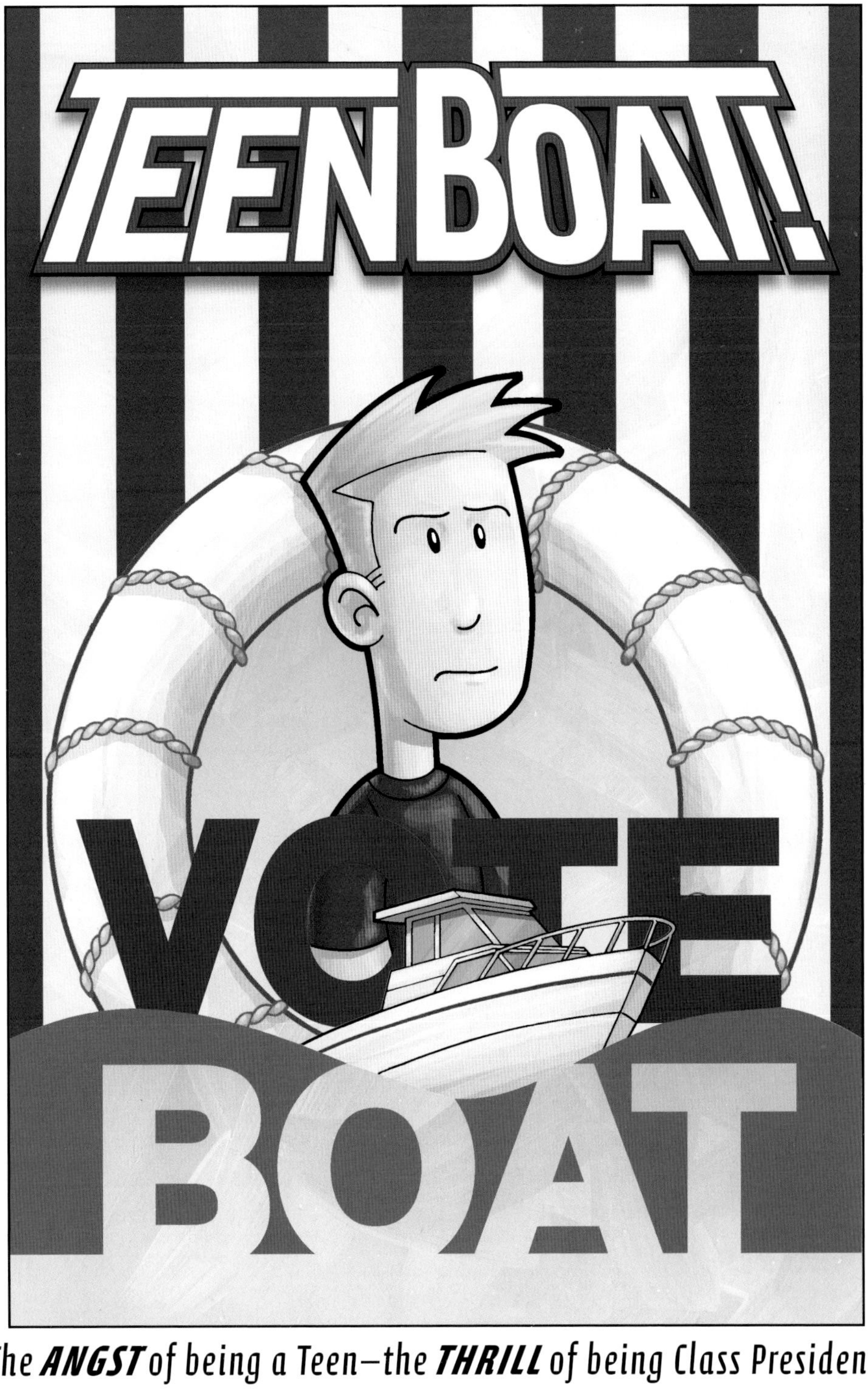
TEEN BOAT!
VOTE
BOAT
The ***ANGST*** *of being a Teen—the* ***THRILL*** *of being Class President!*

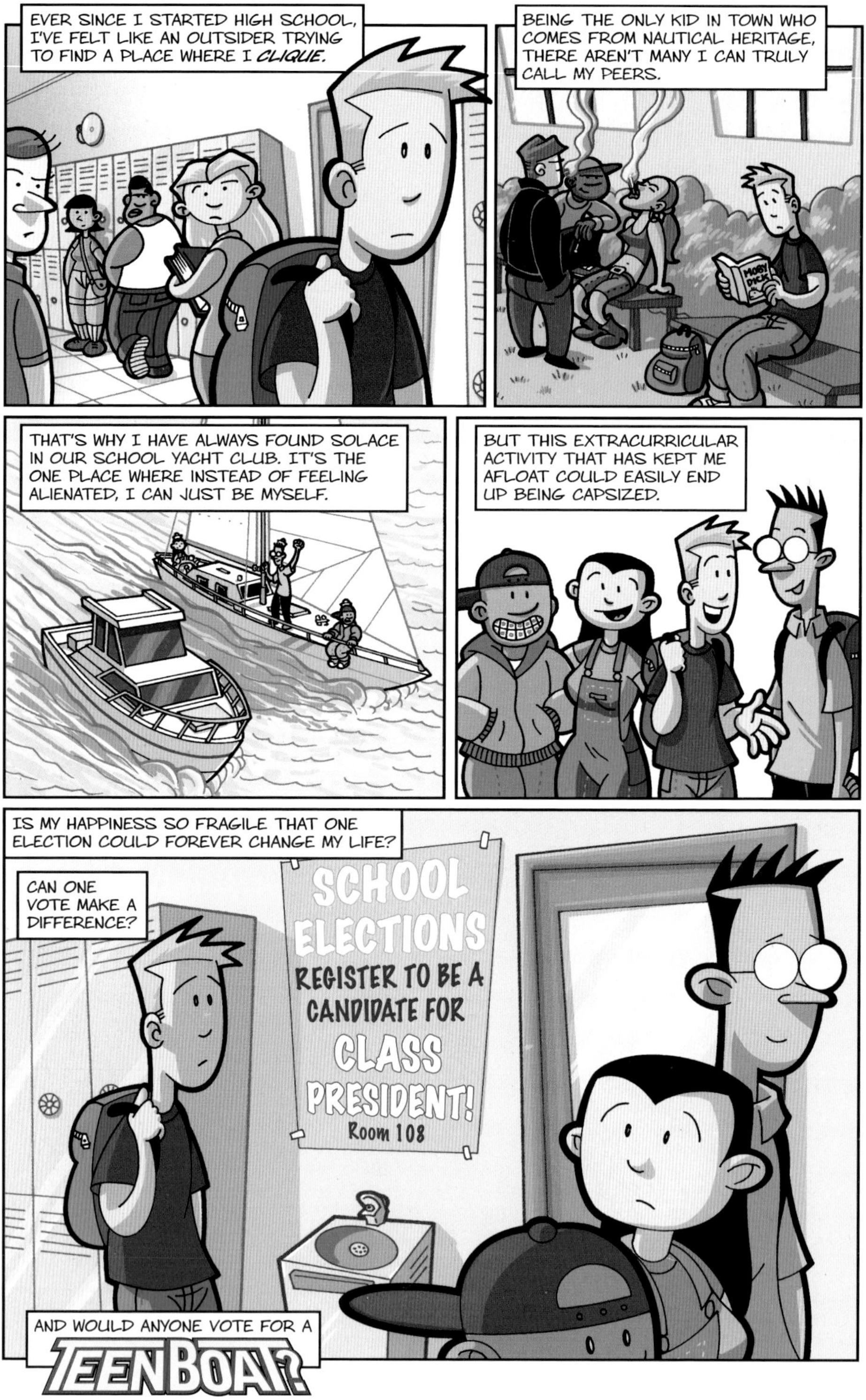
EVER SINCE I STARTED HIGH SCHOOL, I'VE FELT LIKE AN OUTSIDER TRYING TO FIND A PLACE WHERE I *CLIQUE.*
BEING THE ONLY KID IN TOWN WHO COMES FROM NAUTICAL HERITAGE, THERE AREN'T MANY I CAN TRULY CALL MY PEERS.
MOBY DICK
THAT'S WHY I HAVE ALWAYS FOUND SOLACE IN OUR SCHOOL YACHT CLUB. IT'S THE ONE PLACE WHERE INSTEAD OF FEELING ALIENATED, I CAN JUST BE MYSELF.
BUT THIS EXTRACURRICULAR ACTIVITY THAT HAS KEPT ME AFLOAT COULD EASILY END UP BEING CAPSIZED.
IS MY HAPPINESS SO FRAGILE THAT ONE ELECTION COULD FOREVER CHANGE MY LIFE?
CAN ONE VOTE MAKE A DIFFERENCE?
SCHOOL ELECTIONS
REGISTER TO BE A CANDIDATE FOR
CLASS PRESIDENT!
Room 108
AND WOULD ANYONE VOTE FOR A
TEEN BOAT?

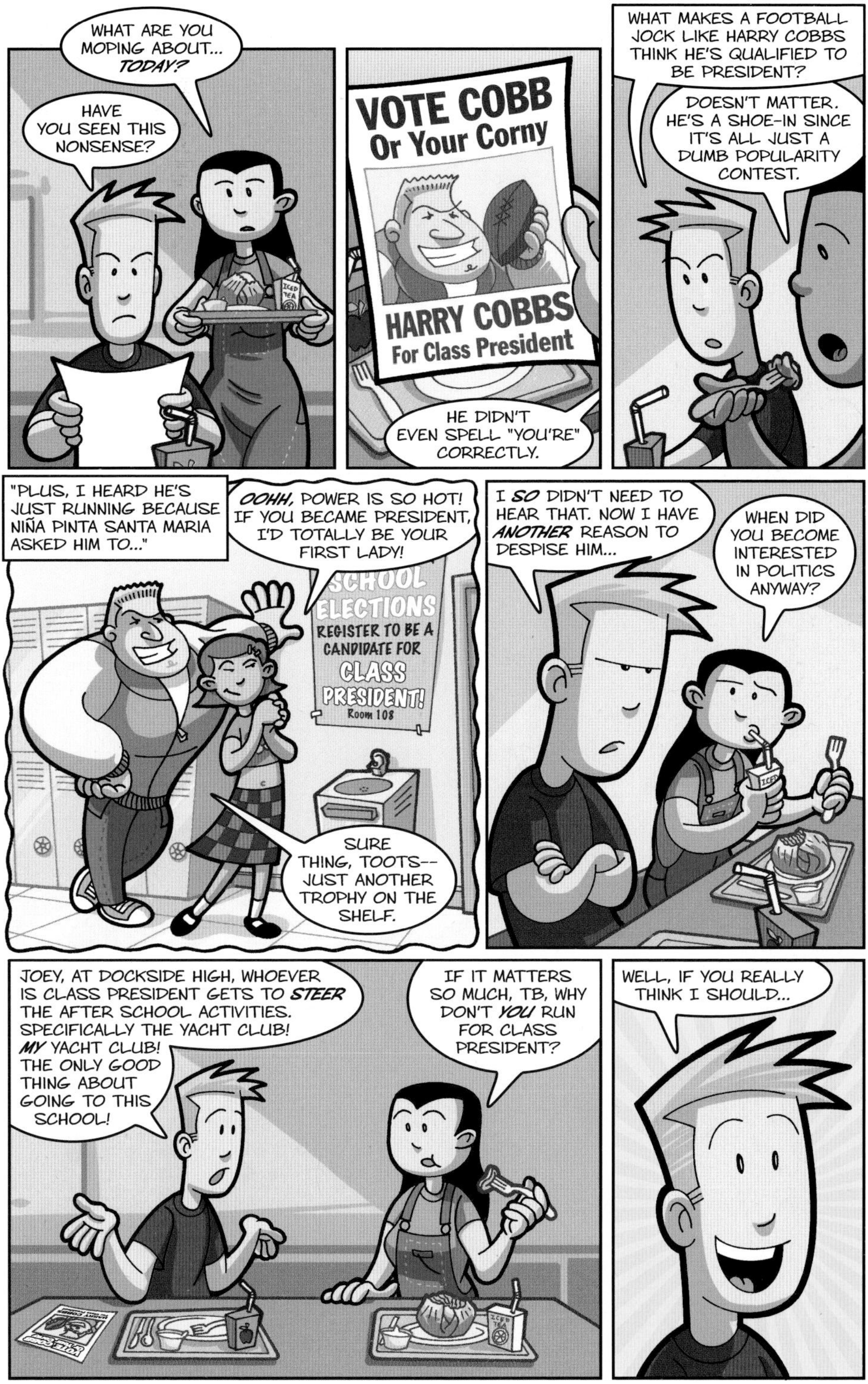
WHAT ARE YOU MOPING ABOUT... TODAY?
HAVE YOU SEEN THIS NONSENSE?
VOTE COBB Or Your Corny
HARRY COBBS For Class President
HE DIDN'T EVEN SPELL "YOU'RE" CORRECTLY.
WHAT MAKES A FOOTBALL JOCK LIKE HARRY COBBS THINK HE'S QUALIFIED TO BE PRESIDENT?
DOESN'T MATTER. HE'S A SHOE-IN SINCE IT'S ALL JUST A DUMB POPULARITY CONTEST.
"PLUS, I HEARD HE'S JUST RUNNING BECAUSE NIÑA PINTA SANTA MARIA ASKED HIM TO..."
OOHH, POWER IS SO HOT! IF YOU BECAME PRESIDENT, I'D TOTALLY BE YOUR FIRST LADY!
SCHOOL ELECTIONS REGISTER TO BE A CANDIDATE FOR CLASS PRESIDENT! Room 108
SURE THING, TOOTS-- JUST ANOTHER TROPHY ON THE SHELF.
I SO DIDN'T NEED TO HEAR THAT. NOW I HAVE ANOTHER REASON TO DESPISE HIM...
WHEN DID YOU BECOME INTERESTED IN POLITICS ANYWAY?
JOEY, AT DOCKSIDE HIGH, WHOEVER IS CLASS PRESIDENT GETS TO STEER THE AFTER SCHOOL ACTIVITIES. SPECIFICALLY THE YACHT CLUB! MY YACHT CLUB! THE ONLY GOOD THING ABOUT GOING TO THIS SCHOOL!
IF IT MATTERS SO MUCH, TB, WHY DON'T YOU RUN FOR CLASS PRESIDENT?
WELL, IF YOU REALLY THINK I SHOULD...

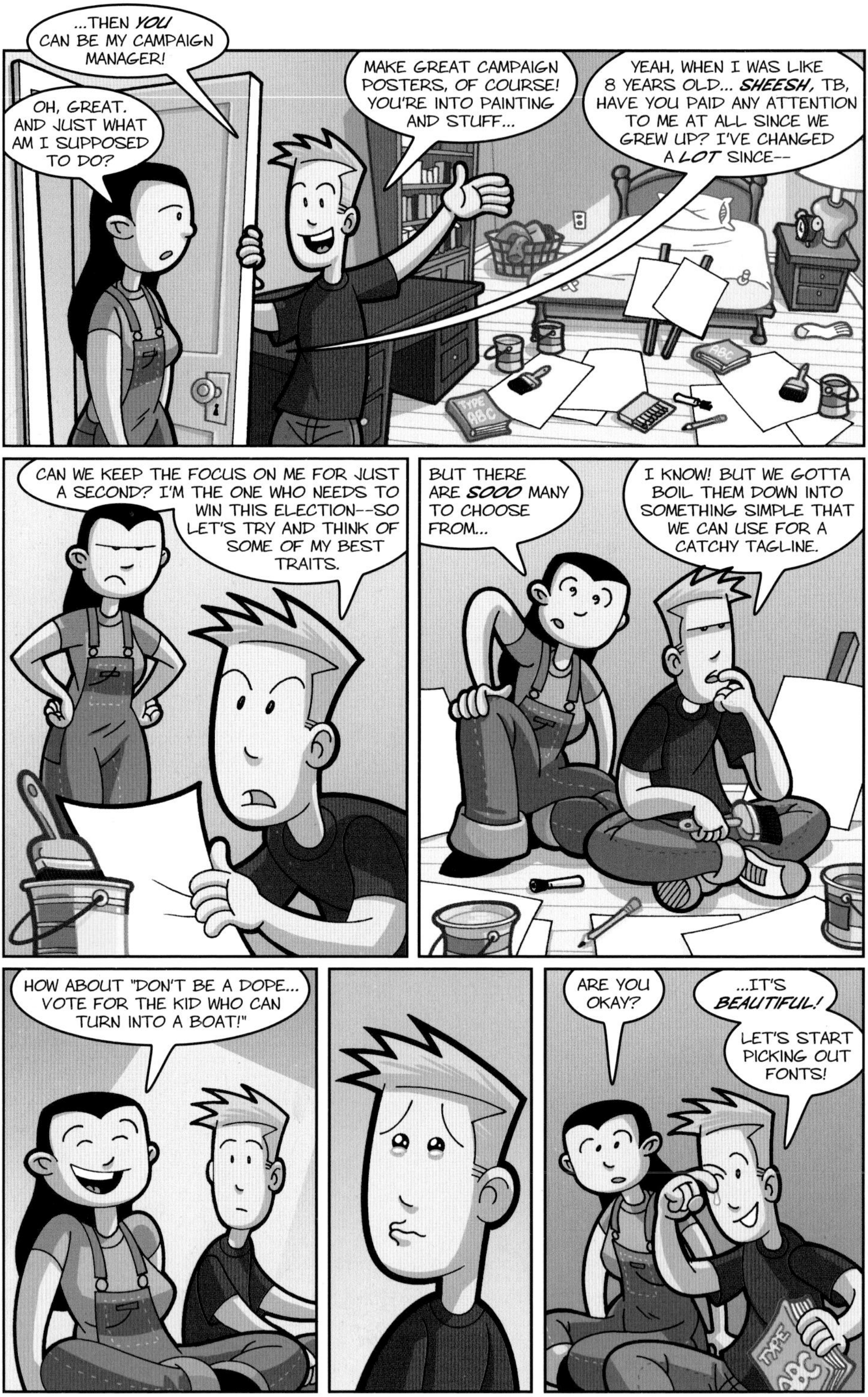
...THEN *YOU* CAN BE MY CAMPAIGN MANAGER!
OH, GREAT. AND JUST WHAT AM I SUPPOSED TO DO?
MAKE GREAT CAMPAIGN POSTERS, OF COURSE! YOU'RE INTO PAINTING AND STUFF...
YEAH, WHEN I WAS LIKE 8 YEARS OLD... *SHEESH,* TB, HAVE YOU PAID ANY ATTENTION TO ME AT ALL SINCE WE GREW UP? I'VE CHANGED A *LOT* SINCE--
TYPE ABC
ABC
CAN WE KEEP THE FOCUS ON ME FOR JUST A SECOND? I'M THE ONE WHO NEEDS TO WIN THIS ELECTION--SO LET'S TRY AND THINK OF SOME OF MY BEST TRAITS.
BUT THERE ARE *SOOO* MANY TO CHOOSE FROM...
I KNOW! BUT WE GOTTA BOIL THEM DOWN INTO SOMETHING SIMPLE THAT WE CAN USE FOR A CATCHY TAGLINE.
HOW ABOUT "DON'T BE A DOPE... VOTE FOR THE KID WHO CAN TURN INTO A BOAT!"
ARE YOU OKAY?
...IT'S *BEAUTIFUL!*
LET'S START PICKING OUT FONTS!
TYPE ABC

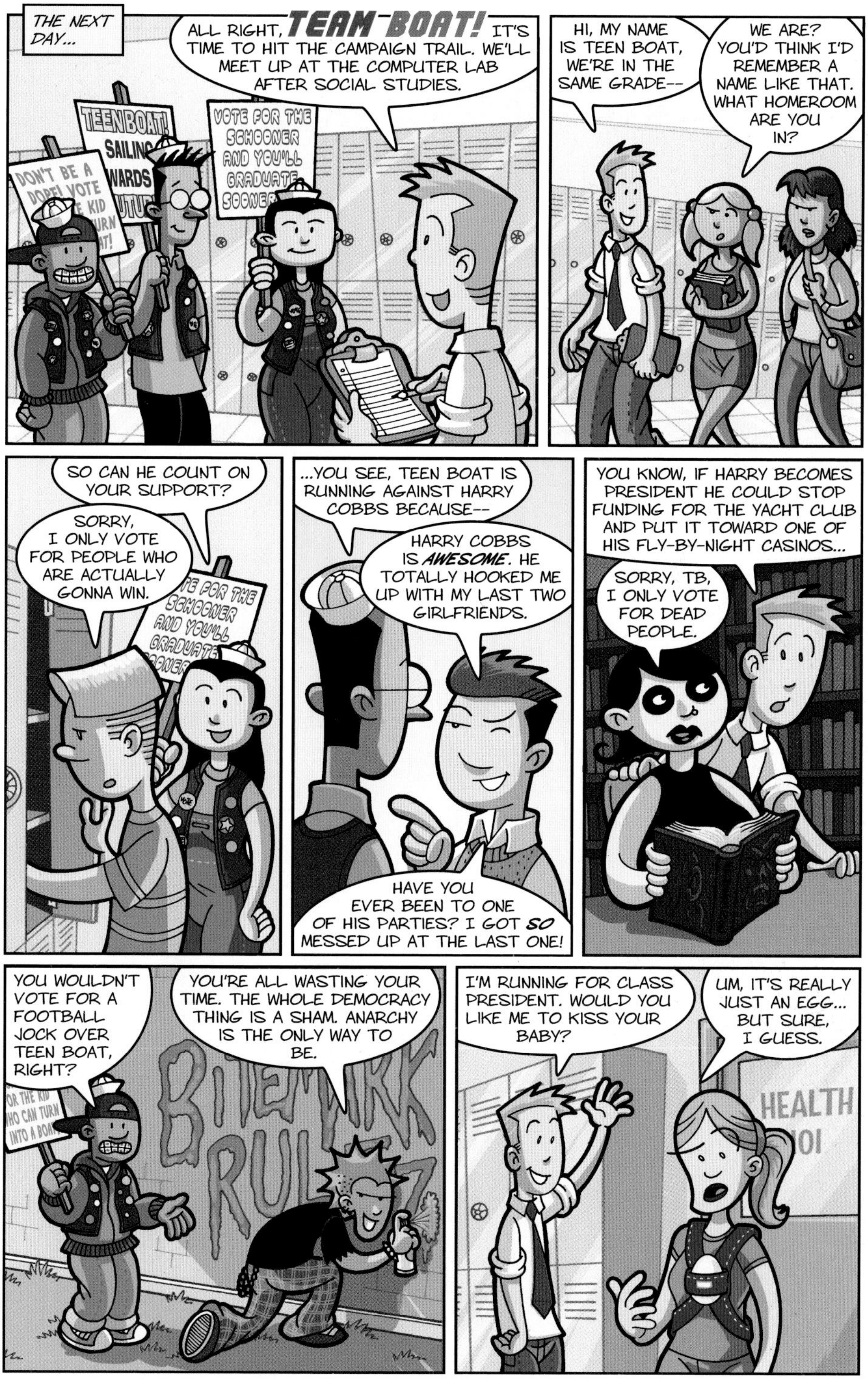
THE NEXT DAY...
ALL RIGHT, TEAM BOAT! IT'S TIME TO HIT THE CAMPAIGN TRAIL. WE'LL MEET UP AT THE COMPUTER LAB AFTER SOCIAL STUDIES.
DON'T BE A DORF! VOTE
TEENBOAT! SAILING
VOTE FOR THE SCHOONER AND YOU'LL GRADUATE SOONER
HI, MY NAME IS TEEN BOAT, WE'RE IN THE SAME GRADE--
WE ARE? YOU'D THINK I'D REMEMBER A NAME LIKE THAT. WHAT HOMEROOM ARE YOU IN?
SO CAN HE COUNT ON YOUR SUPPORT?
SORRY, I ONLY VOTE FOR PEOPLE WHO ARE ACTUALLY GONNA WIN.
...YOU SEE, TEEN BOAT IS RUNNING AGAINST HARRY COBBS BECAUSE--
HARRY COBBS IS AWESOME. HE TOTALLY HOOKED ME UP WITH MY LAST TWO GIRLFRIENDS.
HAVE YOU EVER BEEN TO ONE OF HIS PARTIES? I GOT SO MESSED UP AT THE LAST ONE!
YOU KNOW, IF HARRY BECOMES PRESIDENT HE COULD STOP FUNDING FOR THE YACHT CLUB AND PUT IT TOWARD ONE OF HIS FLY-BY-NIGHT CASINOS...
SORRY, TB, I ONLY VOTE FOR DEAD PEOPLE.
YOU WOULDN'T VOTE FOR A FOOTBALL JOCK OVER TEEN BOAT, RIGHT?
YOU'RE ALL WASTING YOUR TIME. THE WHOLE DEMOCRACY THING IS A SHAM. ANARCHY IS THE ONLY WAY TO BE.
I'M RUNNING FOR CLASS PRESIDENT. WOULD YOU LIKE ME TO KISS YOUR BABY?
UM, IT'S REALLY JUST AN EGG... BUT SURE, I GUESS.
HEALTH 101

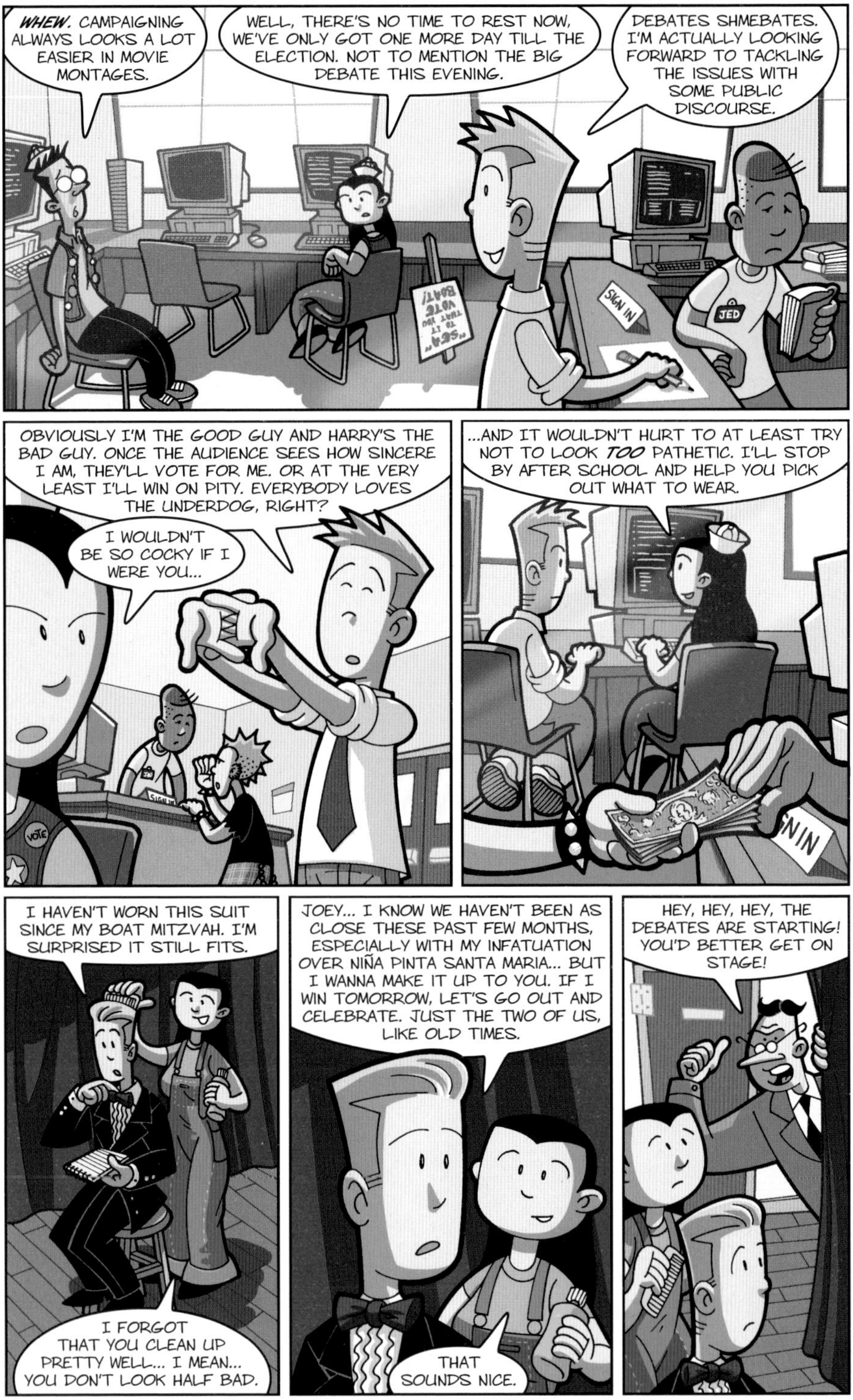
WHEW. CAMPAIGNING ALWAYS LOOKS A LOT EASIER IN MOVIE MONTAGES.
WELL, THERE'S NO TIME TO REST NOW, WE'VE ONLY GOT ONE MORE DAY TILL THE ELECTION. NOT TO MENTION THE BIG DEBATE THIS EVENING.
DEBATES SHMEBATES. I'M ACTUALLY LOOKING FORWARD TO TACKLING THE ISSUES WITH SOME PUBLIC DISCOURSE.
SIGN IN
JED
OBVIOUSLY I'M THE GOOD GUY AND HARRY'S THE BAD GUY. ONCE THE AUDIENCE SEES HOW SINCERE I AM, THEY'LL VOTE FOR ME. OR AT THE VERY LEAST I'LL WIN ON PITY. EVERYBODY LOVES THE UNDERDOG, RIGHT?
I WOULDN'T BE SO COCKY IF I WERE YOU...
VOTE
...AND IT WOULDN'T HURT TO AT LEAST TRY NOT TO LOOK TOO PATHETIC. I'LL STOP BY AFTER SCHOOL AND HELP YOU PICK OUT WHAT TO WEAR.
I HAVEN'T WORN THIS SUIT SINCE MY BOAT MITZVAH. I'M SURPRISED IT STILL FITS.
I FORGOT THAT YOU CLEAN UP PRETTY WELL... I MEAN... YOU DON'T LOOK HALF BAD.
JOEY... I KNOW WE HAVEN'T BEEN AS CLOSE THESE PAST FEW MONTHS, ESPECIALLY WITH MY INFATUATION OVER NIÑA PINTA SANTA MARIA... BUT I WANNA MAKE IT UP TO YOU. IF I WIN TOMORROW, LET'S GO OUT AND CELEBRATE. JUST THE TWO OF US, LIKE OLD TIMES.
THAT SOUNDS NICE.
HEY, HEY, HEY, THE DEBATES ARE STARTING! YOU'D BETTER GET ON STAGE!

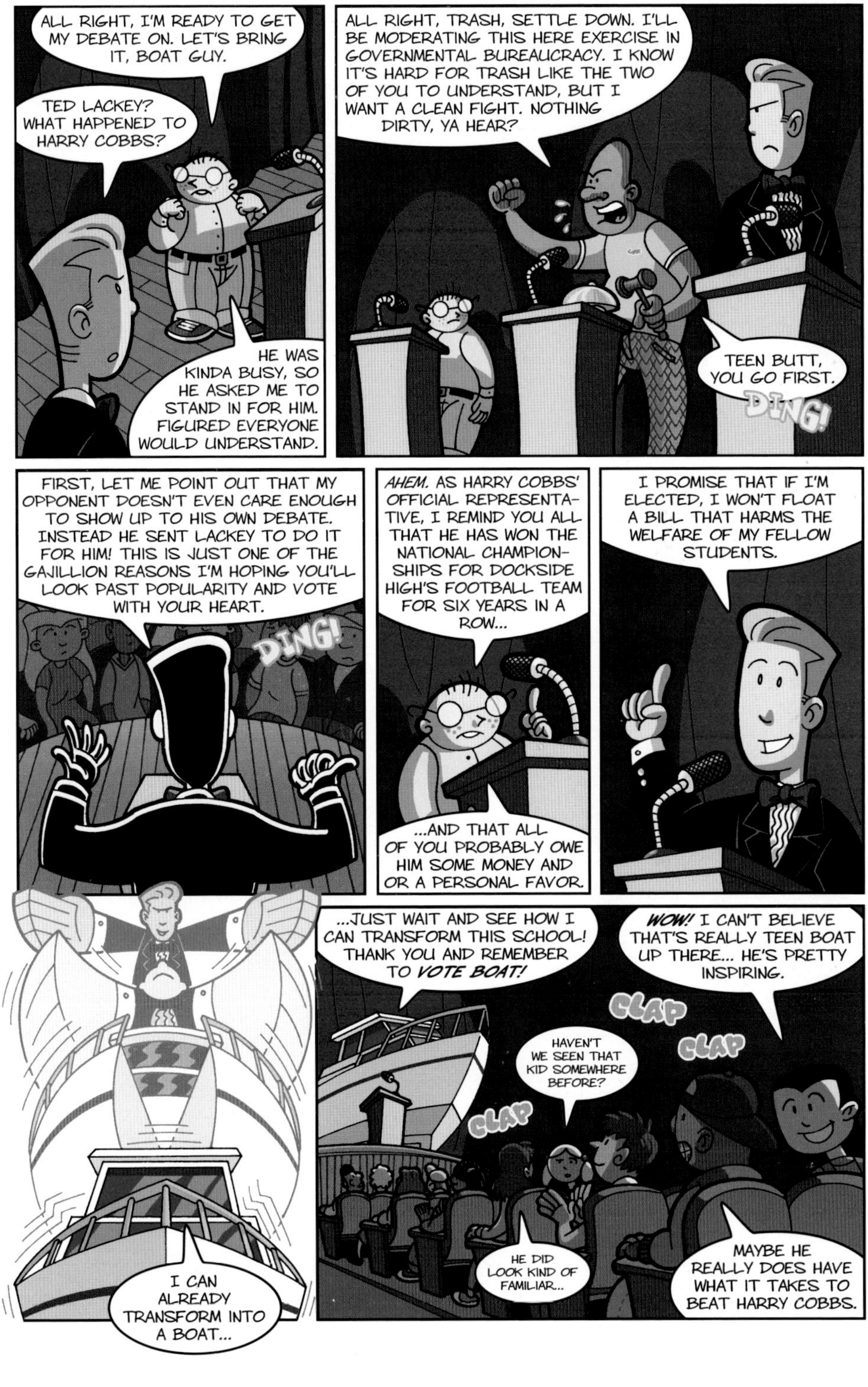
ALL RIGHT, I'M READY TO GET MY DEBATE ON. LET'S BRING IT, BOAT GUY.
TED LACKEY? WHAT HAPPENED TO HARRY COBBS?
HE WAS KINDA BUSY, SO HE ASKED ME TO STAND IN FOR HIM. FIGURED EVERYONE WOULD UNDERSTAND.
ALL RIGHT, TRASH, SETTLE DOWN. I'LL BE MODERATING THIS HERE EXERCISE IN GOVERNMENTAL BUREAUCRACY. I KNOW IT'S HARD FOR TRASH LIKE THE TWO OF YOU TO UNDERSTAND, BUT I WANT A CLEAN FIGHT. NOTHING DIRTY, YA HEAR?
TEEN BUTT, YOU GO FIRST.
DING!
FIRST, LET ME POINT OUT THAT MY OPPONENT DOESN'T EVEN CARE ENOUGH TO SHOW UP TO HIS OWN DEBATE. INSTEAD HE SENT LACKEY TO DO IT FOR HIM! THIS IS JUST ONE OF THE GAJILLION REASONS I'M HOPING YOU'LL LOOK PAST POPULARITY AND VOTE WITH YOUR HEART.
DING!
AHEM. AS HARRY COBBS' OFFICIAL REPRESENTATIVE, I REMIND YOU ALL THAT HE HAS WON THE NATIONAL CHAMPIONSHIPS FOR DOCKSIDE HIGH'S FOOTBALL TEAM FOR SIX YEARS IN A ROW...
...AND THAT ALL OF YOU PROBABLY OWE HIM SOME MONEY AND OR A PERSONAL FAVOR.
I PROMISE THAT IF I'M ELECTED, I WON'T FLOAT A BILL THAT HARMS THE WELFARE OF MY FELLOW STUDENTS.
I CAN ALREADY TRANSFORM INTO A BOAT...
...JUST WAIT AND SEE HOW I CAN TRANSFORM THIS SCHOOL! THANK YOU AND REMEMBER TO VOTE BOAT!
WOW! I CAN'T BELIEVE THAT'S REALLY TEEN BOAT UP THERE... HE'S PRETTY INSPIRING.
CLAP
CLAP
HAVEN'T WE SEEN THAT KID SOMEWHERE BEFORE?
CLAP
HE DID LOOK KIND OF FAMILIAR...
MAYBE HE REALLY DOES HAVE WHAT IT TAKES TO BEAT HARRY COBBS.

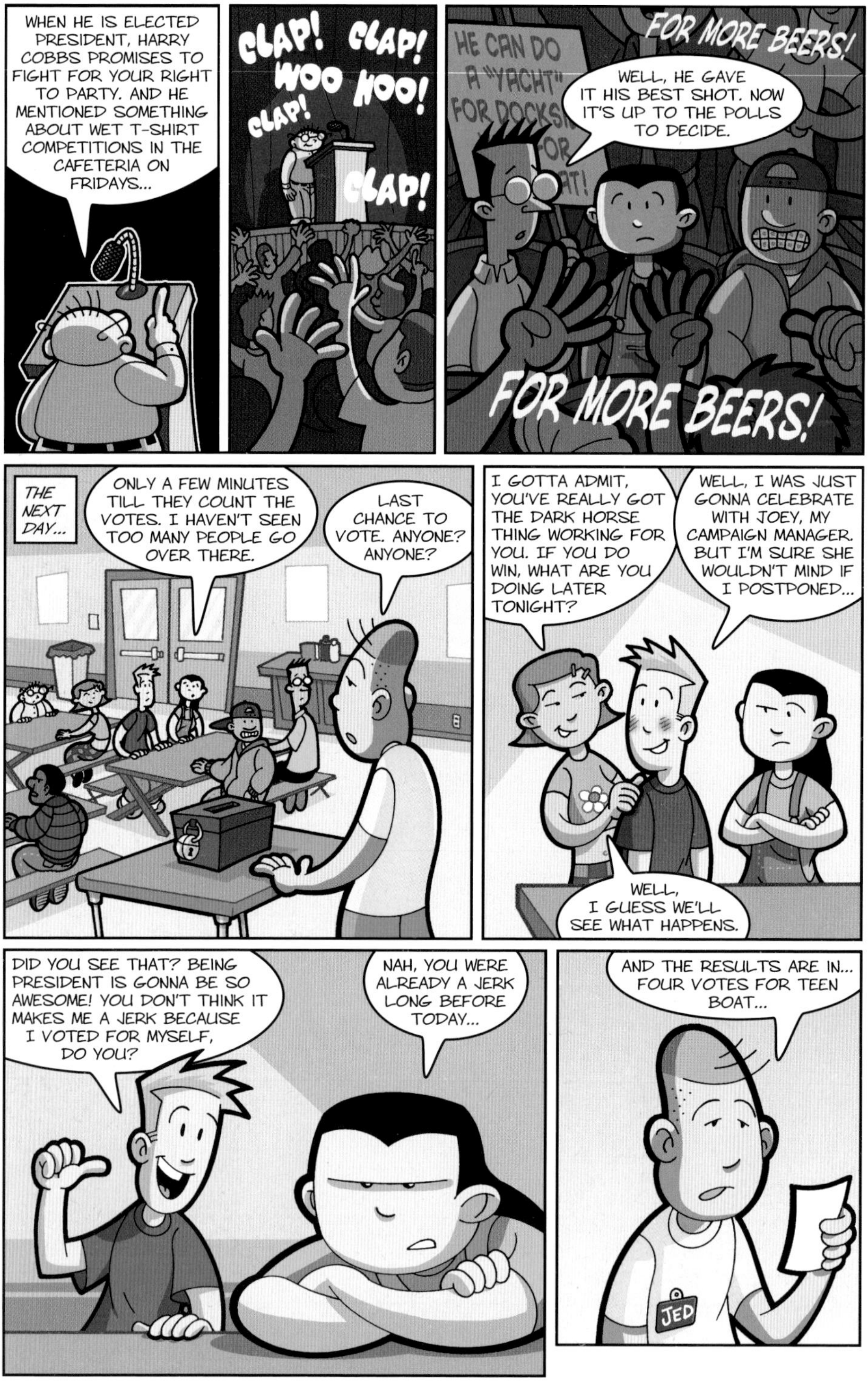
WHEN HE IS ELECTED PRESIDENT, HARRY COBBS PROMISES TO FIGHT FOR YOUR RIGHT TO PARTY. AND HE MENTIONED SOMETHING ABOUT WET T-SHIRT COMPETITIONS IN THE CAFETERIA ON FRIDAYS...
CLAP! CLAP!
WOO HOO!
CLAP!
CLAP!
HE CAN DO A "YACHT" FOR DOCKS
FOR MORE BEERS!
WELL, HE GAVE IT HIS BEST SHOT. NOW IT'S UP TO THE POLLS TO DECIDE.
FOR MORE BEERS!
THE NEXT DAY...
ONLY A FEW MINUTES TILL THEY COUNT THE VOTES. I HAVEN'T SEEN TOO MANY PEOPLE GO OVER THERE.
LAST CHANCE TO VOTE. ANYONE? ANYONE?
I GOTTA ADMIT, YOU'VE REALLY GOT THE DARK HORSE THING WORKING FOR YOU. IF YOU DO WIN, WHAT ARE YOU DOING LATER TONIGHT?
WELL, I WAS JUST GONNA CELEBRATE WITH JOEY, MY CAMPAIGN MANAGER. BUT I'M SURE SHE WOULDN'T MIND IF I POSTPONED...
WELL, I GUESS WE'LL SEE WHAT HAPPENS.
DID YOU SEE THAT? BEING PRESIDENT IS GONNA BE SO AWESOME! YOU DON'T THINK IT MAKES ME A JERK BECAUSE I VOTED FOR MYSELF, DO YOU?
NAH, YOU WERE ALREADY A JERK LONG BEFORE TODAY...
AND THE RESULTS ARE IN... FOUR VOTES FOR TEEN BOAT...
JED

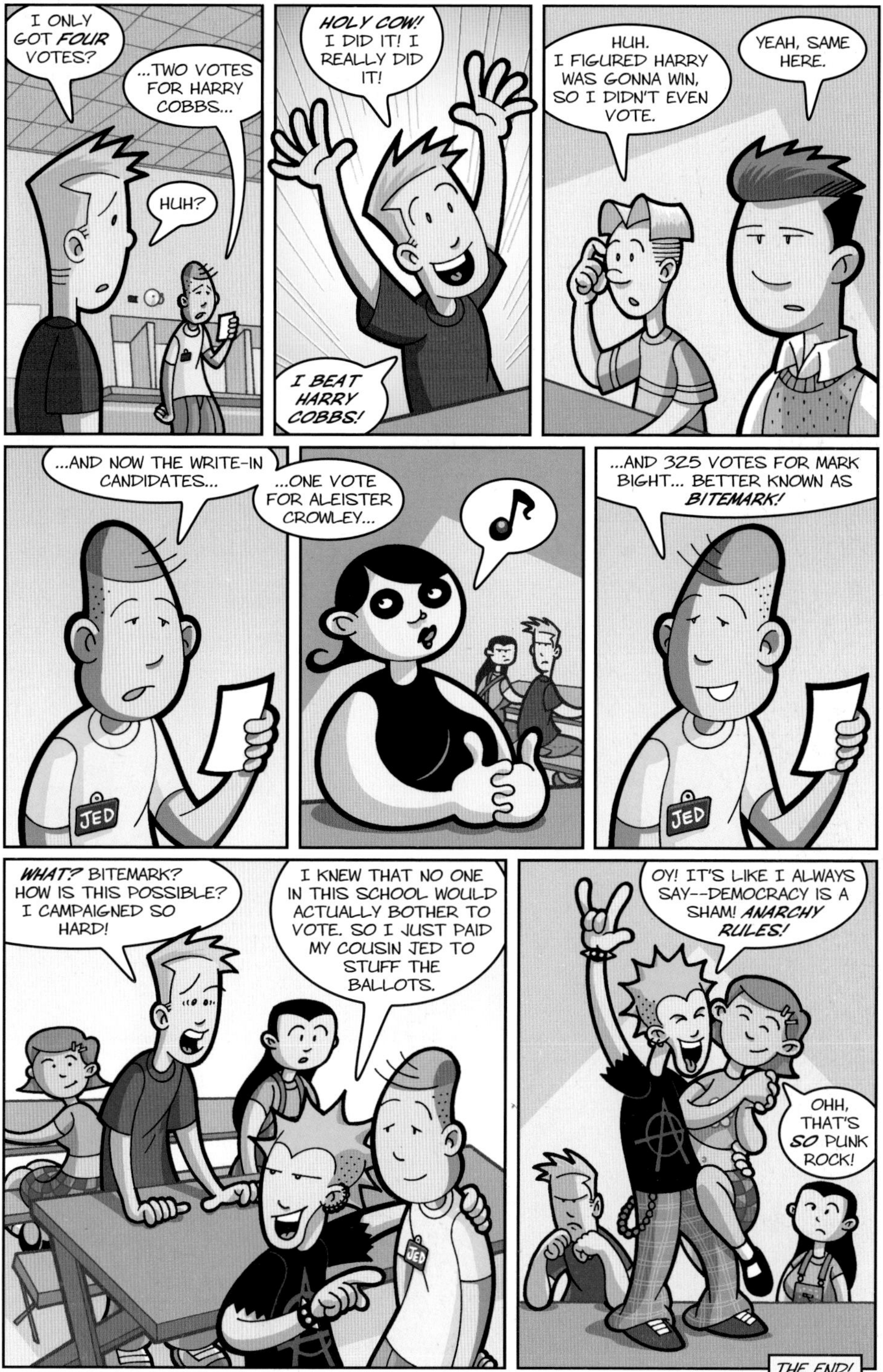
I ONLY GOT FOUR VOTES?
...TWO VOTES FOR HARRY COBBS...
HUH?
HOLY COW! I DID IT! I REALLY DID IT!
I BEAT HARRY COBBS!
HUH. I FIGURED HARRY WAS GONNA WIN, SO I DIDN'T EVEN VOTE.
YEAH, SAME HERE.
...AND NOW THE WRITE-IN CANDIDATES...
...ONE VOTE FOR ALEISTER CROWLEY...
JED
...AND 325 VOTES FOR MARK BIGHT... BETTER KNOWN AS BITEMARK!
JED
WHAT? BITEMARK? HOW IS THIS POSSIBLE? I CAMPAIGNED SO HARD!
I KNEW THAT NO ONE IN THIS SCHOOL WOULD ACTUALLY BOTHER TO VOTE. SO I JUST PAID MY COUSIN JED TO STUFF THE BALLOTS.
JED
OY! IT'S LIKE I ALWAYS SAY--DEMOCRACY IS A SHAM! ANARCHY RULES!
OHH, THAT'S SO PUNK ROCK!
THE END!

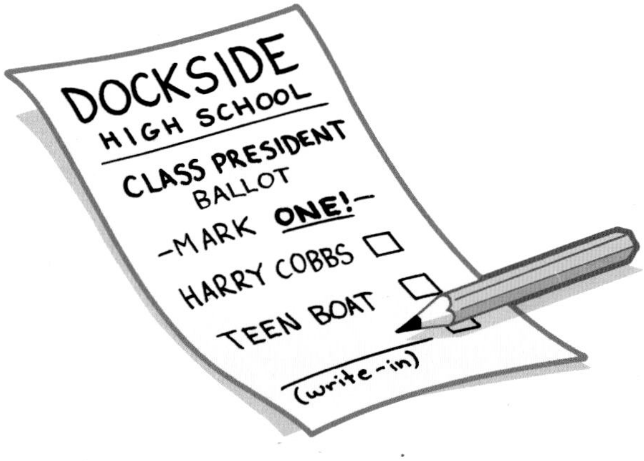
DOCKSIDE
HIGH SCHOOL
CLASS PRESIDENT
BALLOT
-MARK ONE!-
HARRY COBBS
TEEN BOAT
(write-in)

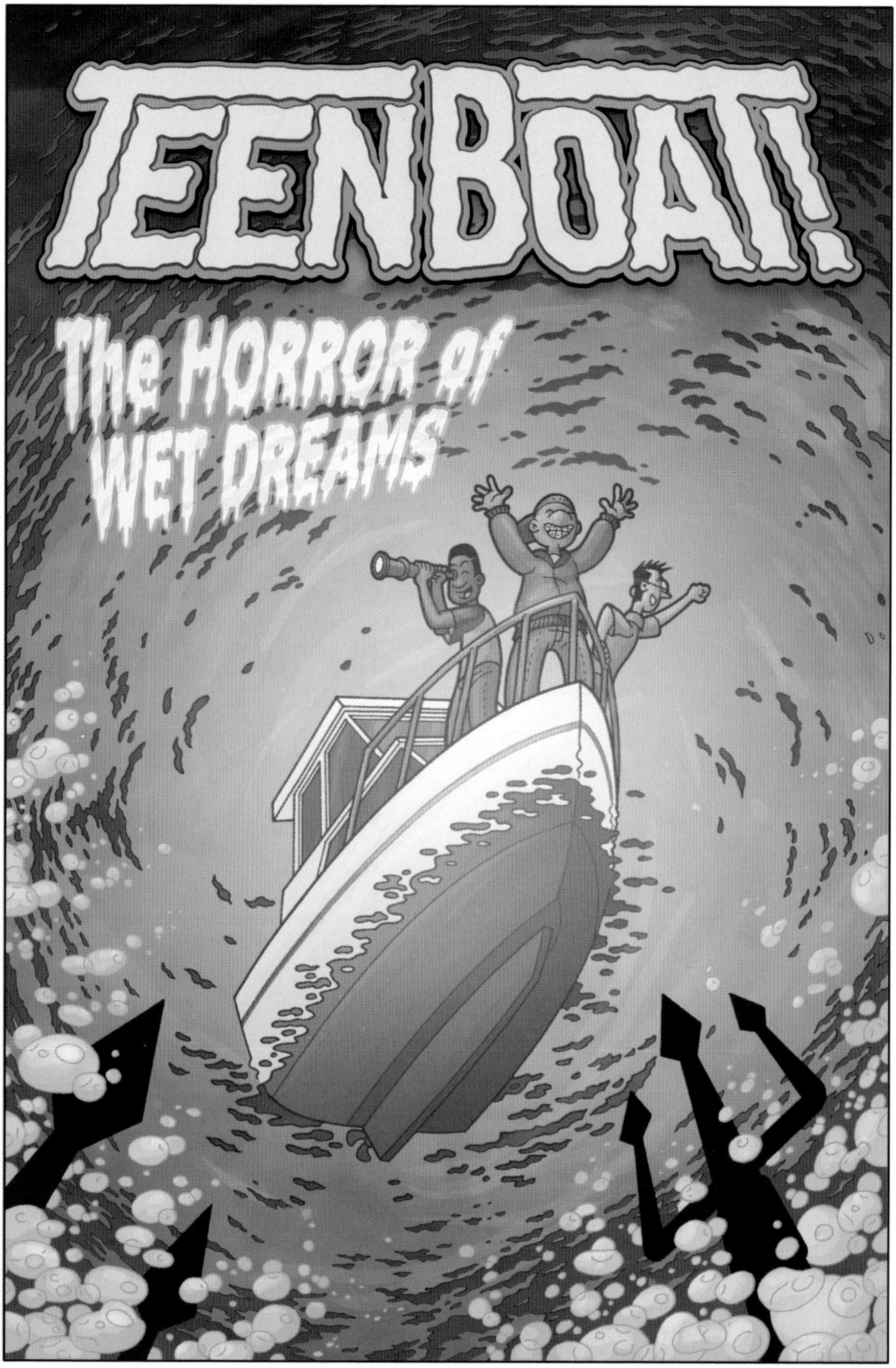
TEENBOAT!
The HORROR of WET DREAMS

The ***ANGST*** of being a Teen—the ***THRILL*** of being a Boat!

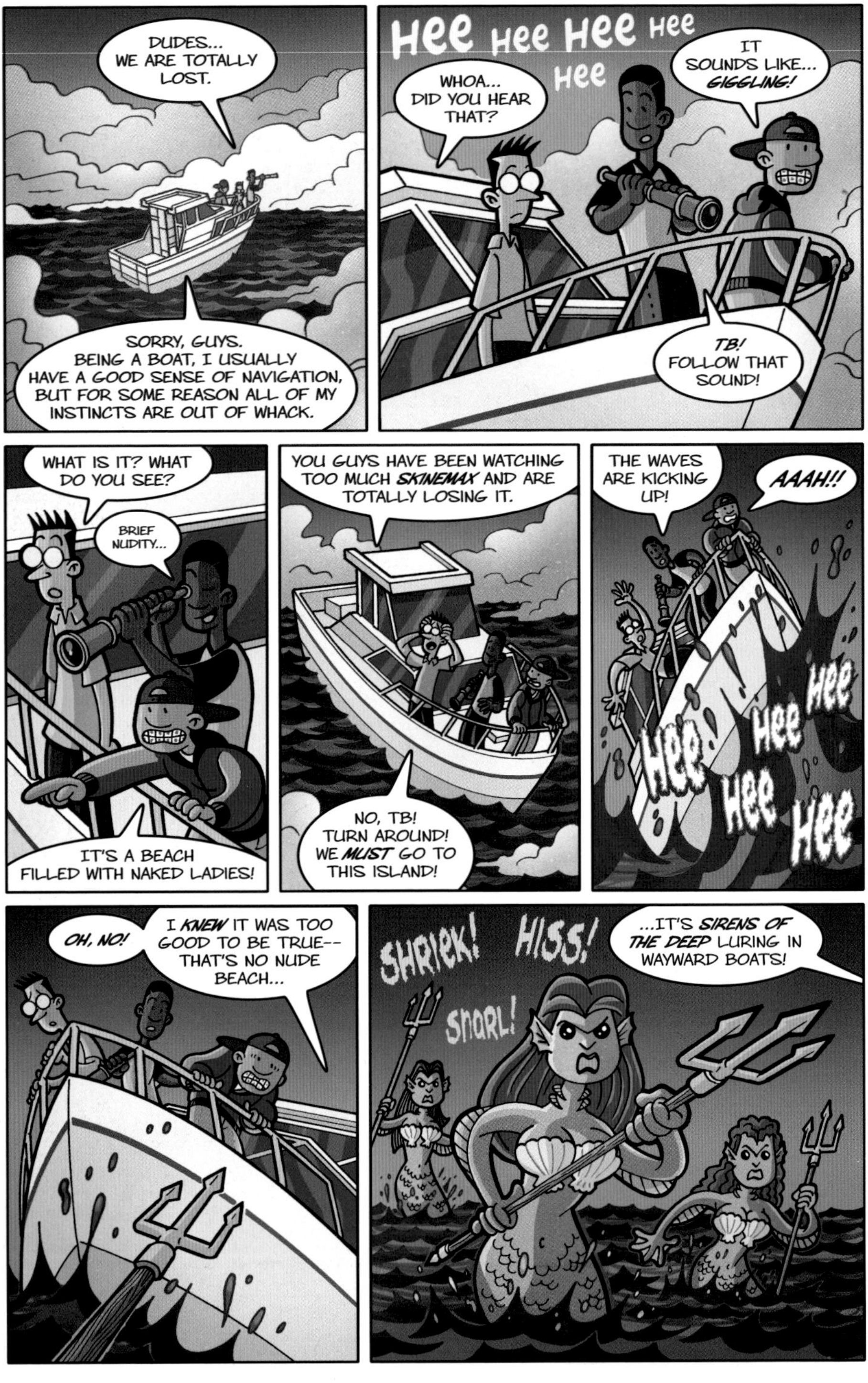
DUDES... WE ARE TOTALLY LOST.
SORRY, GUYS. BEING A BOAT, I USUALLY HAVE A GOOD SENSE OF NAVIGATION, BUT FOR SOME REASON ALL OF MY INSTINCTS ARE OUT OF WHACK.
Hee Hee Hee Hee Hee
WHOA... DID YOU HEAR THAT?
IT SOUNDS LIKE... GIGGLING!
TB! FOLLOW THAT SOUND!
WHAT IS IT? WHAT DO YOU SEE?
BRIEF NUDITY...
IT'S A BEACH FILLED WITH NAKED LADIES!
YOU GUYS HAVE BEEN WATCHING TOO MUCH SKINEMAX AND ARE TOTALLY LOSING IT.
NO, TB! TURN AROUND! WE MUST GO TO THIS ISLAND!
THE WAVES ARE KICKING UP!
AAAH!!
Hee Hee Hee Hee Hee
OH, NO!
I KNEW IT WAS TOO GOOD TO BE TRUE-- THAT'S NO NUDE BEACH...
SHRIEK! HISS! SNARL!
...IT'S SIRENS OF THE DEEP LURING IN WAYWARD BOATS!

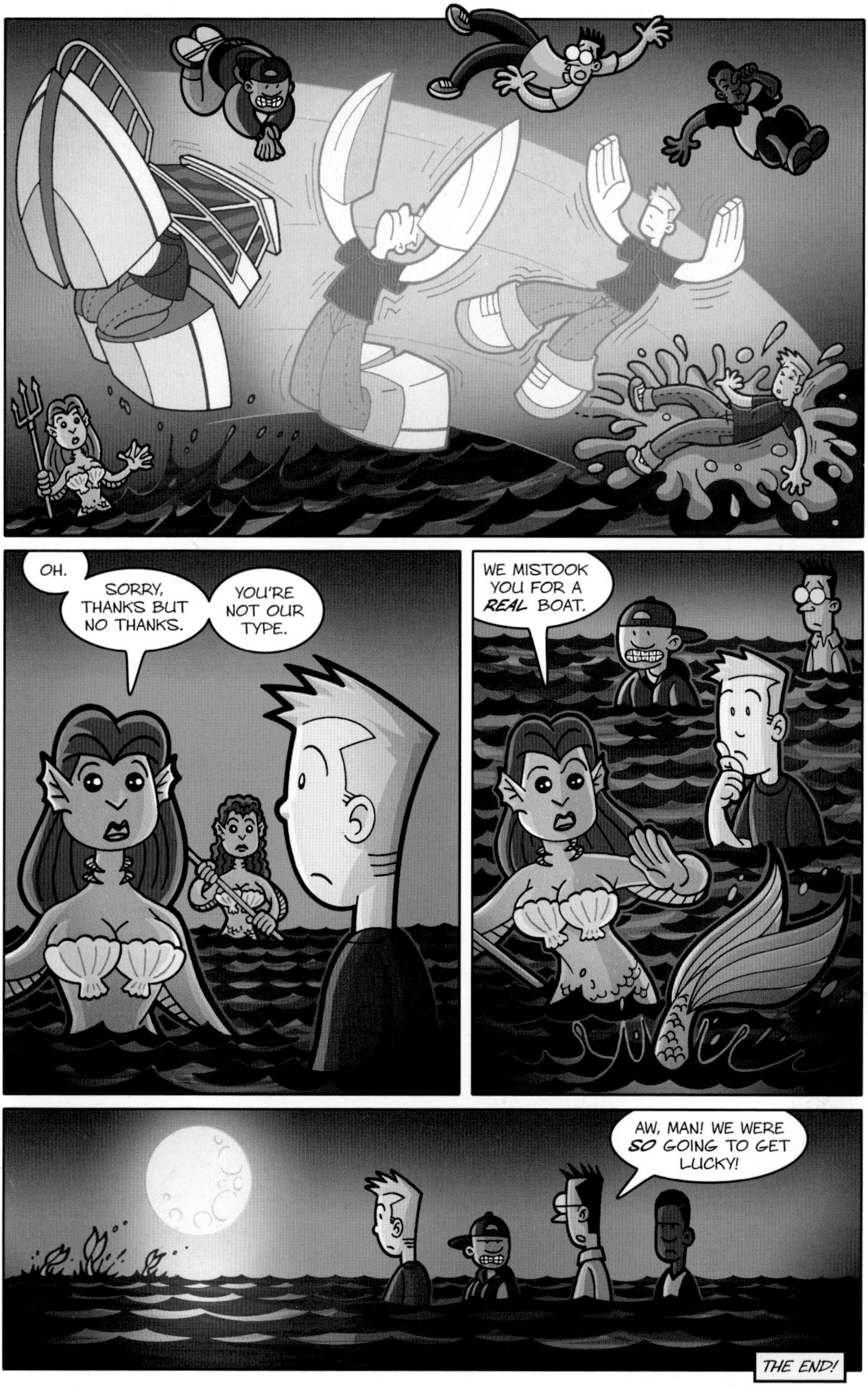

OH.
SORRY, THANKS BUT NO THANKS.
YOU'RE NOT OUR TYPE.
WE MISTOOK YOU FOR A *REAL* BOAT.
AW, MAN! WE WERE *SO* GOING TO GET LUCKY!
THE END!

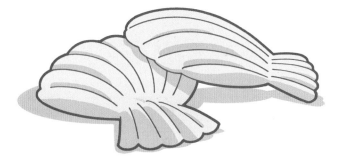

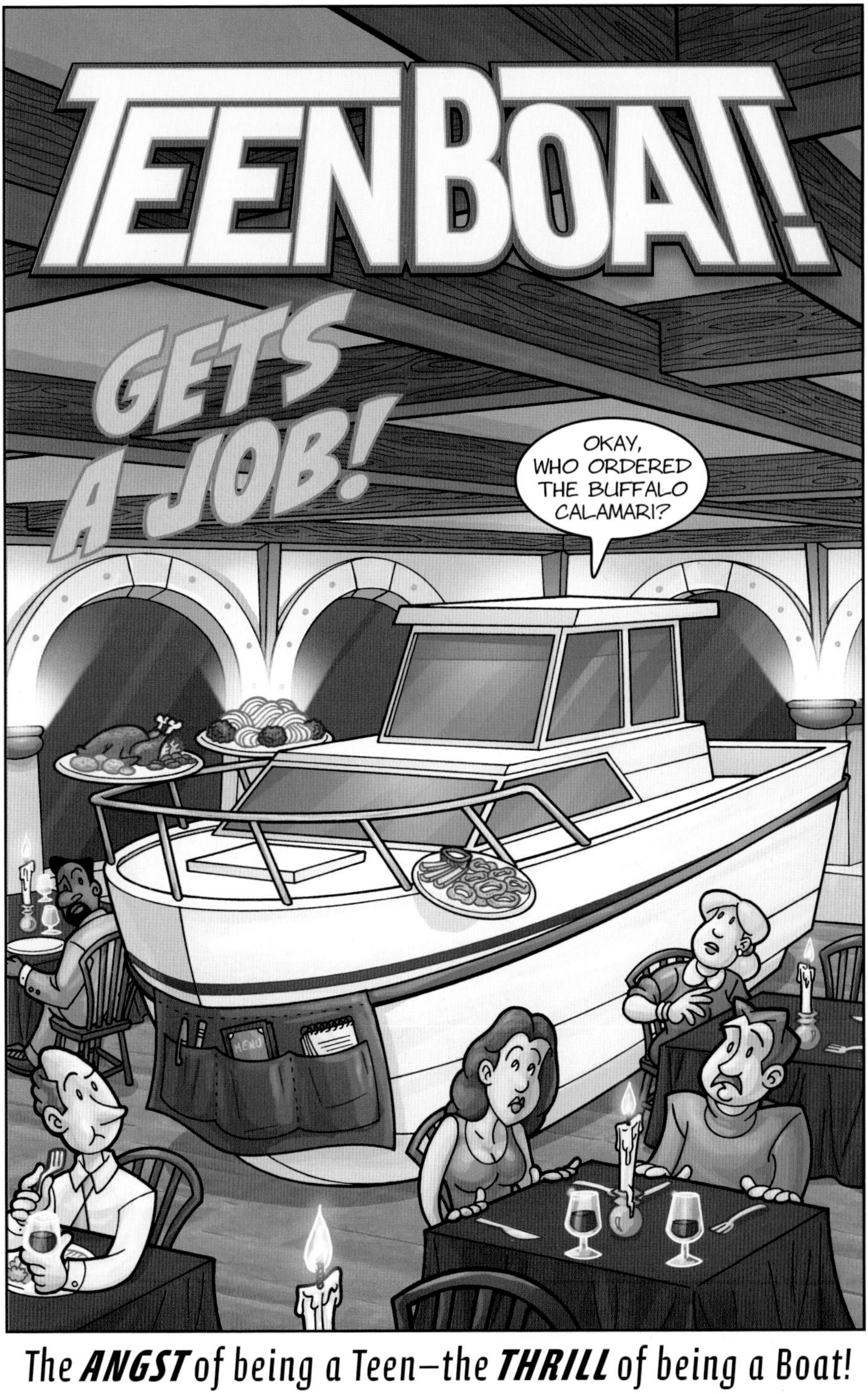
TEENBOAT!
GETS A JOB!
OKAY, WHO ORDERED THE BUFFALO CALAMARI?
MENU

The ***ANGST*** of being a Teen—the ***THRILL*** of being a Boat!

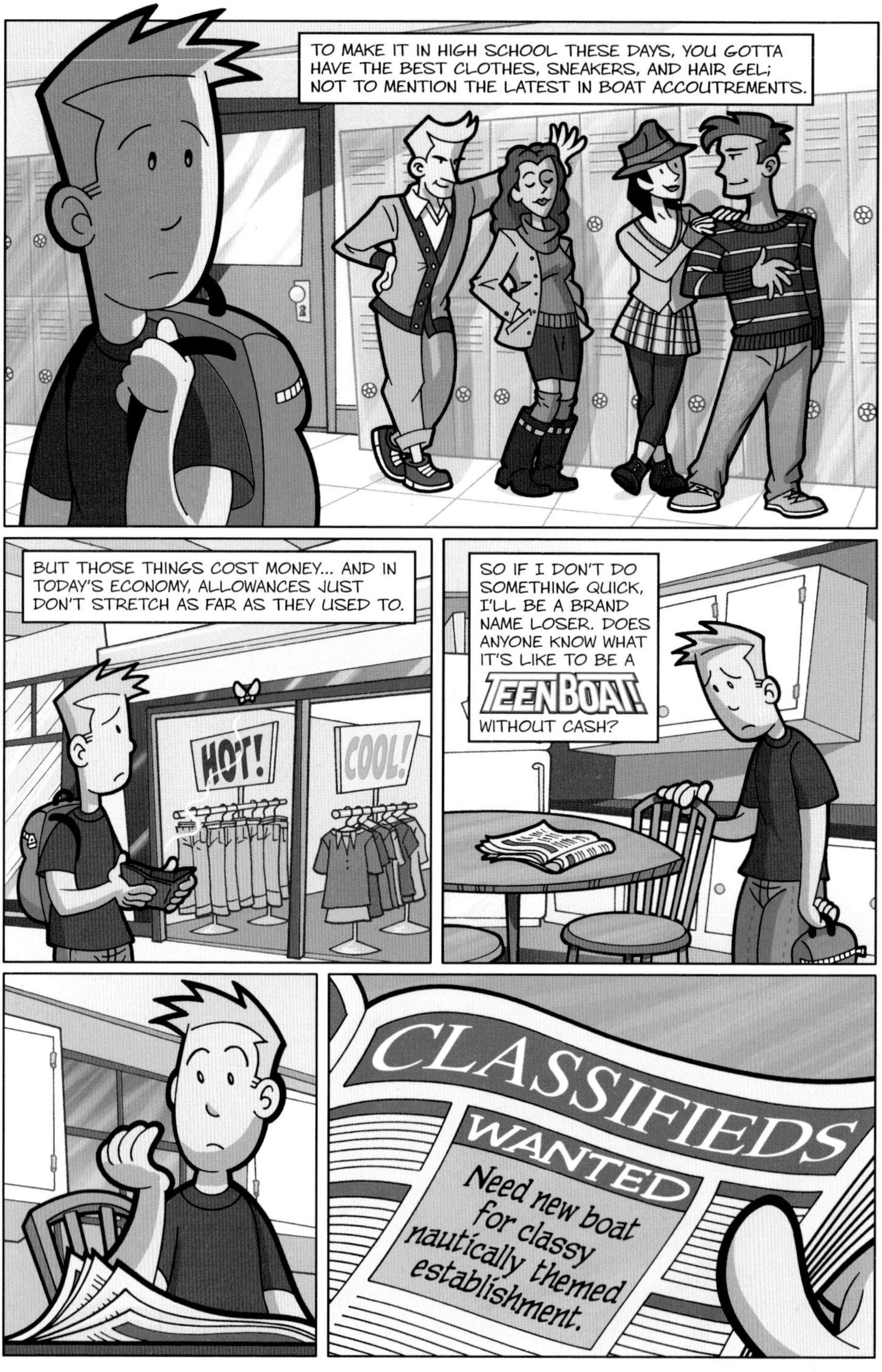
TO MAKE IT IN HIGH SCHOOL THESE DAYS, YOU GOTTA HAVE THE BEST CLOTHES, SNEAKERS, AND HAIR GEL; NOT TO MENTION THE LATEST IN BOAT ACCOUTREMENTS.
BUT THOSE THINGS COST MONEY... AND IN TODAY'S ECONOMY, ALLOWANCES JUST DON'T STRETCH AS FAR AS THEY USED TO.
HOT!
COOL!
SO IF I DON'T DO SOMETHING QUICK, I'LL BE A BRAND NAME LOSER. DOES ANYONE KNOW WHAT IT'S LIKE TO BE A TEENBOAT! WITHOUT CASH?
CLASSIFIEDS
WANTED
Need new boat for classy nautically themed establishment.

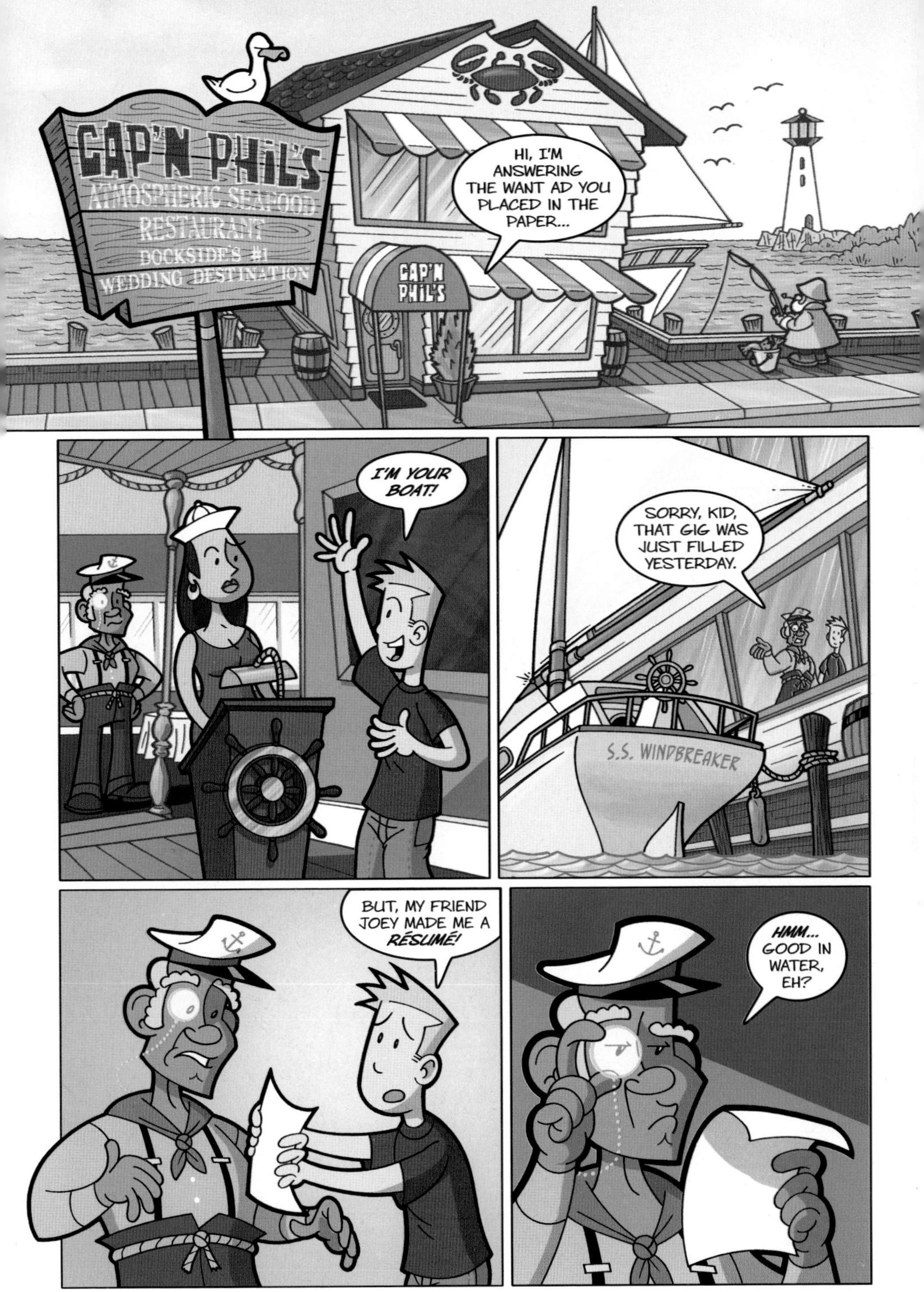
CAP'N PHIL'S
ATMOSPHERIC SEAFOOD
RESTAURANT
DOCKSIDE'S #1
WEDDING DESTINATION
CAP'N PHIL'S
HI, I'M ANSWERING THE WANT AD YOU PLACED IN THE PAPER...
I'M YOUR BOAT!
SORRY, KID, THAT GIG WAS JUST FILLED YESTERDAY.
S.S. WINDBREAKER
BUT, MY FRIEND JOEY MADE ME A RÉSUMÉ!
HMM... GOOD IN WATER, EH?

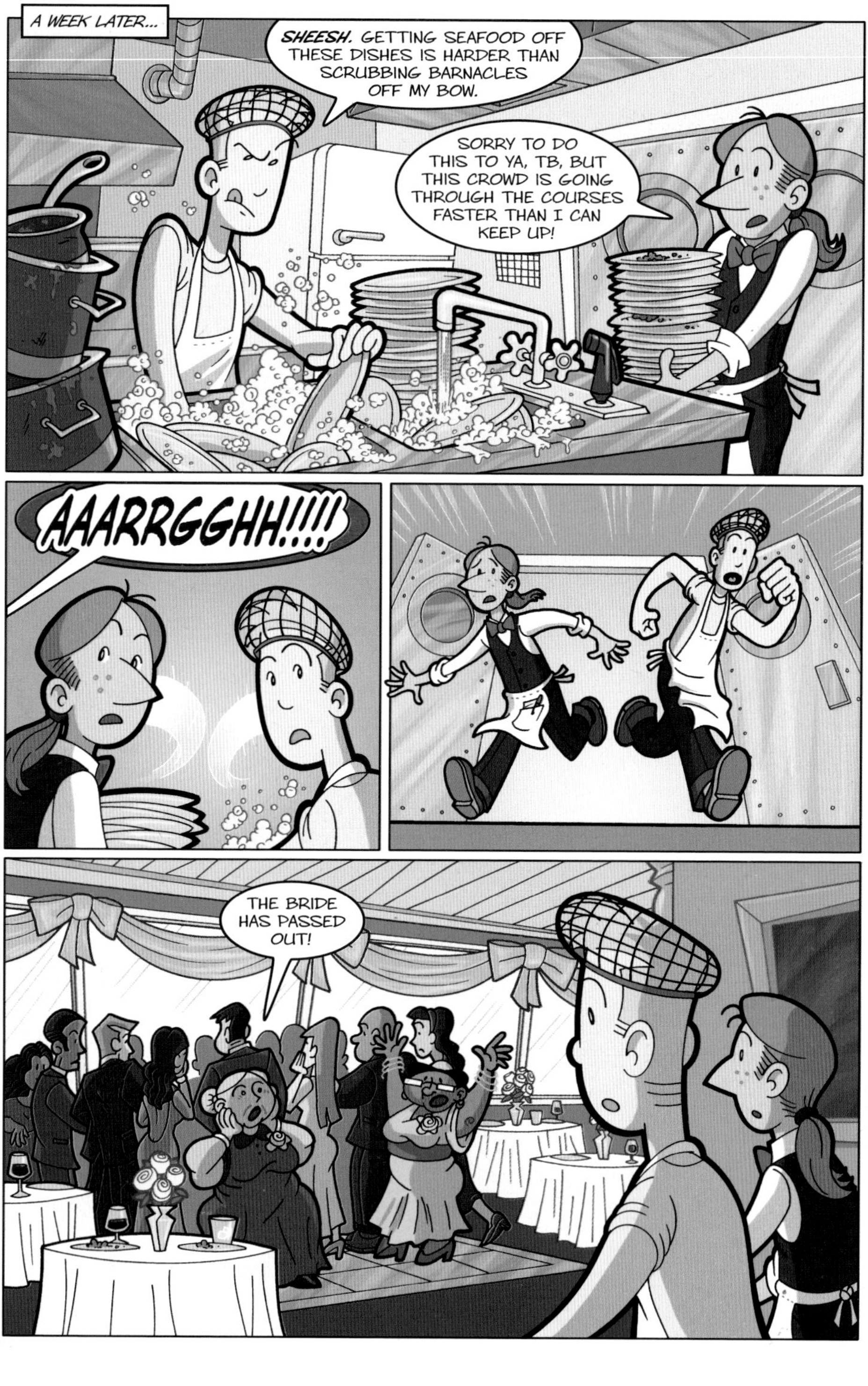
A WEEK LATER...
SHEESH. GETTING SEAFOOD OFF THESE DISHES IS HARDER THAN SCRUBBING BARNACLES OFF MY BOW.
SORRY TO DO THIS TO YA, TB, BUT THIS CROWD IS GOING THROUGH THE COURSES FASTER THAN I CAN KEEP UP!
AAARRGGHH!!!!
THE BRIDE HAS PASSED OUT!

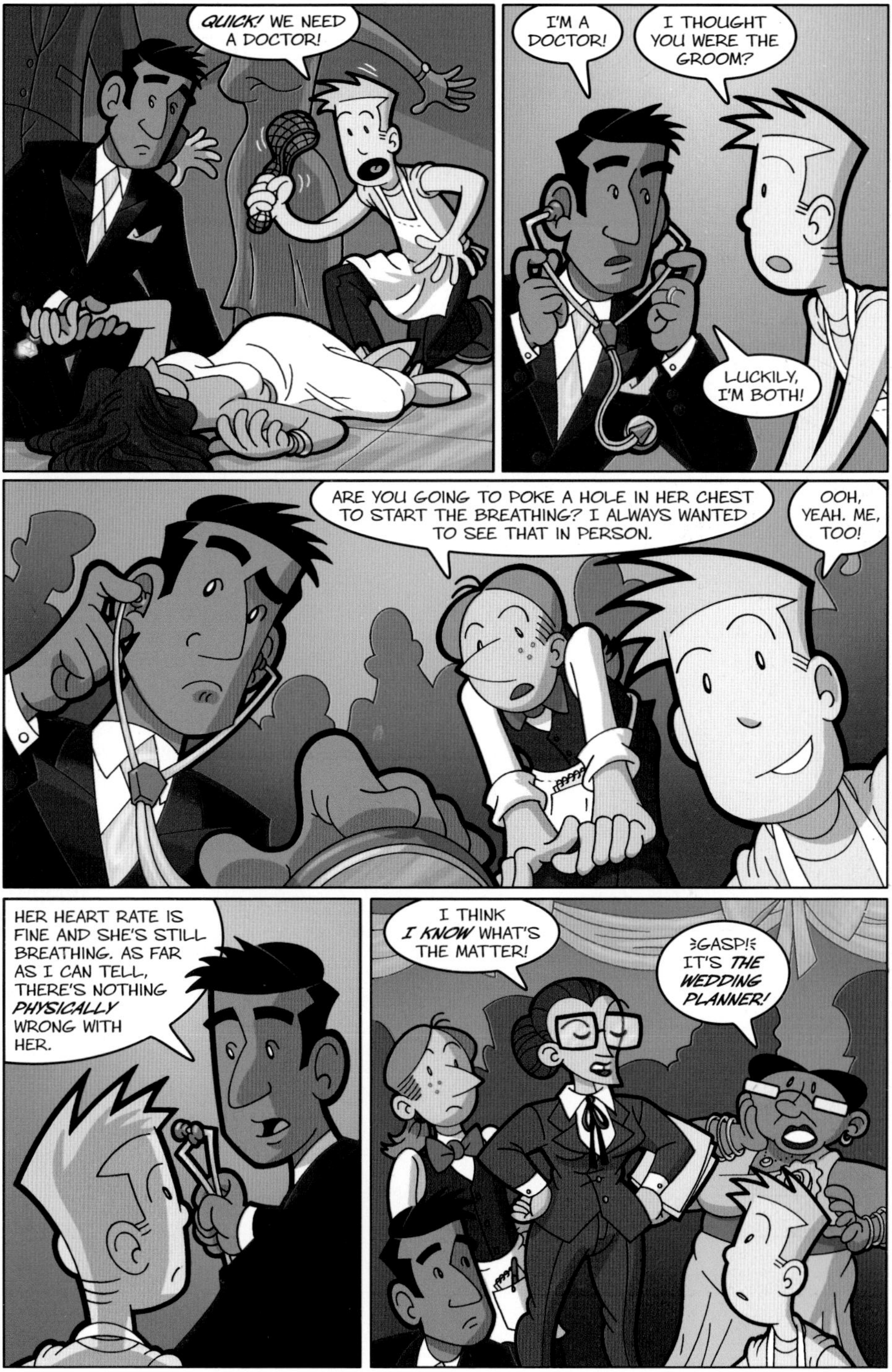
QUICK! WE NEED A DOCTOR!
I'M A DOCTOR!
I THOUGHT YOU WERE THE GROOM?
LUCKILY, I'M BOTH!
ARE YOU GOING TO POKE A HOLE IN HER CHEST TO START THE BREATHING? I ALWAYS WANTED TO SEE THAT IN PERSON.
OOH, YEAH. ME, TOO!
HER HEART RATE IS FINE AND SHE'S STILL BREATHING. AS FAR AS I CAN TELL, THERE'S NOTHING PHYSICALLY WRONG WITH HER.
I THINK I KNOW WHAT'S THE MATTER!
GASP! IT'S THE WEDDING PLANNER!

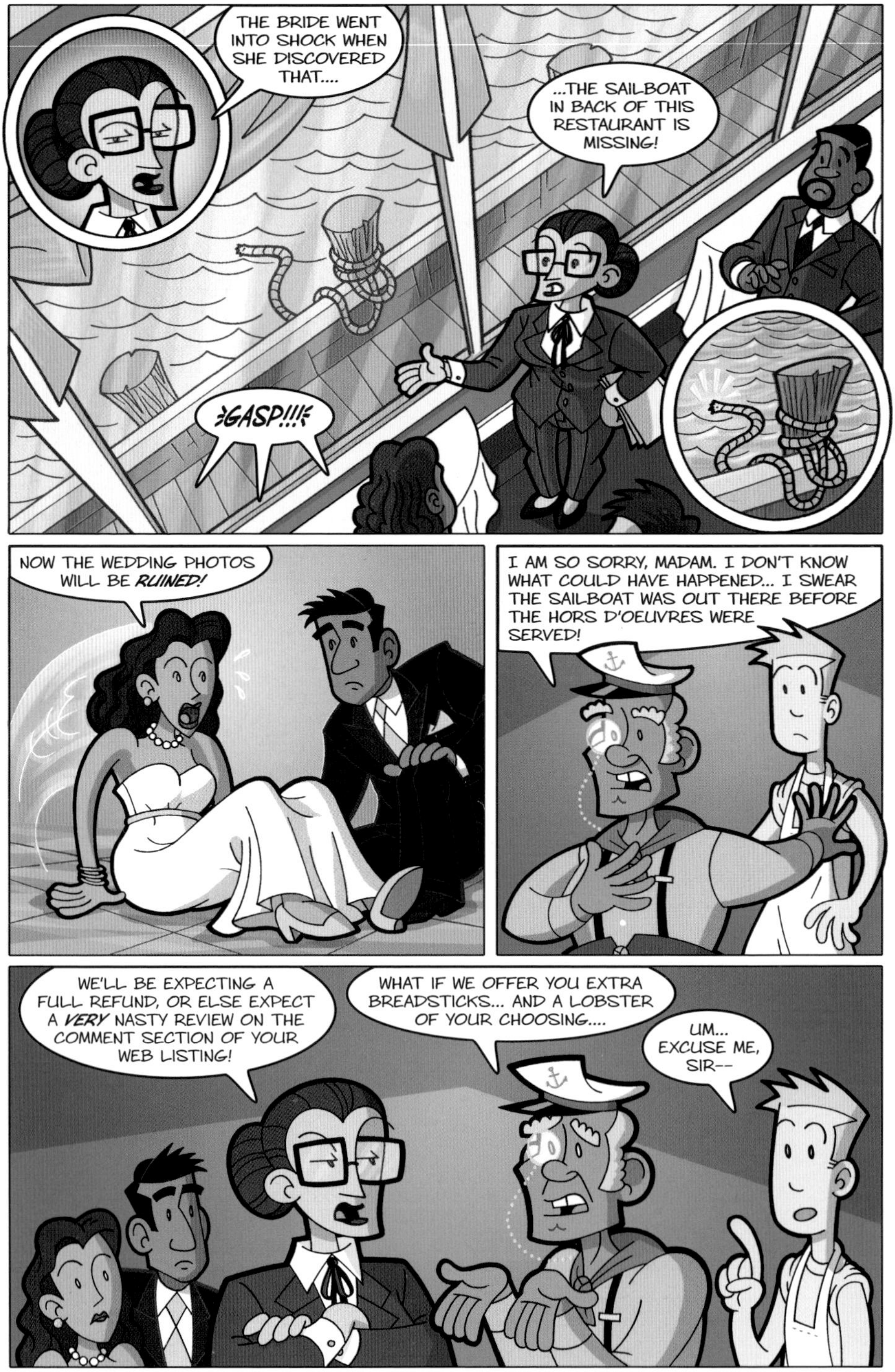
THE BRIDE WENT INTO SHOCK WHEN SHE DISCOVERED THAT....
...THE SAILBOAT IN BACK OF THIS RESTAURANT IS MISSING!
GASP!!!
NOW THE WEDDING PHOTOS WILL BE *RUINED!*
I AM SO SORRY, MADAM. I DON'T KNOW WHAT COULD HAVE HAPPENED... I SWEAR THE SAILBOAT WAS OUT THERE BEFORE THE HORS D'OEUVRES WERE SERVED!
WE'LL BE EXPECTING A FULL REFUND, OR ELSE EXPECT A *VERY* NASTY REVIEW ON THE COMMENT SECTION OF YOUR WEB LISTING!
WHAT IF WE OFFER YOU EXTRA BREADSTICKS... AND A LOBSTER OF YOUR CHOOSING....
UM... EXCUSE ME, SIR--

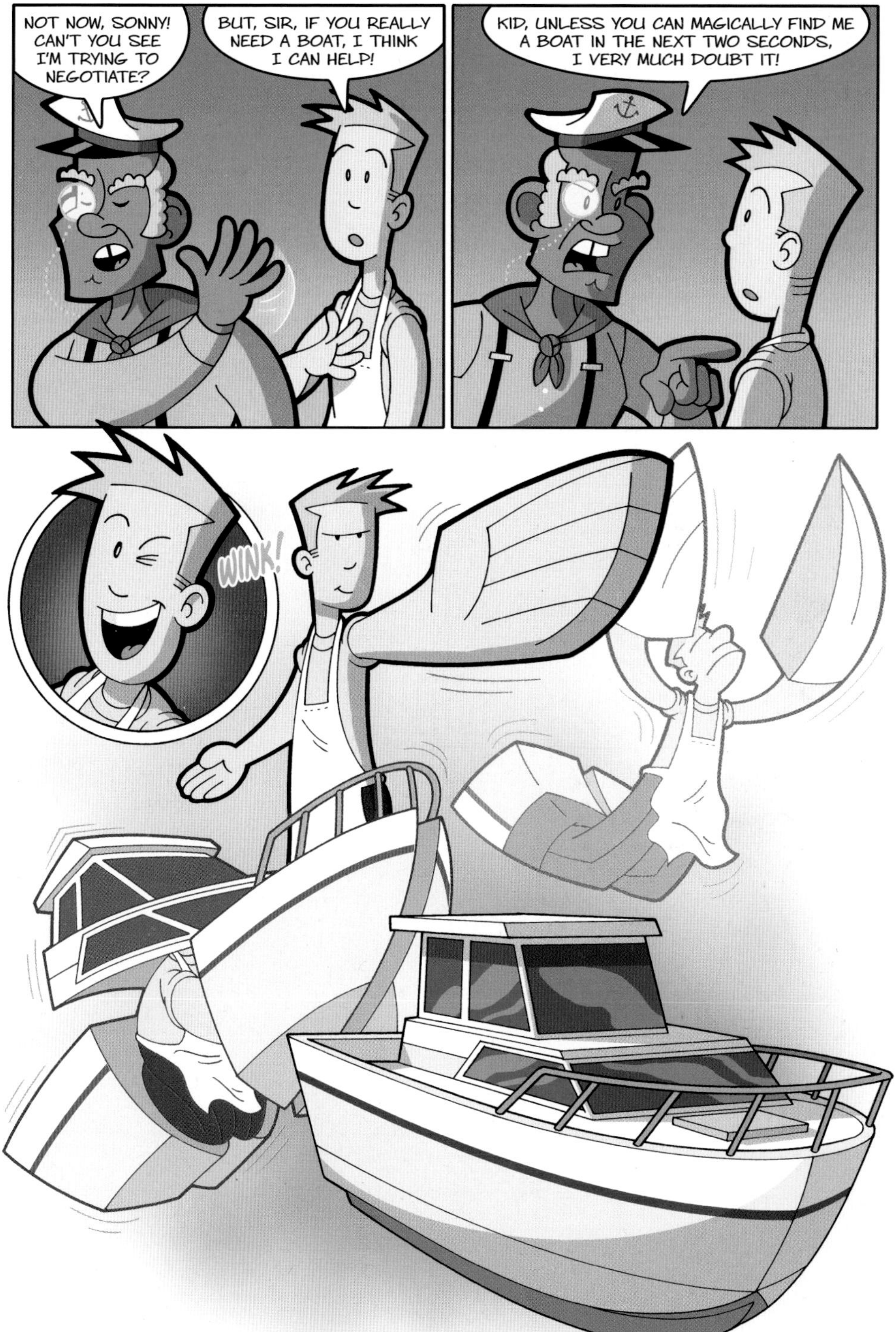
NOT NOW, SONNY! CAN'T YOU SEE I'M TRYING TO NEGOTIATE?
BUT, SIR, IF YOU REALLY NEED A BOAT, I THINK I CAN HELP!
KID, UNLESS YOU CAN MAGICALLY FIND ME A BOAT IN THE NEXT TWO SECONDS, I VERY MUCH DOUBT IT!
WINK!

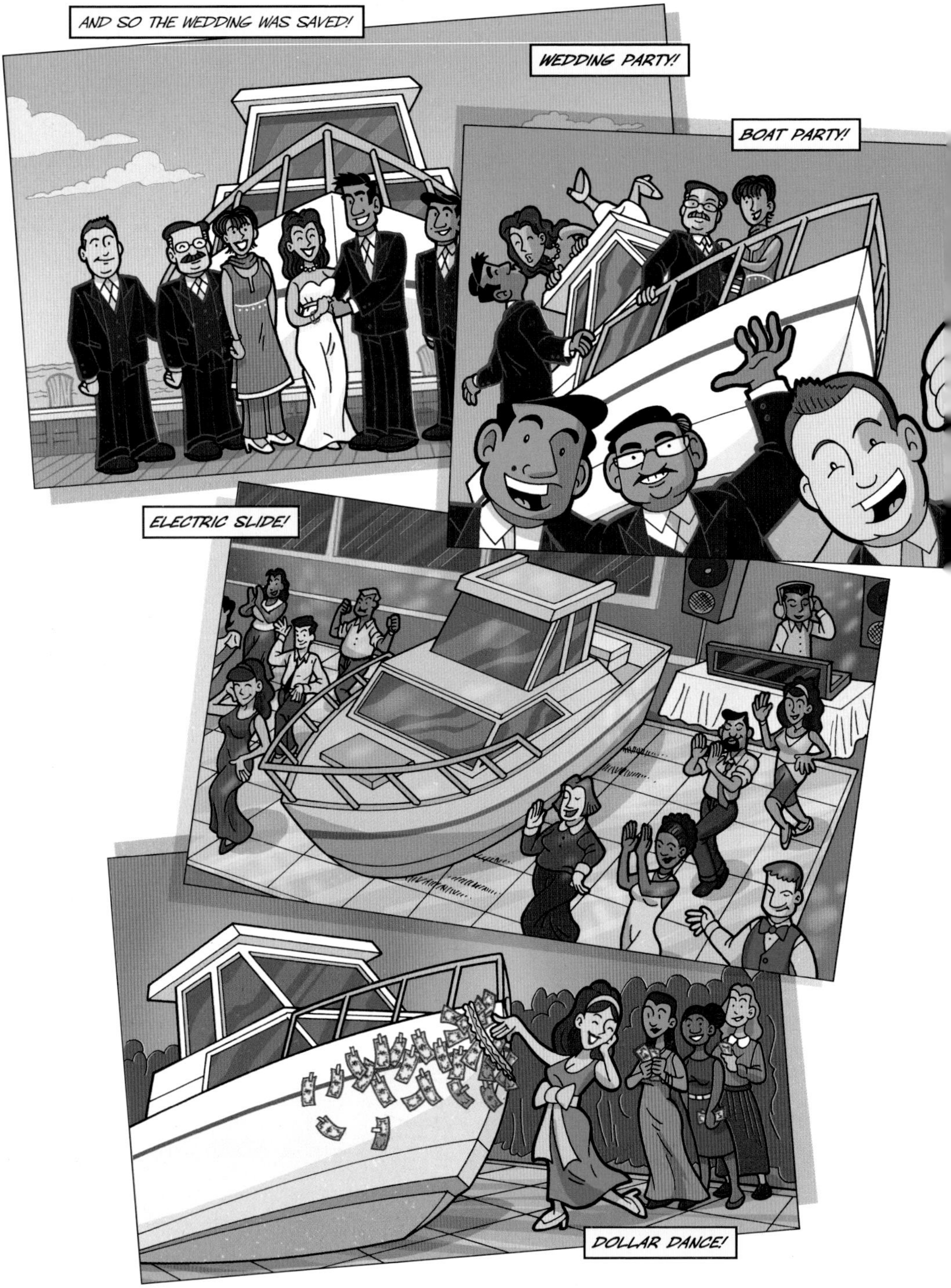
AND SO THE WEDDING WAS SAVED!
WEDDING PARTY!
BOAT PARTY!
ELECTRIC SLIDE!
DOLLAR DANCE!

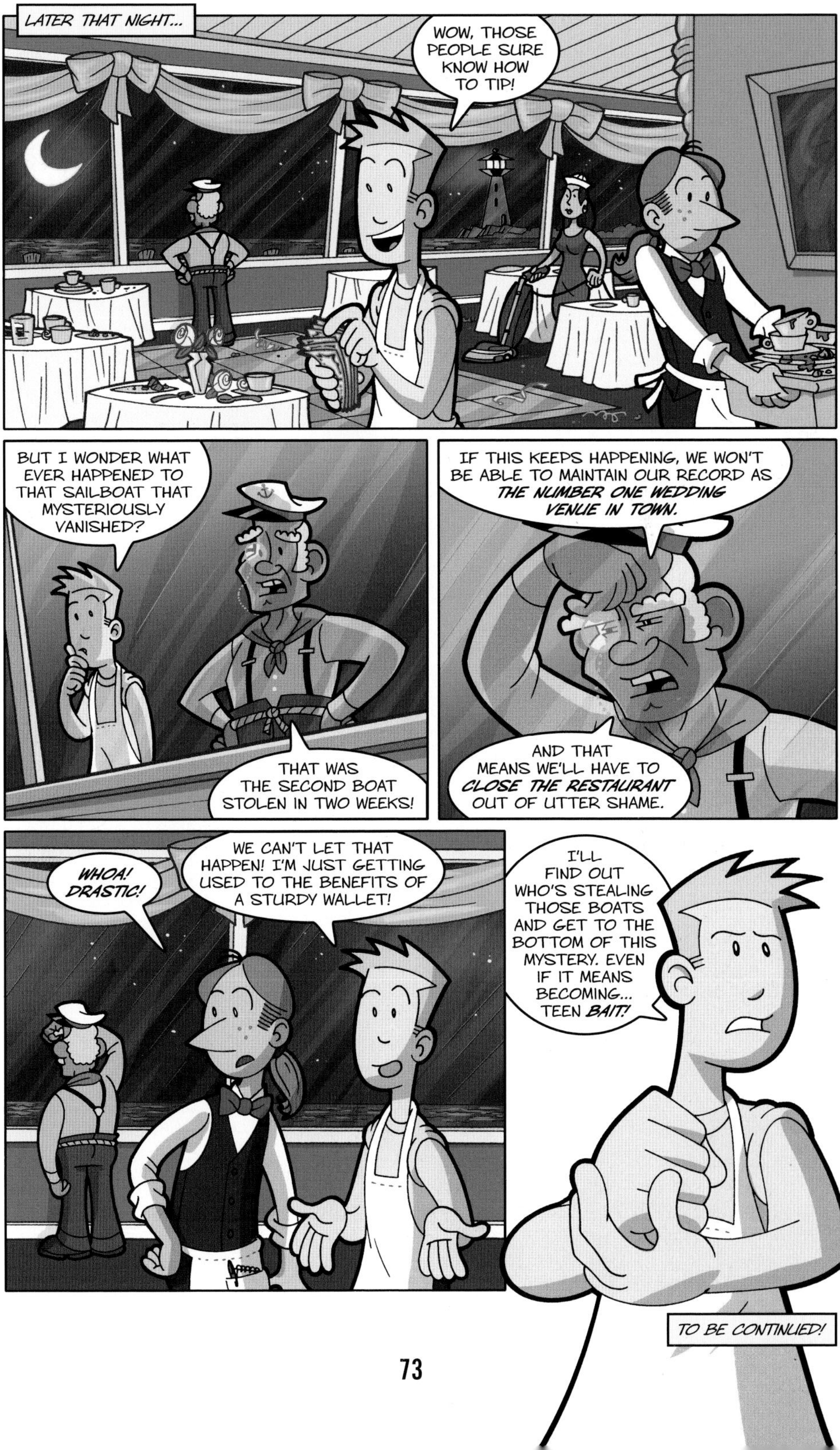
LATER THAT NIGHT...
WOW, THOSE PEOPLE SURE KNOW HOW TO TIP!
BUT I WONDER WHAT EVER HAPPENED TO THAT SAILBOAT THAT MYSTERIOUSLY VANISHED?
THAT WAS THE SECOND BOAT STOLEN IN TWO WEEKS!
IF THIS KEEPS HAPPENING, WE WON'T BE ABLE TO MAINTAIN OUR RECORD AS THE NUMBER ONE WEDDING VENUE IN TOWN.
AND THAT MEANS WE'LL HAVE TO CLOSE THE RESTAURANT OUT OF UTTER SHAME.
WHOA! DRASTIC!
WE CAN'T LET THAT HAPPEN! I'M JUST GETTING USED TO THE BENEFITS OF A STURDY WALLET!
I'LL FIND OUT WHO'S STEALING THOSE BOATS AND GET TO THE BOTTOM OF THIS MYSTERY. EVEN IF IT MEANS BECOMING... TEEN BAIT!
TO BE CONTINUED!

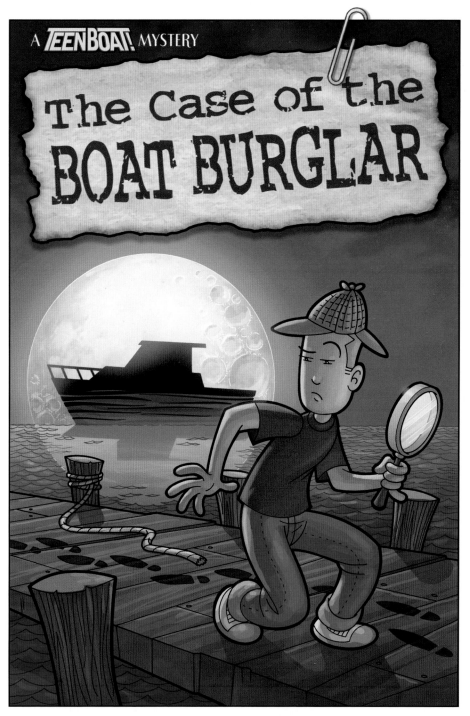

The Case of the BOAT BURGLAR

The **ANGST** of being a Teen—the **THRILL** of being a Boat!

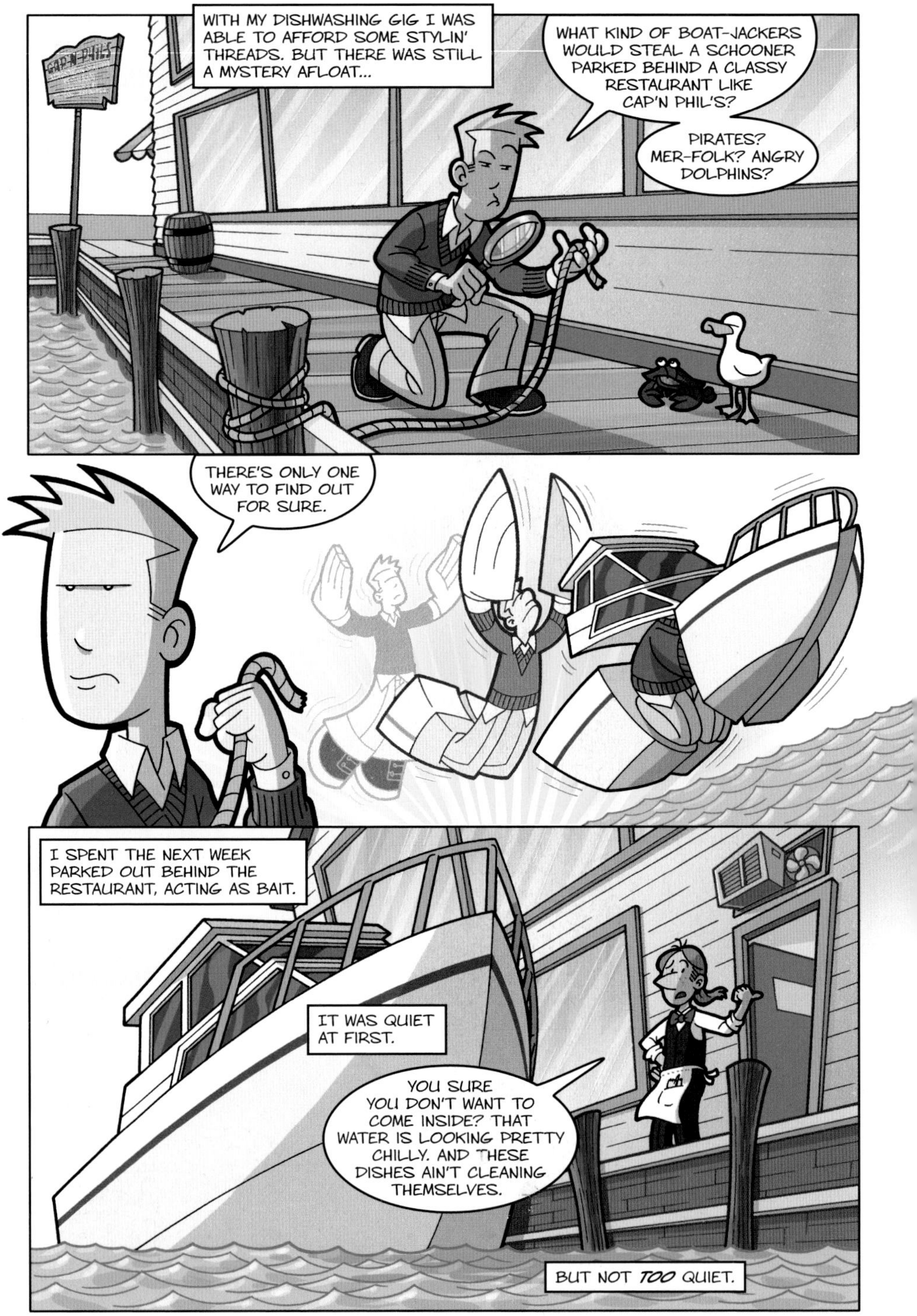
WITH MY DISHWASHING GIG I WAS ABLE TO AFFORD SOME STYLIN' THREADS. BUT THERE WAS STILL A MYSTERY AFLOAT...
WHAT KIND OF BOAT-JACKERS WOULD STEAL A SCHOONER PARKED BEHIND A CLASSY RESTAURANT LIKE CAP'N PHIL'S?
PIRATES? MER-FOLK? ANGRY DOLPHINS?
THERE'S ONLY ONE WAY TO FIND OUT FOR SURE.
I SPENT THE NEXT WEEK PARKED OUT BEHIND THE RESTAURANT, ACTING AS BAIT.
IT WAS QUIET AT FIRST.
YOU SURE YOU DON'T WANT TO COME INSIDE? THAT WATER IS LOOKING PRETTY CHILLY. AND THESE DISHES AIN'T CLEANING THEMSELVES.
BUT NOT *TOO* QUIET.

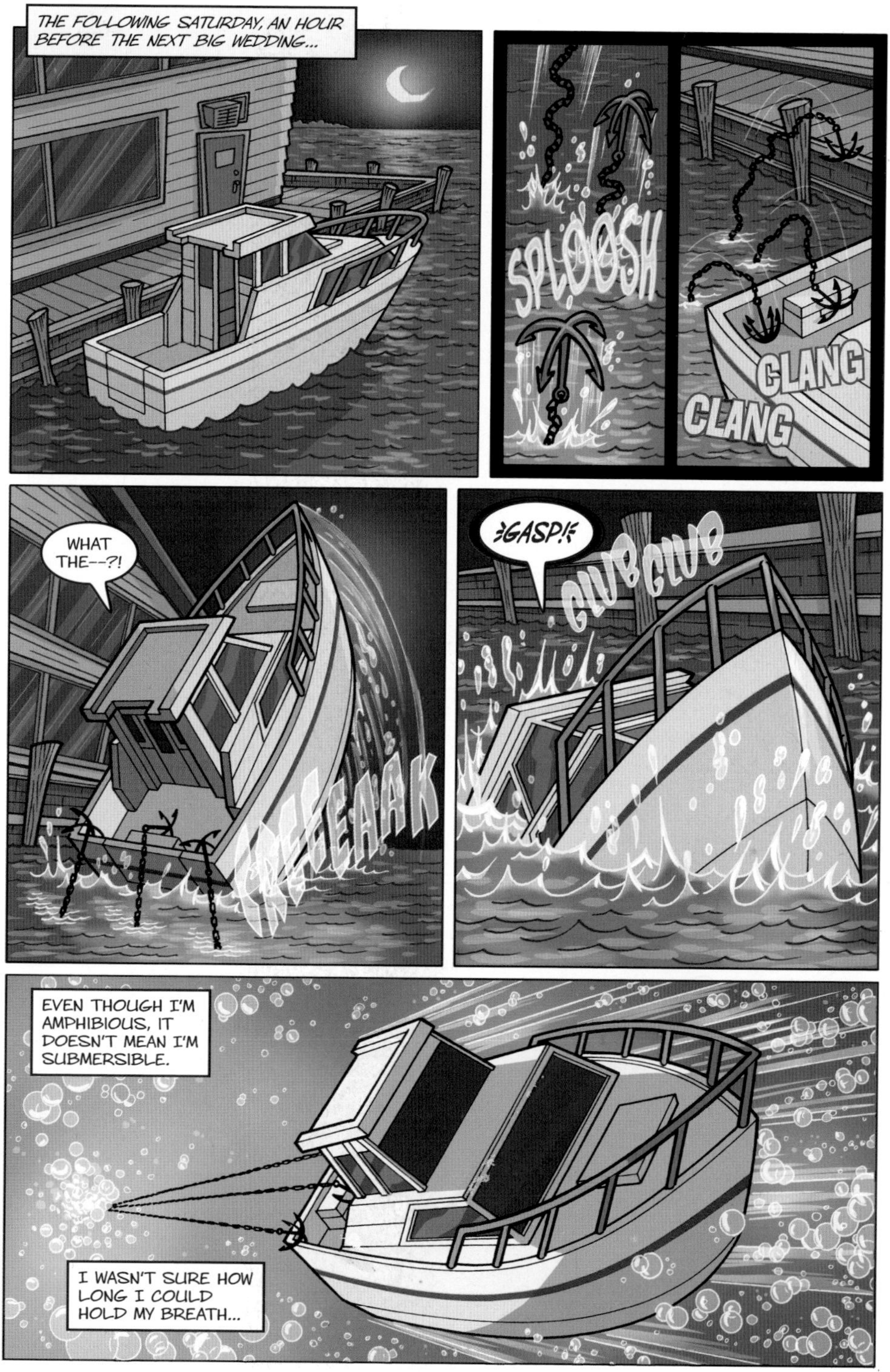
THE FOLLOWING SATURDAY, AN HOUR BEFORE THE NEXT BIG WEDDING...
SPLOOSH
CLANG
CLANG
WHAT THE--?!
CREEEAAK
GASP!
GLUB GLUB
EVEN THOUGH I'M AMPHIBIOUS, IT DOESN'T MEAN I'M SUBMERSIBLE.
I WASN'T SURE HOW LONG I COULD HOLD MY BREATH...

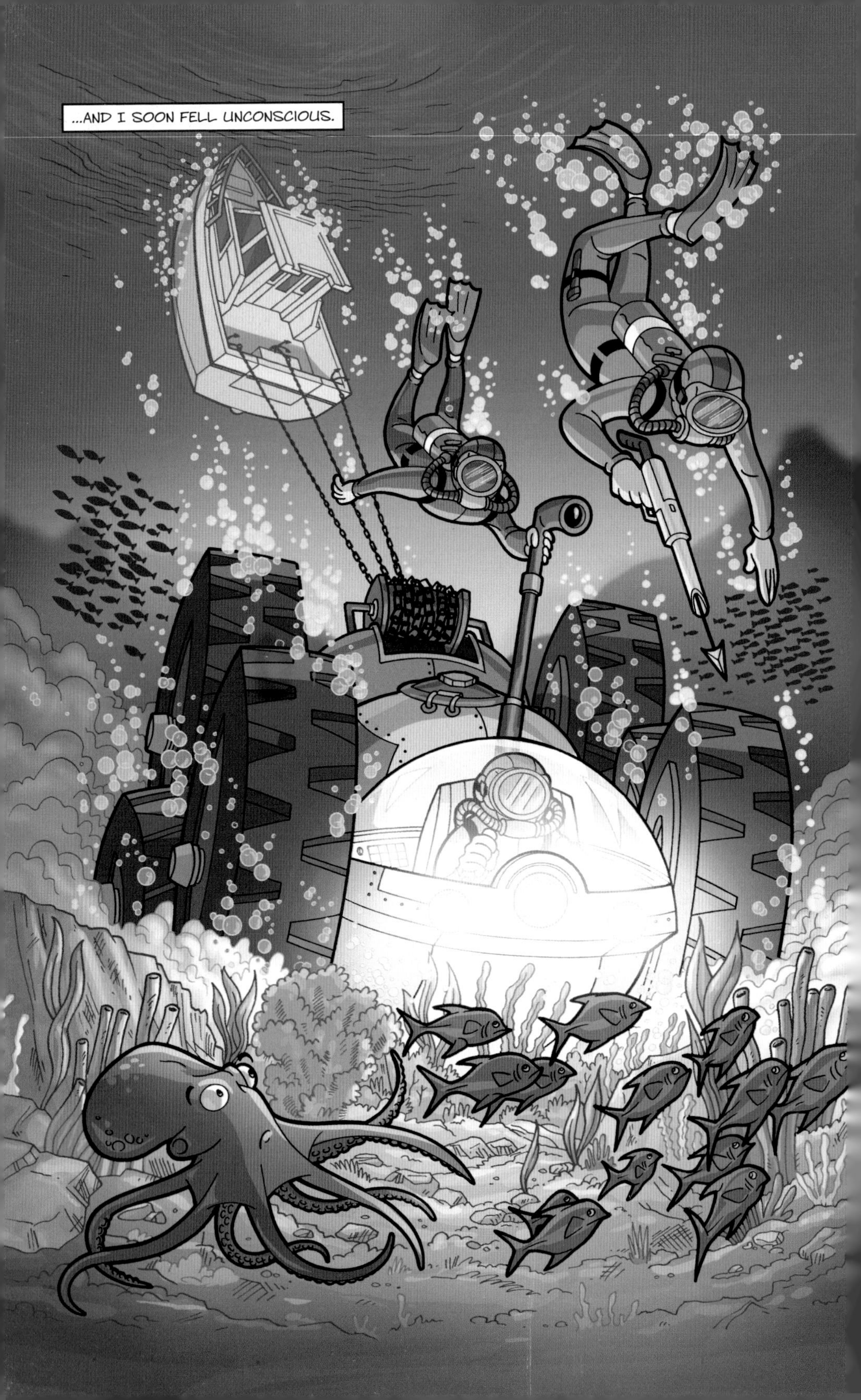
...AND I SOON FELL UNCONSCIOUS.

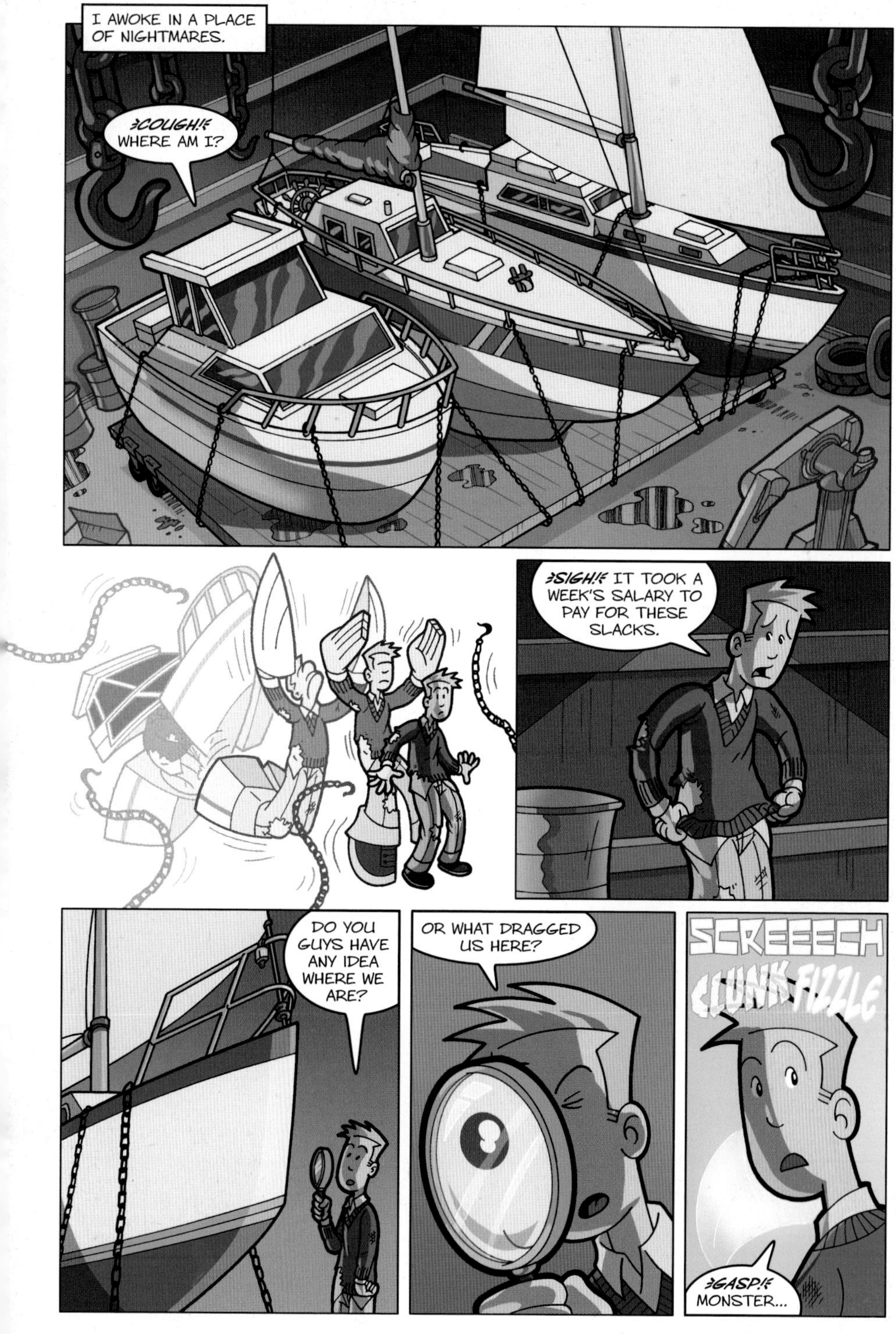
I AWOKE IN A PLACE OF NIGHTMARES.
COUGH! WHERE AM I?
SIGH! IT TOOK A WEEK'S SALARY TO PAY FOR THESE SLACKS.
DO YOU GUYS HAVE ANY IDEA WHERE WE ARE?
OR WHAT DRAGGED US HERE?
SCREEECH
CLUNK
FIZZLE
GASP! MONSTER...

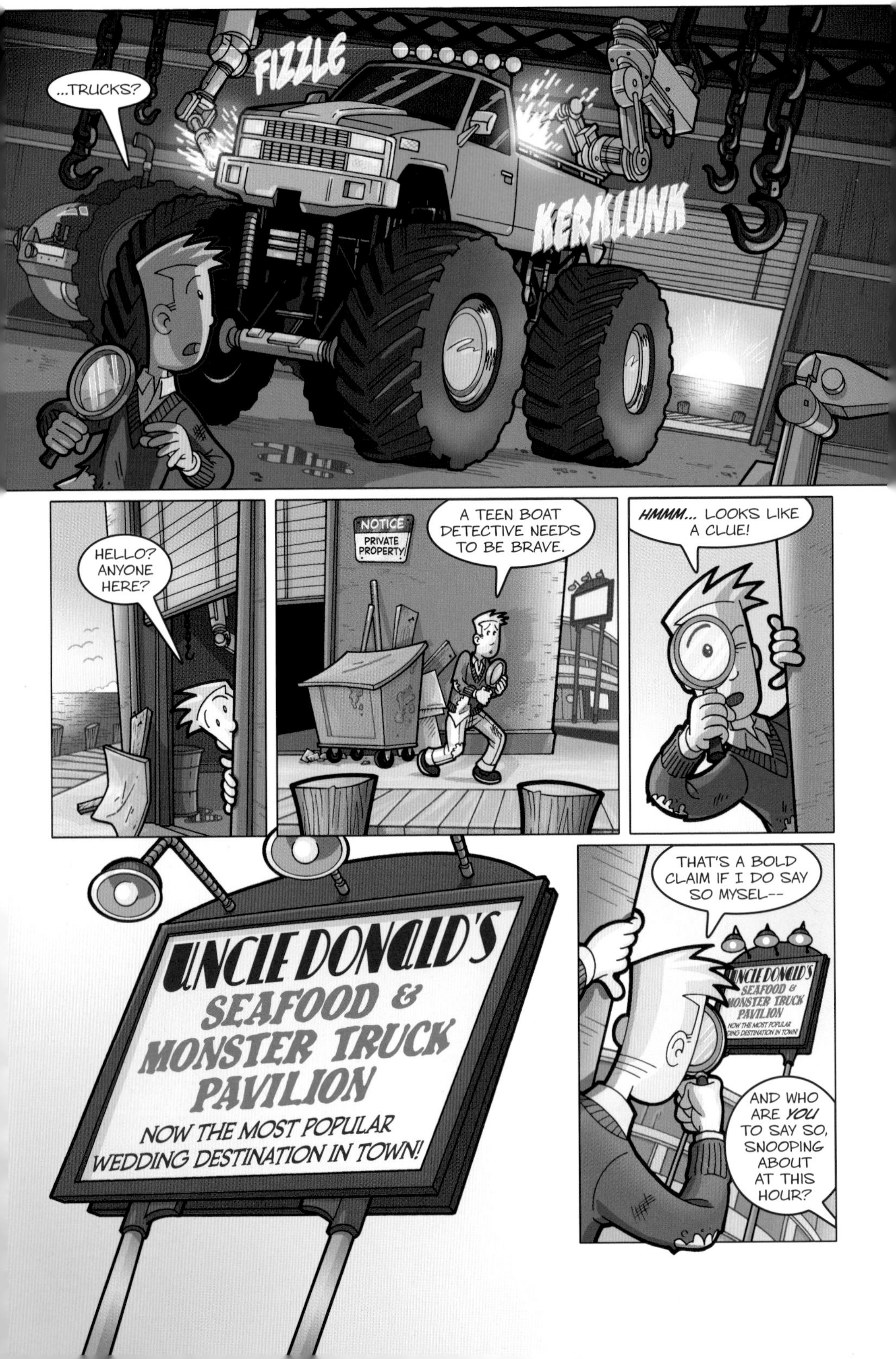
...TRUCKS?
FIZZLE
KERKLUNK
HELLO? ANYONE HERE?
NOTICE
PRIVATE PROPERTY
A TEEN BOAT DETECTIVE NEEDS TO BE BRAVE.
HMMM... LOOKS LIKE A CLUE!
UNCLE DONALD'S
SEAFOOD &
MONSTER TRUCK
PAVILION
NOW THE MOST POPULAR
WEDDING DESTINATION IN TOWN!
THAT'S A BOLD CLAIM IF I DO SAY SO MYSEL--
AND WHO ARE YOU TO SAY SO, SNOOPING ABOUT AT THIS HOUR?

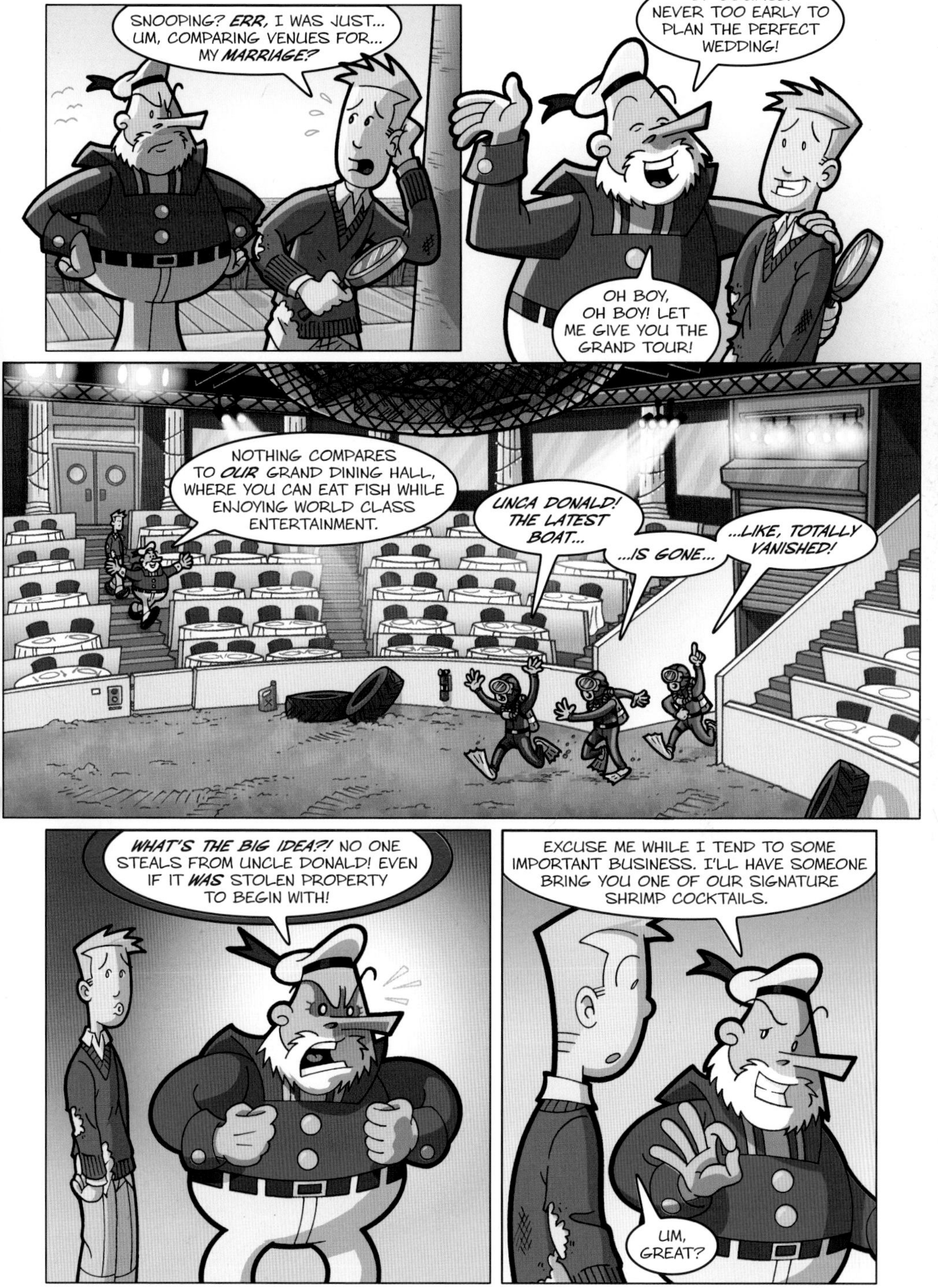
SNOOPING? ERR, I WAS JUST... UM, COMPARING VENUES FOR... MY MARRIAGE?
OF COURSE! NEVER TOO EARLY TO PLAN THE PERFECT WEDDING!
OH BOY, OH BOY! LET ME GIVE YOU THE GRAND TOUR!
NOTHING COMPARES TO OUR GRAND DINING HALL, WHERE YOU CAN EAT FISH WHILE ENJOYING WORLD CLASS ENTERTAINMENT.
UNCA DONALD! THE LATEST BOAT...
...IS GONE...
...LIKE, TOTALLY VANISHED!
WHAT'S THE BIG IDEA?! NO ONE STEALS FROM UNCLE DONALD! EVEN IF IT WAS STOLEN PROPERTY TO BEGIN WITH!
EXCUSE ME WHILE I TEND TO SOME IMPORTANT BUSINESS. I'LL HAVE SOMEONE BRING YOU ONE OF OUR SIGNATURE SHRIMP COCKTAILS.
UM, GREAT?

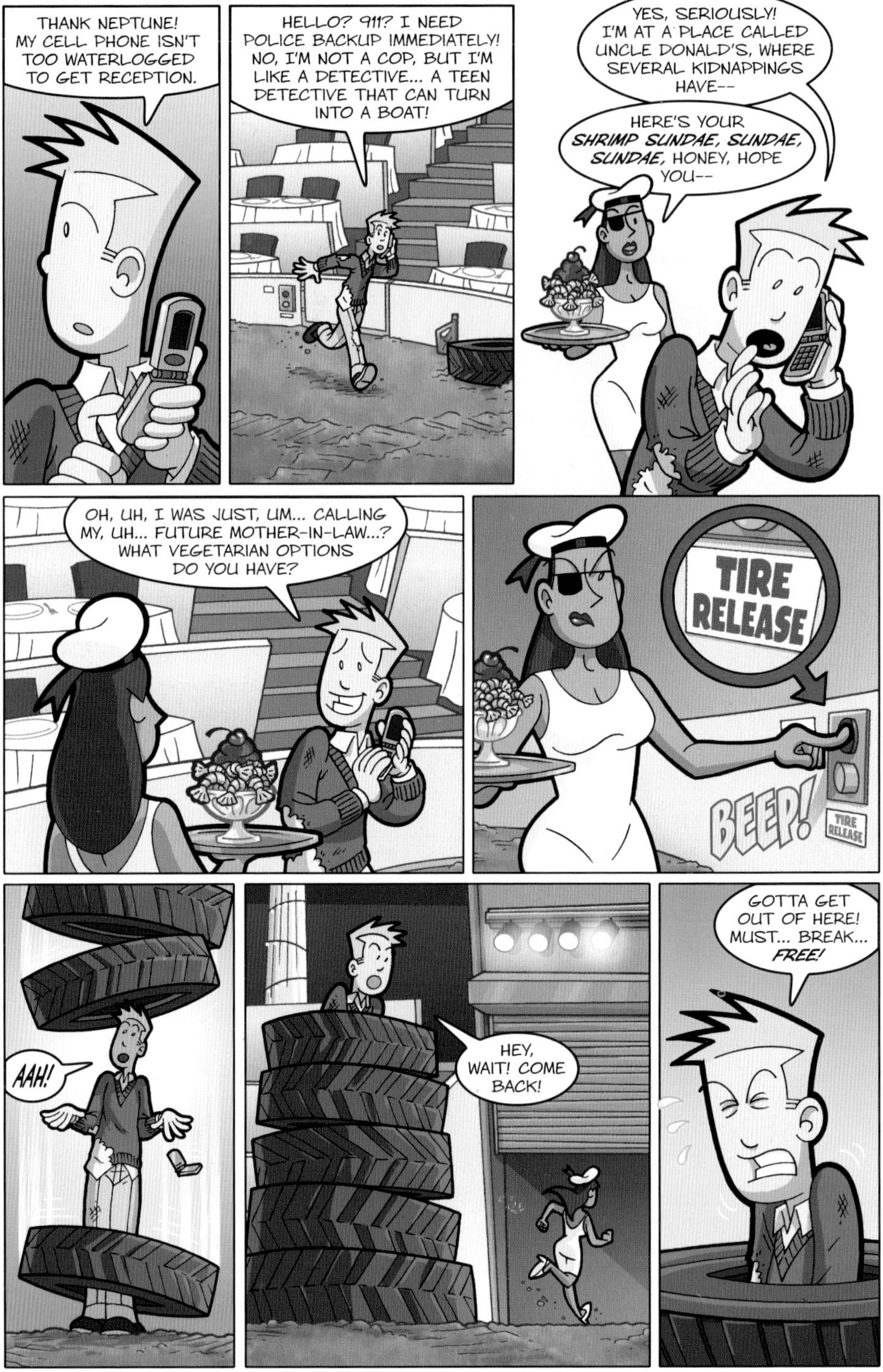
THANK NEPTUNE! MY CELL PHONE ISN'T TOO WATERLOGGED TO GET RECEPTION.
HELLO? 911? I NEED POLICE BACKUP IMMEDIATELY! NO, I'M NOT A COP, BUT I'M LIKE A DETECTIVE... A TEEN DETECTIVE THAT CAN TURN INTO A BOAT!
YES, SERIOUSLY! I'M AT A PLACE CALLED UNCLE DONALD'S, WHERE SEVERAL KIDNAPPINGS HAVE--
HERE'S YOUR ***SHRIMP SUNDAE, SUNDAE, SUNDAE,*** HONEY, HOPE YOU--
OH, UH, I WAS JUST, UM... CALLING MY, UH... FUTURE MOTHER-IN-LAW...? WHAT VEGETARIAN OPTIONS DO YOU HAVE?
TIRE RELEASE
BEEP!
TIRE RELEASE
AAH!
HEY, WAIT! COME BACK!
GOTTA GET OUT OF HERE! MUST... BREAK... ***FREE!***

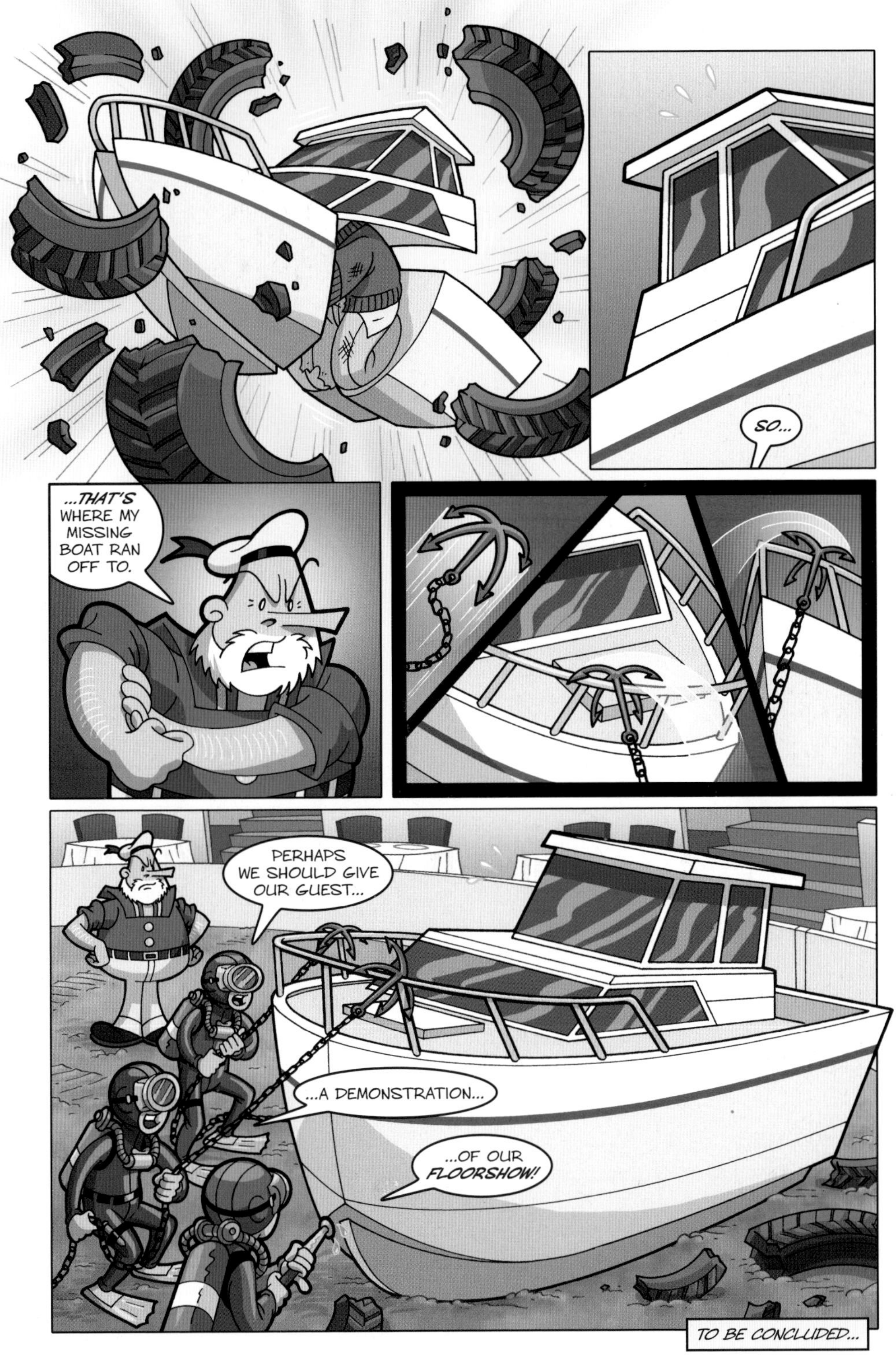
SO...
...THAT'S WHERE MY MISSING BOAT RAN OFF TO.
PERHAPS WE SHOULD GIVE OUR GUEST...
...A DEMONSTRATION...
...OF OUR FLOORSHOW!
TO BE CONCLUDED...

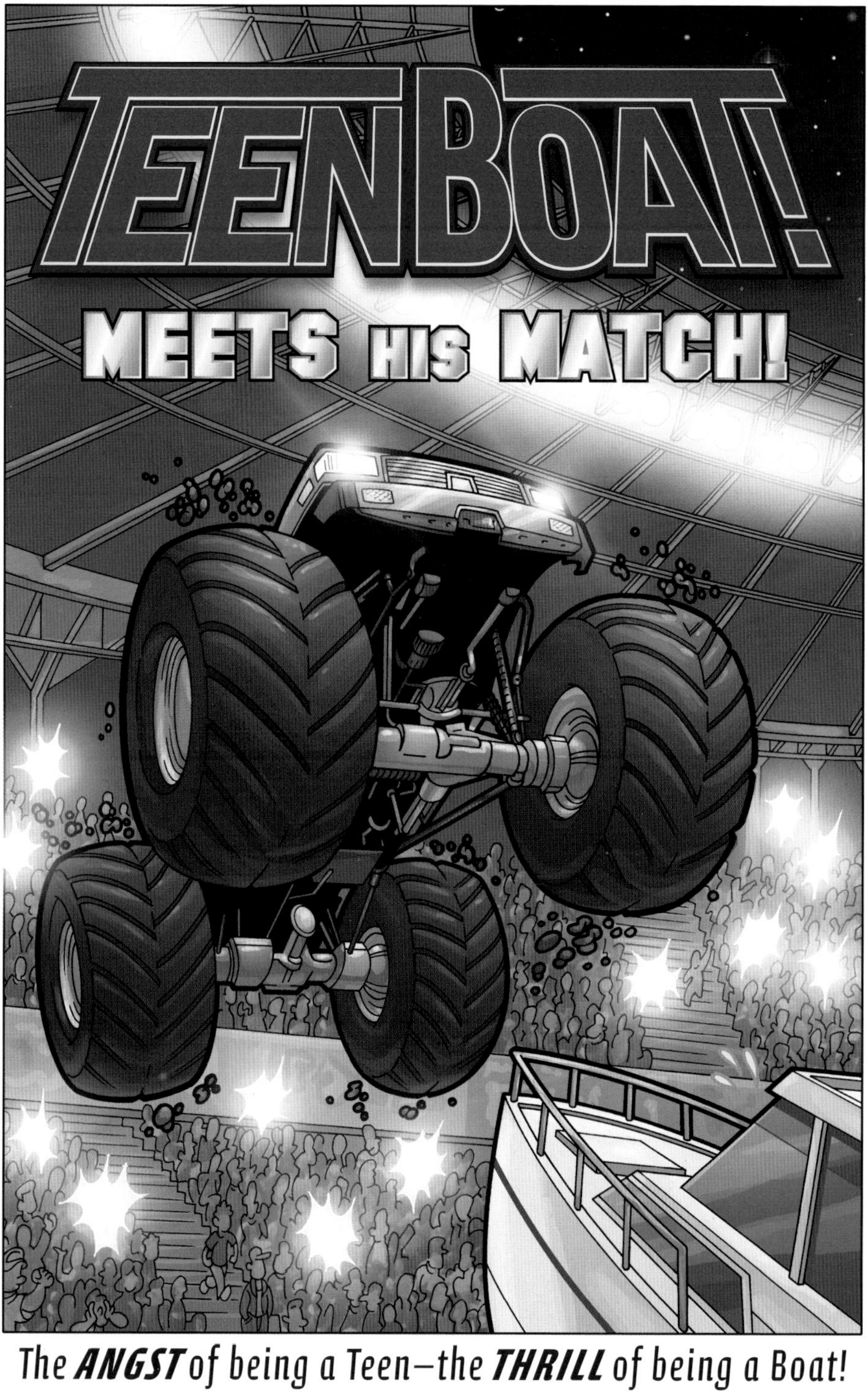
TEENBOAT!
MEETS HIS MATCH!

The ***ANGST*** of being a Teen—the ***THRILL*** of being a Boat!

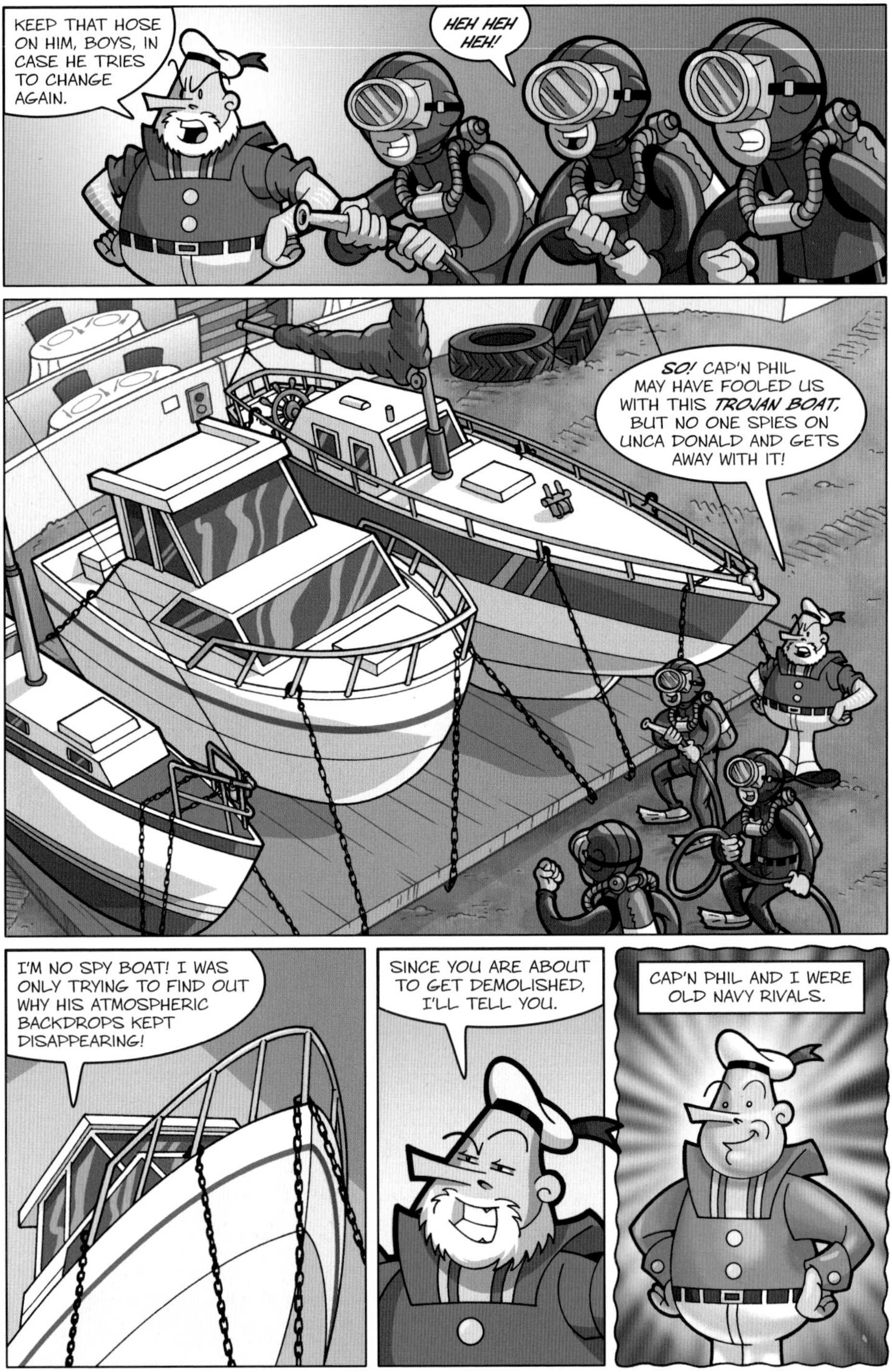
KEEP THAT HOSE ON HIM, BOYS, IN CASE HE TRIES TO CHANGE AGAIN.
HEH HEH HEH!
SO! CAP'N PHIL MAY HAVE FOOLED US WITH THIS TROJAN BOAT, BUT NO ONE SPIES ON UNCA DONALD AND GETS AWAY WITH IT!
I'M NO SPY BOAT! I WAS ONLY TRYING TO FIND OUT WHY HIS ATMOSPHERIC BACKDROPS KEPT DISAPPEARING!
SINCE YOU ARE ABOUT TO GET DEMOLISHED, I'LL TELL YOU.
CAP'N PHIL AND I WERE OLD NAVY RIVALS.

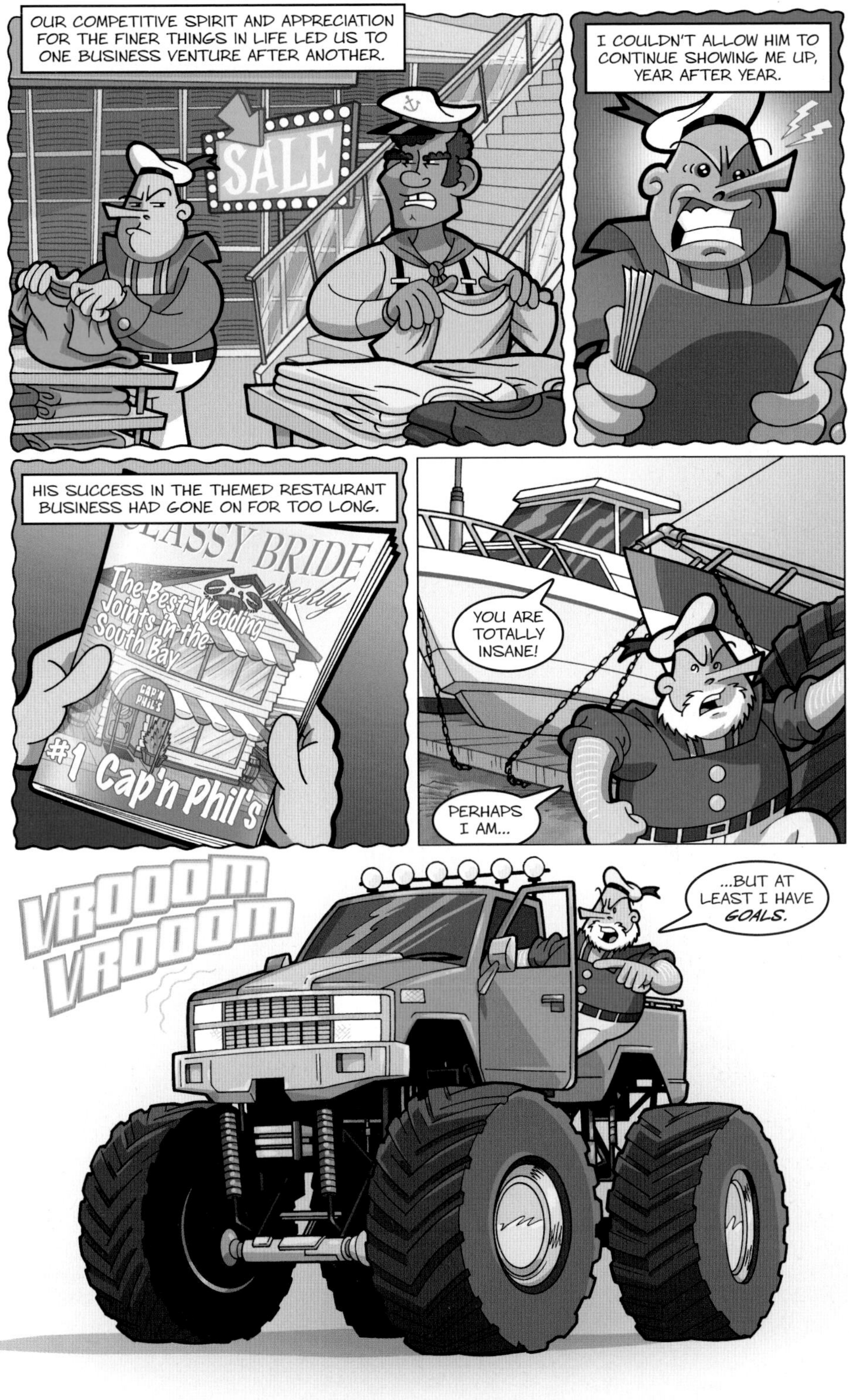

OUR COMPETITIVE SPIRIT AND APPRECIATION FOR THE FINER THINGS IN LIFE LED US TO ONE BUSINESS VENTURE AFTER ANOTHER.
SALE
I COULDN'T ALLOW HIM TO CONTINUE SHOWING ME UP, YEAR AFTER YEAR.
HIS SUCCESS IN THE THEMED RESTAURANT BUSINESS HAD GONE ON FOR TOO LONG.
LASSY BRIDE
weekly
The Best Wedding Joints in the South Bay
CAP'N PHIL'S
#1 Cap'n Phil's
YOU ARE TOTALLY INSANE!
PERHAPS I AM...
VROOOM VROOOM
...BUT AT LEAST I HAVE *GOALS.*

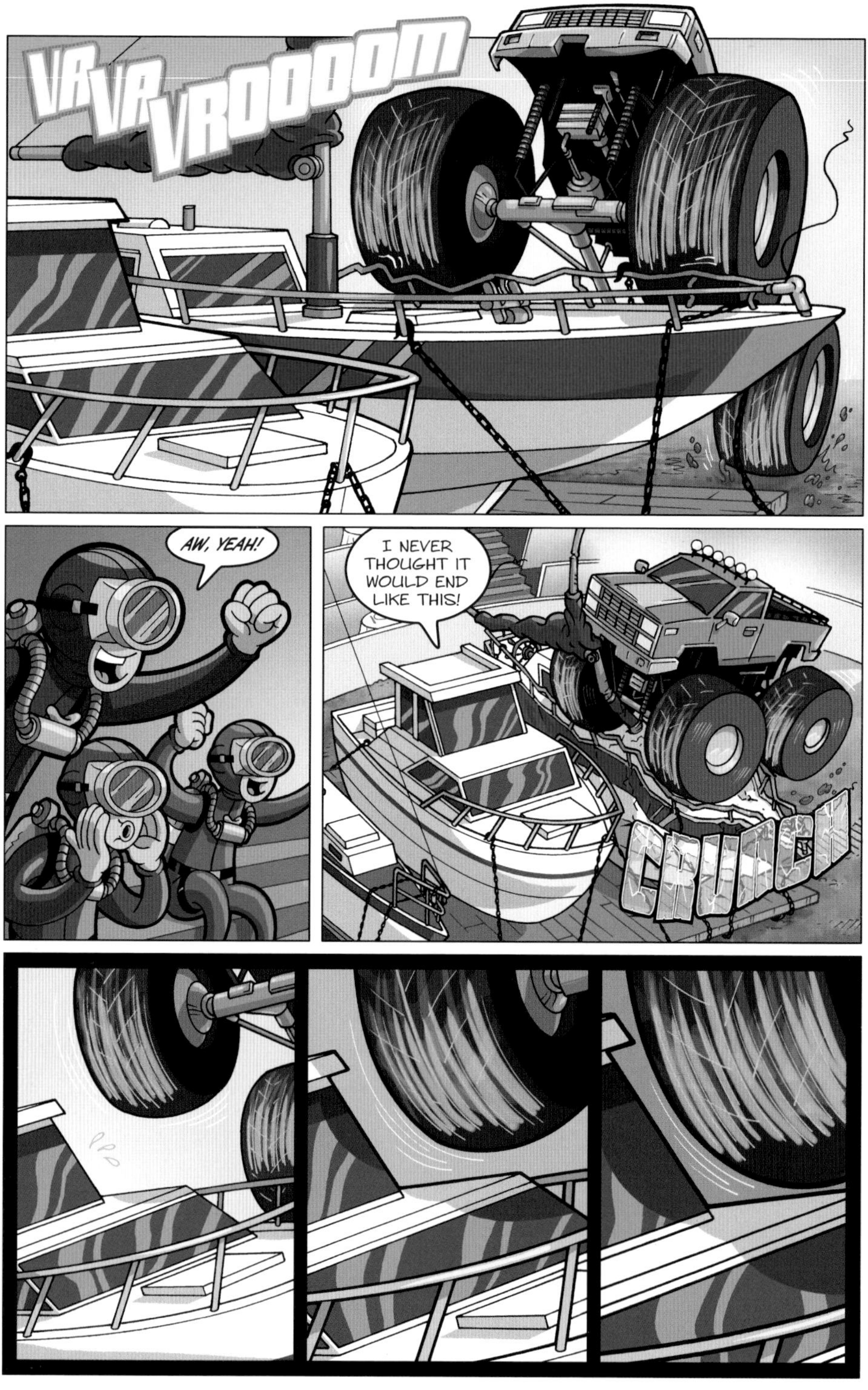
VR VR VROOOOM
AW, YEAH!
I NEVER THOUGHT IT WOULD END LIKE THIS!
CRUNCH

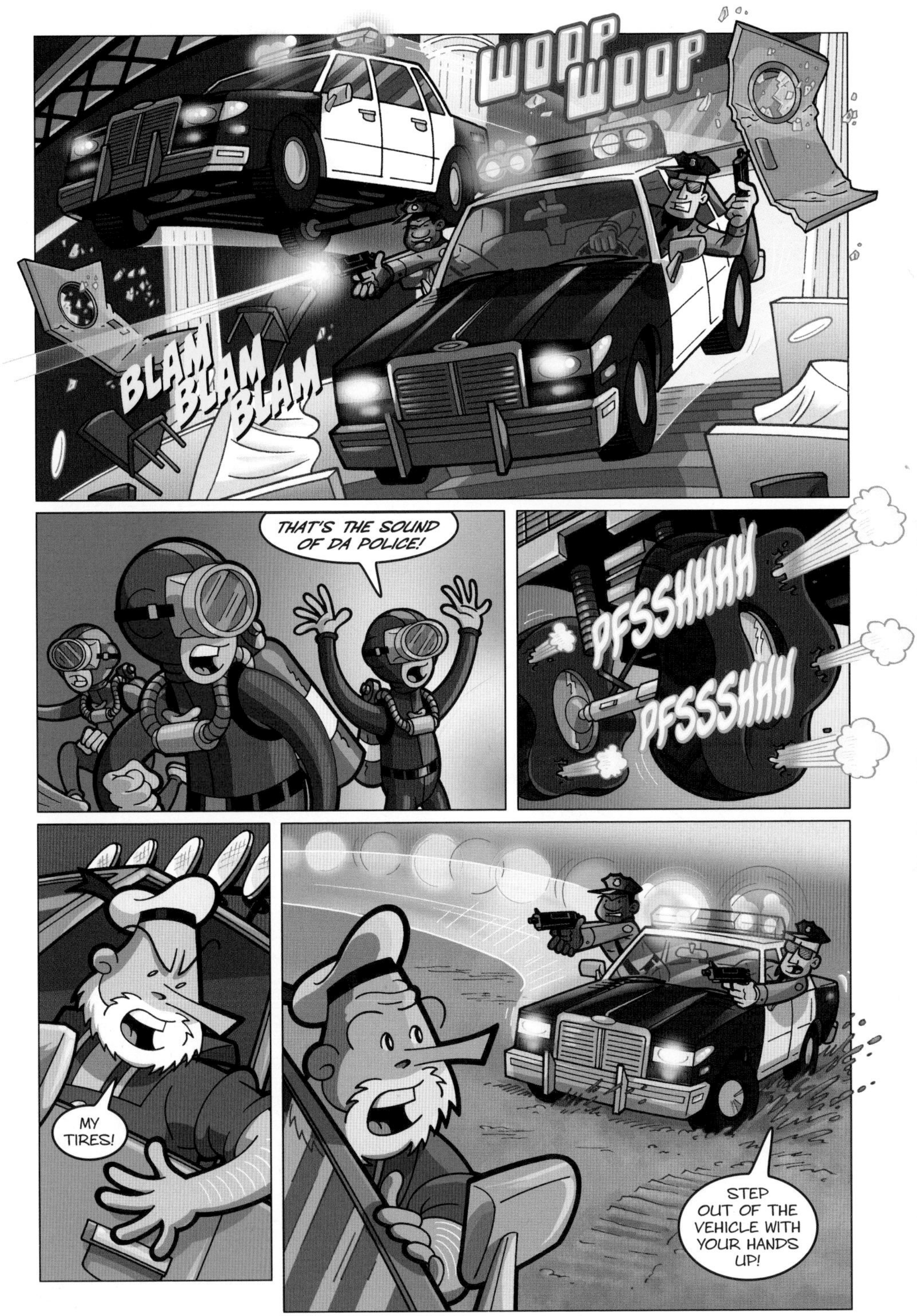
WOOP WOOP
BLAM BLAM BLAM
THAT'S THE SOUND OF DA POLICE!
PFSSHHHH
PFSSSHHH
MY TIRES!
STEP OUT OF THE VEHICLE WITH YOUR HANDS UP!

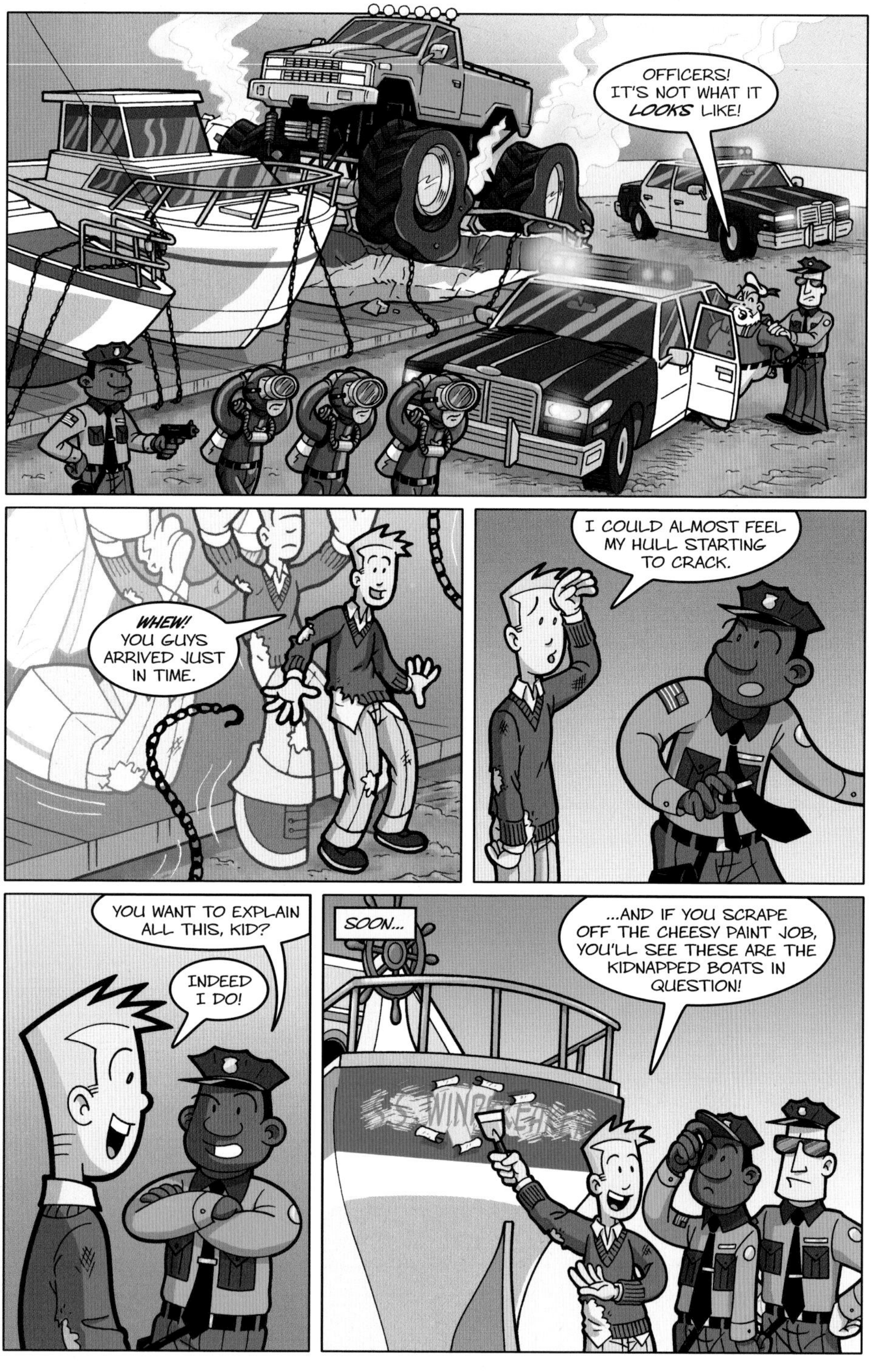
OFFICERS! IT'S NOT WHAT IT *LOOKS* LIKE!
WHEW! YOU GUYS ARRIVED JUST IN TIME.
I COULD ALMOST FEEL MY HULL STARTING TO CRACK.
YOU WANT TO EXPLAIN ALL THIS, KID?
INDEED I DO!
SOON...
...AND IF YOU SCRAPE OFF THE CHEESY PAINT JOB, YOU'LL SEE THESE ARE THE KIDNAPPED BOATS IN QUESTION!

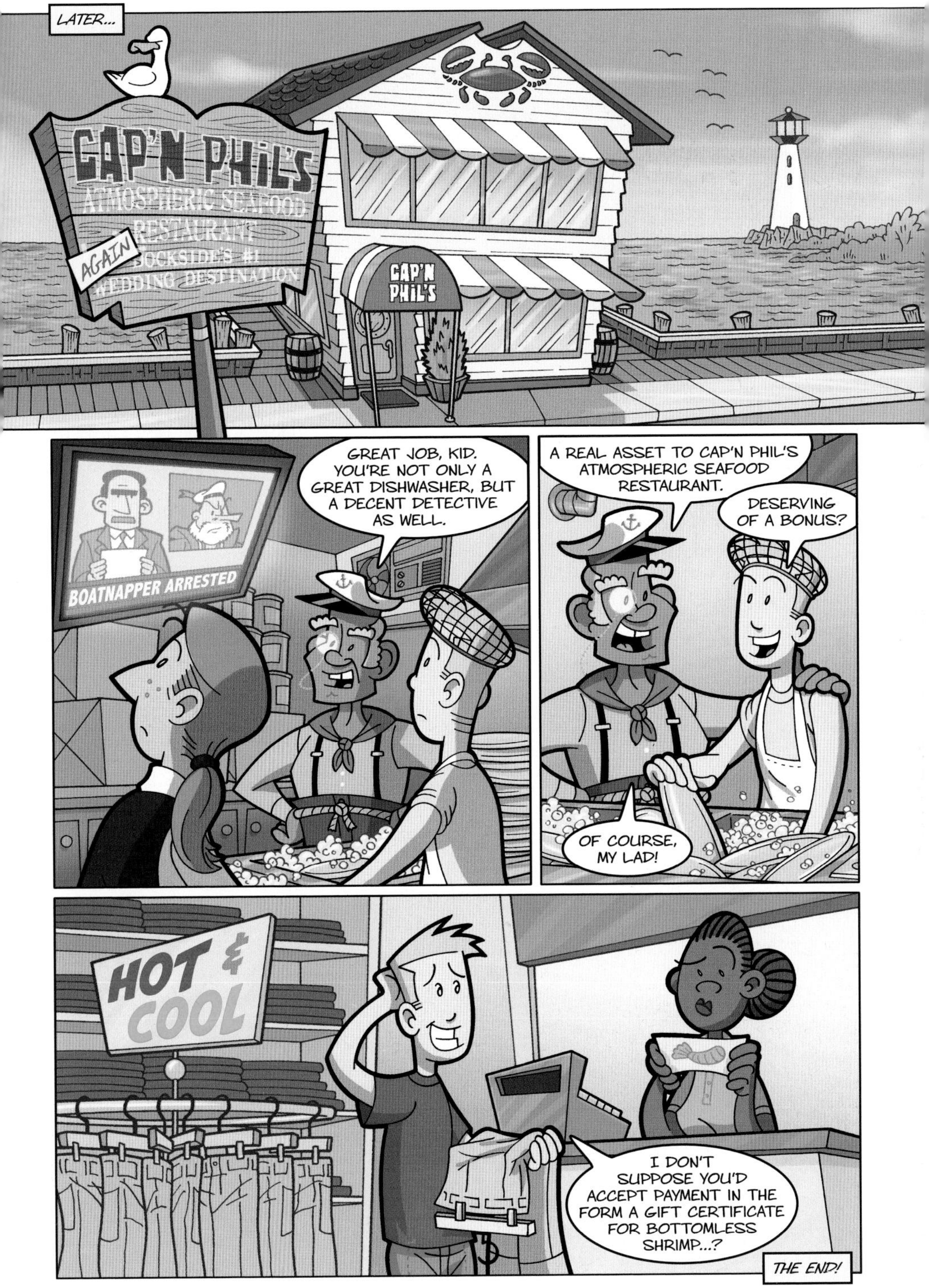
LATER...
CAP'N PHIL'S
ATMOSPHERIC SEAFOOD
RESTAURANT
AGAIN
DOCKSIDE'S #1
WEDDING DESTINATION
CAP'N PHIL'S
BOATNAPPER ARRESTED
GREAT JOB, KID. YOU'RE NOT ONLY A GREAT DISHWASHER, BUT A DECENT DETECTIVE AS WELL.
A REAL ASSET TO CAP'N PHIL'S ATMOSPHERIC SEAFOOD RESTAURANT.
DESERVING OF A BONUS?
OF COURSE, MY LAD!
HOT & COOL
I DON'T SUPPOSE YOU'D ACCEPT PAYMENT IN THE FORM A GIFT CERTIFICATE FOR BOTTOMLESS SHRIMP...?
THE END!

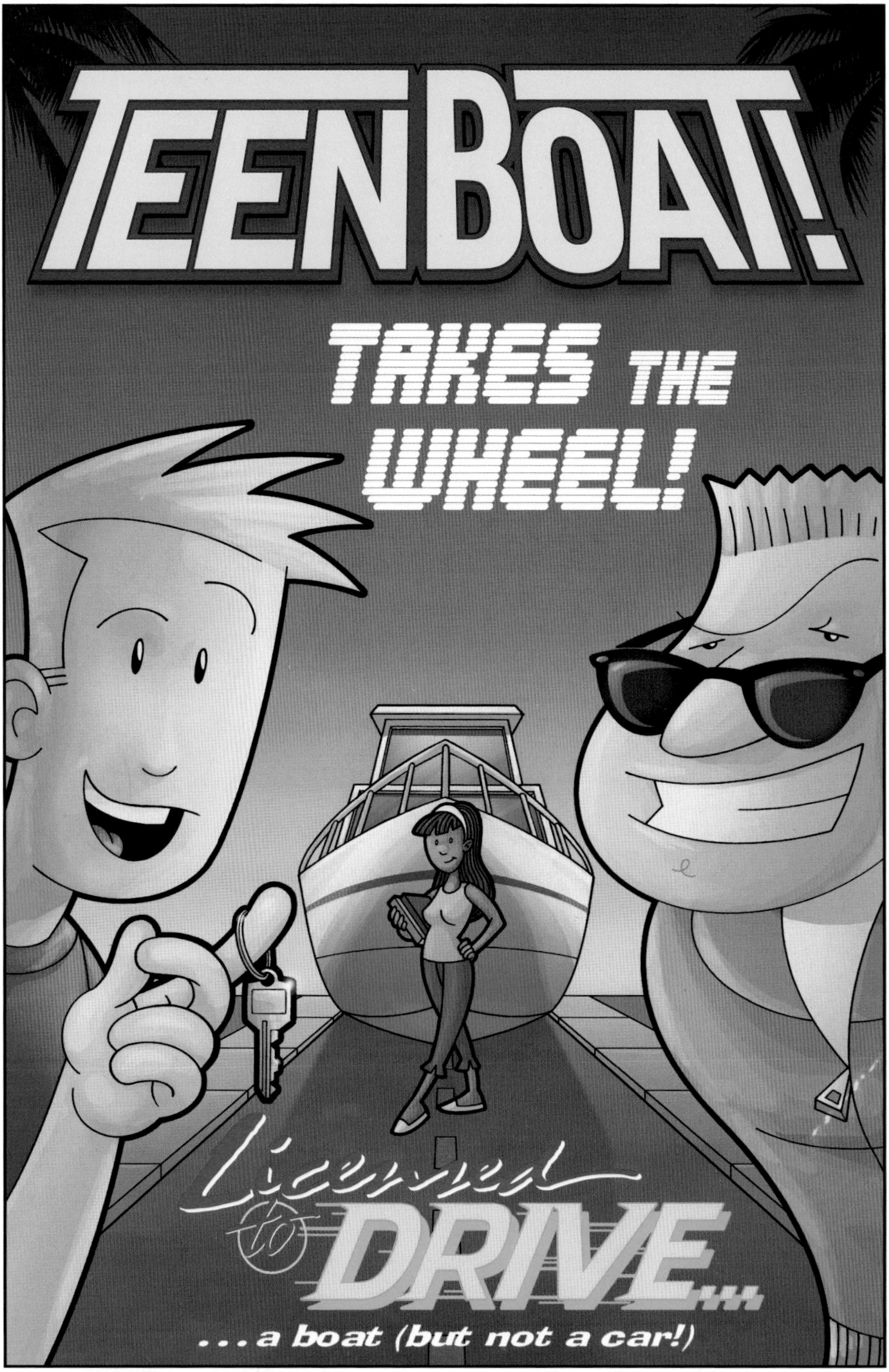
TEENBOAT!
TAKES THE
WHEEL!
Licensed to
DRIVE...
...a boat (but not a car!)

The ***ANGST*** of being a Teen—the ***THRILL*** of being a Boat!

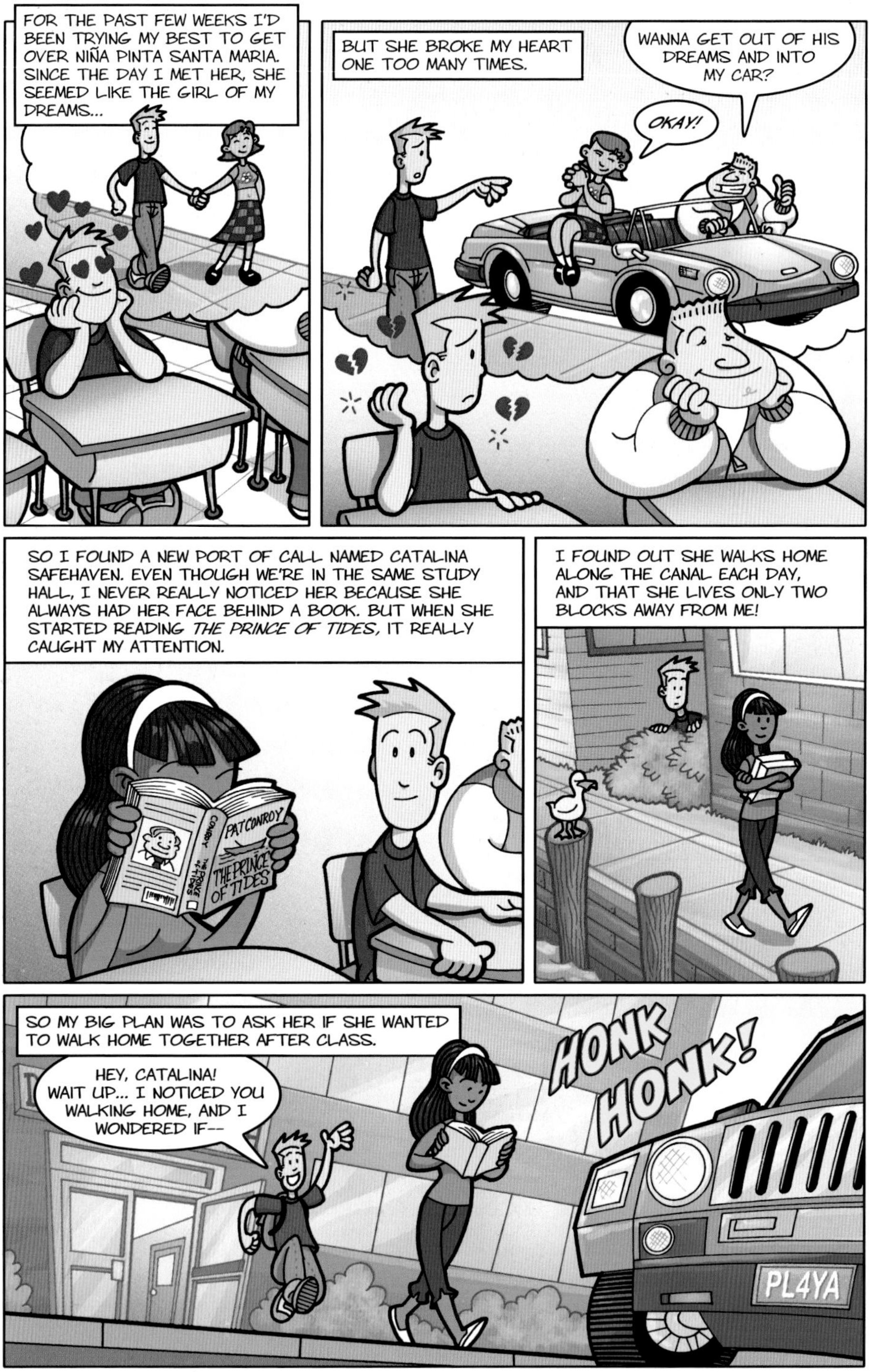

FOR THE PAST FEW WEEKS I'D BEEN TRYING MY BEST TO GET OVER NIÑA PINTA SANTA MARIA. SINCE THE DAY I MET HER, SHE SEEMED LIKE THE GIRL OF MY DREAMS...
BUT SHE BROKE MY HEART ONE TOO MANY TIMES.
WANNA GET OUT OF HIS DREAMS AND INTO MY CAR?
OKAY!
SO I FOUND A NEW PORT OF CALL NAMED CATALINA SAFEHAVEN. EVEN THOUGH WE'RE IN THE SAME STUDY HALL, I NEVER REALLY NOTICED HER BECAUSE SHE ALWAYS HAD HER FACE BEHIND A BOOK. BUT WHEN SHE STARTED READING *THE PRINCE OF TIDES,* IT REALLY CAUGHT MY ATTENTION.
PAT CONROY
THE PRINCE OF TIDES
I FOUND OUT SHE WALKS HOME ALONG THE CANAL EACH DAY, AND THAT SHE LIVES ONLY TWO BLOCKS AWAY FROM ME!
SO MY BIG PLAN WAS TO ASK HER IF SHE WANTED TO WALK HOME TOGETHER AFTER CLASS.
HEY, CATALINA! WAIT UP... I NOTICED YOU WALKING HOME, AND I WONDERED IF--
HONK HONK!
PL4YA

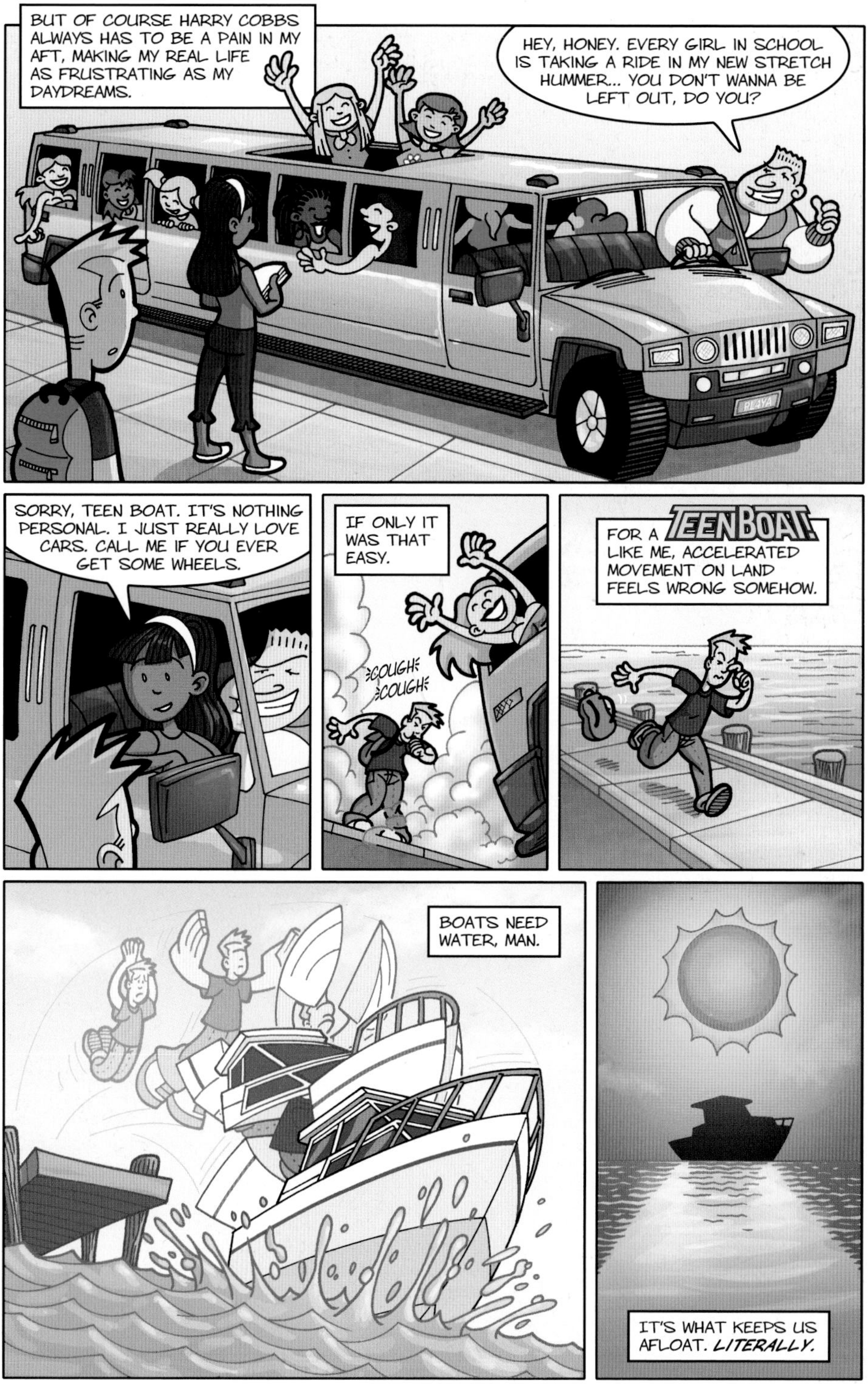
BUT OF COURSE HARRY COBBS ALWAYS HAS TO BE A PAIN IN MY AFT, MAKING MY REAL LIFE AS FRUSTRATING AS MY DAYDREAMS.
HEY, HONEY. EVERY GIRL IN SCHOOL IS TAKING A RIDE IN MY NEW STRETCH HUMMER... YOU DON'T WANNA BE LEFT OUT, DO YOU?
PL4YA
SORRY, TEEN BOAT. IT'S NOTHING PERSONAL. I JUST REALLY LOVE CARS. CALL ME IF YOU EVER GET SOME WHEELS.
IF ONLY IT WAS THAT EASY.
COUGH
COUGH
FOR A TEEN BOAT! LIKE ME, ACCELERATED MOVEMENT ON LAND FEELS WRONG SOMEHOW.
BOATS NEED WATER, MAN.
IT'S WHAT KEEPS US AFLOAT. LITERALLY.

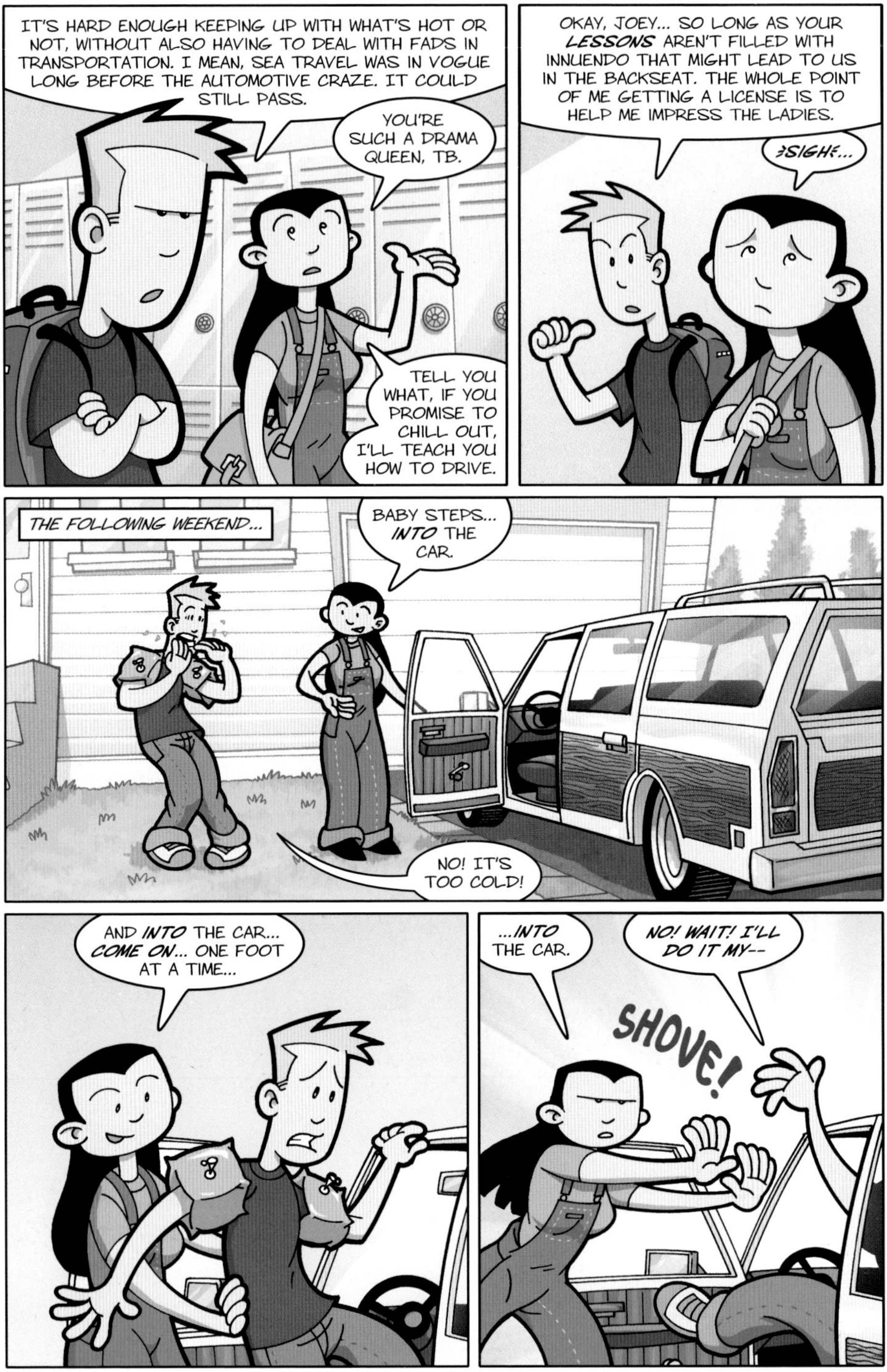
IT'S HARD ENOUGH KEEPING UP WITH WHAT'S HOT OR NOT, WITHOUT ALSO HAVING TO DEAL WITH FADS IN TRANSPORTATION. I MEAN, SEA TRAVEL WAS IN VOGUE LONG BEFORE THE AUTOMOTIVE CRAZE. IT COULD STILL PASS.
YOU'RE SUCH A DRAMA QUEEN, TB.
TELL YOU WHAT, IF YOU PROMISE TO CHILL OUT, I'LL TEACH YOU HOW TO DRIVE.
OKAY, JOEY... SO LONG AS YOUR *LESSONS* AREN'T FILLED WITH INNUENDO THAT MIGHT LEAD TO US IN THE BACKSEAT. THE WHOLE POINT OF ME GETTING A LICENSE IS TO HELP ME IMPRESS THE LADIES.
SIGH...
THE FOLLOWING WEEKEND...
BABY STEPS... *INTO* THE CAR.
NO! IT'S TOO COLD!
AND *INTO* THE CAR... *COME ON*... ONE FOOT AT A TIME...
...*INTO* THE CAR.
NO! WAIT! I'LL DO IT MY--
SHOVE!

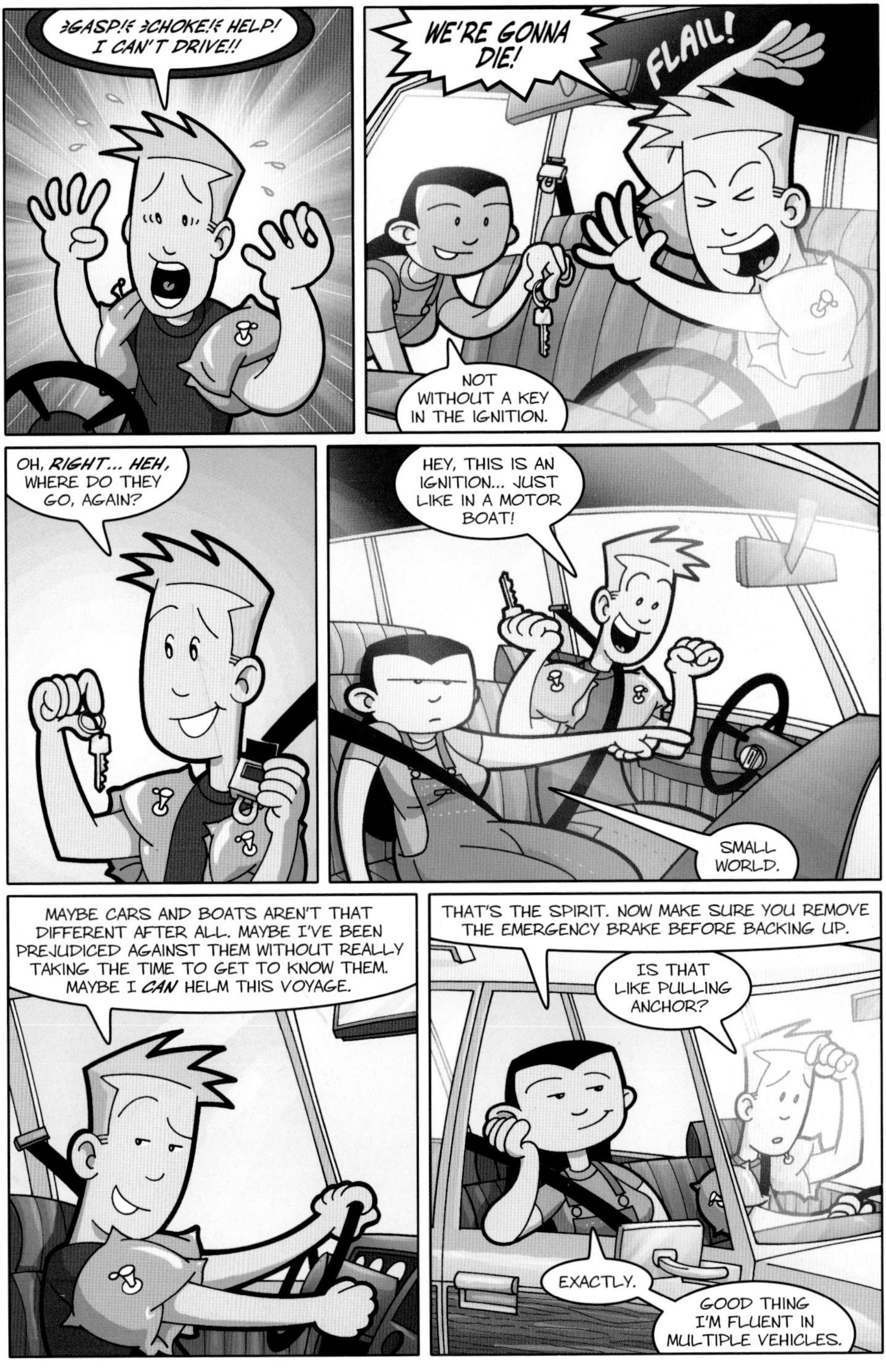

ƎGASP!Ǝ ƎCHOKE!Ǝ HELP! I CAN'T DRIVE!!
WE'RE GONNA DIE!
FLAIL!
NOT WITHOUT A KEY IN THE IGNITION.
OH, RIGHT... HEH, WHERE DO THEY GO, AGAIN?
HEY, THIS IS AN IGNITION... JUST LIKE IN A MOTOR BOAT!
SMALL WORLD.
MAYBE CARS AND BOATS AREN'T THAT DIFFERENT AFTER ALL. MAYBE I'VE BEEN PREJUDICED AGAINST THEM WITHOUT REALLY TAKING THE TIME TO GET TO KNOW THEM. MAYBE I CAN HELM THIS VOYAGE.
THAT'S THE SPIRIT. NOW MAKE SURE YOU REMOVE THE EMERGENCY BRAKE BEFORE BACKING UP.
IS THAT LIKE PULLING ANCHOR?
EXACTLY.
GOOD THING I'M FLUENT IN MULTIPLE VEHICLES.

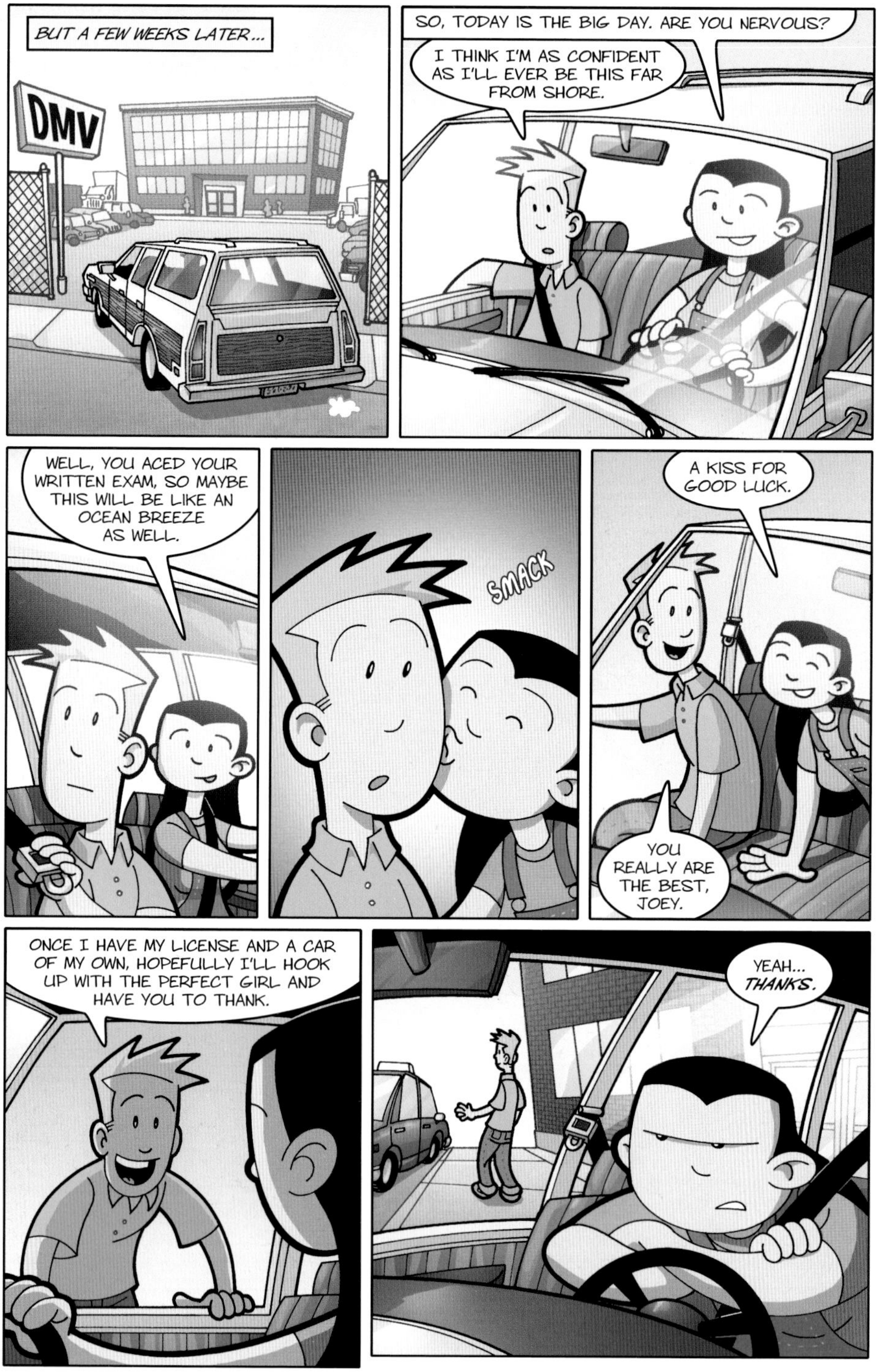
BUT A FEW WEEKS LATER...
DMV
SO, TODAY IS THE BIG DAY. ARE YOU NERVOUS?
I THINK I'M AS CONFIDENT AS I'LL EVER BE THIS FAR FROM SHORE.
WELL, YOU ACED YOUR WRITTEN EXAM, SO MAYBE THIS WILL BE LIKE AN OCEAN BREEZE AS WELL.
SMACK
A KISS FOR GOOD LUCK.
YOU REALLY ARE THE BEST, JOEY.
ONCE I HAVE MY LICENSE AND A CAR OF MY OWN, HOPEFULLY I'LL HOOK UP WITH THE PERFECT GIRL AND HAVE YOU TO THANK.
YEAH... THANKS.

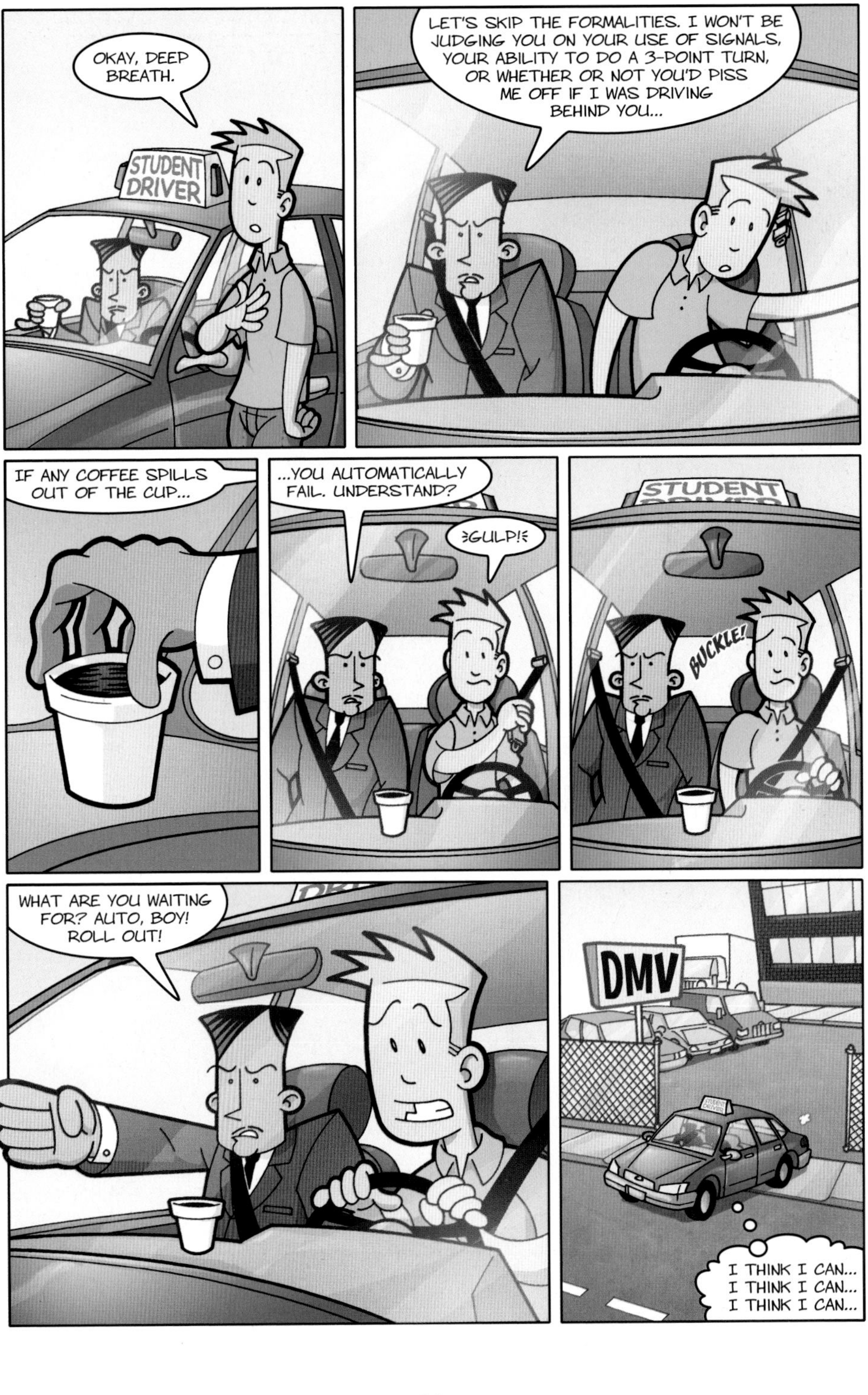
OKAY, DEEP BREATH.
STUDENT DRIVER
LET'S SKIP THE FORMALITIES. I WON'T BE JUDGING YOU ON YOUR USE OF SIGNALS, YOUR ABILITY TO DO A 3-POINT TURN, OR WHETHER OR NOT YOU'D PISS ME OFF IF I WAS DRIVING BEHIND YOU...
IF ANY COFFEE SPILLS OUT OF THE CUP...
...YOU AUTOMATICALLY FAIL. UNDERSTAND?
GULP!
BUCKLE!
WHAT ARE YOU WAITING FOR? AUTO, BOY! ROLL OUT!
DMV
I THINK I CAN...
I THINK I CAN...
I THINK I CAN...

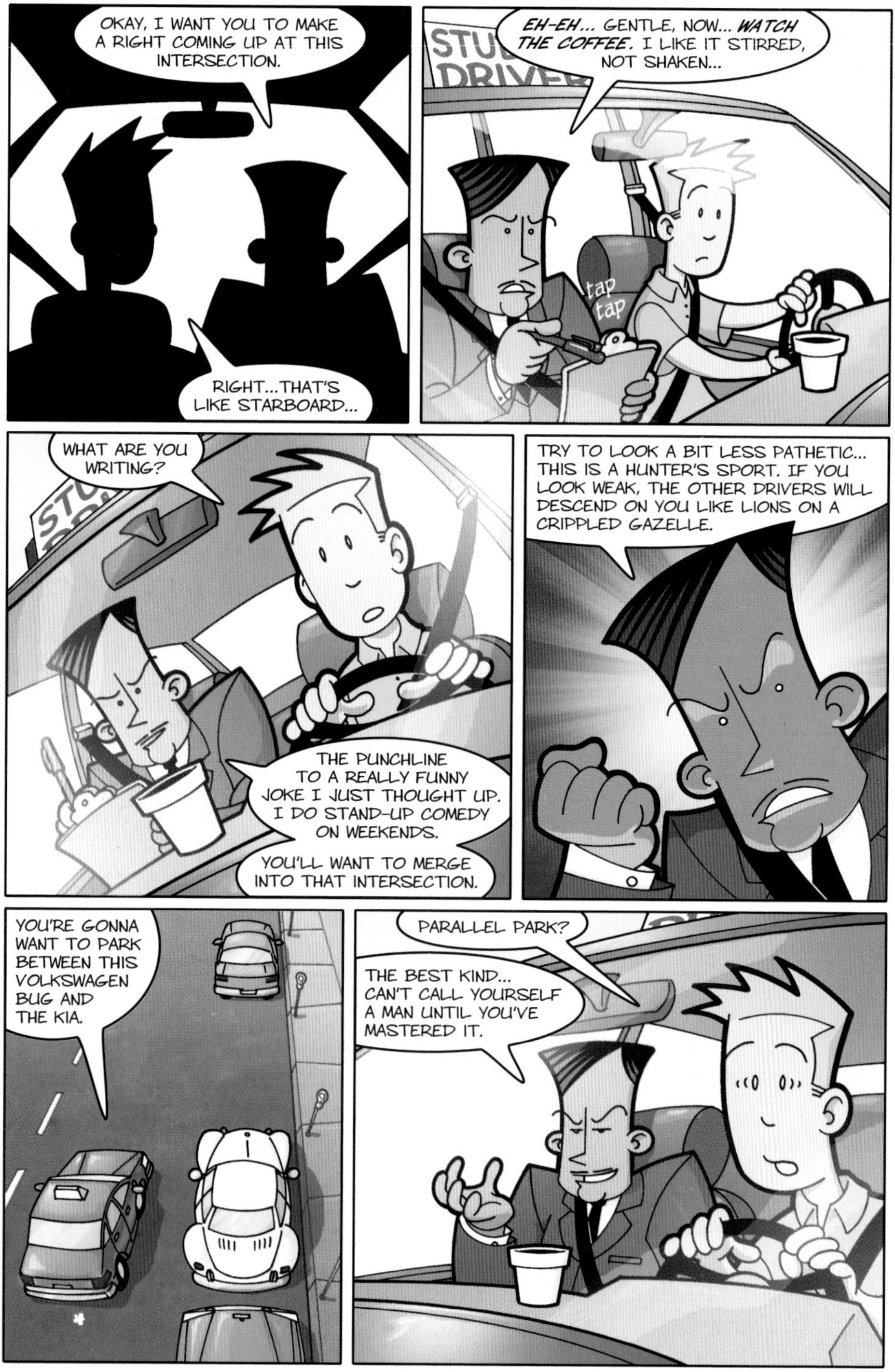
OKAY, I WANT YOU TO MAKE A RIGHT COMING UP AT THIS INTERSECTION.
RIGHT...THAT'S LIKE STARBOARD...
EH-EH... GENTLE, NOW... WATCH THE COFFEE. I LIKE IT STIRRED, NOT SHAKEN...
tap tap
WHAT ARE YOU WRITING?
THE PUNCHLINE TO A REALLY FUNNY JOKE I JUST THOUGHT UP. I DO STAND-UP COMEDY ON WEEKENDS.
YOU'LL WANT TO MERGE INTO THAT INTERSECTION.
TRY TO LOOK A BIT LESS PATHETIC... THIS IS A HUNTER'S SPORT. IF YOU LOOK WEAK, THE OTHER DRIVERS WILL DESCEND ON YOU LIKE LIONS ON A CRIPPLED GAZELLE.
YOU'RE GONNA WANT TO PARK BETWEEN THIS VOLKSWAGEN BUG AND THE KIA.
PARALLEL PARK?
THE BEST KIND... CAN'T CALL YOURSELF A MAN UNTIL YOU'VE MASTERED IT.

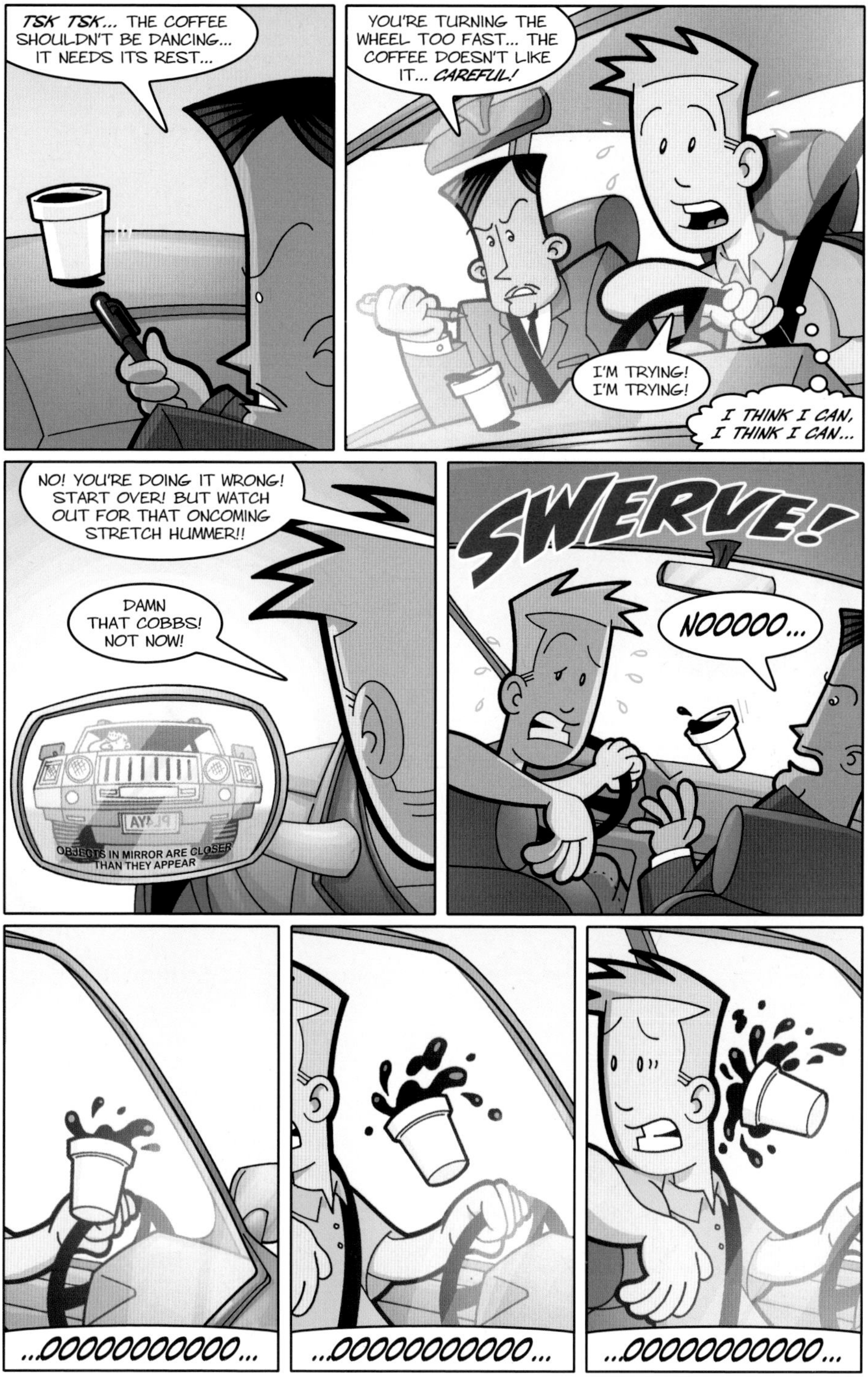
TSK TSK... THE COFFEE SHOULDN'T BE DANCING... IT NEEDS ITS REST...
YOU'RE TURNING THE WHEEL TOO FAST... THE COFFEE DOESN'T LIKE IT... CAREFUL!
I'M TRYING! I'M TRYING!
I THINK I CAN, I THINK I CAN...
NO! YOU'RE DOING IT WRONG! START OVER! BUT WATCH OUT FOR THAT ONCOMING STRETCH HUMMER!!
DAMN THAT COBBS! NOT NOW!
PLAYA
OBJECTS IN MIRROR ARE CLOSER THAN THEY APPEAR
SWERVE!
NOOOOO...
...OOOOOOOOOOO...
...OOOOOOOOOOO...
...OOOOOOOOOOO...

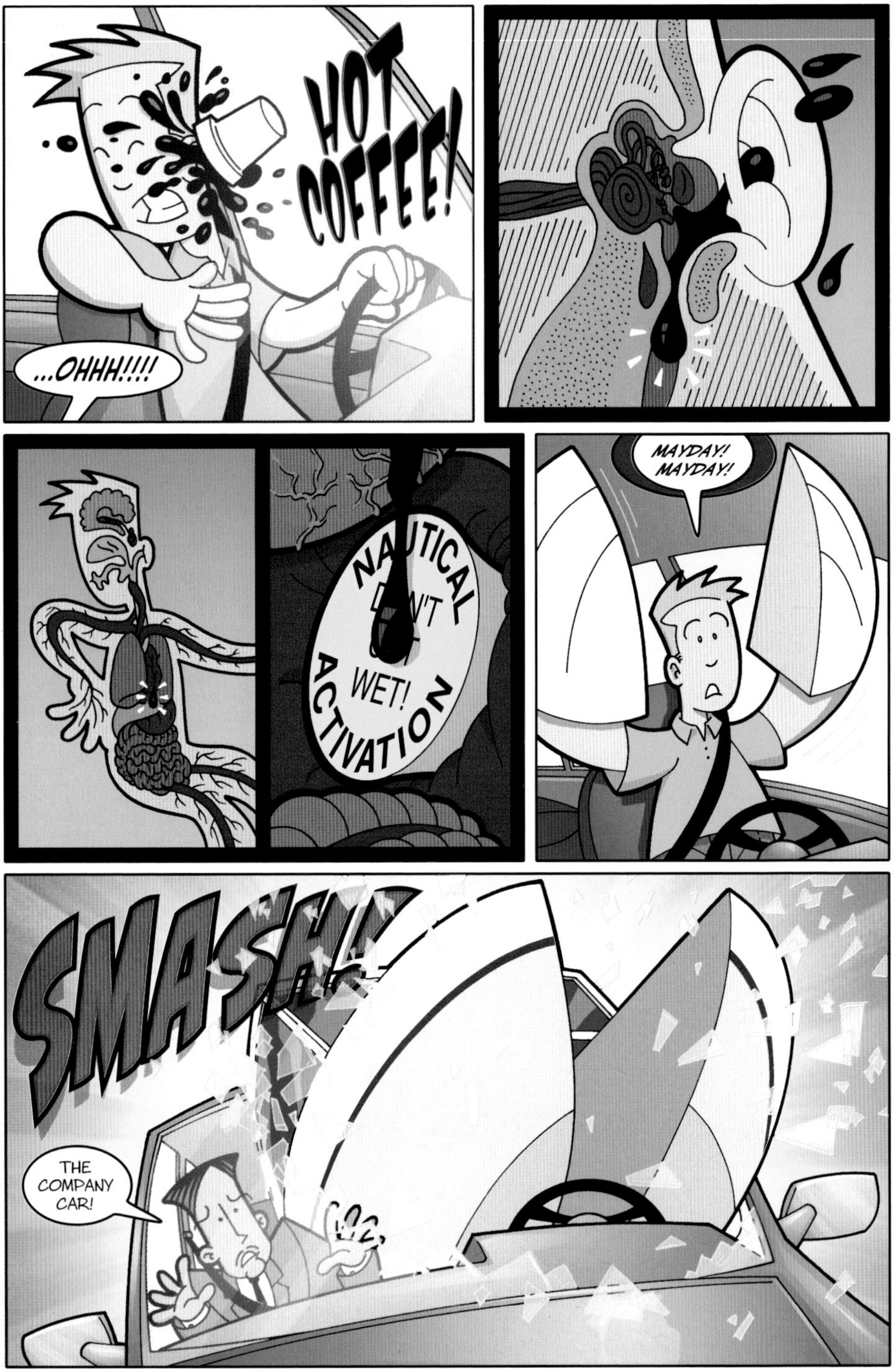
HOT COFFEE!
...OHHH!!!!
NAUTICAL
WET!
ACTIVATION
MAYDAY! MAYDAY!
SMASH
THE COMPANY CAR!

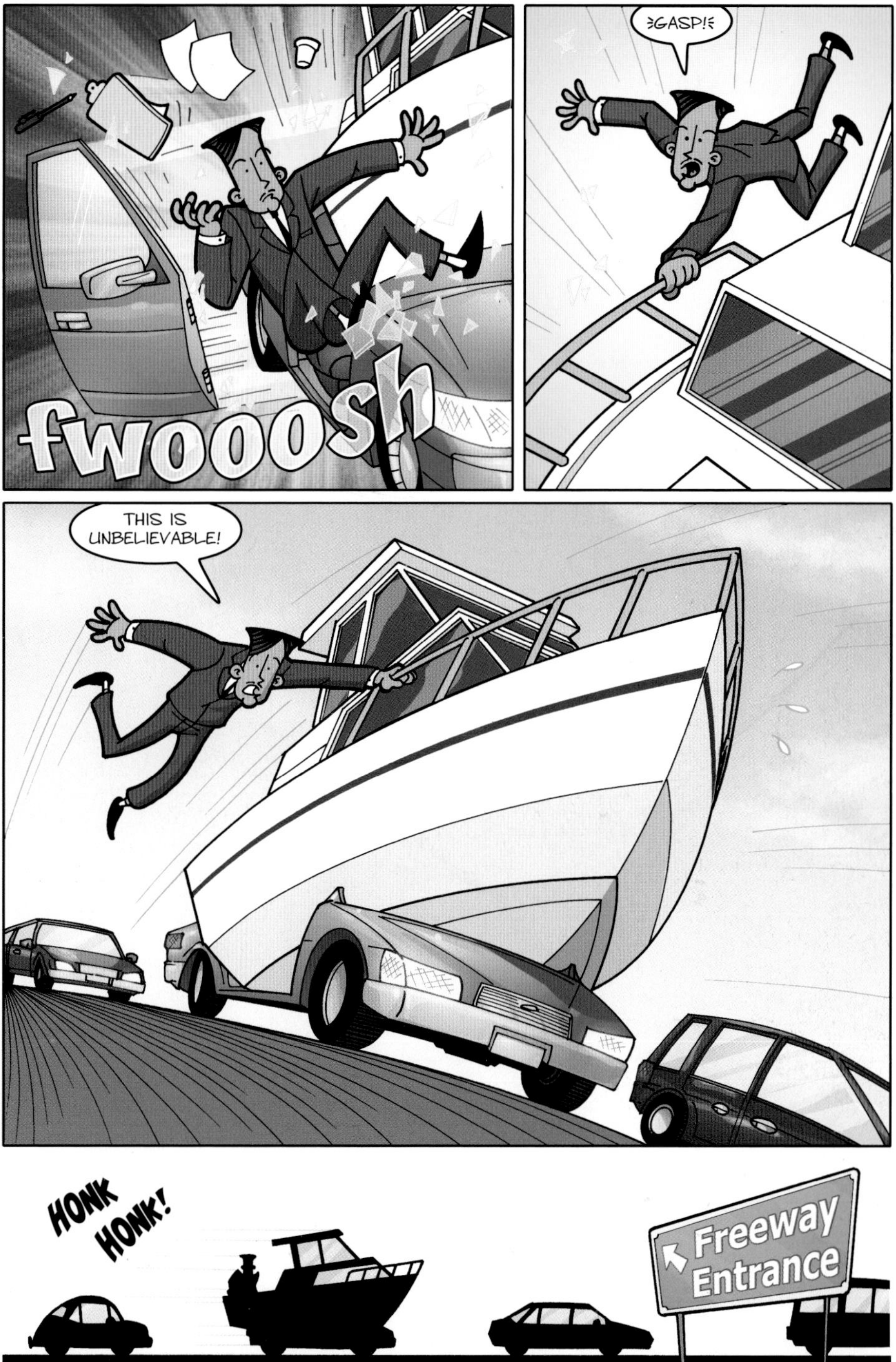
fwooosh
GASP!
THIS IS UNBELIEVABLE!
HONK HONK!
Freeway Entrance

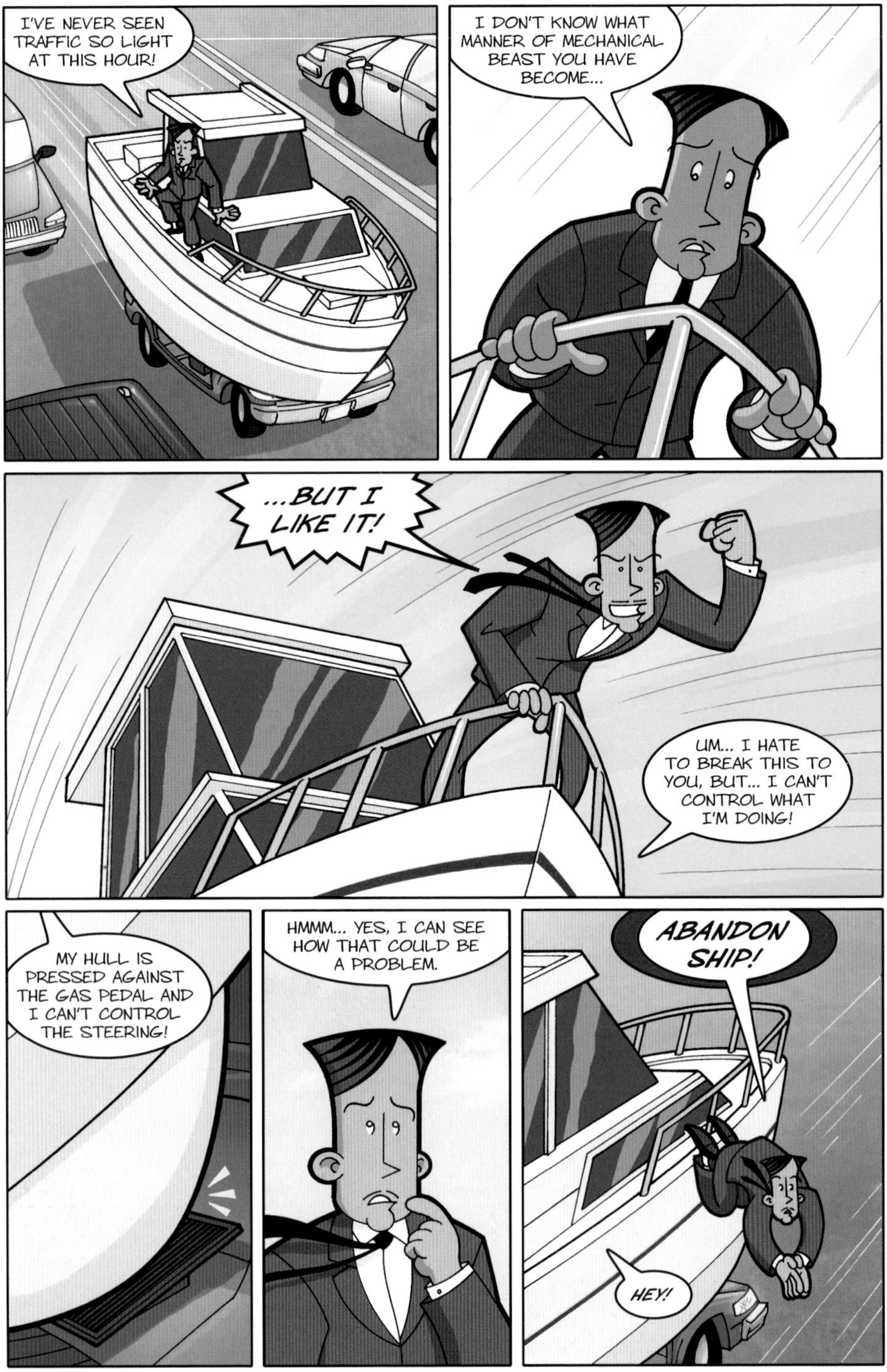
I'VE NEVER SEEN TRAFFIC SO LIGHT AT THIS HOUR!
I DON'T KNOW WHAT MANNER OF MECHANICAL BEAST YOU HAVE BECOME...
...BUT I LIKE IT!
UM... I HATE TO BREAK THIS TO YOU, BUT... I CAN'T CONTROL WHAT I'M DOING!
MY HULL IS PRESSED AGAINST THE GAS PEDAL AND I CAN'T CONTROL THE STEERING!
HMMM... YES, I CAN SEE HOW THAT COULD BE A PROBLEM.
ABANDON SHIP!
HEY!

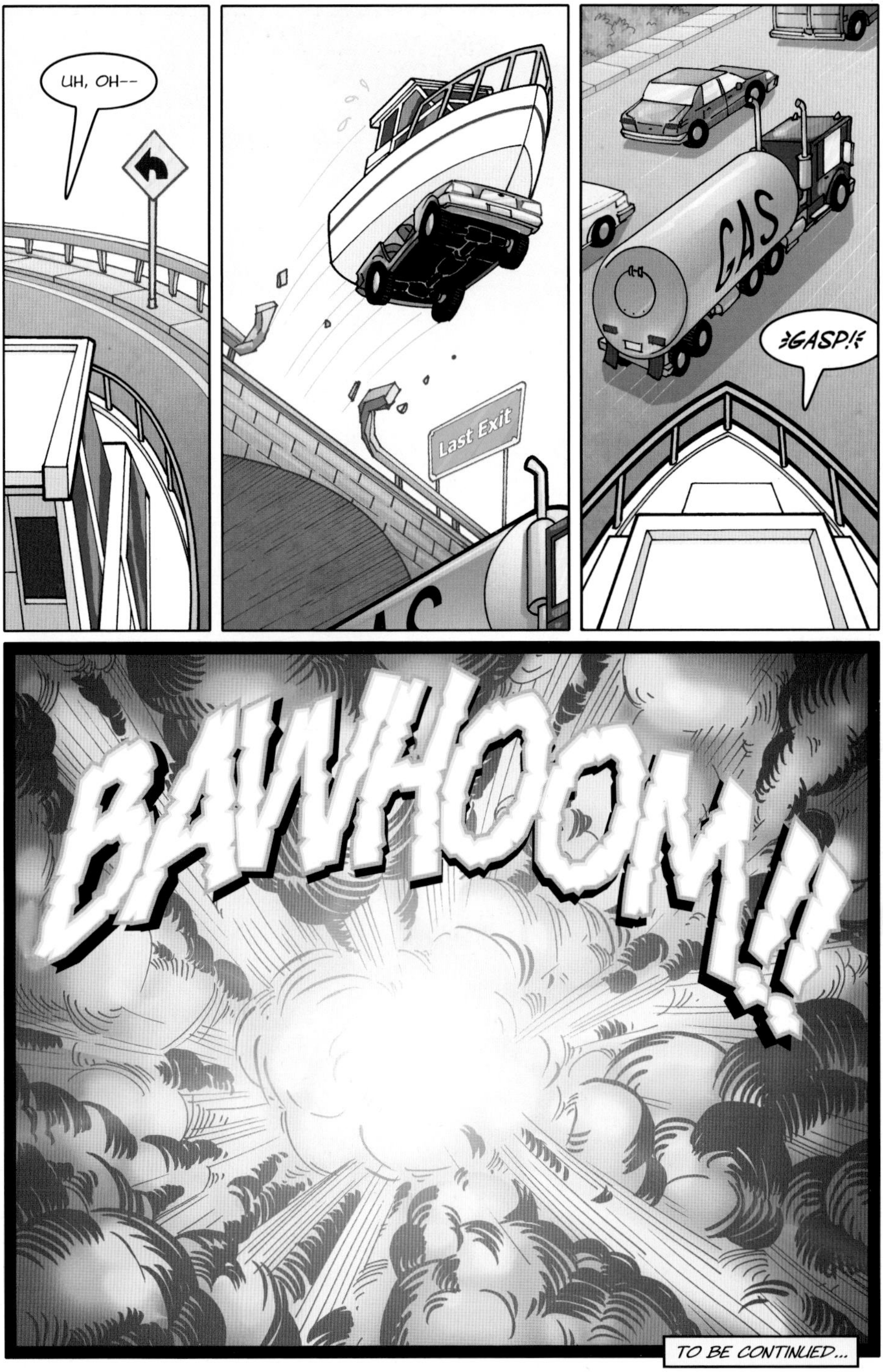
UH, OH--
Last Exit
GAS
GASP!
BAWHOOM!!
TO BE CONTINUED...

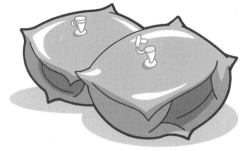

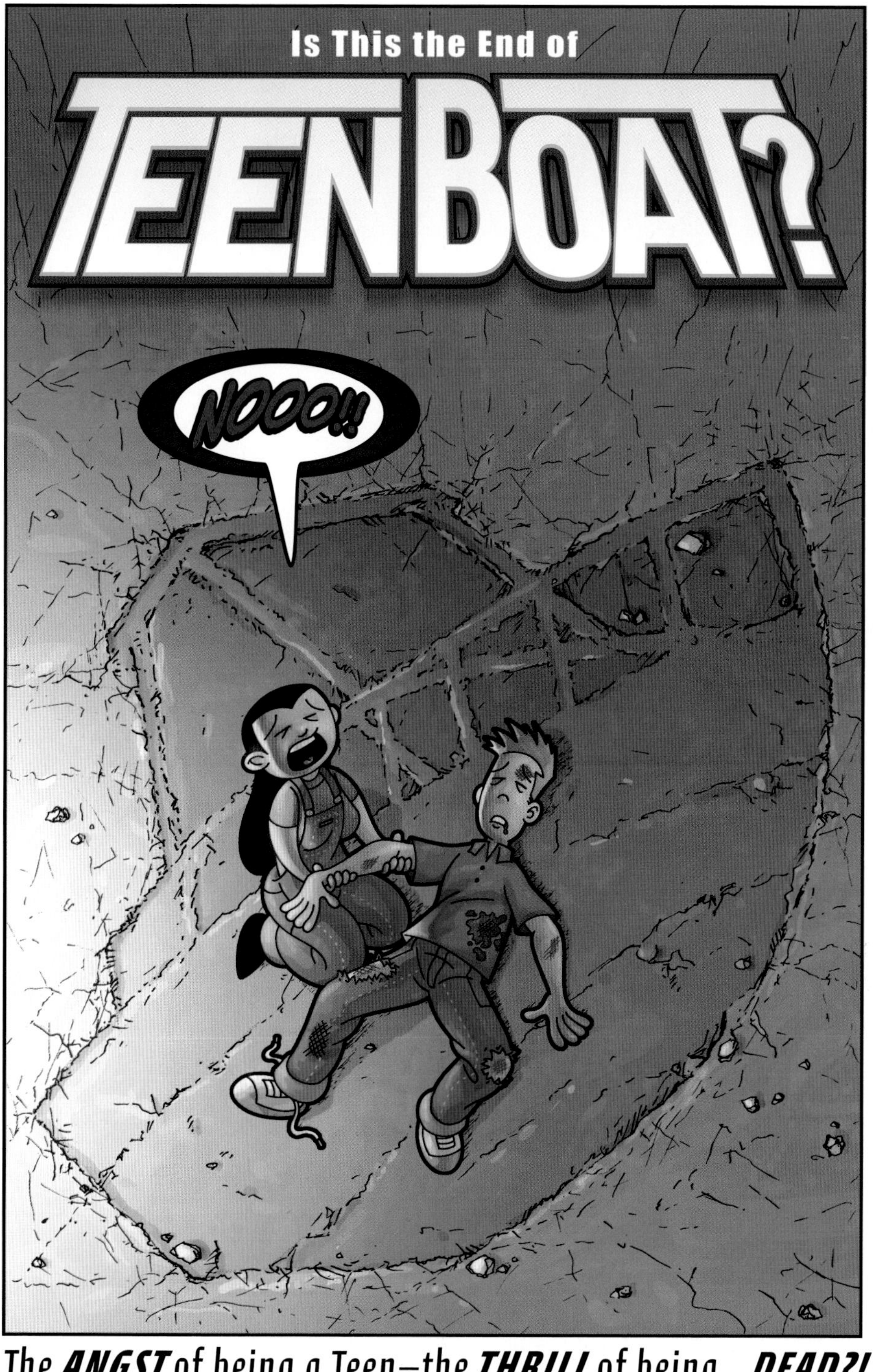
Is This the End of
TEENBOAT?
NOOOO!!

The *ANGST* of being a Teen—the *THRILL* of being... *DEAD?!*

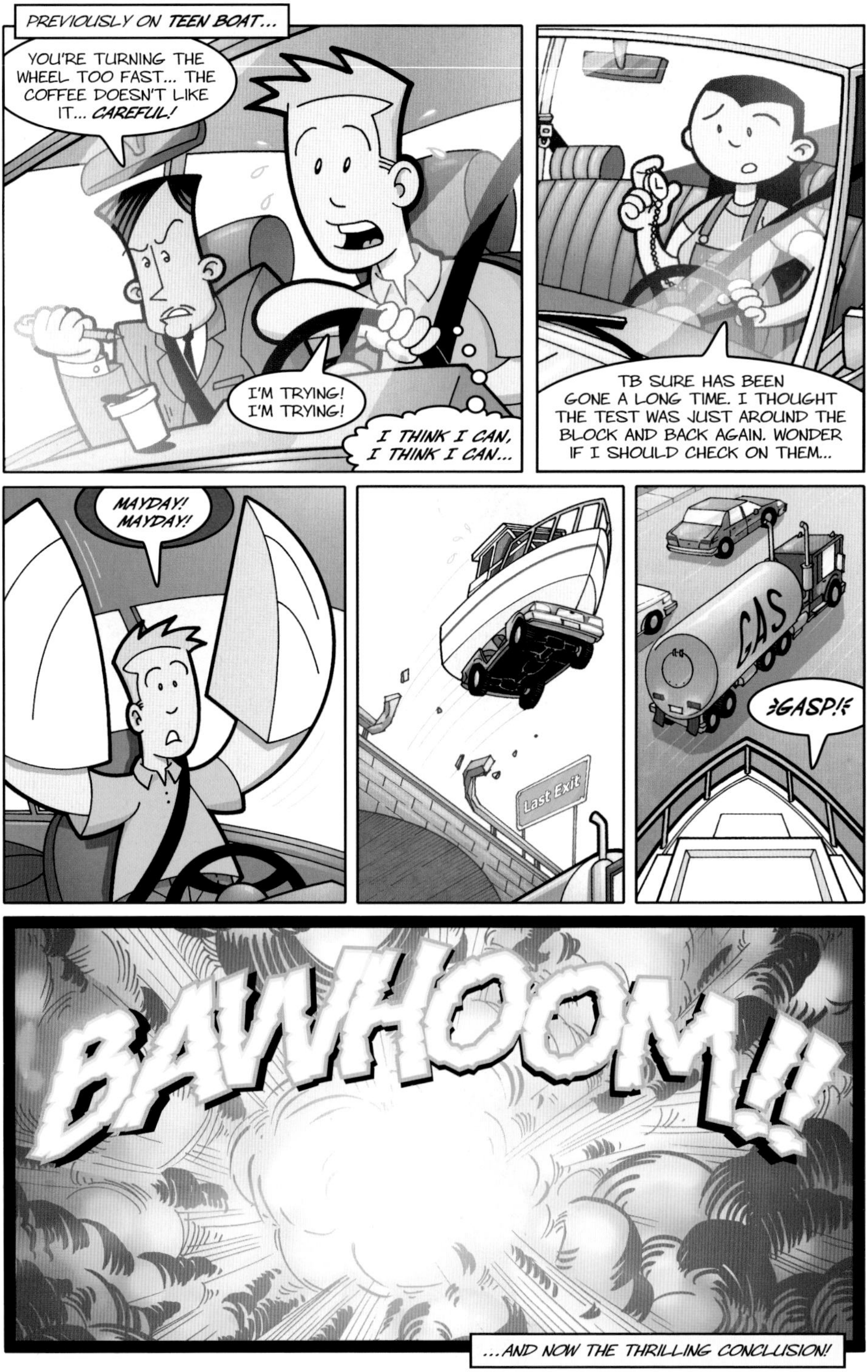
PREVIOUSLY ON TEEN BOAT...
YOU'RE TURNING THE WHEEL TOO FAST... THE COFFEE DOESN'T LIKE IT... CAREFUL!
I'M TRYING! I'M TRYING!
I THINK I CAN, I THINK I CAN...
TB SURE HAS BEEN GONE A LONG TIME. I THOUGHT THE TEST WAS JUST AROUND THE BLOCK AND BACK AGAIN. WONDER IF I SHOULD CHECK ON THEM...
MAYDAY! MAYDAY!
Last Exit
GAS
GASP!
BAWHOOM!!
...AND NOW THE THRILLING CONCLUSION!

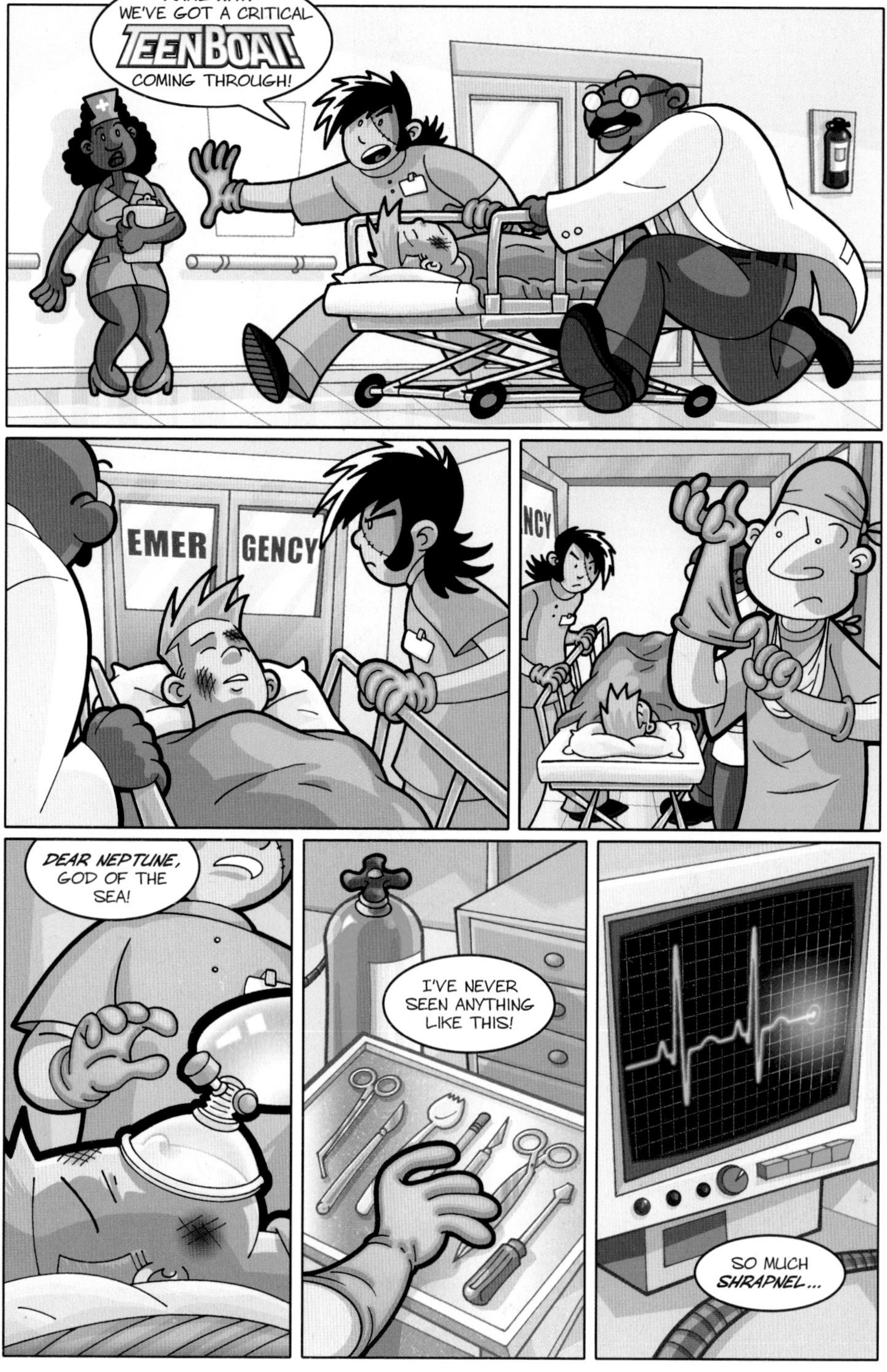
MAKE WAY! WE'VE GOT A CRITICAL TEENBOAT! COMING THROUGH!
EMER GENCY
DEAR NEPTUNE, GOD OF THE SEA!
I'VE NEVER SEEN ANYTHING LIKE THIS!
SO MUCH SHRAPNEL...

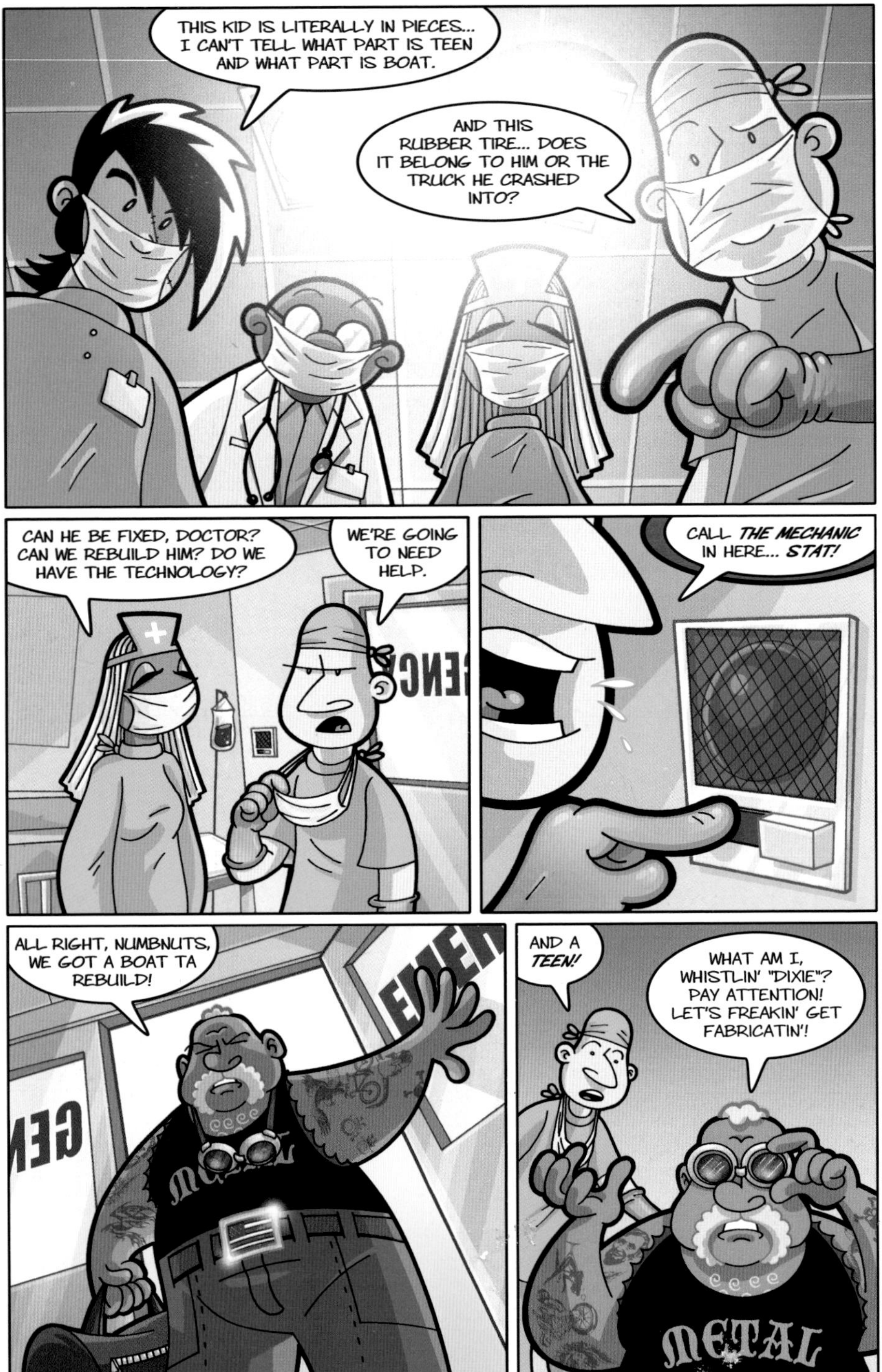
THIS KID IS LITERALLY IN PIECES... I CAN'T TELL WHAT PART IS TEEN AND WHAT PART IS BOAT.
AND THIS RUBBER TIRE... DOES IT BELONG TO HIM OR THE TRUCK HE CRASHED INTO?
CAN HE BE FIXED, DOCTOR? CAN WE REBUILD HIM? DO WE HAVE THE TECHNOLOGY?
WE'RE GOING TO NEED HELP.
CALL *THE MECHANIC* IN HERE... *STAT!*
ALL RIGHT, NUMBNUTS, WE GOT A BOAT TA REBUILD!
AND A *TEEN!*
WHAT AM I, WHISTLIN' "DIXIE"? PAY ATTENTION! LET'S FREAKIN' GET FABRICATIN'!
METAL

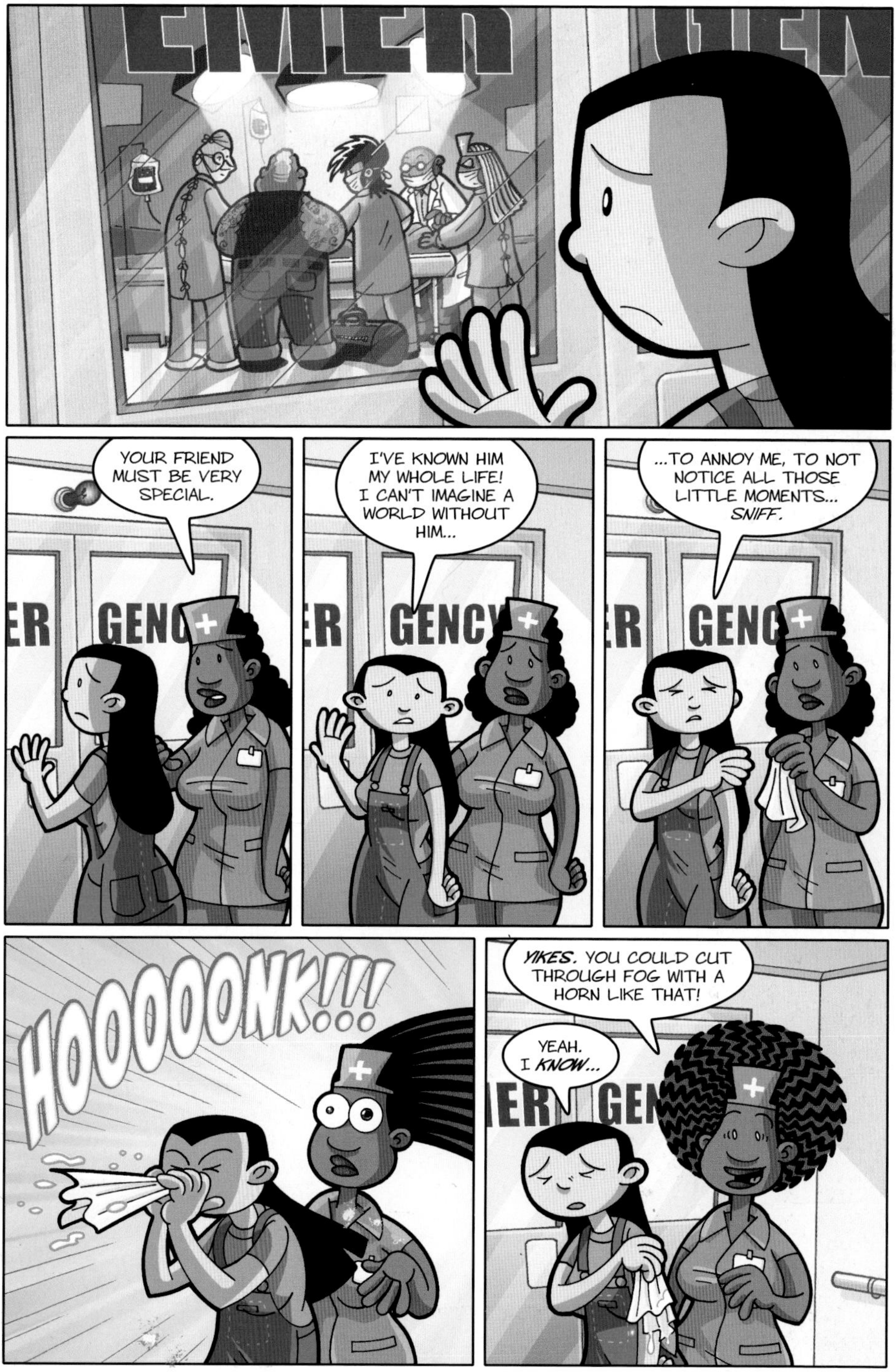
EMER GEN
YOUR FRIEND MUST BE VERY SPECIAL.
ER GENC
I'VE KNOWN HIM MY WHOLE LIFE! I CAN'T IMAGINE A WORLD WITHOUT HIM...
ER GENCY
...TO ANNOY ME, TO NOT NOTICE ALL THOSE LITTLE MOMENTS... SNIFF.
ER GENC
HOOOOONK!!!
YIKES. YOU COULD CUT THROUGH FOG WITH A HORN LIKE THAT!
YEAH. I KNOW...
ER GEN

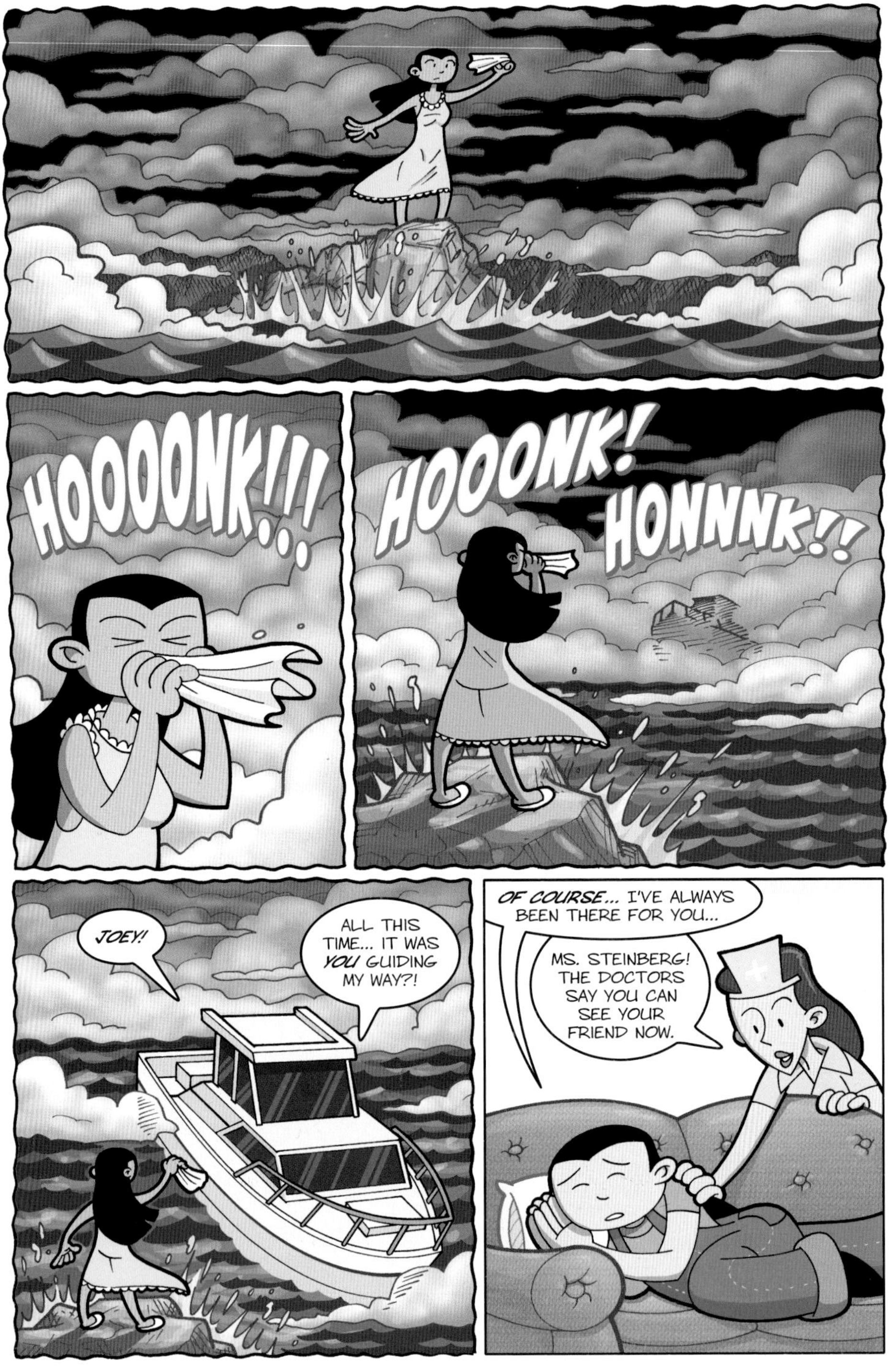
HOOOONK!!!
HOOOONK!
HONNNK!!
JOEY!
ALL THIS TIME... IT WAS YOU GUIDING MY WAY?!
OF COURSE... I'VE ALWAYS BEEN THERE FOR YOU...
MS. STEINBERG! THE DOCTORS SAY YOU CAN SEE YOUR FRIEND NOW.

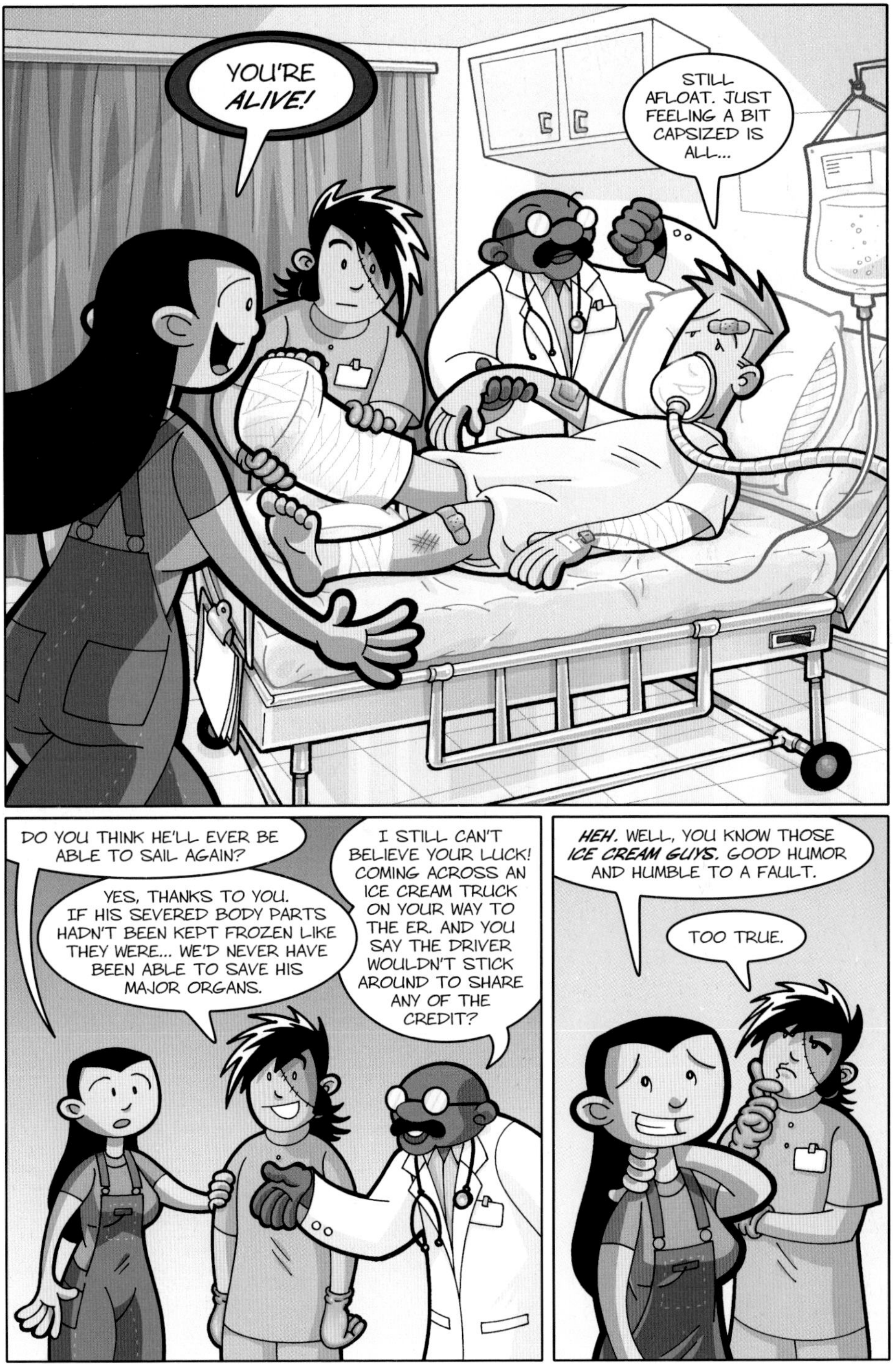

YOU'RE ALIVE!
STILL AFLOAT. JUST FEELING A BIT CAPSIZED IS ALL...
DO YOU THINK HE'LL EVER BE ABLE TO SAIL AGAIN?
YES, THANKS TO YOU. IF HIS SEVERED BODY PARTS HADN'T BEEN KEPT FROZEN LIKE THEY WERE... WE'D NEVER HAVE BEEN ABLE TO SAVE HIS MAJOR ORGANS.
I STILL CAN'T BELIEVE YOUR LUCK! COMING ACROSS AN ICE CREAM TRUCK ON YOUR WAY TO THE ER. AND YOU SAY THE DRIVER WOULDN'T STICK AROUND TO SHARE ANY OF THE CREDIT?
HEH. WELL, YOU KNOW THOSE ICE CREAM GUYS. GOOD HUMOR AND HUMBLE TO A FAULT.
TOO TRUE.

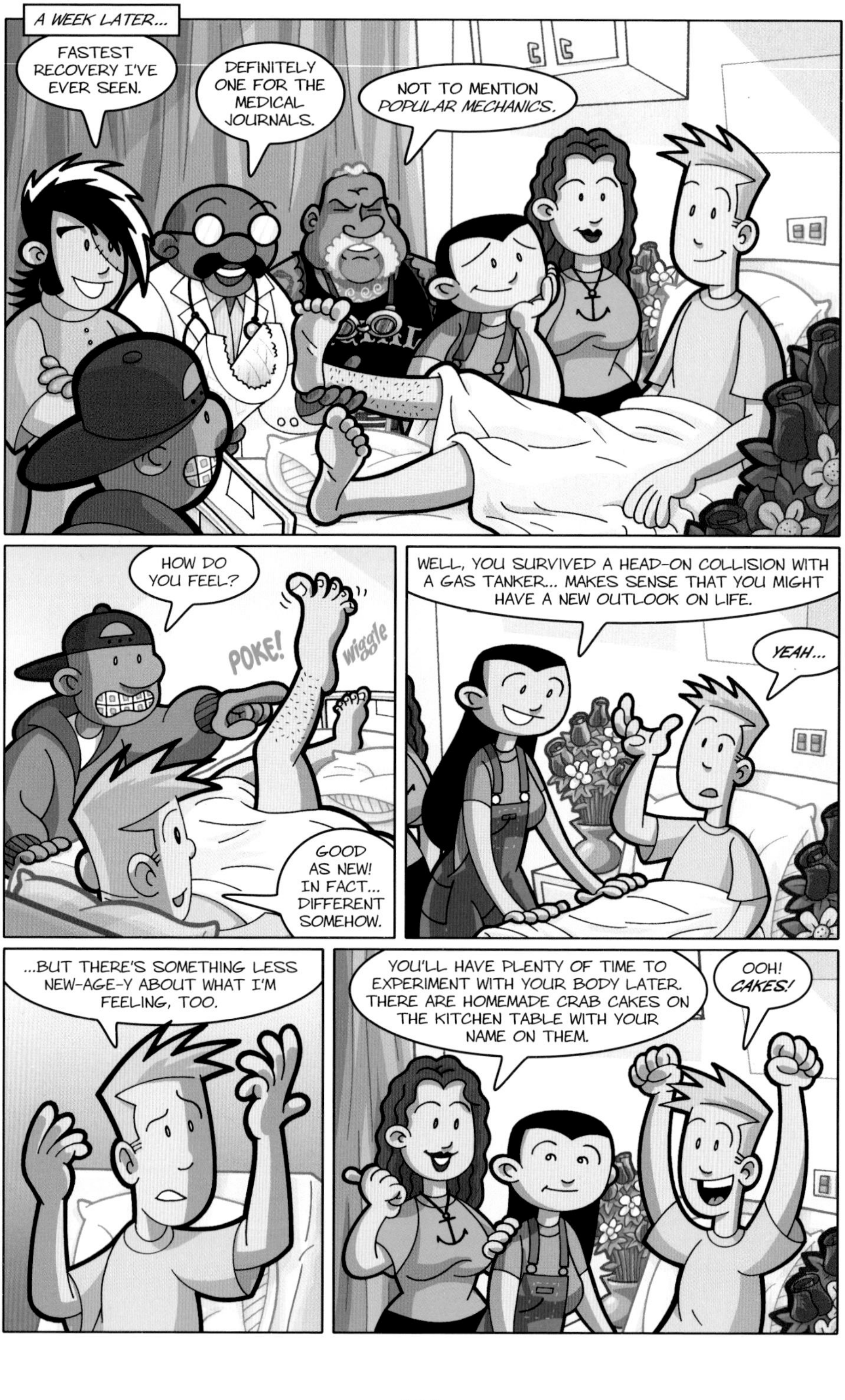
A WEEK LATER...
FASTEST RECOVERY I'VE EVER SEEN.
DEFINITELY ONE FOR THE MEDICAL JOURNALS.
NOT TO MENTION *POPULAR MECHANICS.*
HOW DO YOU FEEL?
POKE!
wiggle
GOOD AS NEW! IN FACT... DIFFERENT SOMEHOW.
WELL, YOU SURVIVED A HEAD-ON COLLISION WITH A GAS TANKER... MAKES SENSE THAT YOU MIGHT HAVE A NEW OUTLOOK ON LIFE.
YEAH...
...BUT THERE'S SOMETHING LESS NEW-AGE-Y ABOUT WHAT I'M FEELING, TOO.
YOU'LL HAVE PLENTY OF TIME TO EXPERIMENT WITH YOUR BODY LATER. THERE ARE HOMEMADE CRAB CAKES ON THE KITCHEN TABLE WITH YOUR NAME ON THEM.
OOH! *CAKES!*

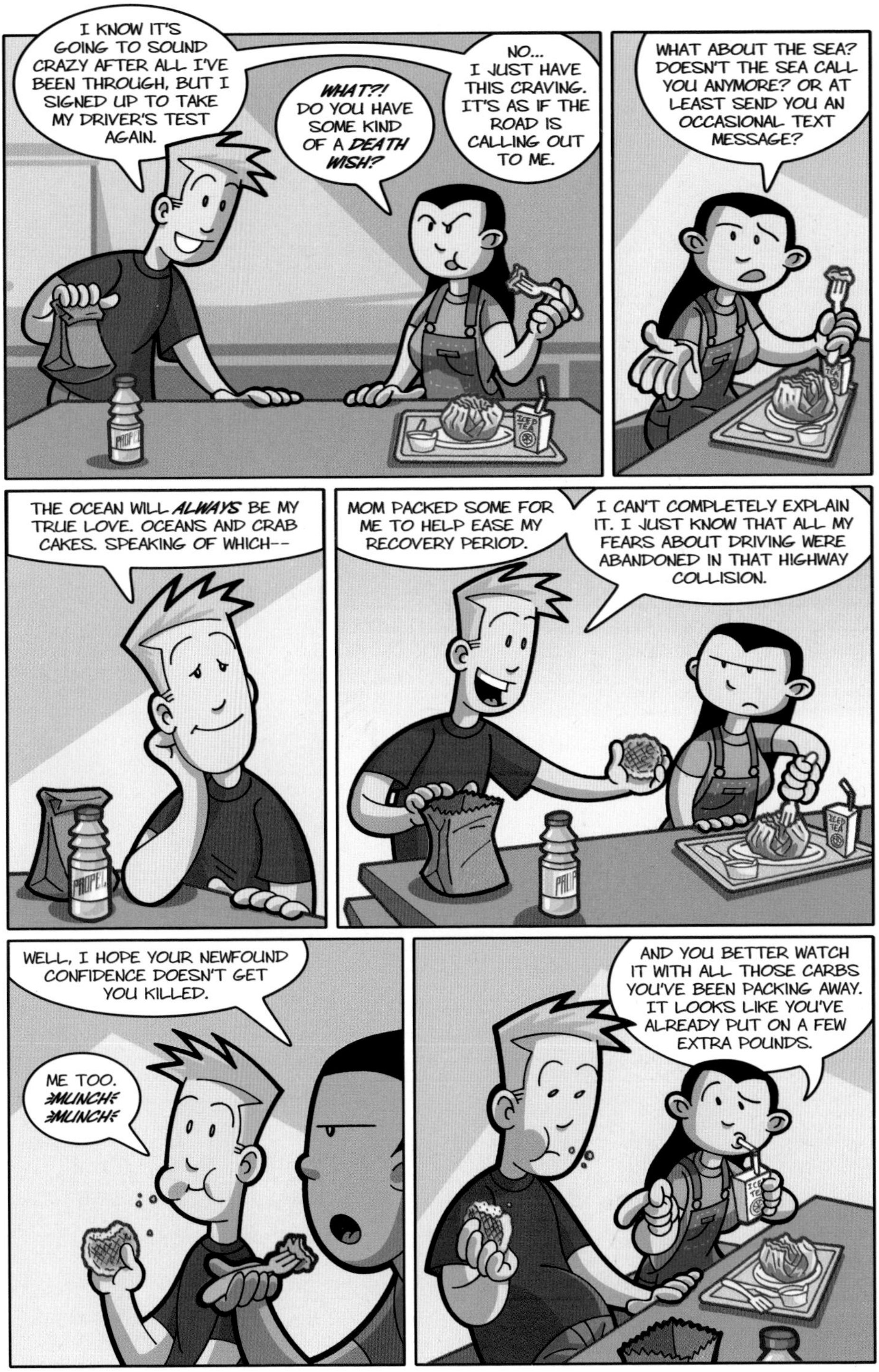
I KNOW IT'S GOING TO SOUND CRAZY AFTER ALL I'VE BEEN THROUGH, BUT I SIGNED UP TO TAKE MY DRIVER'S TEST AGAIN.
WHAT?! DO YOU HAVE SOME KIND OF A DEATH WISH?
NO... I JUST HAVE THIS CRAVING. IT'S AS IF THE ROAD IS CALLING OUT TO ME.
WHAT ABOUT THE SEA? DOESN'T THE SEA CALL YOU ANYMORE? OR AT LEAST SEND YOU AN OCCASIONAL TEXT MESSAGE?
THE OCEAN WILL ALWAYS BE MY TRUE LOVE. OCEANS AND CRAB CAKES. SPEAKING OF WHICH--
MOM PACKED SOME FOR ME TO HELP EASE MY RECOVERY PERIOD.
I CAN'T COMPLETELY EXPLAIN IT. I JUST KNOW THAT ALL MY FEARS ABOUT DRIVING WERE ABANDONED IN THAT HIGHWAY COLLISION.
WELL, I HOPE YOUR NEWFOUND CONFIDENCE DOESN'T GET YOU KILLED.
ME TOO. MUNCH MUNCH
AND YOU BETTER WATCH IT WITH ALL THOSE CARBS YOU'VE BEEN PACKING AWAY. IT LOOKS LIKE YOU'VE ALREADY PUT ON A FEW EXTRA POUNDS.

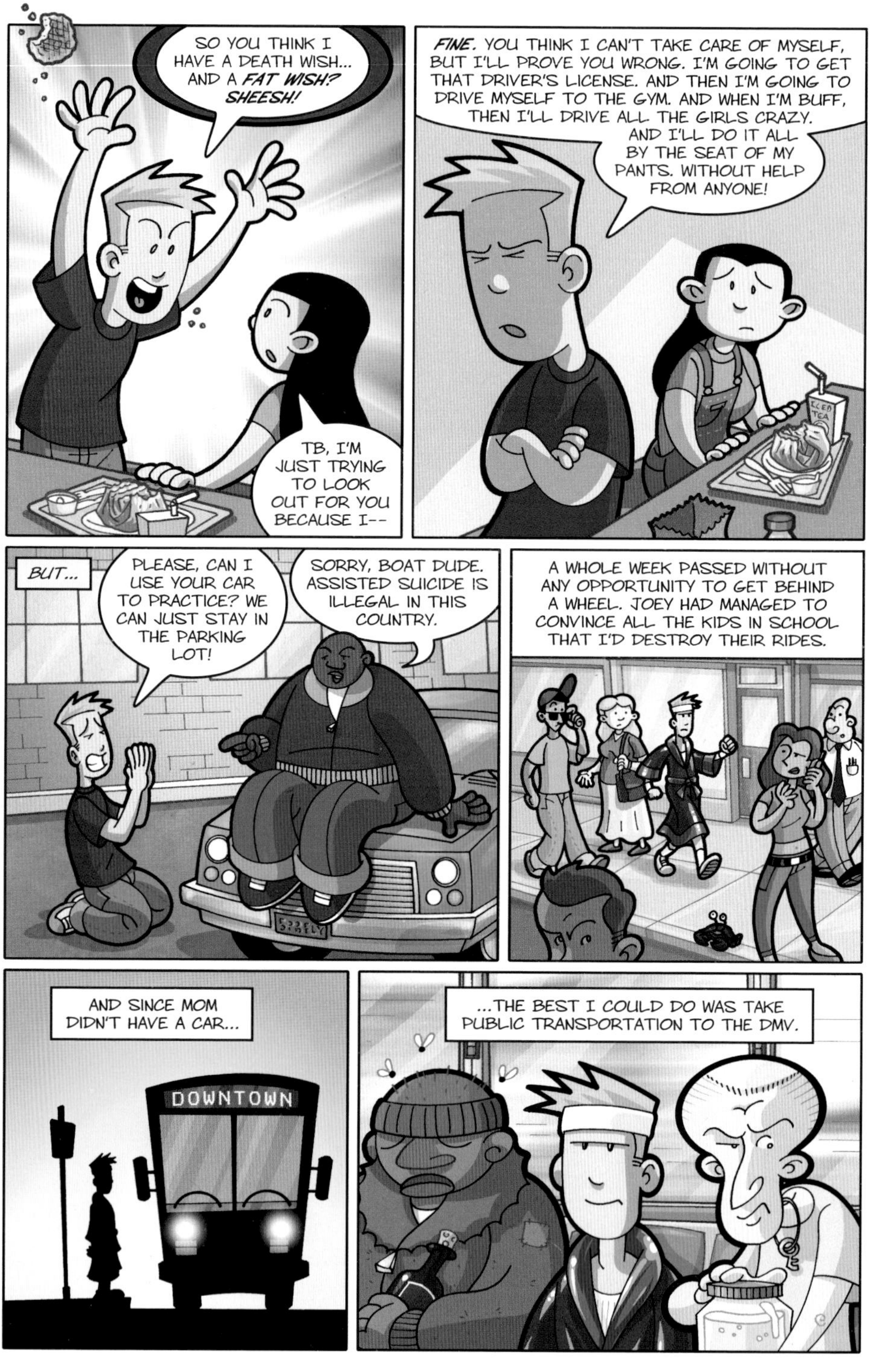
SO YOU THINK I HAVE A DEATH WISH... AND A FAT WISH? SHEESH!
TB, I'M JUST TRYING TO LOOK OUT FOR YOU BECAUSE I--
FINE. YOU THINK I CAN'T TAKE CARE OF MYSELF, BUT I'LL PROVE YOU WRONG. I'M GOING TO GET THAT DRIVER'S LICENSE. AND THEN I'M GOING TO DRIVE MYSELF TO THE GYM. AND WHEN I'M BUFF, THEN I'LL DRIVE ALL THE GIRLS CRAZY.
AND I'LL DO IT ALL BY THE SEAT OF MY PANTS. WITHOUT HELP FROM ANYONE!
ICED TEA
BUT...
PLEASE, CAN I USE YOUR CAR TO PRACTICE? WE CAN JUST STAY IN THE PARKING LOT!
SORRY, BOAT DUDE. ASSISTED SUICIDE IS ILLEGAL IN THIS COUNTRY.
A WHOLE WEEK PASSED WITHOUT ANY OPPORTUNITY TO GET BEHIND A WHEEL. JOEY HAD MANAGED TO CONVINCE ALL THE KIDS IN SCHOOL THAT I'D DESTROY THEIR RIDES.
AND SINCE MOM DIDN'T HAVE A CAR...
DOWNTOWN
...THE BEST I COULD DO WAS TAKE PUBLIC TRANSPORTATION TO THE DMV.

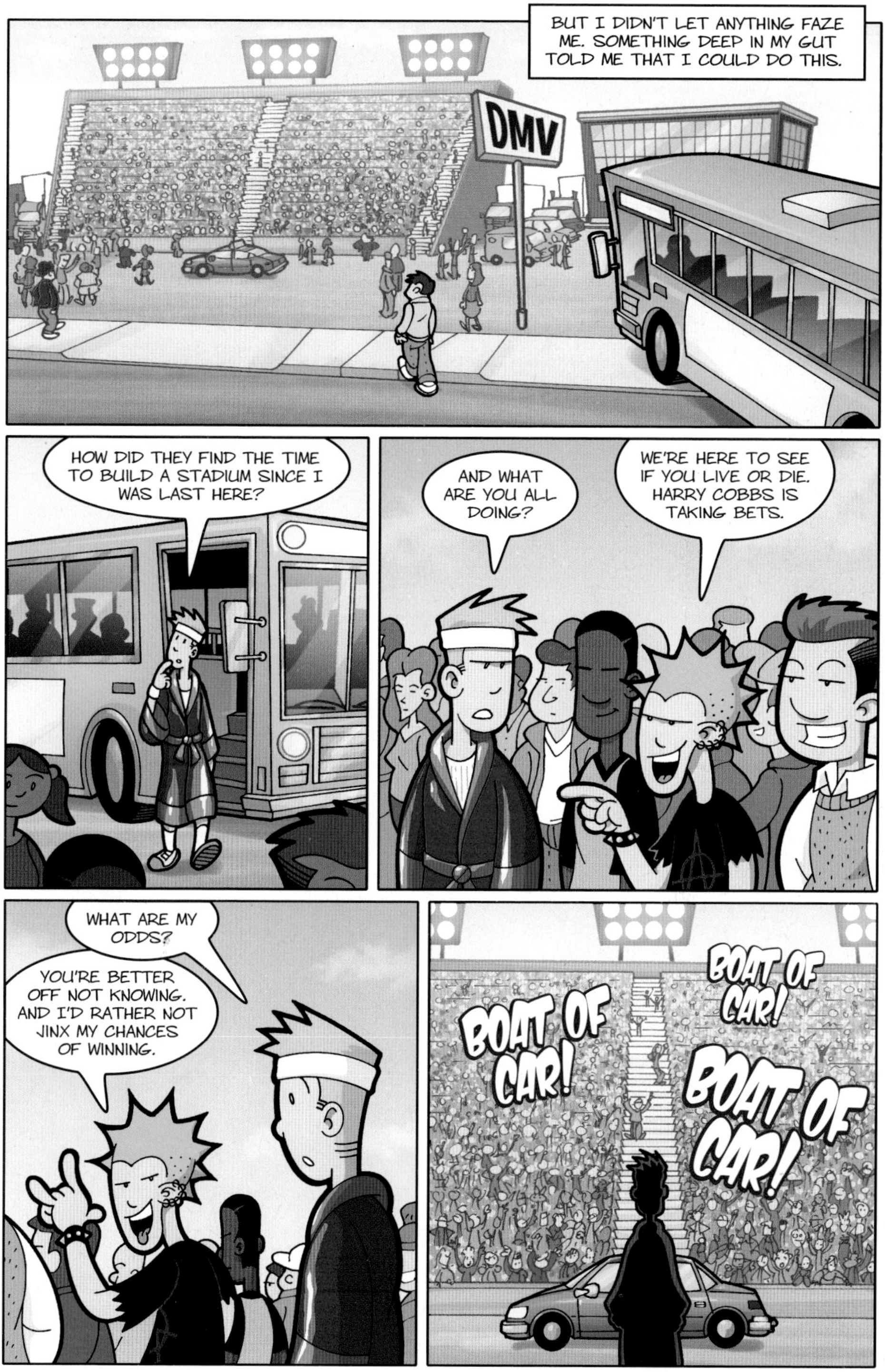
BUT I DIDN'T LET ANYTHING FAZE ME. SOMETHING DEEP IN MY GUT TOLD ME THAT I COULD DO THIS.
DMV
HOW DID THEY FIND THE TIME TO BUILD A STADIUM SINCE I WAS LAST HERE?
AND WHAT ARE YOU ALL DOING?
WE'RE HERE TO SEE IF YOU LIVE OR DIE. HARRY COBBS IS TAKING BETS.
WHAT ARE MY ODDS?
YOU'RE BETTER OFF NOT KNOWING. AND I'D RATHER NOT JINX MY CHANCES OF WINNING.
BOAT OF CAR!
BOAT OF CAR!
BOAT OF CAR!

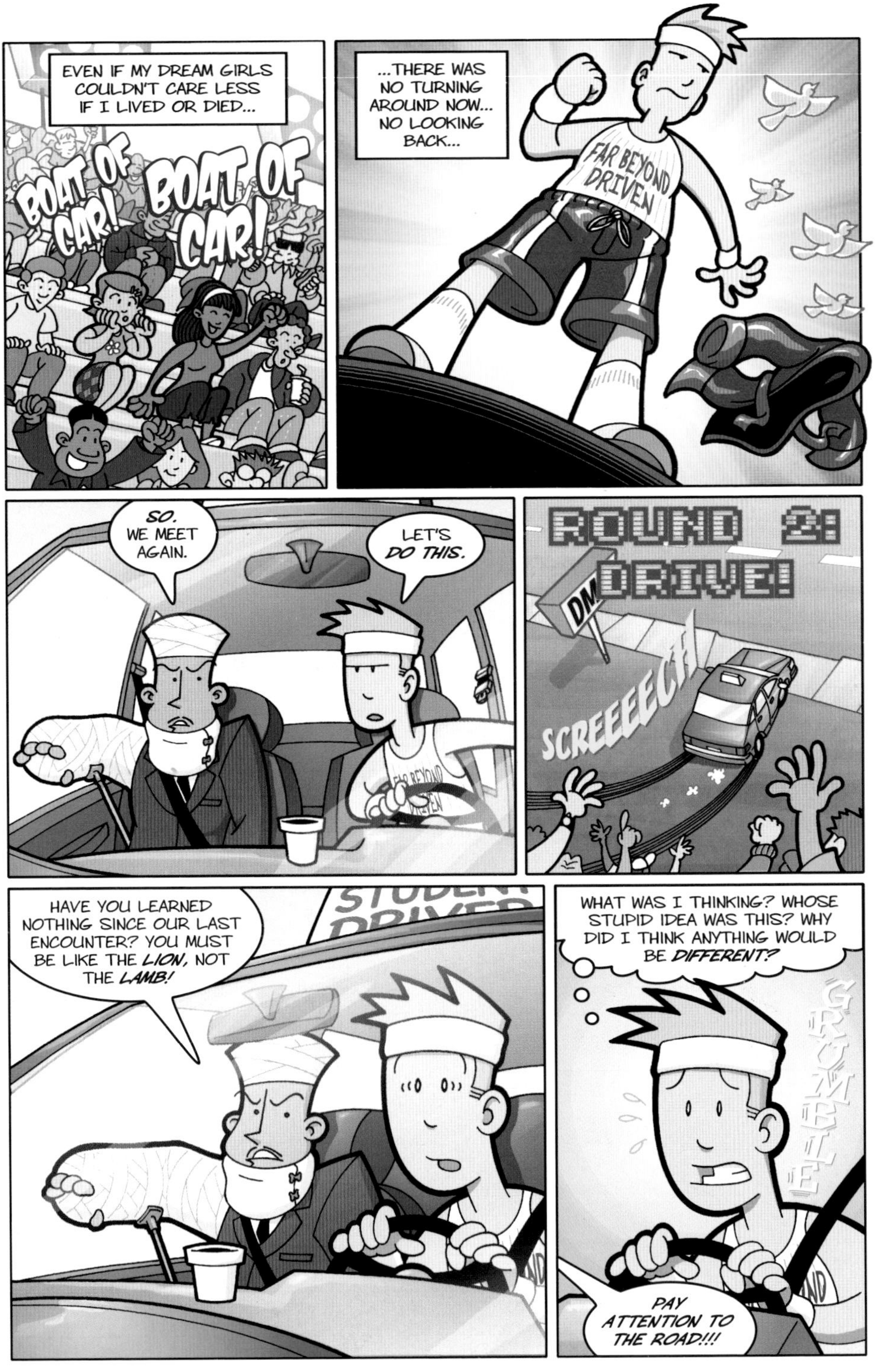
EVEN IF MY DREAM GIRLS COULDN'T CARE LESS IF I LIVED OR DIED...
BOAT OF CAR! BOAT OF CAR!
...THERE WAS NO TURNING AROUND NOW... NO LOOKING BACK...
FAR BEYOND DRIVEN
SO. WE MEET AGAIN.
LET'S DO THIS.
ROUND 2: DRIVE!
DM
SCREEEECH
HAVE YOU LEARNED NOTHING SINCE OUR LAST ENCOUNTER? YOU MUST BE LIKE THE LION, NOT THE LAMB!
WHAT WAS I THINKING? WHOSE STUPID IDEA WAS THIS? WHY DID I THINK ANYTHING WOULD BE DIFFERENT?
GRUMBLE
PAY ATTENTION TO THE ROAD!!!

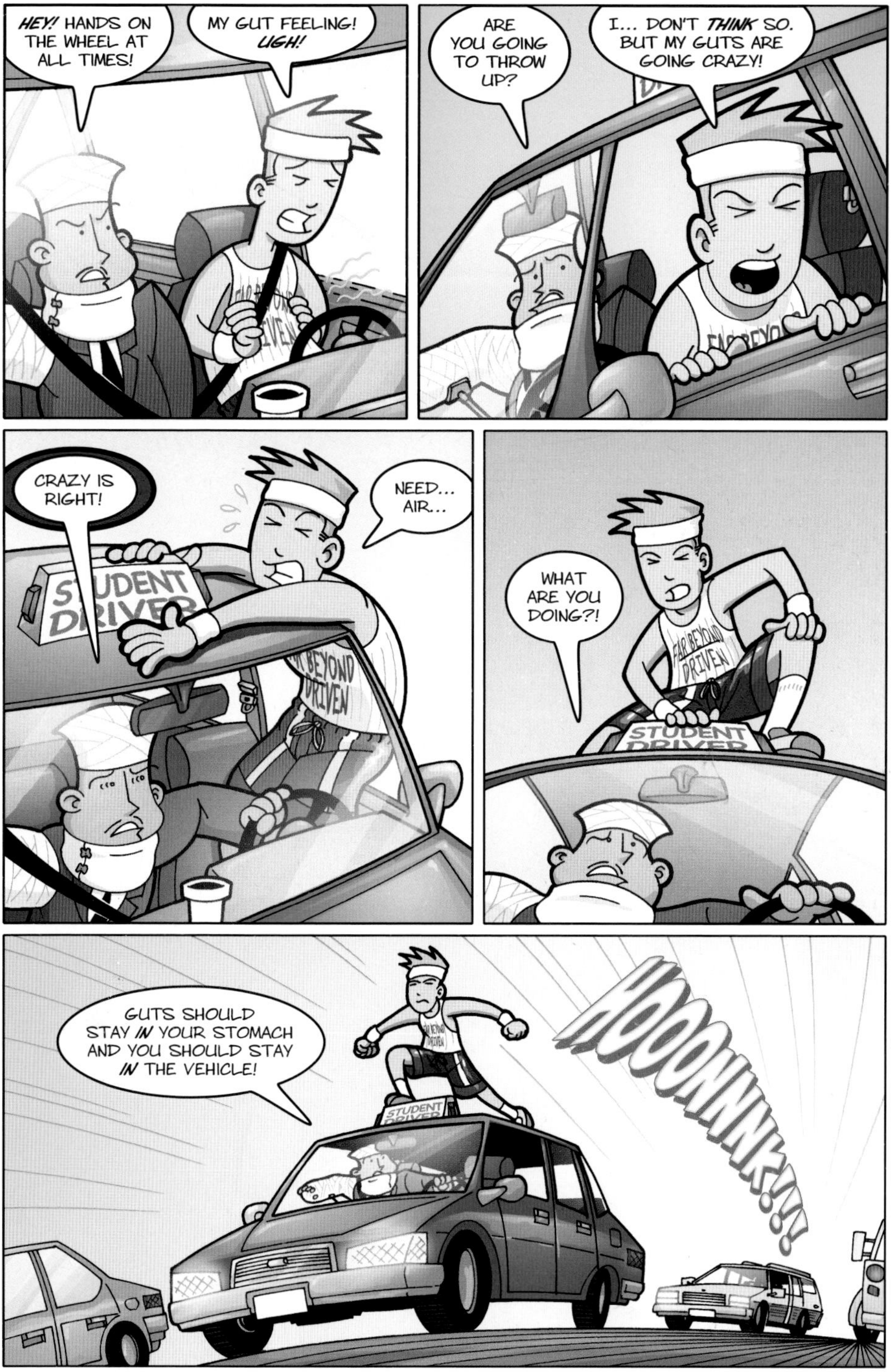
HEY! HANDS ON THE WHEEL AT ALL TIMES!
MY GUT FEELING! UGH!
ARE YOU GOING TO THROW UP?
I... DON'T THINK SO. BUT MY GUTS ARE GOING CRAZY!
CRAZY IS RIGHT!
NEED... AIR...
STUDENT DRIVER
WHAT ARE YOU DOING?!
GUTS SHOULD STAY IN YOUR STOMACH AND YOU SHOULD STAY IN THE VEHICLE!
HOOONNNK!!!

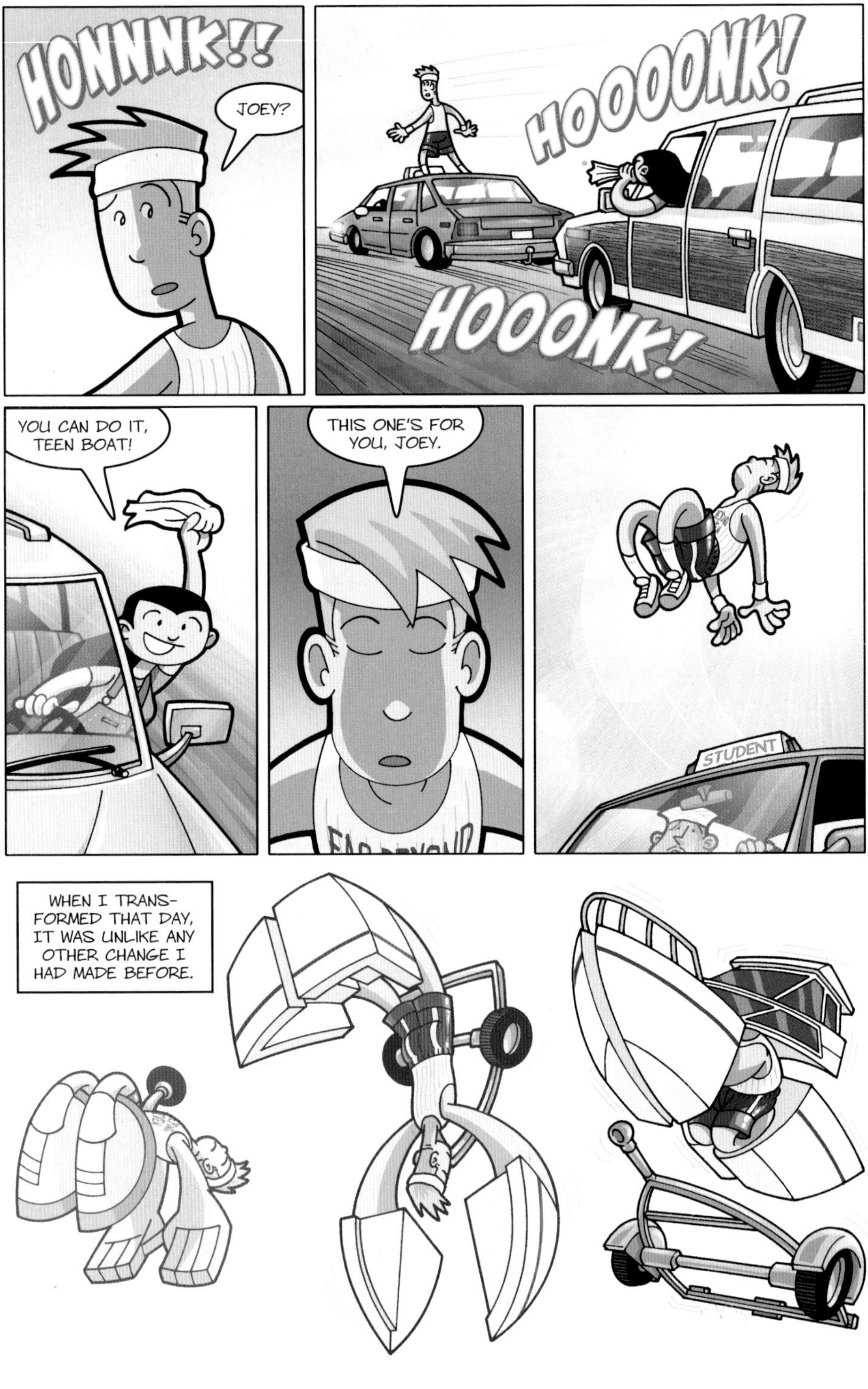
HONNNK!!
JOEY?
HOOOONK!
HOOONK!
YOU CAN DO IT, TEEN BOAT!
THIS ONE'S FOR YOU, JOEY.
STUDENT
WHEN I TRANSFORMED THAT DAY, IT WAS UNLIKE ANY OTHER CHANGE I HAD MADE BEFORE.

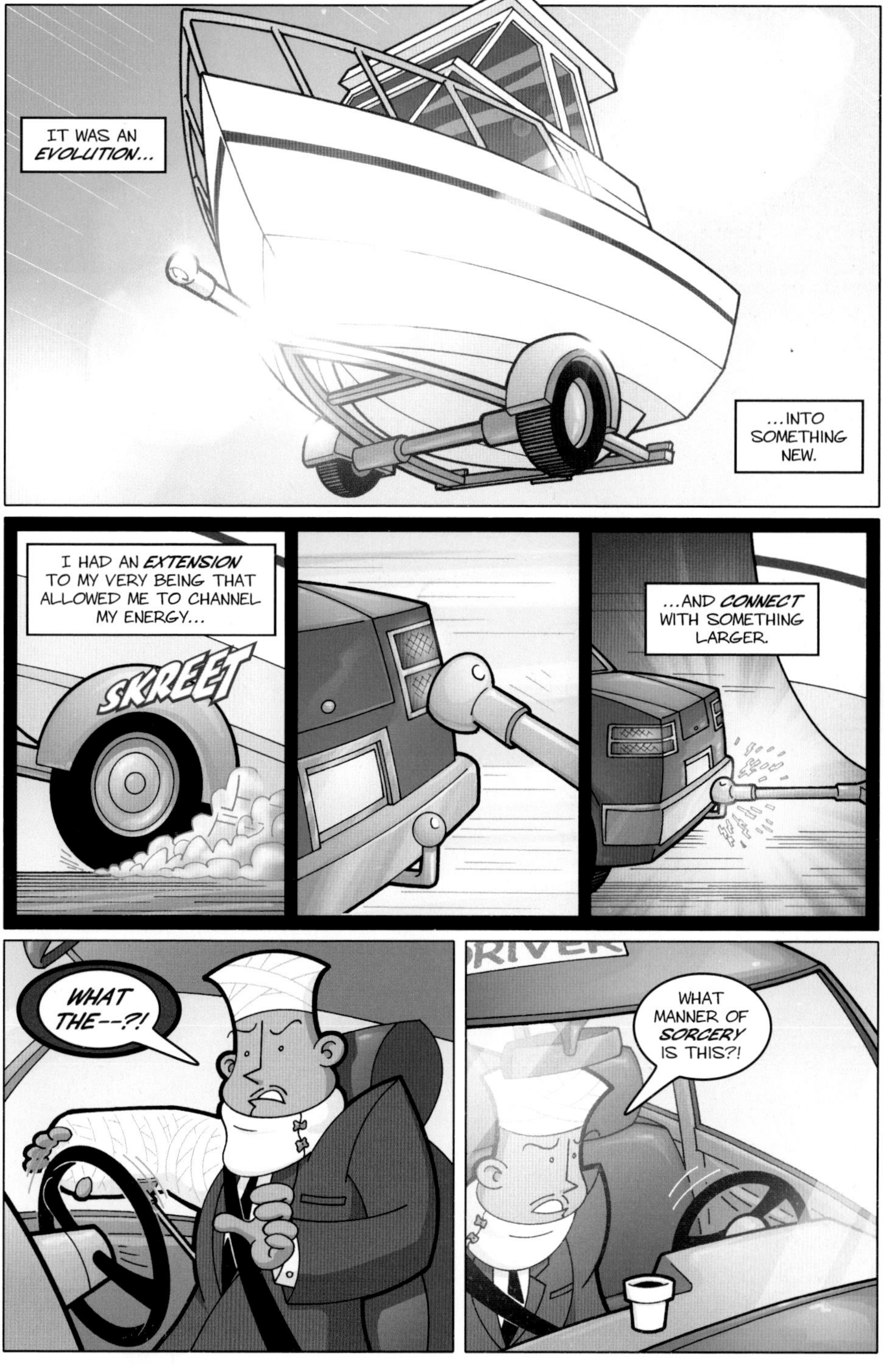
IT WAS AN *EVOLUTION*...
...INTO SOMETHING NEW.
I HAD AN *EXTENSION* TO MY VERY BEING THAT ALLOWED ME TO CHANNEL MY ENERGY...
SKREET
...AND *CONNECT* WITH SOMETHING LARGER.
WHAT THE--?!
DRIVER
WHAT MANNER OF *SORCERY* IS THIS?!

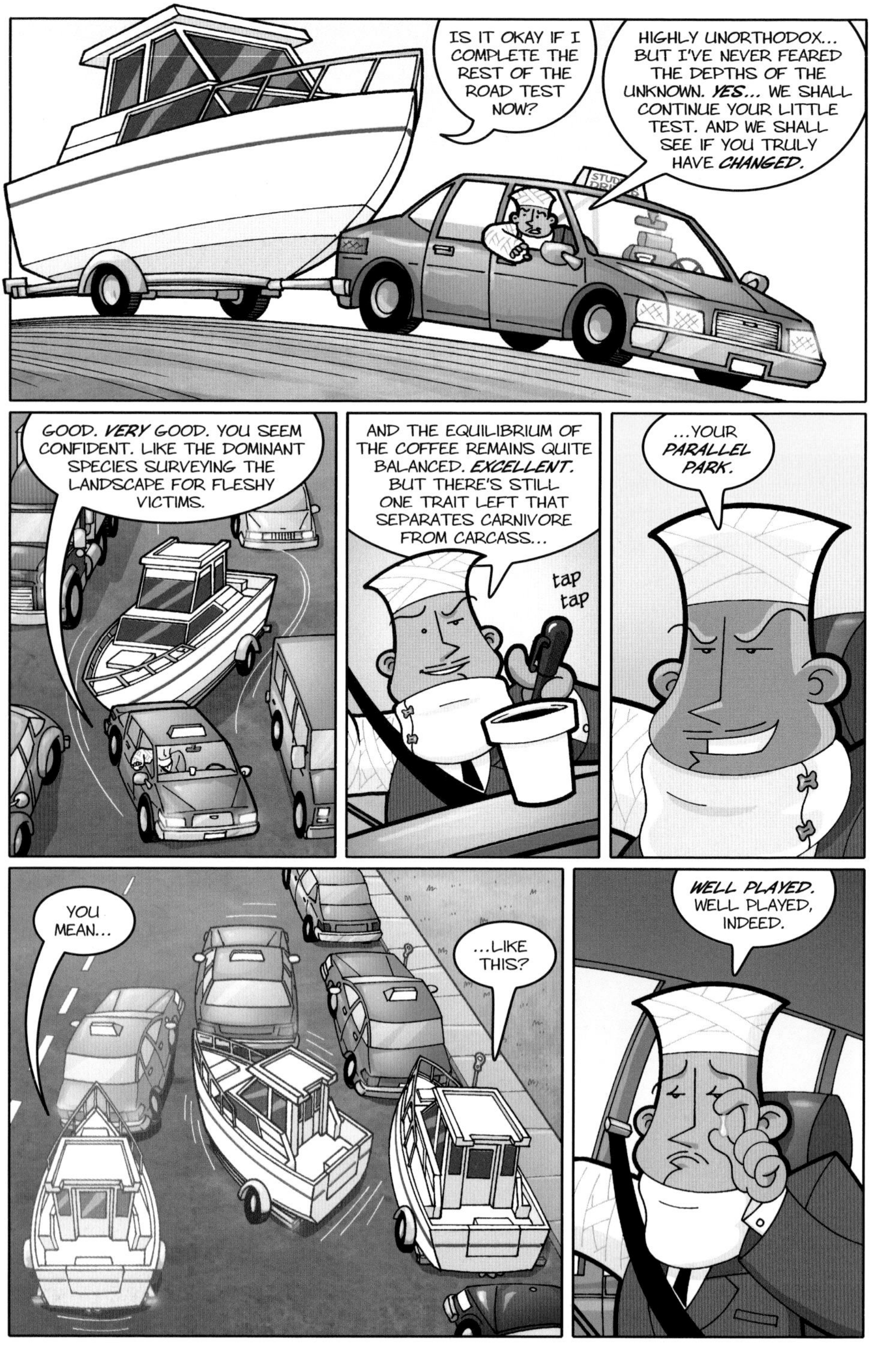
IS IT OKAY IF I COMPLETE THE REST OF THE ROAD TEST NOW?
HIGHLY UNORTHODOX... BUT I'VE NEVER FEARED THE DEPTHS OF THE UNKNOWN. ***YES...*** WE SHALL CONTINUE YOUR LITTLE TEST. AND WE SHALL SEE IF YOU TRULY HAVE ***CHANGED.***
GOOD. ***VERY*** GOOD. YOU SEEM CONFIDENT. LIKE THE DOMINANT SPECIES SURVEYING THE LANDSCAPE FOR FLESHY VICTIMS.
AND THE EQUILIBRIUM OF THE COFFEE REMAINS QUITE BALANCED. ***EXCELLENT.*** BUT THERE'S STILL ONE TRAIT LEFT THAT SEPARATES CARNIVORE FROM CARCASS...
tap tap
...YOUR ***PARALLEL PARK.***
YOU MEAN...
...LIKE THIS?
WELL PLAYED. WELL PLAYED, INDEED.

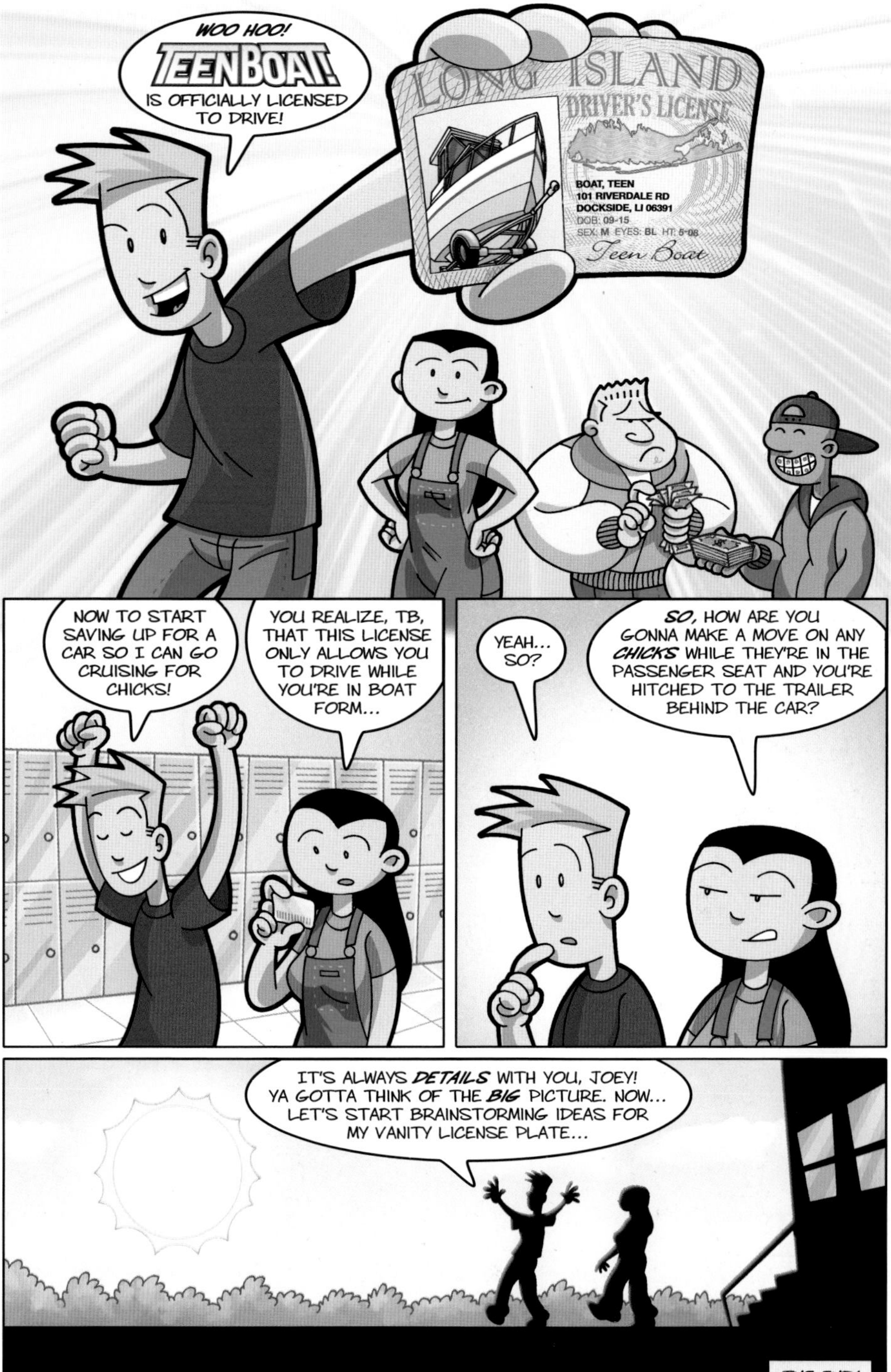
WOO HOO!
TEEN BOAT!
IS OFFICIALLY LICENSED TO DRIVE!
LONG ISLAND
DRIVER'S LICENSE
BOAT, TEEN
101 RIVERDALE RD
DOCKSIDE, LI 06391
DOB: 09-15
SEX: M EYES: BL HT: 5-08
Teen Boat
NOW TO START SAVING UP FOR A CAR SO I CAN GO CRUISING FOR CHICKS!
YOU REALIZE, TB, THAT THIS LICENSE ONLY ALLOWS YOU TO DRIVE WHILE YOU'RE IN BOAT FORM...
YEAH... SO?
SO, HOW ARE YOU GONNA MAKE A MOVE ON ANY CHICKS WHILE THEY'RE IN THE PASSENGER SEAT AND YOU'RE HITCHED TO THE TRAILER BEHIND THE CAR?
IT'S ALWAYS DETAILS WITH YOU, JOEY! YA GOTTA THINK OF THE BIG PICTURE. NOW... LET'S START BRAINSTORMING IDEAS FOR MY VANITY LICENSE PLATE...
THE END!

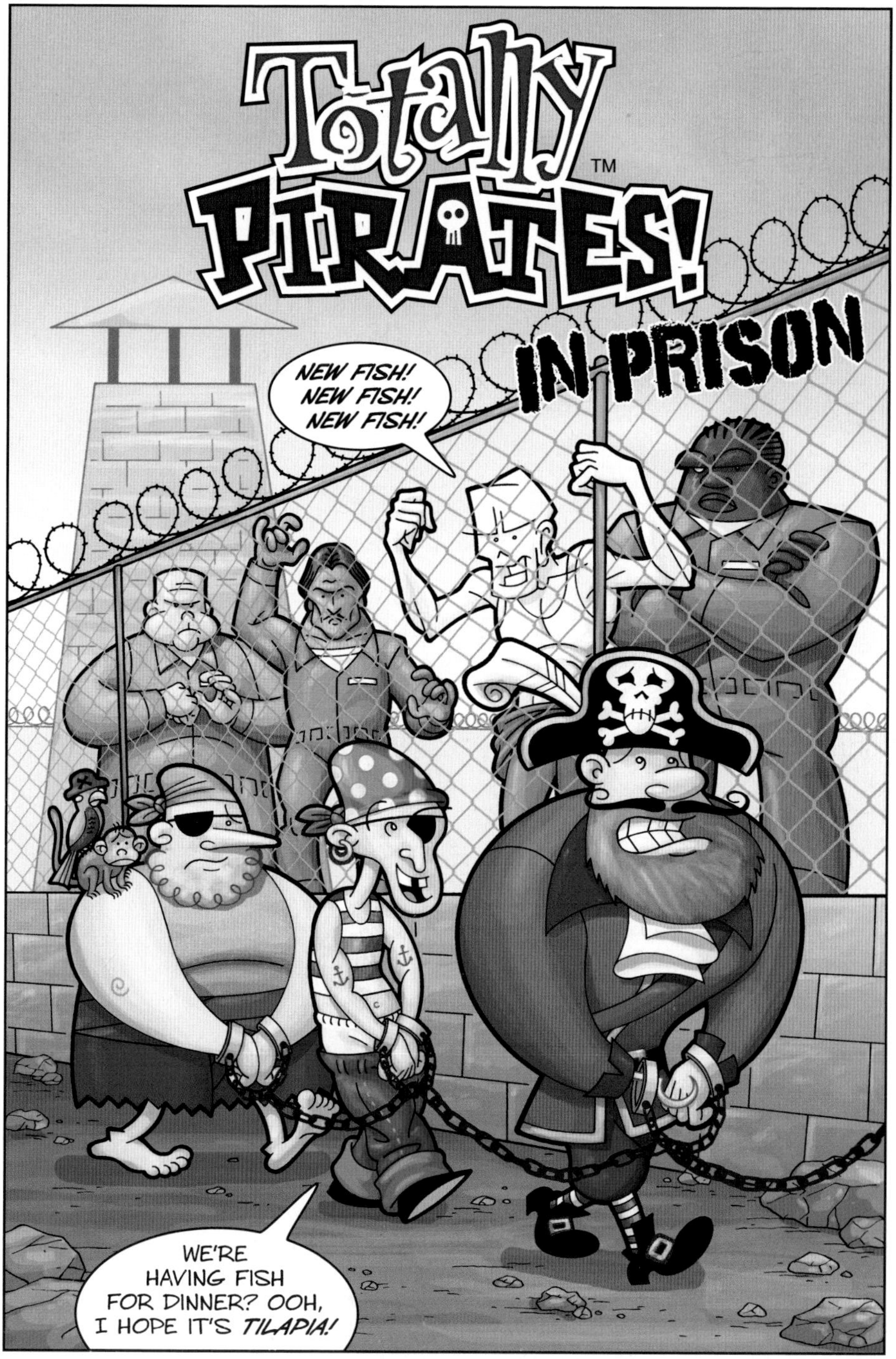
Totally PIRATES! IN PRISON
NEW FISH! NEW FISH! NEW FISH!
WE'RE HAVING FISH FOR DINNER? OOH, I HOPE IT'S TILAPIA!

The ***ANGST*** of being in prison—the ***THRILL*** of being a pirate!

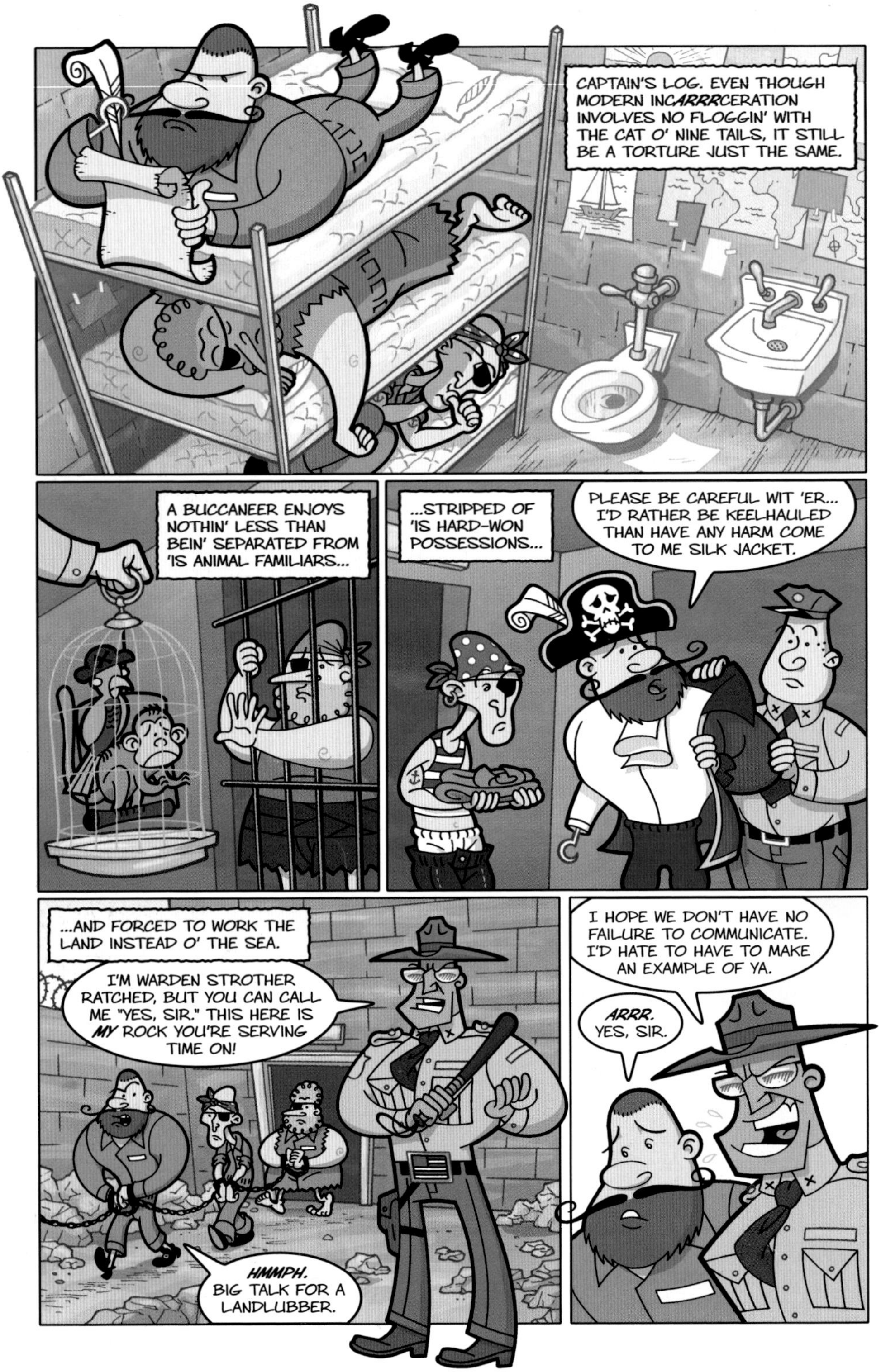
CAPTAIN'S LOG. EVEN THOUGH MODERN INCARRRCERATION INVOLVES NO FLOGGIN' WITH THE CAT O' NINE TAILS, IT STILL BE A TORTURE JUST THE SAME.
A BUCCANEER ENJOYS NOTHIN' LESS THAN BEIN' SEPARATED FROM 'IS ANIMAL FAMILIARS...
...STRIPPED OF 'IS HARD-WON POSSESSIONS...
PLEASE BE CAREFUL WIT 'ER... I'D RATHER BE KEELHAULED THAN HAVE ANY HARM COME TO ME SILK JACKET.
...AND FORCED TO WORK THE LAND INSTEAD O' THE SEA.
I'M WARDEN STROTHER RATCHED, BUT YOU CAN CALL ME "YES, SIR." THIS HERE IS MY ROCK YOU'RE SERVING TIME ON!
HMMPH. BIG TALK FOR A LANDLUBBER.
I HOPE WE DON'T HAVE NO FAILURE TO COMMUNICATE. I'D HATE TO HAVE TO MAKE AN EXAMPLE OF YA.
ARRR. YES, SIR.

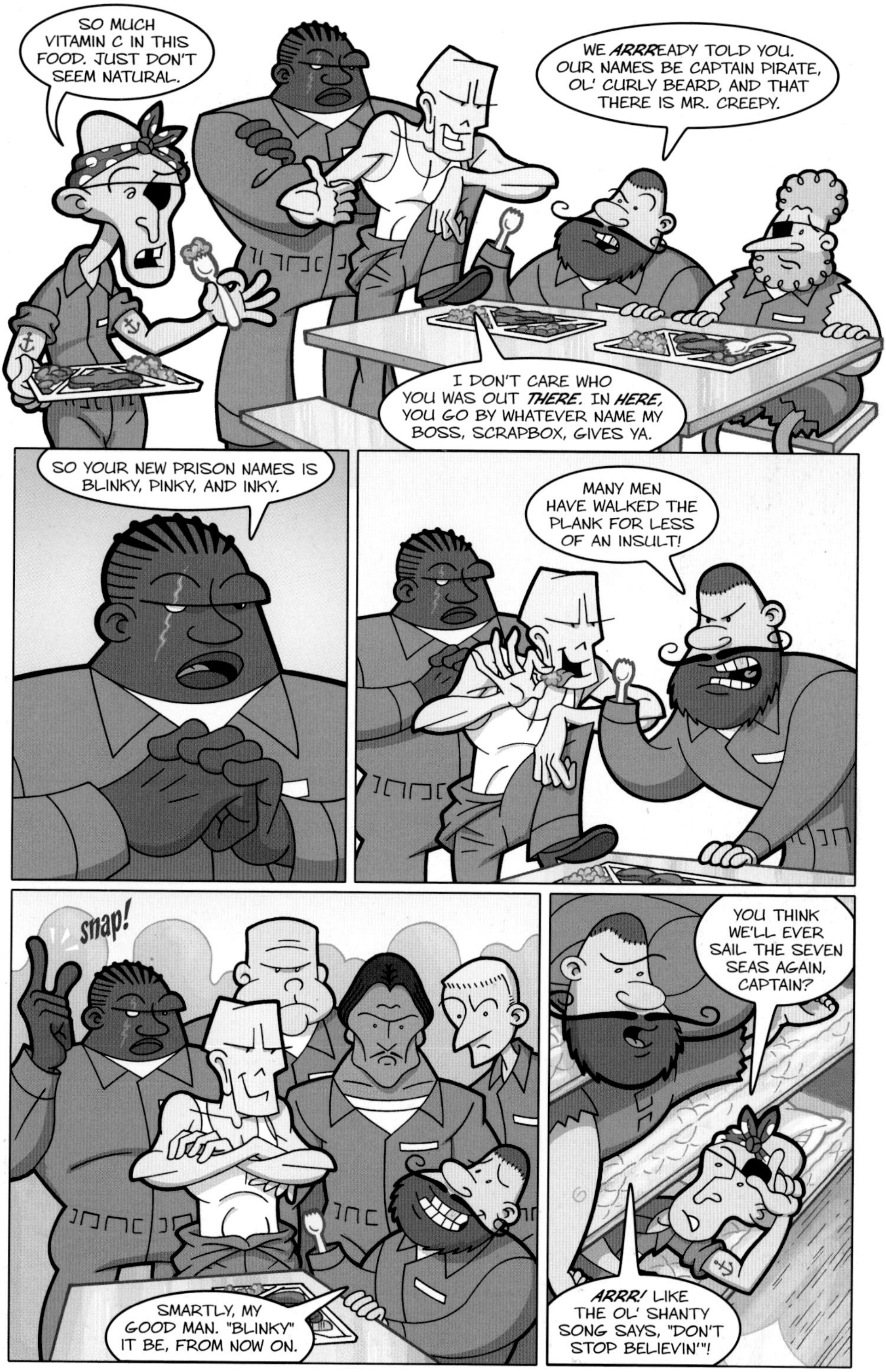
SO MUCH VITAMIN C IN THIS FOOD. JUST DON'T SEEM NATURAL.
WE ARRREADY TOLD YOU. OUR NAMES BE CAPTAIN PIRATE, OL' CURLY BEARD, AND THAT THERE IS MR. CREEPY.
I DON'T CARE WHO YOU WAS OUT THERE. IN HERE, YOU GO BY WHATEVER NAME MY BOSS, SCRAPBOX, GIVES YA.
SO YOUR NEW PRISON NAMES IS BLINKY, PINKY, AND INKY.
MANY MEN HAVE WALKED THE PLANK FOR LESS OF AN INSULT!
snap!
SMARTLY, MY GOOD MAN. "BLINKY" IT BE, FROM NOW ON.
YOU THINK WE'LL EVER SAIL THE SEVEN SEAS AGAIN, CAPTAIN?
ARRR! LIKE THE OL' SHANTY SONG SAYS, "DON'T STOP BELIEVIN'"!

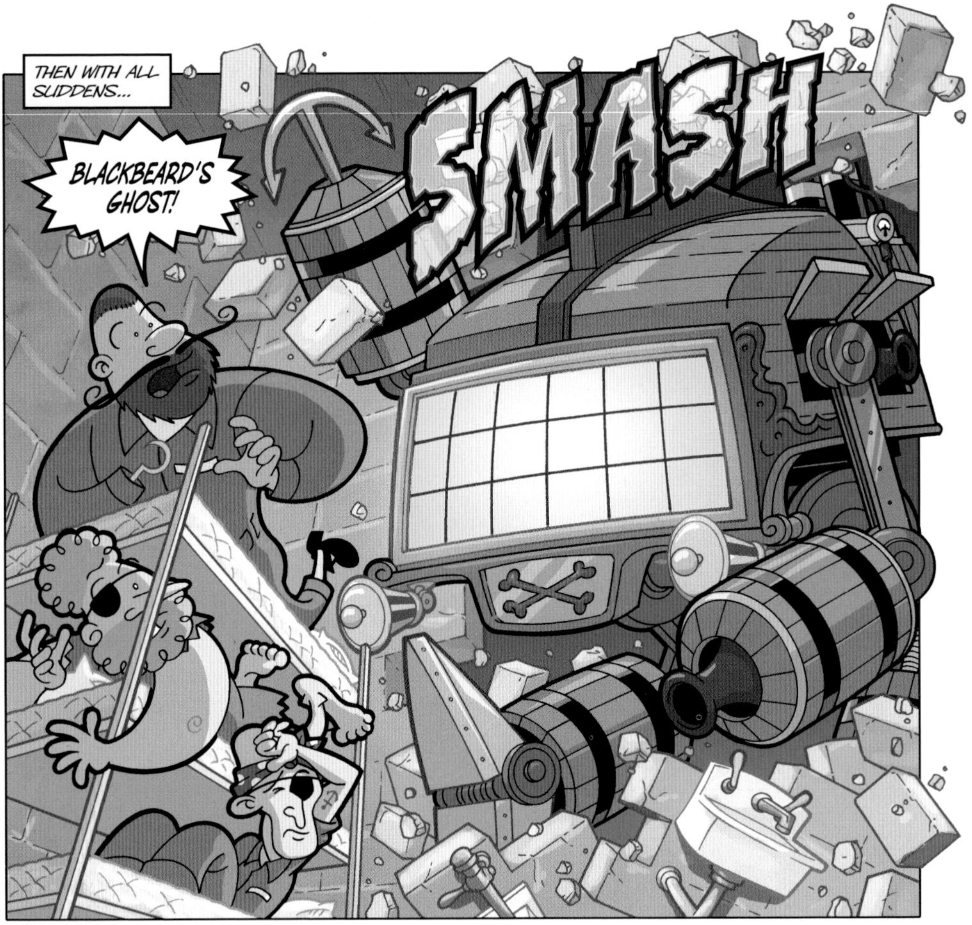
THEN WITH ALL SUDDENS...
BLACKBEARD'S GHOST!
SMASH

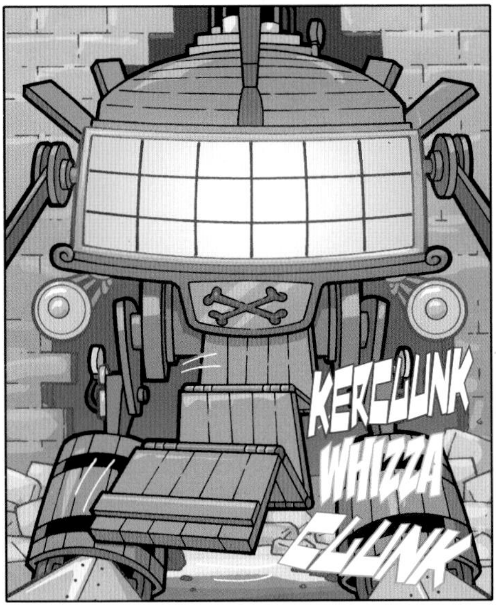
KERCLUNK
WHIZZA
CLUNK

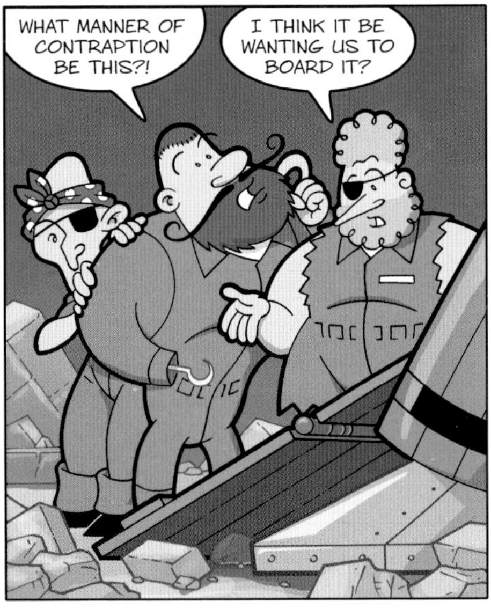
WHAT MANNER OF CONTRAPTION BE THIS?!
I THINK IT BE WANTING US TO BOARD IT?

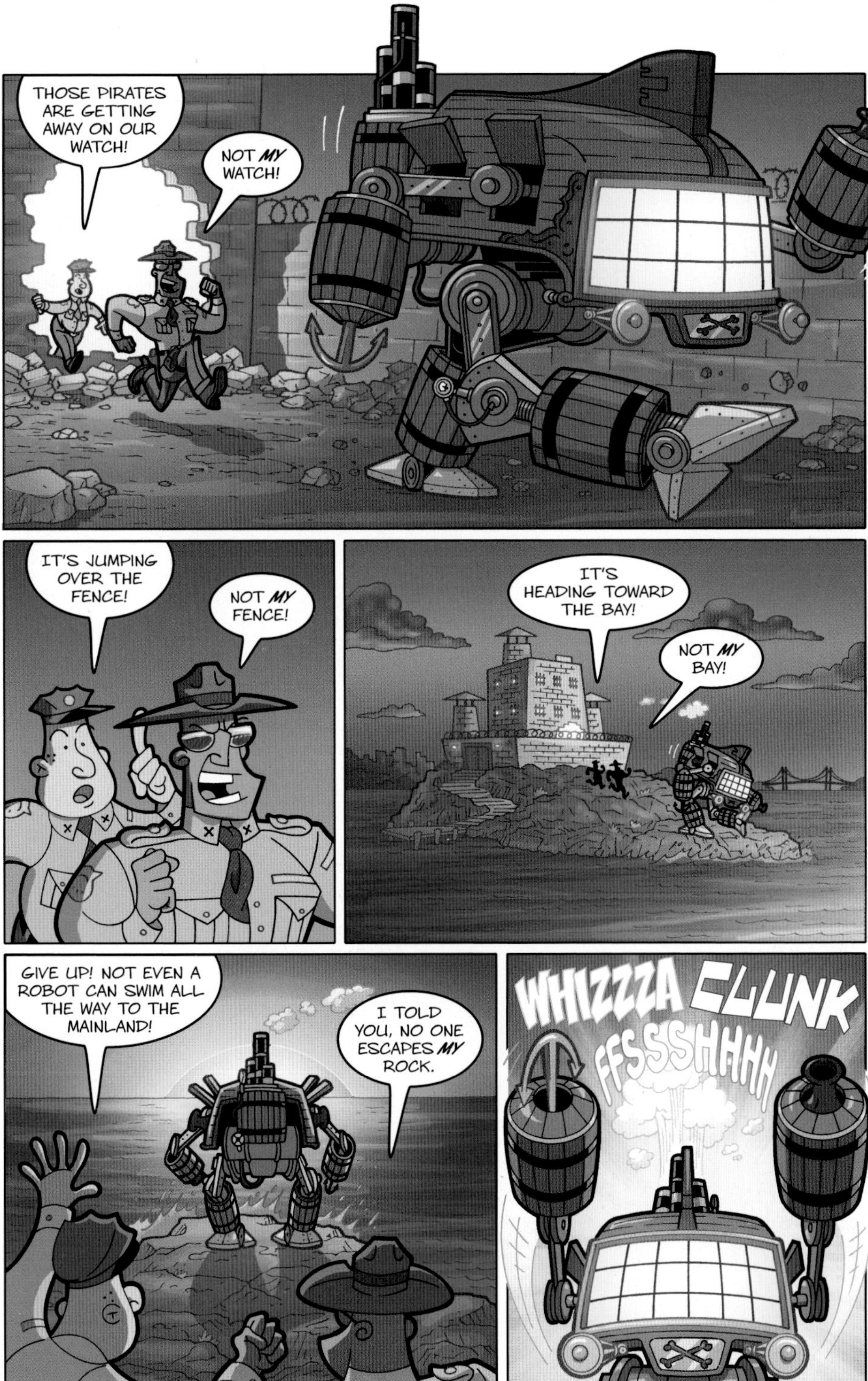
THOSE PIRATES ARE GETTING AWAY ON OUR WATCH!
NOT MY WATCH!
IT'S JUMPING OVER THE FENCE!
NOT MY FENCE!
IT'S HEADING TOWARD THE BAY!
NOT MY BAY!
GIVE UP! NOT EVEN A ROBOT CAN SWIM ALL THE WAY TO THE MAINLAND!
I TOLD YOU, NO ONE ESCAPES MY ROCK.
WHIZZZA CLUNK
FFSSSHHHH

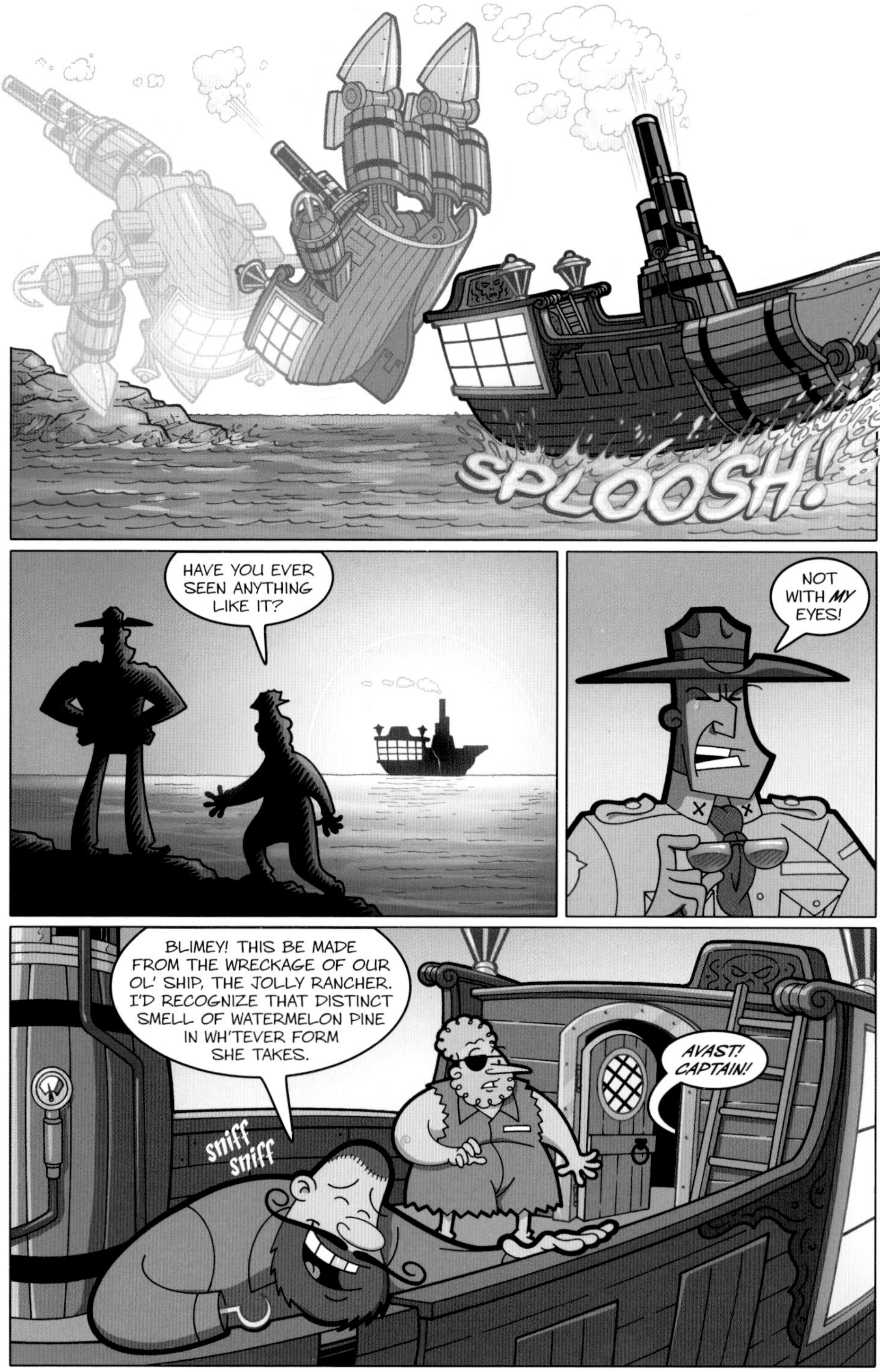
SPLOOSH!
HAVE YOU EVER SEEN ANYTHING LIKE IT?
NOT WITH MY EYES!
BLIMEY! THIS BE MADE FROM THE WRECKAGE OF OUR OL' SHIP, THE JOLLY RANCHER. I'D RECOGNIZE THAT DISTINCT SMELL OF WATERMELON PINE IN WH'TEVER FORM SHE TAKES.
sniff sniff
AVAST! CAPTAIN!

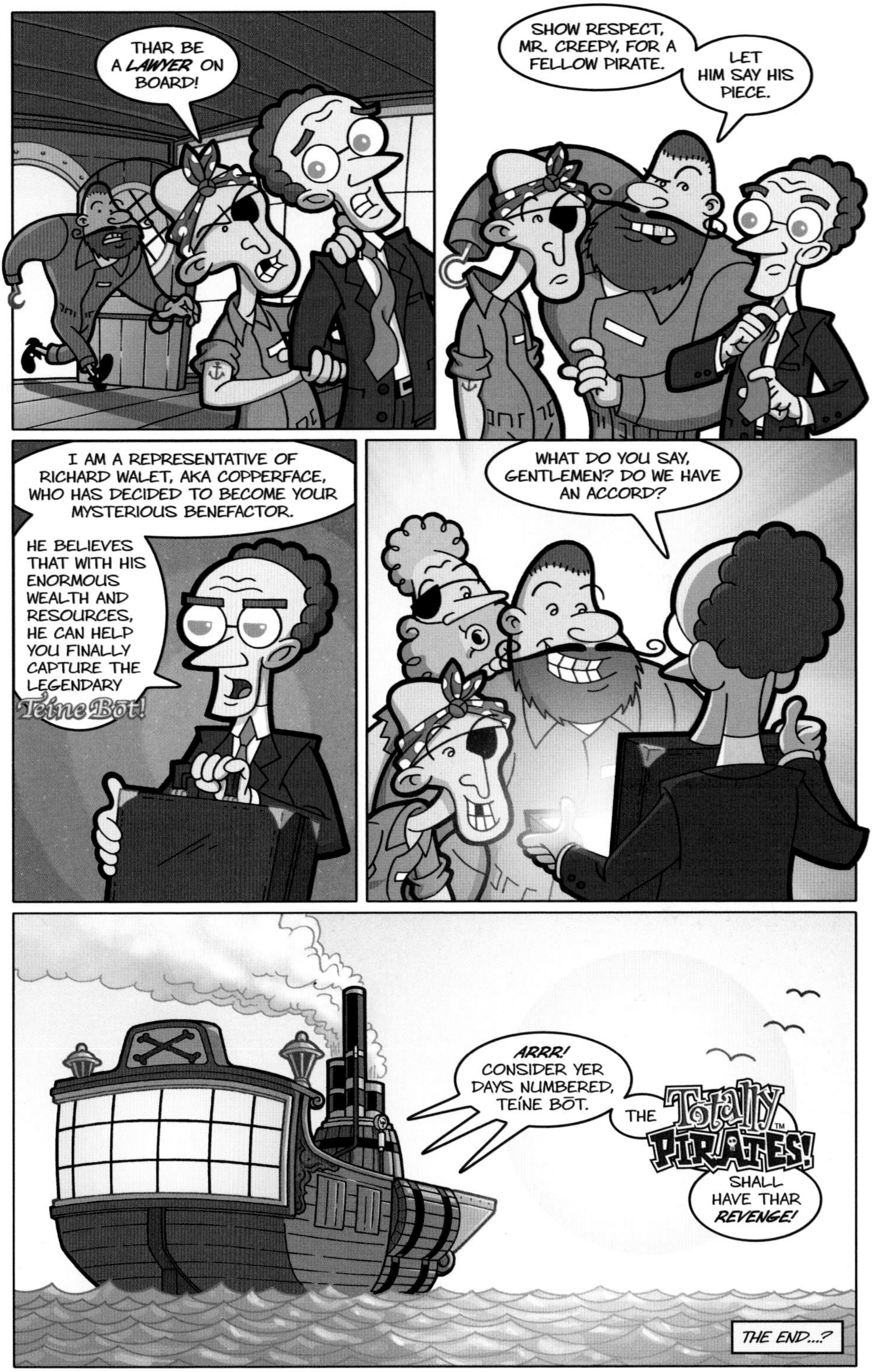
THAR BE A LAWYER ON BOARD!
SHOW RESPECT, MR. CREEPY, FOR A FELLOW PIRATE.
LET HIM SAY HIS PIECE.
I AM A REPRESENTATIVE OF RICHARD WALET, AKA COPPERFACE, WHO HAS DECIDED TO BECOME YOUR MYSTERIOUS BENEFACTOR.
HE BELIEVES THAT WITH HIS ENORMOUS WEALTH AND RESOURCES, HE CAN HELP YOU FINALLY CAPTURE THE LEGENDARY Teíne Bōt!
WHAT DO YOU SAY, GENTLEMEN? DO WE HAVE AN ACCORD?
ARRR! CONSIDER YER DAYS NUMBERED, TEíNE BŌT.
THE Totally PIRATES!™
SHALL HAVE THAR REVENGE!
THE END...?

THANKS TO

the Green family, the Roman family, Raina Telgemeier, Marion Vitus, Lisa Fernandez, Mar-Mar & BeauPa, Daniel Nayeri, Judith Hansen, Gina Gagliano, Erin Houlihan, Steve Behling, Chris Duffy, Art Baltazar, Kristina & Amit Saxena, Kevin Bramer of Optical Sloth, Tony Shenton, Adam Lore & Mr. Door, Abby Denson, Jordan Cooper, Small Press Expo, the '80s, John Hughes, Kevin Williamson, Sea Spray and the rest of the Autobots, Turbo Teen, the Gobots, and Venice, Italy.

We'd also like to thank anyone else who has supported or inspired *Teen Boat!* May your lives be free of ANGST and full of THRILLS.

dave & John

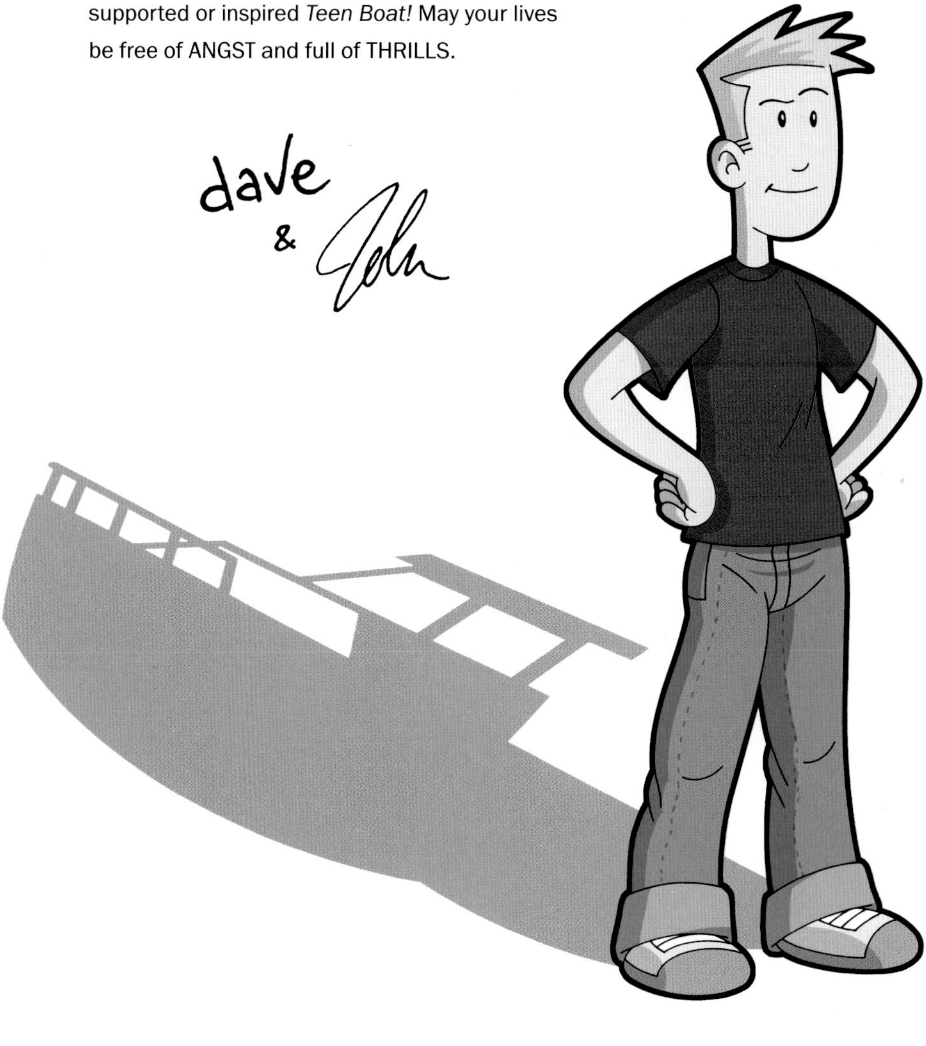

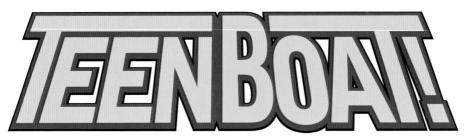

TEEN BOAT!

The *ANGST* of being Graphic—the *THRILL* of being Novel!

Here's a peek at how **DAVE** and **JOHN** transformed their ideas and hard work into the book you hold in your hands today . . .

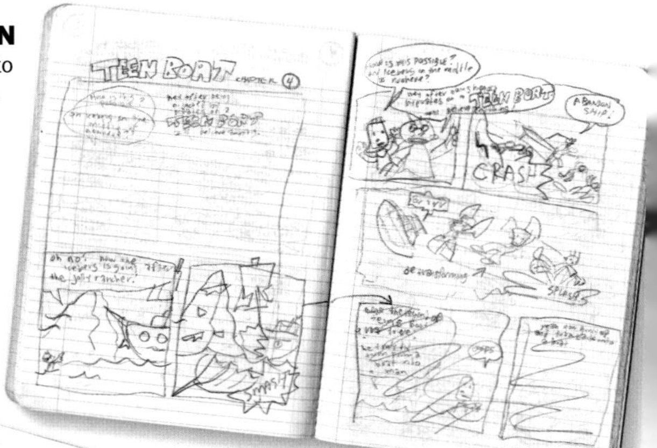

TEEN BOAT chapter 4
CRASH
SPLASH

A portion of Dave's original script to chapter two.

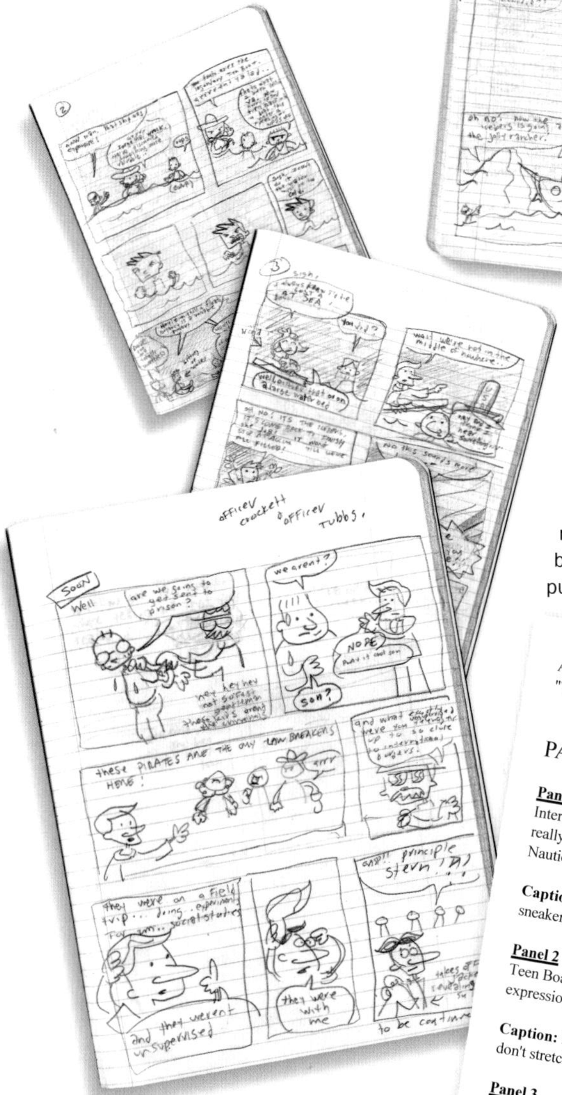

officer crockett & officer Tubbs.
Soon
are we going to get sent to prison?
we aren't?
NOPE
son?
these PIRATES ARE THE ONLY LAW BREAKERS HERE!
they were on a field trip... doing... experiments for um.. social studies
and they weren't unsupervised
they were with me
to be continued

SCRIPT

After hashing out the story for each chapter, Dave writes up the script, detailing what happens in each panel and what the characters say. For some of the early chapters, he even drew the scripts as comics in a notebook. These came in handy for John, but eventually Dave started to write them purely as text in the format seen below.

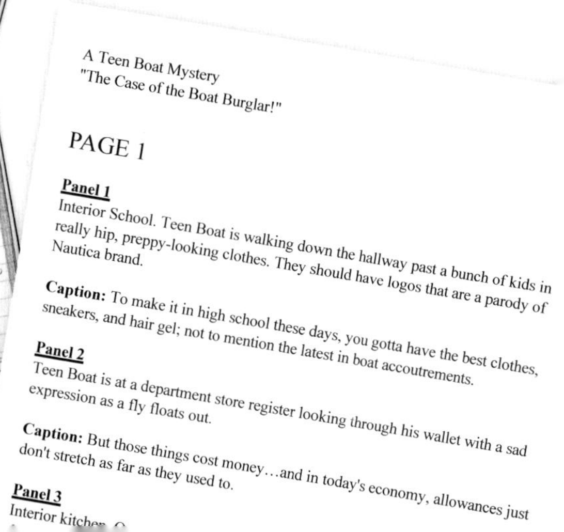
A Teen Boat Mystery
"The Case of the Boat Burglar!"

PAGE 1

Panel 1
Interior School. Teen Boat is walking down the hallway past a bunch of kids in really hip, preppy-looking clothes. They should have logos that are a parody of Nautica brand.

Caption: To make it in high school these days, you gotta have the best clothes, sneakers, and hair gel; not to mention the latest in boat accoutrements.

Panel 2
Teen Boat is at a department store register looking through his wallet with a sad expression as a fly floats out.

Caption: But those things cost money…and in today's economy, allowances just don't stretch as far as they used to.

Panel 3
Interior kitchen. O

Dave's very first sketch of Teen
Boat's transformation sequence.

Feet &
HANDS
Stretch
into
parts
of BOAT.

NOSE
stretches

HEAD
FLIPS
BACK

Ghostface

Scrapbot

Lawyer
A

Lawyer
B

Warden

Guard

Capt Bill

SKETCHES

Dave sends the script and any
sketches to John, who then does
sketches of his own of the characters.
This step is invaluable, and Dave and John
spend a lot of time going back and forth
on how things look. It's not easy figuring out
how to draw a robot made out of a pirate ship,
or how a teen transforms into a boat!

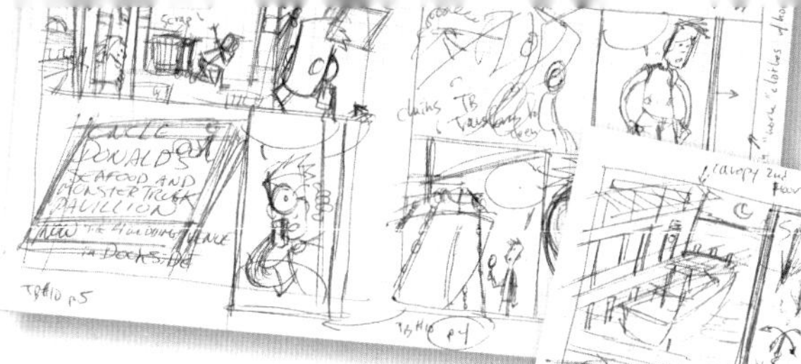

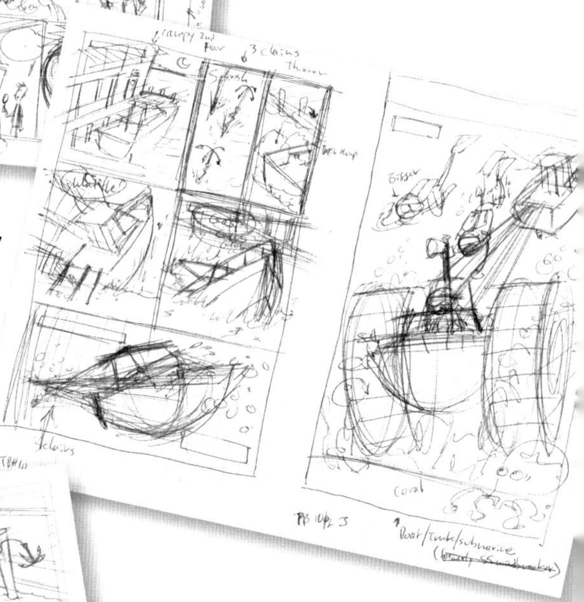

THUMBNAILS

Similar to how Dave wrote the early chapters, John sketches out small versions of every page based on Dave's script. This helps John figure out if everything written will fit in each panel, or if more panels are needed, or if any should be moved to another page.

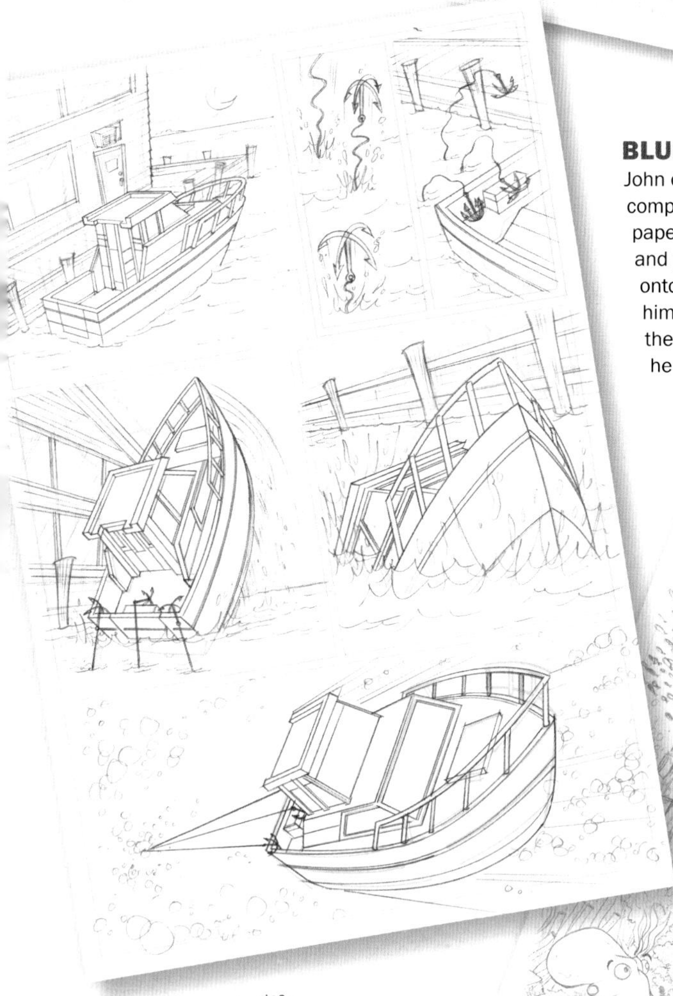

BLUE LINES

John often scans his thumbnails into a computer, enlarges them for 11″ x 14″ paper, resizes panels or other elements, and prints them out in light blue directly onto smooth Bristol paper. This gives him a handy guide for penciling, and the blue printing won't show up when he scans the art again.

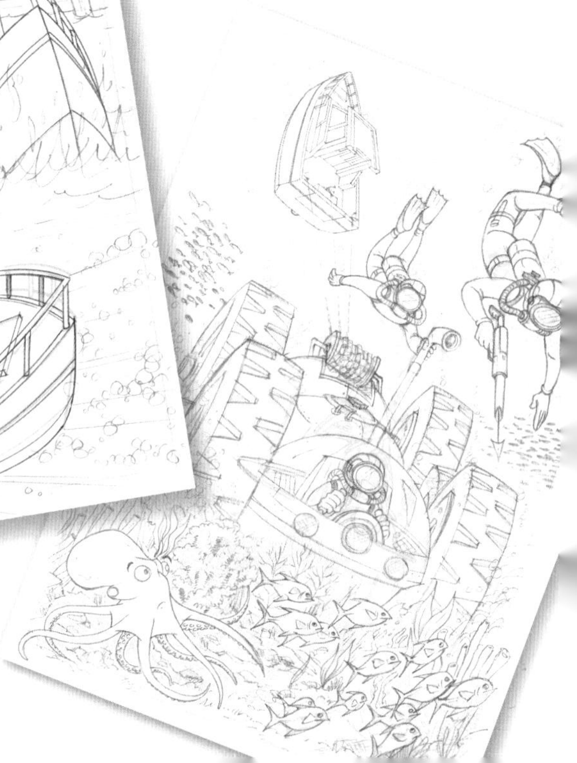

Blue lines from chapter nine .

PENCILS

To the right you can see what a penciled page looks like once scanned and the blue lines are removed. John likes to use a mechanical pencil, but nothing fancy—the ones you can get on "Back-to-School" sales do the trick just fine!

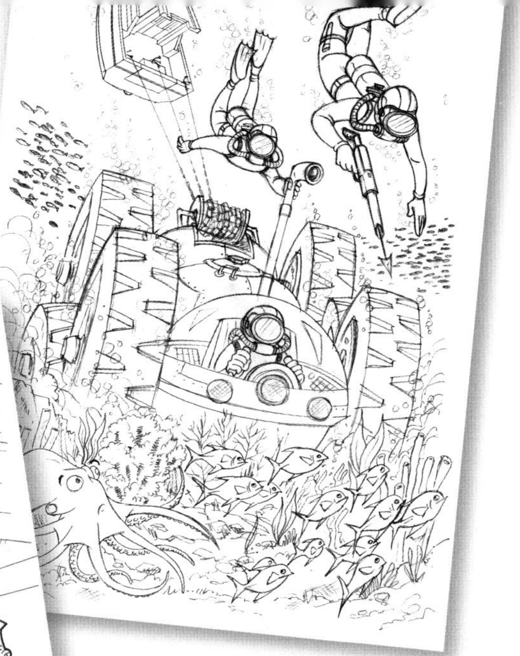

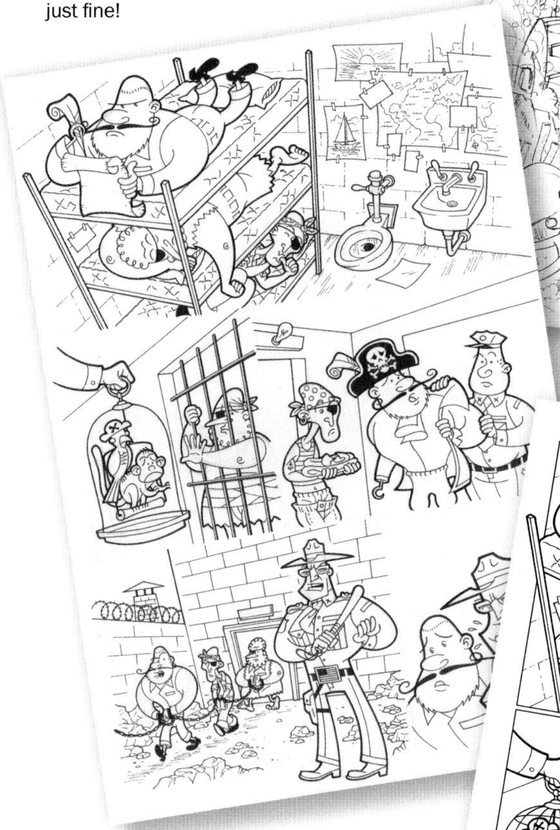

An inked page before cleanup.

INKS

For *Teen Boat!,* John inked over the pencil art almost exclusively in Micron pens, with the occasional Sharpie thrown into the mix. After erasing the pencil marks, he scans the inks into Photoshop. Any leftover blue lines are dropped out, the panel borders are added, and the tedious process of making digital corrections begins!

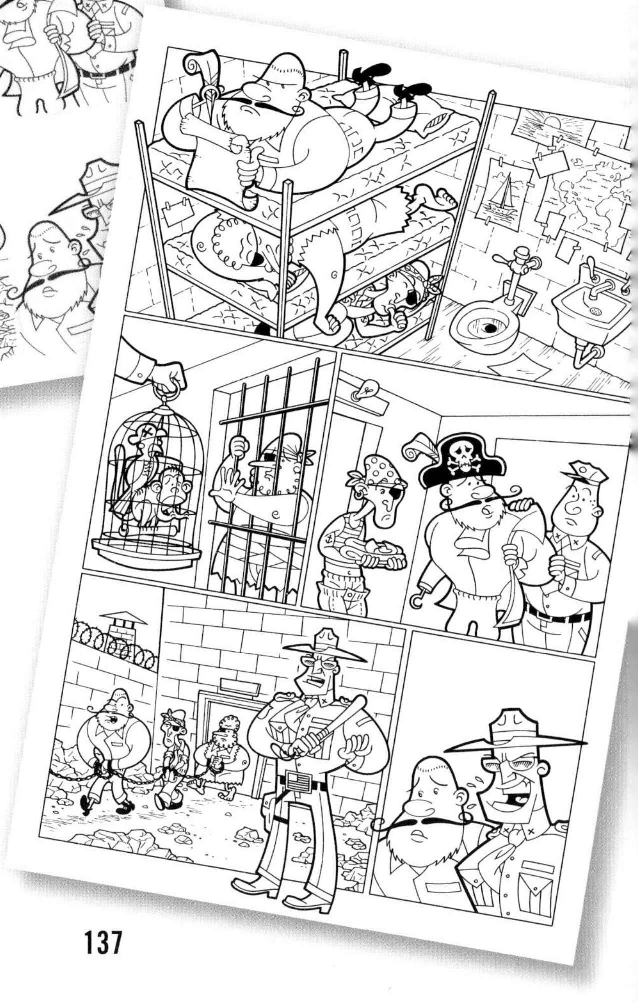

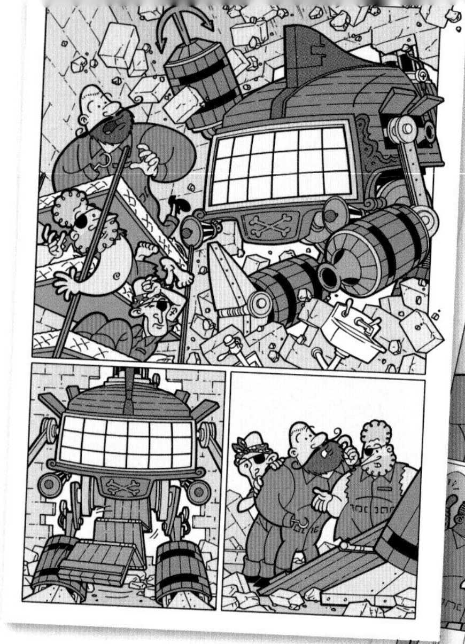

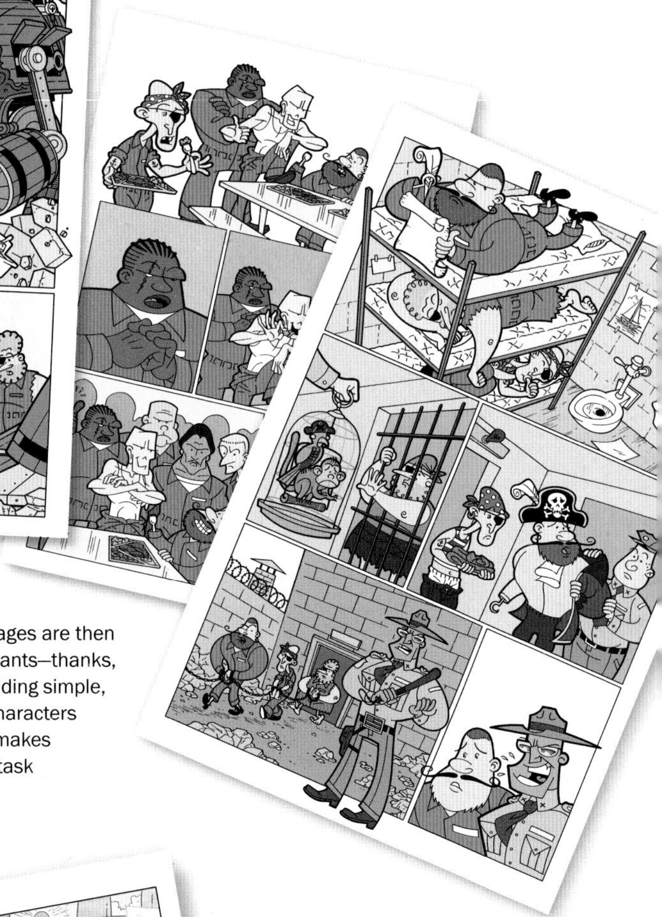

FLATS

The digital versions of the inked pages are then "flatted" (often by friends or assistants—thanks, guys!). Basically, flatting means adding simple, solid color to all the objects and characters on the page, as seen above. This makes selecting each element an easier task for our colorists.

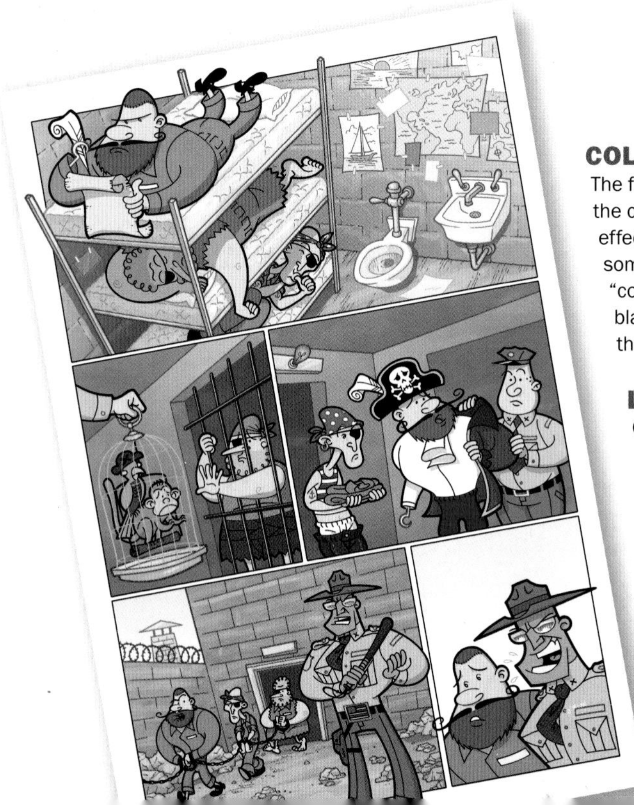

COLORS

The flat color pages are then sent to the colorists, who add shadows, special effects, and textures, and drop out some of the ink lines. "Drop outs" or "color holds" are when lines that are black are turned a color, like most of the background line art.

LETTERS

One of the final steps is for John to place the text and word balloons. This is done in Adobe Illustrator, and to see the final result, just flip through the book!

COVER SKETCHES

Here you can see a selection of the numerous cover ideas John sketched out. You can see how certain elements, from Teen Boat's pose, to his boat shadow, to the logo design, made it into the final cover.

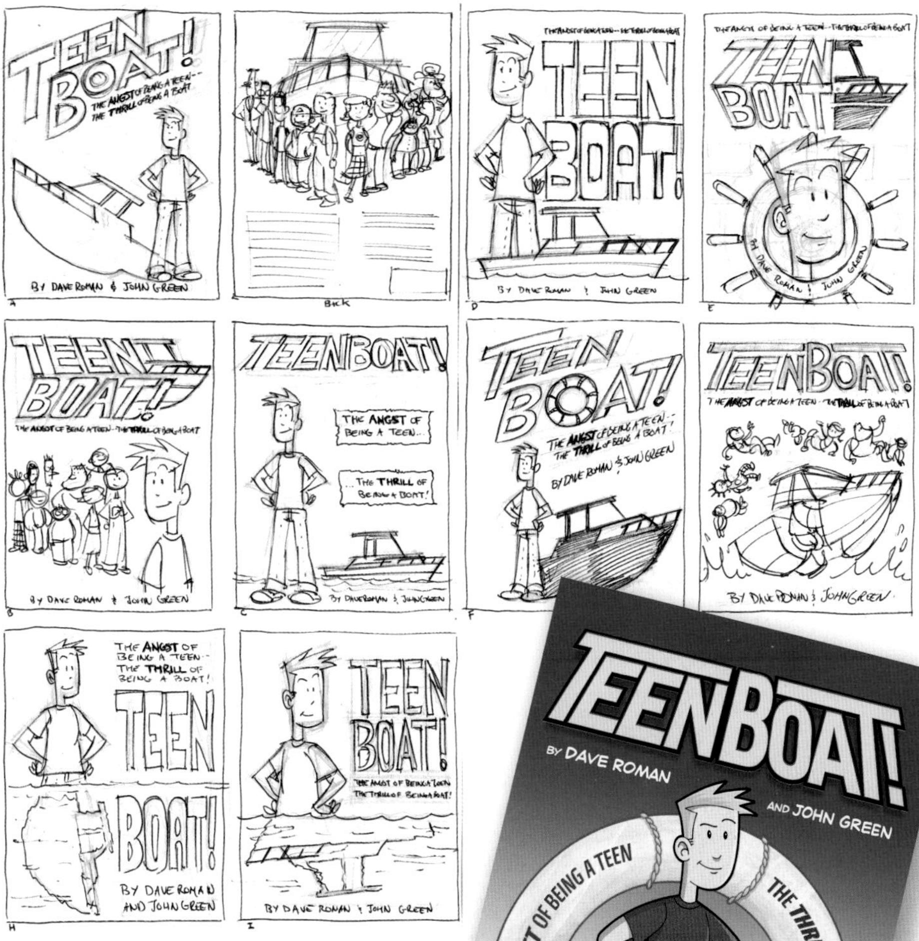

TEEN BOAT!
BY DAVE ROMAN & JOHN GREEN
THE ANGST OF BEING A TEEN...
...THE THRILL OF BEING A BOAT!
TEEN BOAT!
THE ANGST OF BEING A TEEN--
THE THRILL OF BEING A BOAT!
BY DAVE ROMAN AND JOHN GREEN

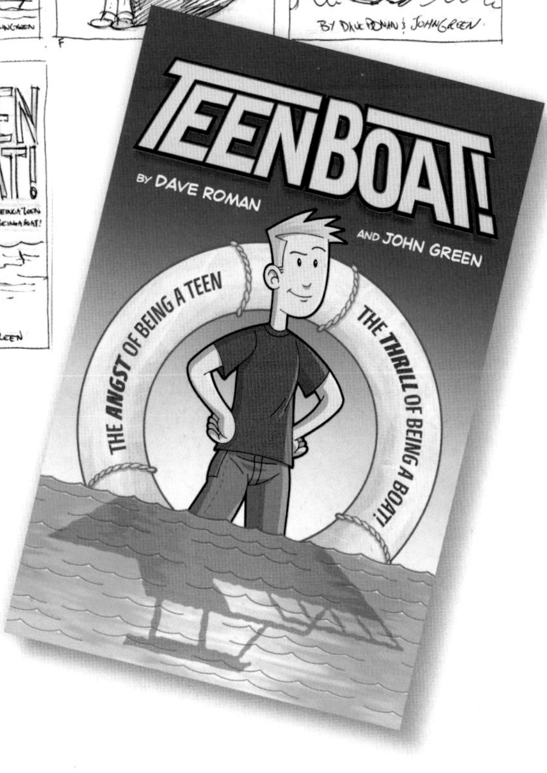

TEEN BOAT!
BY DAVE ROMAN
AND JOHN GREEN
THE ANGST OF BEING A TEEN
THE THRILL OF BEING A BOAT!

FINAL BOOK

Of course, let's not forget the editors, designers, publicists, and countless production sea monkeys who were part of the process. But lo and behold, everyone's hard work all comes together to form the fine piece of literature you see before you!

Bon voyage!

DAVE ROMAN is the creator of *Astronaut Academy: Zero Gravity* and *Agnes Quill: An Anthology of Mystery.* He has contributed stories to the Flight series, and is the coauthor of two *New York Times* best-selling graphic novels, *X-Men: Misfits* and *The Last Airbender: Zuko's Story.* He is also the writer of *Jax Epoch and the Quicken Forbidden,* which he cocreated with John Green while they were students at the School of Visual Arts. Dave worked as an editor for the groundbreaking *Nickelodeon* magazine and lives in New York City with his wife, Raina. See more of Dave's work at **yaytime.com**.

JOHN GREEN grew up on Long Island and has worked in New York City ever since graduating from the School of Visual Arts for Graphic Design in 1997. He was the comics consultant for *Disney Adventures* magazine, and in addition to Disney has written, illustrated, or otherwise worked on comics for Nickelodeon, Dreamworks, Scholastic, DC Comics, and First Second Books. When not drawing comics, John creates artwork for video games, such as *Emerald City Confidential, Puzzle Bots,* and *Nearly Departed.* See more of John's work at **johngreenart.com**.